Fae

The Wild Hunt

Book One of the Riven Wyrde Saga

by Graham Austin-King

Third Edition

THE RIVEN WYRDE SAGA

Fae - The Wild Hunt
Fae - The Realm of Twilight
Fae - The Sins of the Wyrde

For Gillian

Savarel
Widdengate
Kavtrin
ANLAN
Celstwin
Feldane

Hesk
The Barren Isles.
The Vorstelv
N
W
E
S

Chapter One

Miriam gazed through the small window at the sun as it sank slowly behind the tiled rooftops of Kavtrin. Smoke was rising from the chimney pots, lending a contrast that painted a dirty stain of indigo across the flaming skies. It was a sunset for young lovers and poets, but Miriam was blind to it. Once there had been a time when the sight would have struck a chord within her, but those days seemed long gone to her now. She traced her fingertips idly over the worn and knife-scarred worktop, and sighed as she picked up a damp cloth and began to run it back and forth over the surface. There was nothing to wipe up. The counter was as clean as anyone could make it, but hands need to feel busy and the cloth worked almost unnoticed by her as she stared unseeing out of the window.

She caught sight of her reflection as she turned and she froze in place, one hand coming up to touch her cheek. Her face was lined and drawn. Her once lustrous brown hair was tied back into a severe bun, which only served to highlight the faint touch of grey at her temples. She looked... old? She wondered at herself. Who was this woman looking back at her? How long had it been since she'd really looked at herself? How long since she'd really been herself?

She turned to stir the pot resting on the woodstove, and glanced nervously at the door. The stew was catching again, but he probably wouldn't notice unless it was really badly burned. She was a good cook, she knew she was, but there was only so much a person could do to keep food hot once it was ready. The mutton had stewed for a good six hours and she had been trying to keep it hot for the last four. She glanced at the door again and tutted as she caught herself doing so. Sliding the iron vent in the base of the stove closed, she lifted the pot with a grunt and placed it onto the heavy table.

Her eyes drifted to the simple cot in the corner and she padded over on quiet feet. The only joy she had found in the last fifteen years of her marriage lay sleeping soundly in this small bed. Caerl hadn't really wanted children, but she'd hoped that it would mellow his temper and when Devin came along, he'd seemed to calm for a time. Then of course, he had taken up the drink again.

Creaks and mutterings drifted in from the stairs. She turned, with a smile carefully arranged on her face, as the door opened and Caerl slumped against the frame. She took in all of his appearance in a single glance. The stained and slovenly clothing, the unwashed and unkempt hair, the filthy and scraggly beard. Where, under all of this filth, was the man she had married? The man who had stolen moments with her, risking her father's wrath when she'd been little more than a child herself.

"Hello dear," she said, forcing lightness into her voice. "How was the marketplace? Would you like some dinner? I made your favourite."

Caerl grunted, a non-committal noise that could have meant any number of things, and staggered the three steps to the sturdy table before collapsing into a chair. Miriam busied herself with the stew, spooning out a healthy portion into a large earthenware bowl and setting a hunk of bread on the side. She put it down in front of Caerl's slouched form, and stepped quickly away to busy herself in the tiny kitchen. Not that anything needed doing, the rooms were spotless. Living in fear of Caerl's dark moods had turned her into an efficient cleaner, and the fewer reasons she could give him to start off with her, the better.

Caerl dunked the dark peasant bread into the stew and chewed. He shovelled a spoonful into his mouth, and then grimaced and spat. His dark eyes sought her out and seemed to flash in the light from the fire and the oil lamps on the walls.

"This is burnt, woman." He slurred, seeming to chew out the words from a mouth slack from drink.

"I'm sorry Caerl," Miriam said, hating herself for the way she sounded. "I tried to keep it warm for you, but it must have caught."

"Dammit girl, how hard can it be to put some food in a man's belly?" He pressed his hands to the tabletop and stood in a sudden burst, knocking the simple wooden chair to the floor. It made a sharp crack as it splintered. "I run those damned carts all day long for you. Put food on the table and a roof over the head of you and your brat, and you can't even make a decent meal?"

Miriam rankled at him starting on the boy. She knew she ought to keep her head down, just as a rabbit will stay in the warren when a storm is coming, but somehow

Caerl always knew what would set her off.

"Well, maybe if you had been home instead of in the tavern three hours ago, it wouldn't have caught," she muttered, the words spilling from her lips before her good sense could stop them.

Caerl stopped and stared at her with dark eyes for a long moment. A slow smile spread over his stubbled face.

"So, it's my fault is it?"

"No, Caerl. I didn't mean it like that." She took a step back away from him and began edging along the wall towards the window.

"I work all damned day and this is what I get? Burnt slop I wouldn't feed a dog!" He slammed his hands down on the table, making the bowl jump.

Miriam flinched and turned quickly to see if Devin had woken.

"Dammit, woman. Look at me when I'm talking to you!" He snatched up the bowl and hurled it at the fireplace. It shattered on the woodstove, splattering stew over the walls and onto the hearth where it bubbled and hissed.

Miriam cried out as the bowl smashed, ducking involuntarily as though it had struck her. She cowered down, her hands shielding her face as Caerl stormed towards her with rage dancing in his eyes. She drew back as he came closer and grabbed for her, then skittered along the wall towards the woodstove and the doorway to their own tiny room. Caerl followed swiftly, his movements unimpeded by the ale he stank of, as if the rage had burned the alcohol from him.

"Caerl, don't. Please?" She backed into the darkness of the bedroom. "You'll wake the boy. Try to calm down."

"Don't *you* tell me what to do." He reached for her and managed to grab her hair, pulling it free from the bun, as she twisted and tried to dart away from him. "Who in the hells do you think *you* are, telling me what to do?"

He yanked savagely on her hair, bending her backwards and off-balance as her eyes filled with tears. "You're *nothing*!" he spat. "That's what you are woman. You know it, and I know it."

He let go, dropping her to the floor and she curled up tight, balling her fists and pressing them to her face as if to ward off the hate.

"Say it," he whispered, but she lay silent, biting her cheek to hold in the tears.

"Say it!" he roared, drawing back his foot and kicking her savagely in the ribs with his heavy boot.

Miriam gasped as the pain flooded through her. Her vision was blurred by her tears and she felt him crouch down and grab her by the throat, wrenching her towards him. His calloused hands were rough on the delicate skin of her throat, and she fought to draw in a ragged breath as he squeezed at her neck.

"Don't you *ever* tell me what to do." His spittle sprayed onto her cheeks with his words and the stench of stale beer turned her stomach. She began to sob silently as she fled inside herself. Her silence seemed to enrage him more than her defiance had, and he struck her with the back of his hand, the force throwing her to the floor.

"Da?" A small voice carried in from the doorway.

Miriam's eyes flew open in horror and her pain was forgotten. Devin was a slight boy and the nightshirt made him seem all the smaller as he looked up at his father.

"Da, don't hit her," he said, a world of reproach in his voice.

Miriam flew to her feet as Caerl turned and bristled at the lad.

"You telling me what to do, boy?" he asked in a low dangerous voice as he moved toward the doorway.

"Don't you touch him, Caerl," she warned. "Don't you *dare* touch him."

"Boy needs to know his place," he muttered, almost to himself, as he looked down at the dark-haired child backing away from him.

Desperately, she reached for him and clung to his arm, trying to hold him back as he dragged her into the kitchen again. Snarling out a curse Caerl struggled to throw her off, turning to face her once more. His face was a mask of pure rage as he struck her with his open hand across the face. This was no slap, his hand was rigid and she staggered backwards into the wall, her head ringing. He stalked towards her as she dashed the tears from her eyes and looked up at him. Her face throbbed and one eye was already starting to swell.

He staggered suddenly as Devin launched himself on his back screaming like a feral cat. Caerl's eyes went wide in shock and then pain as the boy's nails clawed at his neck. He reached back almost casually, grasping a handful of the nightshirt and threw the boy at his mother.

"You both got no damned respect," he spat and began to undo the thick leather belt he wore.

"That's enough Caerl," Miriam snapped, her lips white with anger as she got to her feet, clutching Devin to her skirts as they moved sideways towards the fireplace. He laughed coldly and shook out the belt. Miriam reached out behind her, her hand scrabbling for something, anything. She took up the first thing she touched, the heavy iron ladle from the pot.

"So help me Caerl, if you touch this boy..."

His laugh was frost as she thrust Devin behind her awkwardly. She shrieked as he feinted towards her and she swung wildly with the ladle, missing and spraying stew across the room.

He grinned and lunged again, but this time his balance or the ale betrayed him and he had none of the grace of moments ago. She lashed out, screaming, and the ladle caught him solidly on the temple with a sickening crunch.

Caerl staggered backwards and fell, crashing through the chairs and table before hitting the floor. The silence when it fell, was louder than her screams had ever been. She stood frozen, holding the ladle with both hands. She was dimly aware of Devin behind her, both arms gripping her dress and his face buried in the cloth. Extricating herself from his grasp she crept towards Caerl's prone figure. Blood was seeping slowly from his temple and one nostril, and his eyes were half closed. She looked carefully, but saw no signs of movement. He lay still, seemingly out cold. She felt a wild exultation in her breast but then, just as powerfully, the reality of what she had done washed over her and Miriam was filled with a fear deeper than she had ever known. He would kill her. Her and the boy both, that much was certain. If he didn't kill her, he'd either make her pay so savagely that she begged for death, or he'd have her up before the Justice.

"Devin, sweetheart?" she called softly. "Let's take a trip, just you and me. We'll have an adventure."

The boy looked at her with huge dark eyes. "Without Da?" he asked in a quiet voice. Miriam nodded.

"Good." His young face was stone, hard and cold.

Forcing a smile onto her face, she set about grabbing clothes and what little food they had in the house, filling bags while Devin dressed. Taking his hand, she led him to the door and reminded herself to walk normally and calmly into the hallway and down the stairs, even as her mind screamed at her to run.

Kavtrin was not a small city and even at this time in the evening the streets were filled with people. Miriam held tight to Devin with one hand, and the bags with the other, as she tried to thread her way through the crowded streets. Many people were still making their way home from work. Some few hawkers shouted out from street corners, trying to sell this and that. Miriam noticed first one, and then several more evening girls coming to stand under the, as yet, unlit street lamps with their lost and hopeless eyes.

She hurried Devin along the cobbled streets, trying to keep from being forced into the gutters by the sheer weight of traffic. They darted over to the side from time to time to avoid the carts that clattered through with their drivers flicking the whip at the horses and cursing at all who stood in their way. She was only dimly aware of where she was going. It had been so long, she was surprised she even remembered the way. Devin had been silent since they left the house, and she desperately needed to get him into the warm.

Miriam didn't notice the rain when it first started, a soft misting drizzle that was more like spray, but which soon began to soak through her simple woollen dress. It slowly changed into a steady downpour that plastered her long brown hair to her face and made her dress cling to her legs with each step. They were both soaked to the skin as they finally crossed the high cobbled bridge and saw the golden glow of the lamplight coming from the windows of the Broom and Badger. Miriam made her way around to the rear of the inn and pounded on the large oak door as Devin pressed himself hard against her hip. The boy was shaking, not simply shivering, but a solid trembling. Miriam drew in a breath to speak as the door finally opened, but the wide-eyed girl in the doorway pulled them both out of the wet with a gasp.

"Lords and Ladies, look at the state of you two." she exclaimed. "Boy'll catch his death out in that. So will you! An' what's wrong with the front door anyway?"

"Shalin said I could call on her if ever I needed anything," Miriam told the blonde girl in a tiny broken voice. The girl looked at her, taking in the deepening bruises, and her face softened. "Ah darlin', you've been through it, haven't you, love?" She hurried them through into the warm kitchen, still filled with the aromas of dinner, and sat them close to the fire set in the long wall.

"You two sit here and I'll find Shalin. I expect you could use something hot inside you too." She bustled around and set a large bowl in front of Devin, before leaving through the double doors that led into the inn proper.

The kitchen was long and low-beamed, with huge cast-iron ovens set against one wall and a long table filling the centre of the room. It was well-lit with the oil lamps on the walls shedding a warm, comforting light. It smelled of chicken, freshly baked bread, and hope. Miriam let the warmth from the fire soak slowly into her body and watched Devin devour a large bowl of warm apple pie as only a ten year old boy could.

"My stars, Miriam, I never thought I'd see you again!" exclaimed a slim blonde woman from the doorway. Shalin seemed determined to overcome every stereotype about innkeeper's wives. She was tall and willowy, with a figure that made other women hate her on sight. She was neither matronly nor blousy, though that was not to say she was not beautiful. She had long hair the colour of fine honey, and piercing blue eyes. It would be easy to assume that she was just some young thing the innkeeper had been lucky enough to end up with, but Shalin was far more than a pretty face. She ran the inn with a brisk efficiency that showed in her eyes. This was a woman that commanded loyalty and who no man with a whit of sense would cross. She had once been Miriam's closest friend, and the last things Miriam had said to her had been lies.

"Shalin," she said with relief as she made her way to the doorway.

"Lords and Ladies woman, look at the state of you," Shalin muttered as she drew Miriam close into a fierce embrace, ignoring the water that was pooling by her feet. "What's happened to you?"

Miriam sucked in one shuddering breath before spitting out, "Caerl." The name tore from her throat and carried all the years of venom and fear. All the love and betrayal, the hurt and every bruise. She clung to Shalin, taking strength from the simple knowledge that another adult cared for her. Shalin stroked her hair softly, making hushing noises. "Deena," she called through into the hallway. "Why don't you get the lad a warm bath and wrap him up in Thomas' old room?"

The girl nodded, smiling at Devin as she held out her hand. "That pie was good wasn't it? I always feel better after coming in from the wet, when I can get something hot inside me. Now, how about we get you out of those wet clothes, into a hot bath, and then find you a nice warm bed?" Devin nodded sleepily and allowed himself to be herded from the room.

"He'll be fine," Shalin said, stepping back to look at Miriam. "Now, how about we get you warm and you can tell me just what is going on? Go on with Deena and she'll get you one of my robes. You can wrap up in that for now and get dry."

The blonde girl led them both up the stairs and pointed Miriam towards a bedroom door, "There should be a robe or two on the back of the door. Just leave your dress in there and I'll see it's cleaned for you."

Miriam nodded her thanks and crouched a little to give Devin a quick hug before stepping into the room.

Shalin smiled at her as she came back into the kitchen and waved her back into the chair. The robe was soft and with the warmth from the fire she was beginning to thaw. "Right then, now that you look more like the woman I knew and less like a drowning kitten, why don't you tell me what's going on? The last time I saw you, your Caerl had gotten a new job in Savarel and you were moving up there."

"We were never going to Savarel," Miriam admitted in a small voice. "I lied because he'd lost his job, again, and we were being thrown out of our home."

"Why didn't you say something?" Shalin gasped. "I had no idea! You know I would have helped you."

"When you've got nothing, Shalin, sometimes pride is all you can to cling to," Miriam said simply.

"Hmm, you're right." said Shalin. "We were so poor when I was a little'un we made the birds look rich, but our doorstep was scrubbed daily." She folded her arms across herself. "So, what's happened now? I mean, it's been what, eight years? Nine?"

"It's been eleven, Shalin, almost twelve." Miriam walked over to the fireplace and stared deep into the flames. "He drank," she began. "Most men drink, but he drank and then he got mean with it. I could cope with that well enough, I suppose, but it was almost every day in the end." Her head bowed as if she were speaking to the floor, confessing like a naughty child. "And he would hit me. Nothing I did would be good enough, Shalin. I tried. I *really tried!* There would be days when he would come home and it seemed like he was searching for something to start off on. Then tonight, he beat me and Devin woke up."

"Your boy?" Shalin asked quietly.

Miriam nodded silently. "Caerl was always careful not to wake him, either that or Devin always made out like he was sleeping. He'd never stir." She breathed deeply before pressing on. "Caerl had me on the floor and he just kept *kicking* me. All I could think was, this is it. This is the night that he's finally going to kill me. Then, Devin was there, throwing himself on Caerl and he grabbed him and threw him at me. He actually threw my boy, Shalin! He was taking his belt off to beat the both of us."

"How did you end up like this, Miriam? You were always so strong, when I knew you."

"He wasn't always like this. When we first met, he was so sweet you wouldn't believe he was the same person."

"How did you meet him? You never did tell me, you know?" She stood and took down a kettle from a hook, filling it from the pump over the double sinks. "I expect you could use some tea to start with?" She cocked an eyebrow at Miriam over one shoulder.

"He was a caravan guard. He used to come into my father's inn every few months, doing the route from Savarel to Kavtrin."

"And I bet you thought he held the sun in one hand and the moon in the other, didn't you?" Shalin said as she set the kettle to boil.

"And then some," Miriam admitted. "He was everything my father hated, and of course, everything I wanted. I was all of fifteen when we started sneaking about together." Her face twisted as she spoke. "Eventually, he talked me into running away with him and that was that. I snuck out of the window one night with nothing but a small pack of clothing and keepsakes." She picked up the mug and blew softly at the steam curling from the top. "At fifteen, I knew all there was to know, and so I turned my back on my family, friends and my home. All for a man I really, barely knew."

"You don't need to tell me if you don't want to," the woman said softly.

"No, it's good. It sort of helps, you know, to talk about it? I don't think I've ever told anyone the whole thing before."

Shalin nodded, setting the steaming mug down in front of Miriam and moving back to her own chair, cradling her cup in her elegant hands.

"We settled here in Kavtrin. He found work easily enough in the marketplace and on the docks. I found easy work in a tavern. We had a lovely room in a nice area overlooking some of the gardens by the park. It wasn't anything especially wonderful, but it was ours, and it felt like a home. Things were wonderful. I mean truly storybook wonderful, until he started drinking." She cleared her throat and looked down at the table as she continued. "First, he started drinking after work with the boys from the marketplace. I didn't mind or blame him. It's hot and heavy work, and a man needs to spend time with the folks he works with.

"Then, he started drinking during lunch with the dockhands. Before long, he was drinking more than he was working. That was when he lost the first job. He was so ashamed that he hid it from me for almost a week before he finally admitted it. He'd still been going out to work in the mornings and not back until dusk, but I knew something wasn't right. A woman always knows. So, he swore off the drink again and we muddled through. He found more work and things were back to normal, until it happened again." She drew in a deep shuddering breath and sighed it out slowly. "This is harder than I thought," she said, looking at Shalin with an apologetic smile.

"You're doing fine Miriam, just take your time."

Miriam nodded and drained her tea, setting the mug down and clasping her hands in her lap. "After we lost the third home, I told him straight. One more time, one *last* time, and that was all the chances I was giving him." She sniffed and then gave a wry smile, "We hadn't really planned for a family. Oh, we hadn't exactly avoided it. I'd stopped drinking moon-tea soon after we settled down again. If I'm honest with myself, it had been my price for keeping us together, and that had been the idea really. Maybe I thought that if we concentrated on starting a family, then things would be better. Of course, you need to be home to start a family. It helps if you're conscious and not snoring ale fumes into the kitchen floor. I'd been right on the verge of telling him we were done, when along came Devin, just like that." She laughed then, a bitter little laugh that held no joy.

"He changed. Overnight he changed, and it was like none of the strife or struggles had ever been there." She glanced up at Shalin and smiled with tear-rimmed eyes. "He helped through the pregnancy. He worked harder, was home earlier and looked after me like I was made of glass. Sometimes too much! When Devin was born he was there, though he bolted outside as soon as the midwife arrived and wouldn't come back into the building until he heard the babe squall. Life was back to the storybook for almost four years, four blissful years."

"So, what happened? What changed?" she heard Shalin ask.

"Honestly? I have no idea." She shook her head. "I wondered for a while if he'd been having an affair and it had ended or something like that. Between one month and the next he shifted, he became distant. He came home twice with ale on his breath, though I pretended I hadn't smelt it. The following week, it was spirits he reeked of. Then it seemed it was every night. You know the funny thing?" Shalin shook her head quietly and Miriam smiled a sad smile. "It was only then, that I began to realise how alone I'd become. We lost most of our friends when we'd had to move the first time. There's nothing quite like pride to rob a person of their good sense is there? Oh, I'd reached out a couple of times, but after we'd moved the third time, I was so ashamed I never bothered trying to keep in touch again. Then Devin came along and my days were filled with him and what work I could find. Caerl had been so good to me that I almost didn't notice that I never really saw anyone else. Until of course, I needed somebody else. Until it all began again. And then I was alone. So, so alone."

Shalin moved to take her in her arms as the tears began to fall. Her body shook with silent sobs, and she allowed the willowy blonde to pull her head into her shoulder. For a time they just sat in silence, until Miriam pushed herself away with a sniff. "Look at me, crying like a babe."

Shalin produced a handkerchief, a faint smile on her face. "Where were you working?"

Miriam snuffled into the hanky, "I still worked in a couple of taverns. It was hard to find one where I could bring Devin. But then, when he got old enough, he worked as a scullion while I worked in the kitchen or the laundry. I'd tried working as a serving girl again, but any man who smelled of ale reminded me of Caerl. I tried a few places, but in the end I realised it wasn't the inn, it was me. A girl working in an inn needs to be able to laugh and banter and flirt a bit. I couldn't do it. I couldn't find it in me. Any man so much as spoke to me and I ran off like a startled rabbit. So I stayed in the kitchens, preparing meals and washing linens.

"Through all of it, Caerl was the same. He ran in cycles. He would drink himself to almost rock bottom before swearing off the stuff. He was true to his word too. He wouldn't touch it or go to the inn with the others. He'd come back from his work early. He'd be calmer, kinder, more attentive, and then it would begin again. Always the same, every time. It would start with one drink with the boys on a Friday. Then it would become Wednesday too, then a touch of wine with dinner. Before too long, he'd be cursing that we had nothing in the place to drink. He'd be coming back from the marketplace later and later, stinking like the bottom of an ale barrel. The more he drank, the blacker his mood seemed to get and then, before long, I was back to never knowing when he was coming home, or who he might be when he arrived.

"Some men are happy drunks. We've both seen them, laughing and carrying on. Some become depressed and snuffle into a tankard in the corner. Caerl wasn't either of these. He would fall in through the doors with a shadow in his eyes, and then it would start. It seemed some days he almost had to search for something to get angry about, but he always found something. Everything was meant as a hurt when the mood was on him. If the fire was built too high, I was squandering his money. If the food was too simple or the rooms weren't spotless I was failing as a wife. But he never actually hit me, until just lately." Her hand crept unnoticed to her face and she fingered the bruises, probing the sore flesh absently as she spoke.

"Always before, even in his darkest place, he stopped at hurling things across the room or kicking over the table. He'd rage and curse at me as I stood in front of Devin's cot and eventually, it was like he'd suddenly see me. Maybe he saw how scared I was or something. But he'd turn and storm out of the door. He'd be back later, stinking of cheap gin and slurring apologies as he pawed at me in the bed.

"And then one time, he did it. He hit me. And it was like, now he'd crossed the line and seen that nothing came from it, he decided it was okay. He never did it in front of the boy, though. It was like he thought beating me was fine, it was okay. But children shouldn't see it. Then tonight, he woke Devin with all his shouting and Devin saw him hit me. My boy actually tried to protect me, Shalin." Her voice was filled with a fierce pride.

"What have you done, Miriam?" Shalin asked, as understanding suddenly dawned on her.

"He was going to beat us both. He was taking off his belt!"

"What have you done, Miriam?" she repeated in a soft voice.

"I went for him with a pot ladle. It caught him in the face, just here." She touched her temple. "He fell hard. And...and, we just left."

"Is he dead?"

Miriam gasped. "I don't know," she admitted as her hand flew to her mouth. "I didn't think to check. Oh, Lords and Ladies! What if I've killed him?"

Shalin took her by the hands, and looked at her firmly. "Now, listen here. You did what you needed to do. Nobody in this room is going to blame you or think less of you for that. You were keeping your boy safe and that's what counts. If he's dead, well then he got what was coming to him. Less than I would have given him!" She stood abruptly and left the room, returning quickly with two glasses and a dark bottle.

"Take this, you look like you could use a good drink," she said, pressing the brandy into Miriam's hands.

Miriam drank the fiery liquid down without comment and held her glass out for another. Shalin chuckled and poured, before giving her a serious look. "Have you thought what you might do?"

Miriam shook her head.

"I'd have you here, Miriam, you know that. But you must realise it's going to be one of the first places he looks, if he comes looking for you. If he's dead, well then, better you were gone from Kavtrin completely."

"Maybe I should just go to the Justice, Shalin. I mean, if he's dead?"

"Now don't talk stupid, girl!" Shalin snapped. "You've done the right thing. You got yourself out, you looked after your lad. You've walked all the way here, and *now* you talk about going to the Justice?"

"If he's dead though..." She trailed off.

"What? Because it's the law?" Shalin scoffed. "You know as well as I do, people die in this city every day. Caerl wasn't rich or important, they won't bat an eye. IF he's even dead!" She took a deep drink, and set down her glass again. "Now, before you started on that nonsense, I was about to ask if you have anywhere you could go. Somewhere outside of Kavtrin, until you get on your feet? Are you in touch with your family at all?"

Miriam shook her head. "No. And it's been too long. I couldn't just turn up, not now. To be honest, I don't even know if they're still there."

"It's a start, Miriam. Go there and see. It gets you away from any... problems here. And it gets you moving off your behind, girl!"

"I don't have any money, Shalin. I hadn't really thought past maybe someday getting away from Caerl, and finding a job somewhere with just me and Devin. It was all just rainy day dreams, but now..."

Shalin took a deep breath, visibly biting back words which were too harsh for the moment. "Wait here," she said tersely and strode from the room. Miriam sat by the fire, listening to the sounds of raucous laughter and merriment from the common room. She was dimly aware of Shalin's voice in the hallway. The words were indistinct, but the tone spoke volumes. A few moments later, she stepped back into the kitchen.

"I've a few things to organise, but we *will* sort you out, Miriam. For now, I think you probably need a bed. You look like you're about to drop off your feet. Why don't you head up and climb in with your boy? We'll talk more in the morning."

Chapter Two

Devin woke in confusion at the unfamiliar creak and clatter of the wagons as they made their way along the road. He sat up on the hard wooden bench-seat, swinging his legs down, thankful for the folded blankets that were acting as a cushion under him. Realising that the figure next to him was not his mother, he sat upright with a lurch, wiping the drool from his face and looking around uncertainly.

"She's in the back, lad," said the man next to him as he clucked the horses on. "I'm Garret, you're Devin, and now we're not strangers. So now there's no need to be nervous, see?" He smiled down at the boy.

Devin gave a tight smile back at the strange man and took in his surroundings. They were trundling along on a wide, well-travelled road with broad, sweeping fields on either side of them. Nodding heads of wheat stirred in the slight breeze and bright blue birds swooped and dove for insects in the morning sunlight. In the distance, Devin could see the fields giving way to trees as the road rose into the hills.

Garret was a grizzled and daunting looking man that Devin would probably have been scared to approach if he hadn't introduced himself in such a way. He was dressed in dark and hardened leathers under a rough cloak. Devin was a young boy, but not so unobservant as to not notice the long knife at the man's belt or the scars on his face.

"In the back?" Devin asked, in hushed tones.

"She was tired. I told her to go and get some sleep and I'd drive for a bit. Now that you're awake, do you think you can handle the cart for a few minutes?"

"Me?" gaped Devin. "I don't know. I mean, I've never..."

"It's not hard, boy. The horses'll follow the wagon in front anyway, and I'll only be gone a few minutes. This here's Beth," he said, gesturing towards the piebald horse on the left. "An' this one's Bunion. He used to be a bit of a handful, but he's settled down these days." He handed the boy the leather reins, and watched him for a few minutes until he was satisfied. Then he reached out a short hunting bow from behind the seat and grabbed up a quiver of arrows. With a grin, he hopped off the cart and was gone. Leaning over the side, Devin saw him smoothly unhitch his horse from the back of the cart and haul himself into the saddle before turning sharply and riding back down the line of wagons. Clearly, this was something he'd done more than a few times. Remembering his responsibilities, Devin turned his attention back to the road and held the reins seriously. The horses didn't seem to notice overly much, and plodded along at the same pace.

They were travelling in a team of six wagons which had been moving since before light. Devin vaguely remembered being put into the wagon and wrapped up in blankets, whilst his mother quietly said her goodbyes to Shalin, and then they were off. It had all seemed very exciting as they passed through the city and then moved out through the gates and onto the roads. Very quickly though, it had become dull and boring and he'd fallen into a half-doze as he slumped down next to his mother.

The wagons were serviceable, but showed signs of heavy wear. To Devin's inexperienced eyes, though, they looked quite fine. They were all heavily loaded with various wares from Kavtrin, and the team of fifteen caravan guards served to demonstrate the value of the cargo. The guards seemed a hard-bitten lot, an impression reinforced by the selection of hard boiled leather and varied bits of mail. They rode on either side of the caravan, their eyes sweeping the fields frequently, armed with both bows and swords and saying little.

The wagon shook as Garret appeared next to him in the seat and grinned at him. "All okay, then? No broken wheels? No fighting off bandits?"

Devin laughed and shook his head.

"Good work then, lad. We'll make a guard of you yet!"

"You're a caravan guard?" wondered Devin. "I thought you were just a driver."

"What did you think the bow was for lad? Shooting squirrels?" Garret laughed again.

"I don't know, I didn't think about it," replied Devin. He decided he liked the man. He had a ready laugh and an easy way about him.

"No, I'm no driver lad, but I hope on this trip all I'll be shooting *is* dinner."

Devin looked at him, the unspoken question must have been obvious on his face.

"Killing a man is no small thing, lad. You take all he is and all he could be with one stroke," Garret explained, his eyes faraway. "I don't know a man who has done it and not regretted it in some way. An' those that say they don't, are either liars or less than men."

The day passed pleasantly for Devin, as Garret regaled him with tales of travelling to distant lands and time spent hunting.

Miriam woke just past noon and sat in silence, watching. It felt good to see him with a man and not be on edge for once. She had avoided thinking about whatever might have happened to Caerl. He had brought all of it upon himself. Her change of attitude was, in no small part, due to another lecture from Shalin that morning. She had been awakened at dawn and informed that Shalin had arranged passage with a caravan of wagons to Savarel for both her and Devin. They were leaving within the hour, and as she gasped and made weak protestations, Shalin had rushed her around the inn, packing old clothes for both Miriam and Devin from her and her son's rooms. The final straw had come as she stood outside the inn, when Shalin forced a fat purse into her hands.

"You'll need something to set you up in Savarel," she'd advised and refused to take no for an answer.

Miriam had eventually accepted with tears in her eyes, promising to repay her friend as soon as she could, though who knew when that might be.

She sat up on the improvised bed in the back of the wagon, just behind the seat. Watching the scenery idly for a time, she listened to Devin pepper Garret with questions. Eventually, she fell into a light doze whilst watching Devin's hero worship grow.

That evening, the wagons drew into a circle with a fire pit dug at the centre. Devin sat entranced, as a driver named Mika played on a wooden flute. Miriam made her way over to the fire and spoke to the woman at the pots. She was soon humming contentedly to herself as she cut vegetables on a long wooden board.

Dinner was a rough stew, but delicately seasoned, and Devin devoured it before asking for a second helping. Mika picked up his flute as soon as his bowl was empty, and Devin sang along and laughed at the wagoneer's tales as he nestled close to his mother. She sat, not really listening, her eyes and mind elsewhere as she picked disinterestedly at her food. How sad it was that Devin was only just now discovering simple pleasures. The guards, Miriam noticed, did not join in with the merriment. They ghosted amongst the trees, with only one or two at a time coming in to the fire for food every half an hour, until they were all fed.

"That was a wonderful meal, Ma'am," Garret hunkered down beside them. "Nancy is a good wife to Mika but she can't cook worth a damn, if you'll excuse my language."

Miriam laughed. "I've heard far worse than that, Garret, and it's Miriam. Please?"

"As you wish, Miriam," he replied with a smile. He stood and moved off to speak to one of the guards for a moment before sitting back down beside her.

"It looks like your lad here's day is done." He nodded at Devin with a smile.

Miriam looked down and saw Devin's eyes were closed. A half-empty bowl of stew was tilted dangerously in his hand. She reached down and took the bowl quickly, setting it on the ground beside them.

"He's had a rough couple of days," she admitted. "I should probably get him bedded down."

"It looks like you both have," the grizzled man said gently. "I can put him down easily enough. It looks like he's good and gone. You stay here and I'll bring you something to drink."

He moved quickly before she could protest and carried Devin over to the wagons. He was as good as his word though, and returned swiftly with a leather wineskin and two wooden cups. He poured out a good-sized measure of rich red wine and handed a cup to her. "So, what brings a lovely young lady like yourself to be running?" he asked with a smile.

"Not running," she replied smoothly, as she sipped the wine, "Just travelling."

"I think it's a bit more than that," Garret said, nodding at her face. Her eyes widened for second and her free hand drifted to her face and the bruise that had yet to fade.

"A man like that usually gets what's coming to him," Garret muttered.

"My husband," she admitted as she stared into the dark wine.

"Well, I suspect you're better off without a man like that," he said and took a deep drink. She copied him and they sat in a companionable silence for a time.

"What about you?" she asked, mostly to break the silence. "No one waiting by the door for you?"

"I was married, years ago." He spoke slowly, as if dredging through something unpleasant.

"What happened?" Miriam asked, curiosity getting the better of her manners.

"I lost her to the red fever," Garret said with a tightness to his voice.

"Oh!" Her hand flew to her mouth. "I'm sorry, Garret. I didn't mean to drag up painful memories."

"It's fine," he said, smiling sadly. "It was a long time ago."

"Not that long, surely? I mean, you can't be more than thirty-five summers."

"Are you enquiring after my age, madam?" he said, his lips twitching as he fought against a smile at her instant blush. He refilled their cups and nodded towards the wagons. "He's a good lad though. Your boy I mean. So it can't have been all bad."

"No," she said softly. "No, it wasn't. It was wonderful in the beginning."

"So, what happened?" he asked, looking into the fire.

"This stuff," she tapped the edge of the cup with a fingernail.

"Wine?"

"Wine, or ale. Anything that did the job in the end."

Garret gave a slow nod. "I've known a few men like that myself. The kind that are fine on the street, but their woman's eyes tell another story."

Miriam sniffed into her cup and took another deep drink. The wine was strong but smooth, and slipping down entirely too easily.

"So, how did you meet him then?" Garret asked.

"He was a caravan guard actually," she admitted with a smile.

"Like me?" he said, raising his eyebrows.

"No," she replied quickly. "No, he was nothing like you. He was young and brash and, well, everything that a stupid girl finds attractive."

"Am I so very old and ugly, then?" he smiled as she blushed again.

"You're a rotten tease, is what you are," she said laughing, swatting at his arm.

"No, he was fine when we first met. He promised me the moon and I believed he'd get it for me too." Her lips tilted up at the memory, the expression at odds with the purple and yellow bruising on her cheek. Garret sat in silence, waiting for her to go on.

"Then he started with the drinking. He'd be fine for a time, and then he'd go too far and we'd be struggling for a bit." She looked at him. "We moved around quite a bit. Rent. Well, you can imagine how it was." Garret nodded, sipping his wine and holding her gaze.

"Then along came Devin." She laughed suddenly. "We'd tried for a bit, but nothing came of it. Then, just as things were hitting rock bottom and I was ready to pack my bags, along he came." She twisted her lips wryly. "Actually it couldn't have come at a worse time."

"How did he take it?" Garret asked.

"He was wonderful." she smiled. "I mean, he changed overnight. He was kind, considerate. He stopped with this." She held out her cup again and Garret refilled it, overflowing it so the wine ran down the back of her hand. She laughed and waved off his apology as she shook her hand and licked off the drips.

"But then it slowly slipped back," she carried on. "He was drinking again and things got bad. Really bad." She touched her face and grimaced unconsciously.

"So, what do you plan to do now?" he asked, ignoring the grimace and taking another drink.

"Well, we're going to go to Savarel," she said, suddenly aware of how much the wine was thickening her tongue. "From there, I'm not sure. Start again, I suppose."

"I spend quite a bit of time in Savarel," he said, and his meaning was clear. She turned to look at him shyly and caught his expression, their eyes met, and then his head was moving slowly towards her. He didn't think...? Did he? She moved back sharply, turning her face away from him and towards the fire.

"I can't," she gasped. "I mean, it's just too soon." She turned to face him, expecting anger or confusion but his face was calm, apologetic even.

"I'm sorry, Miriam," he offered. "I should never have..."

"It's fine." She cut him off. "It's just too soon right now. Maybe once we get to Savarel." She left it hanging but met his eyes for the briefest moment, flashing a smile.

* * *

The days fell into a pattern, with Devin at the reins more often than not and chattering away to Garret. More than once Miriam had offered to tell Devin to leave the poor man alone, but Garret rebuffed her with a smile and a laugh, seeming to enjoy the boy's attention. The fields had long since given way to trees. For close to two weeks, they had been travelling through woodlands, broken here and there by tiny hamlets or farms. By the fifth day however, they had entered the forest proper and the road narrowed as it twisted and snaked its way through the trees.

Devin noticed that the trees on either side of the road had been cleared. Every now and then one of the guards would ride off the path to hack down a sapling. "Why are the trees cut?" he asked Garret curiously.

"This forest used to be a favourite for bandits," Garret explained. "It's been standard practice for all guards to cut down any sapling within two hundred paces of the road for years. Stops them shooting from the trees, see?"

Devin's eyes grew wide. "Real bandits?" he gaped.

"Real enough, lad. I shouldn't worry too much though. This road is well-travelled and we're a bit too large a caravan for most thieves. They usually stick to smaller groups or anyone fool enough to travel alone."

Devin thought back to the few travellers he'd seen on the road. All of them had been in parties of ten or more, save the lone messenger travelling on a powerful-looking horse. "What about the messenger?" he said.

"Messengers are trained to fight, or run. The horse can gallop away from most problems. Plus, they're crazy." Garret grinned. "You couldn't pay me enough for their job. Roads are dangerous places when you're alone, fast horse or not." He watched the boy scanning the trees fearfully, then picked up his bow and laid it on the lad's lap. "Try this for size," he suggested.

Devin lifted the bow, his eyes like saucers as he marvelled at the weapon. It was slightly longer than he was tall and strung with a hemp string. He stood and braced his calf against the seat for balance, drawing back the string and loosing an imaginary arrow.

"Did you get it?" Garret asked with a smile.

"What?" Devin replied, confused.

"The deer. It looked like you did. It was a great shot."

Devin grinned, and then sat quickly as the wagon hit a rut and lurched.

"Be careful, Devin!" Miriam cried from the back of the wagon.

"I'm okay, Mum," he said back over his shoulder.

"Now you've gone and got me in trouble," he muttered sideways to Garret.

"Life's no fun without getting into a little bit of trouble now and then," he said in a stage whisper.

"I heard that," called Miriam sweetly. "Unless you want to be cooking for yourself tonight sir, you'll watch what you say to my son."

Garret laughed and turned his attention back to the road.

The skies had clouded over around mid-morning and a light drizzle had begun to mist down. By mid-afternoon, the rain had settled down and decided to put in a real effort. The wagon slowed and had to fight for every mile as the road surface became less of a road, and more of a muddy track. Devin left the driving to Garret, who was now wrapped up in his cloak with a broad-brimmed hat crammed down on his head. He scowled at the road, as if the rain were a personal affront, and muttered darkly out at the wet.

"Looks like you've made a friend," observed Miriam as he climbed over the back of the wooden seat and into the wagon.

Devin grinned and sat down in the space his mother had created by stacking and shoving the crates and sacks out of the way.

"He's funny," said Devin. "I've never met anyone like him before."

"He does seem to be a nice man," agreed Miriam. "It would be nice if he could visit you, sometimes, once we get to Savarel."

Devin smiled at the thought and then looked at her with serious eyes. "Where are we going, Ma?" he asked. "I mean, I know we are going to Savarel, but where?"

"We'll go and see if we can find your Grandpa first," Miriam said. "If we can't find him, well then, we'll just have to see how things go. It's our adventure, right?"

"I suppose it is," said Devin.

A commotion from the front of the caravan drew their attention, and their wagon came to halt. Garret hopped down to the road in one smooth motion.

"What's going on?" Miriam called after him.

"Not sure yet, Ma'am, I'll be back shortly," he yelled back, without bothering to turn.

Devin looked around at the trees set back from the road, his eyes darting this way and that as Garret's tales of bandits came back into his mind. The rain was slowly turning into a steady downpour and it was hard to see more than a few dozen feet in any direction. He looked at his mother and they shared a smile which they both knew to be false as they waited.

The wagon rocked, heralding Garret's return. "Something wrong with one of the wheels. We're going to be stuck here for a time while they try and fix it." Garret's easy manner was offset by his nervous glance towards the tree-line, while he reached into the wagon for his bow and slung the quiver of arrows over his shoulder.

"Are you expecting trouble?" Miriam asked softly.

"Never hurts to be ready is all, Ma'am." Garret replied. "I can't see any bandit coming out in this though. Weather like this is best suited to being inside a tavern somewhere, trying to get the serving wench onto your lap..." He trailed off suddenly, as if he had just realised who he was talking to. Covering a sudden flush by clearing his throat, he gruffly muttered, "Stay here, and out of sight." He reached down past Devin for a wicked-looking short sword, and climbed out into the rain.

Miriam pulled Devin down into the back of the wagon, and they lay quietly amongst the sacks and crates. The road was oddly silent after the creak and rattle of the caravan. The only noise was the soft hiss made by the rain striking the treated canvas roof of the cart and the sounds of their own breathing. Peering over the back of the seat, she saw Garret talking with two of the other guards and gesturing towards the distant trees, before making his way back towards the wagon.

He hauled himself up and clucked at the horses, taking the wagon off the road, and positioning it into a rough circle to the side of the stricken wagon. As they passed, Miriam could see several of the guards and drivers struggling to hold one side of the wagon up in the air, as others placed thick sections of wood underneath to serve as a brace. One wheel lay on the ground nearby, damaged beyond repair.

"Right," said Garret, twisting around in the seat to speak to the pair. "They'll soon get that wheel changed, and then we can be on our way." He looked at Miriam speculatively. "We may as well have a spot of lunch while we're here?"

"That, sir," said Miriam tartly, "was pathetic."

He stood and as he extended an arm to help Miriam over the back of the bench, an arrow buried itself neatly into the seat beside his hand with a solid thunk. Garret's response was instant. Shoving Miriam hard so she fell back down into the wagon, he used the force of the shove to propel himself out of the seat, and down next to the wheel.

"Stay down!" he shouted, as he nocked an arrow and crept to the corner of the cart.

Shouts of "bandits!" were coming from the rest of the caravan, and the guards flew into action, dropping tools and drawing weapons. Arrows continued to fly from the tree-line, travelling in a low arc to cover the range, but hitting little more than the ground and the occasional wagon.

Devin, lying in the back of the wagon, could just see Garret through a gap where the canvas met the wooden side and saw the confused look on his face. Suddenly, a cry came up from the other side of the camp. Swearing viciously, Garret tore around to the other side of the wagon. Devin flew across the wagon bed, ignoring Miriam who grabbed at him and made frantic hushing motions at him. With a sharp tug, he managed to create another peephole through which to watch the attack.

A group of a dozen or so rough looking men, had made it half-way to the wagons before the ruse had been uncovered, and were now charging with weapons raised. Four of the caravan's guards rushed to meet them, while the rest held bows and fired at the oncoming bandits.

Garret stood tall, loosing arrow after arrow, but they either dropped short or flew off wildly. After four or five shots, the string snapped completely. "Cursed rain." he swore. "Drop the bows and attack," he bellowed, pulling his short-sword from its scabbard and a long knife from his belt as he charged.

The fight was vicious and brutal. Devin saw, almost at once, that the stories he had heard of battle held nothing in common with an actual sword fight. Men slipped and cursed at the wet even as they slashed and hacked at each other in desperate attempts to kill or maim. There was little or no grace in the fight, and Garret was no exception as he slid in the muck and used the opportunity to strike savagely at a man's leg. The blade bit deeply into the bandit's leathers, and he cried out as blood sprayed from the wound. Devin's mouth fell open as he watched the man drop to one knee, only to meet Garret's sword coming the other way.

Three of the guards were rolling on the ground screaming, and half of the bandits were dead or dying in the mud in just a few short minutes. A cry from behind the wagon raised a gasp from Miriam. Garret's head shot round for a moment, before turning back at the last second to save him from a spear thrust that would have taken him in the throat.

The bandit stepped backwards, using short jabbing thrusts to keep Garret at a distance and himself outside the reach of his short-sword. An ugly scar ran down the side of his face and carved a silvery line through his close-cropped black beard. With a fluid grace that had been lacking on the muddied field, Garret stepped into the next thrust, moving the spearhead slightly to the side with the flat of his sword and then sliding it down the shaft before lashing out with his boot at the side of the bandit's knee. Even inside the wagon Devin heard the sickening cracking noise as the man's leg flew out from under him, and he fell to the ground, screaming in agony.

The wagon rocked suddenly, shaking from a sudden weight. Silently Miriam pulled Devin towards the floor. They moved with agonising slowness so as not to alert the bandit who had appeared from the opposite side of the fight, and now taken up a position on the wagon's seat. He pulled a bowstring from a pouch, and strung a short-bow in one quick, practised motion. He drew back on the string and released smoothly, prompting a scream from a guard, before he reached for another arrow.

Devin looked frantically about him, and grabbed the heavy iron pan that Miriam had used to cook with the night before. He crept forward towards the seat, keeping low and praying the wagon wouldn't creak. Rising up behind the bandit, and ignoring Miriam's frantic flapping motions, he swung the pan at the back of the man's head with all of his strength. The pan made a dull ringing sound as it connected, the impact tearing it from Devin's grasp. The bandit shot forwards, but the blow of a small ten year old boy was not enough to knock him out, and he turned to see Devin cowering back away from him. He reached into his belt and the long dagger made a steely hiss as he pulled it free from the sheath.

"You won't regret that for long, boy," he rasped, as he made to step over the seat.

A blade was savagely thrust up into his groin and he screamed a shockingly feminine combination of pain and outrage. Garret reached in and dragged him from the seat before climbing back up and peering into the back. "Everyone alright?" he asked tersely. Miriam nodded, white-faced, and Garret took up the reins and slapped them down hard onto the horses' rumps.

"Let's get out of here then shall we?"

The startled horses leapt forward as he tried to navigate out of the circle and onto the road. Arrows slammed into the seat next to him, and tore through the canvas of the wagon, but they did not slow. It seemed like they were away, until a hook-nosed bandit with hard eyes stepped neatly into the road. In an unhurried fashion he watched as the wagon bore down upon him, then stepped casually to the side and drove his spear into Bunion's neck. The horse screamed and tried to rear against the traces before going down in a twitching heap. Beth struggled as Bunion's weight pulled her sideways and she whinnied in terror. She was fighting a losing battle though, and the wagon lurched violently before crashing onto its side.

Devin and Miriam were hurled violently to the ground. Mercifully, the sacks of goods were between them and the crates, and served as a buffer to some extent. Miriam staggered to her feet and pulled the terrified boy to her, holding his hand and clambering over the crates and sacks as she made her way to the front of the wagon.

Beth was struggling against the traces, but was still hitched firmly to the fallen wagon. Bunion, however, lay still and the scent of his blood was driving the dray horse to hysterics. Miriam climbed gingerly out of the wagon and stepped well away from the flailing horse, looking for Garret.

He stood not far from the wagon, long knife and sword in hand, as he watched the spear-wielding bandit approach. "You evil little bastard," he muttered. The bandit smiled a slow, lazy smile and edged closer.

"Any chance of letting me go with the boy and the woman?" Garret ventured.

"Can't see it," said the man, laconically.

"You've got the whole damned caravan, man. What do you want with a boy and his mother?"

Devin looked around quickly and saw that this was true. The guards had been slaughtered to a man and the two remaining drivers stood some distance behind them against one wagon with bandits surrounding them. Several of the bandits stood watching Garret with cruel amusement on their faces.

"Don't want the boy especially," the man said with a smirk. "Gets cold and lonely in the woods though. A woman like that'd keep a man warm at night."

Miriam stared at the man with a sick horror. What kind of twisted fate had allowed her to escape Caerl only to be a bandit's whore in the woods?

Garret sighed and stepped away from the wagon, giving himself room to move freely. All traces of the man Devin had spent the previous few weeks with had fallen away. The amiable wagon driver was gone. In his place stood the seasoned caravan guard with weapons drawn.

The bandit approached slowly, with his spear already in guard position. Miriam noticed he carried no shield and wondered at that. From her years working in her father's tavern, she knew a man with a spear usually held a shield too. A spear alone was the choice of experts or fools. Miriam found herself fervently hoping he was the latter.

Garret and the man began to circle each other slowly, not yet fighting but testing the other's speed and intent. She looked about her for something that she might use to help, but then she spotted Devin. The boy had run back to the wagon and was rummaging through the wreckage. She opened her mouth to call after him, but the bandit struck and the sound of steel on steel drew her back to the fight.

The bandit used his spear as a bladed staff, spinning and striking with both the blade and haft. Garret backed away from him, looking for all the world as if he had never held a sword before today, a panicked expression on his face. Encouraged by Garret's expression, the hook-nosed bandit lunged at his chest. Garret stepped nimbly to the side and, placing the flat of his long knife against the spear, slid down the shaft and struck savagely with his short-sword at the bandit's arm.

Where his ploy had worked so well before, it failed now and the bandit seemed ready for Garret's move, shifting backwards smoothly and sliding the spear down, past the end of Garret's knife and into his leg. It was a light blow, lacking the strength to do any real damage, but the spear blade looked to be razor sharp and left a clear scar in the leather. He shifted away smoothly, his feet moving lightly and barely seeming to touch the muddy track.

Garret muttered a curse and shifted back and away to give himself room for a moment. His eyes never leaving his opponent as he began to circle once more, he held the short-sword low and his long knife at the ready. The spear thrust at him again and he skipped to the side before lunging back in and slashing viciously at the man's ribs. The blade struck, but the man was already moving away, robbing the blow of the force it needed to cut through the thick leather armour.

He launched a sudden flurry of attacks, feinting to get inside the reach of the spear. It seemed as though he was outmatched, his every strike knocked easily aside as the bandit used both the blade and the shaft of the weapon to parry his strokes, the spear whirling in his hands. Garret's blades danced and slashed independently, as he avoided falling into any pattern, but each strike met only empty air or the shaft of the spear.

The man struck once, twice, three times with the spear, forcing Garret to parry desperately, and then lashed out with his foot, sweeping Garret to the ground. He raised the spear high to strike and then froze as an arrow buried itself in his back.

Both Garret and Miriam looked around in shock as Devin tried to nock another arrow, his hands shaking visibly. The bandit glared back at the boy, the arrow clearly not having penetrated deeply enough through the armour to cause any significant damage. Moving like a snake, Garret took advantage of his distraction and rose to one knee, arms extended as he thrust both blades through the armour and deep into the bandit's belly.

Tearing the weapons free, as the man hissed and sank to the muddy road, Garret beckoned frantically to Devin as he saw the three bandits who had watched the fight motioning in his direction.

"Into the trees!" Garret cried, and grabbed at Devin, half-dragging the boy along as he charged up the bank and plunged headlong into the woods. Miriam scrambled frantically up the bank behind him, looking over her shoulder as the bandits gave chase. Once at the top of the bank, the woods were dense and she fought to keep up as leaves and branches slapped her in the face and caught at her dress. She screamed as the arrows began to hiss through the trees around them. Garret, not even slowing or bothering to turn, lifted Devin into his arms and shifted into a sprint.

The ground sloped down gently, which helped to keep Miriam running, but her breath was already ragged and she could see she was beginning to lag behind. She fell twice in quick succession, tripping over unseen roots, and it was as she clambered to her feet from the second fall that the arrow struck. She felt it tear through her flesh, glancing off the bone high in the side of her thigh and she screamed hard as she fell to the ground again. Garret was there, it seemed in seconds, pulling her to her feet and helping her along. The arrows kept flying, although now they were hitting trees or being foiled by leaves and twigs more often than not.

"Devin lad, you go with your Ma," Garret said gently. "Keep going, I'm going to have a chat with these lads."

"No! Please don't leave us here," pleaded Miriam, but the big man was already moving back towards the bandits, keeping low and moving from tree to tree.

"Go!" he hissed back at them, and then he was gone.

They floundered on through the trees, and she tried not to think about why the arrows had stopped, or the sudden silence behind them. The forest floor was carpeted with old leaves and lush green ferns. It would have been a beautiful sight were it not for the pain lancing through her with every step. She didn't dare stop to look at the wound, but she could feel the blood running down her leg and the flesh tearing as she hobbled along. Devin was moving as if asleep, his eyes glassy and unseeing.

Screams and the distant clash of steel on steel, prompted her to pull Devin to a stop by a thicket of brambles. A natural channel led into the tangle, and she could just make out a hollow inside. Miriam lay down and squirmed her way in, adrenaline dulling the pain in her leg. Devin, being smaller, made it inside with no problems. His face was still pale and drawn, and he flinched with every faint sound of the fight.

The brambles were incredibly dense and Miriam could barely see out. A faint animal smell suggested this had once been a den for some manner of forest creature, but the ground looked undisturbed. They huddled in the thicket, listening to the faint sounds of fighting, and when the silence eventually came she lay, waiting for Garret, wishing she could still hear the swords.

She lay there for what felt like hours, as Devin tried and failed, to lie still beside her. Every time he fidgeted, three or four thorns dug into her side, causing her to flinch away which sent a jolt of pain from her leg. A soft shaking beside her brought her out of her thoughts and she realised with a pang of guilt that Devin was crying, but was too scared to make a noise. She pulled him close and wrapped him in her arms, making soft hushing noises and kissing the top of his head, as silent tears ran down her cheeks. Eventually, giving in to both physical and mental exhaustion, they slept.

She woke hours later to a gnawing agony in her leg and jerked violently away from it, stabbing herself with thorns as she did so. Cursing under her breath, she shook Devin awake, and they made their way out of the brambles. It was time to take control of the situation. Garret hadn't returned so he was either dead or captured. Either way, they were on their own.

With Devin in hand and half asleep, she hobbled back in the direction they had fled. It didn't take long to find Garret. He lay close to one of the bandits, his body torn and broken, obviously dead. She made Devin stand behind a tree while she rummaged through the bodies, taking the long knife and a tinderbox. On a whim she took the bandit's hunting bow as well. The most important thing, was to attend to the wound in her leg. It had been left too long already.

If she sat almost cross-legged with her skirts hitched up she could see where the arrow had ripped through the top of her thigh. The wound was already angry and inflamed. She took Garret's knife and sliced and tore a strip from her skirts to bind her leg up as best she could.

She found Devin curled up beside the tree, rocking back and forth slowly with tears running down his cheeks. Crouching she took him into her arms.

"It'll be okay baby boy," she whispered. "The bad men are gone now." She held him for a time and eventually the tears subsided. At least he was crying now, she thought. Tears were better than being numb.

"Devin, you know what a willow tree and birch tree look like, don't you?" she asked gently.

"The bendy one with the long hair?" Devin asked.

"That's the willow, yes. The birch is the one with the shiny bark," Miriam smiled. "We need to find your Ma a willow or a birch tree so you keep a look out for me okay?"

They wandered for the best part of two hours before Devin spotted a willow tree. Miriam hacked ineffectually at the trunk until she managed to slice enough off to get at the softer bark underneath. It tasted foul and bitter but she knew it would help with the pain of her leg somewhat. This was only half a remedy. She knew that lessening the pain of her wound would do little unless they managed to find some water to clean it with. The willow bark would ease a fever, but this wouldn't help if the wound were to go foul.

Chewing on the bark lessened the pain, eventually, but the acrid taste was making her thirstier. The tall trees of the forest had blocked most of the rain, so the woods that had only been damp to begin with, were now almost completely dry. She kept them travelling downhill, in the hopes they would hit water. Common sense told her that any water must lay down the slope of the forest, and she had decided from the outset to travel away from the site of the ambush. The bandits had to live somewhere in these woods, and she had no intention of going anywhere near them again if she could help it. She felt reasonably confident that they were moving away from any encampment, since the bandits had come from the other side of the road, but still kept a wary eye behind them as they walked.

It was late afternoon when they finally found a small stream, and she and Devin collapsed beside it, leaning out over the water to drink directly from the surface in long gasping gulps. She forced herself to sit up and look at her leg again. The blood had soaked through the makeshift bandage and dried on the back of her thigh. She sent Devin off to collect twigs and small sticks, and set about clearing an area for a fire, digging a hollow with a broken branch. Devin returned shortly with a double armful of twigs, and his fingers stained a dark purple red. He dropped the wood and opened his hands to reveal the half-squashed blackberries. His smile was like the sun coming up, and easily eclipsed the joy she felt at the prospect of food.

They quickly devoured the berries and she sent him off for more, while she tried to start a fire. Garret's tinderbox was well-stocked and before long she had a fire going. She knew she ought to boil water to make clean dressings for her leg, but of course, they had no pot to hold water in. In the end, she settled for ripping more strips from her rapidly shortening skirts, and sent Devin to soak them in the stream before holding them on sticks above the fire until they steamed. It wasn't perfect, and the first two she tried came away blackened with smoke and soot until she caught the trick of it.

They stayed by the stream overnight, devouring the berries and some edible mushrooms. She mentally thanked her father for the trips they had made into the woods when she was a child. As she did, she realised it was the first time she had thought of him fondly in years.

The mushrooms and berries were not enough to fill either of them, and she sent Devin off again to collect acorns. Pounding them into a paste between two flat stones, she tasted it gingerly. Devin spat his out immediately and refused to try it again. She found that by mashing acorns into a pulp, and then baking it on the stones by the fire, it became slightly less disgusting. Even Devin managed to fight down a mouthful.

"Don't like it cold, huh?" she teased. "My little squirrel boy needs his acorns baked."

Devin giggled at this, the first real smile or laugh she'd seen since the ambush, and she took it as a good sign. "Want to go and find me some more acorns and blackberries, little squirrel?" she asked, and Devin scampered off into the trees.

By the end of the second day, it became obvious that they needed to move on. Devin needed real food, as did she. The main reason, she kept hidden from Devin. The flesh surrounding the wound in her leg was now a deep angry red and streaks were tracing down her leg. She knew enough about infection to know she needed to clean it, and she needed more than wet strips of her dress hung over the fire.

* * *

Miriam awoke in the moonlight, soaked in a hot sweat. She stood on unsteady legs and staggered towards the stream, before plunging face first into the shallow water. The splash woke Devin, who helped her up from the water.

"Do you hear the bells, darling?" she asked Devin brightly and smiled at his confused face.

She leaned on him as she stood but then took his hand and led the way through the woods, weaving in and out of the moonlit trees, laughing in delight.

The bells were tinkling lightly in her ears, calling her ever forward. Devin was following close behind, but she didn't think so much about the boy now. He would be fine. Everything was fine. She danced onwards through the trees, the pain in her leg gone, and her soaked dress seemed as light as gossamer.

She could hear horns now, and the sweetest flutes. The music was distant, but she could hear just enough to sing along with a wordless crooning as she danced, twirling and laughing through the trees.

"Mistletoe and berry-wine, sparrow song and ivy climb," she sang, as the words came to her unbidden. "Stream and stone, field and barrow, moonlight, stars bright, bone and marrow."

She darted away from Devin's grasping hands, moving faster and faster through the woods, dancing and spinning as she went, until she burst out of the trees and into a clearing. Moonlight bathed a ring of low stones cast in a rough circle with a taller stone set in the centre. The stones were half covered in moss, as if the forest floor were cradling them in an embrace. A bare patch here and there reflected the light. Thick moss and lush grass filled the clearing and Miriam laughed in delight as she began to weave in and out of the stones, singing and twirling.

* * *

Devin awoke with a start at a loud splash from the stream. He sat up, rubbed at bleary eyes and turned to see his mother lying face down in the water. With a gasp, he rushed to her side and tried to haul her out, but she was far too heavy for him to move. She rolled over and sat in the waist-deep water, laughing at him. Her eyes shone with a sickly sheen in the pale light from the moon and stars, and even soaked in the stream he could feel the heat pouring off her.

"Come on Ma, let's get you out, eh?" he suggested, and she stood agreeably, wading out of the stream and onto the bank.

"Can you hear the bells?" she slurred at him, and then laughed at his concerned face. She staggered off into the trees, lurching this way and that. Devin chased after her, calling her back, but she didn't stop or slow. She was almost running, moving with a painful limping gait, her soaked skirts slapping at her legs.

"Ma, please!" Devin called, close to tears.

Her voice carried back to him through the trees. She was singing, an odd crooning with words he didn't understand. "Lians'antha cu Savenfaer, Arun taer cu Brystlien lair. Tuertha cu Faana, C'rus cu Callow, Lune staer, Lis taer, Fis cu Halow."

She dashed away from him again as he caught up, and crashed through a stand of holly, ignoring and not even seeming to feel the cuts and scratches. Devin skirted around the holly and stopped as he spotted her.

She stood at the centre of a circle of short, mossy stones, swaying back and forth like a willow in a soft breeze. Her head was cocked to one side as if listening and her face was fixed in a jubilant smile. She stood next to a slightly larger stone that was positioned as if it were the hub of a wheel in relation to the rest of the circle. Unlike the other stones, this one had gathered no moss and almost seemed to shine in the moonlight. Devin walked towards her slowly, his eyes darting this way and that. He wasn't especially scared of the dark, but he was still a city boy, and the noises of the forest at night spooked him. A boy who was slightly older might have been terrified, but Devin was young enough to still think his mother could fix anything.

She smiled broadly at him and reached to take his hand. "Dance with me?" she whispered. She held his hands tight and spun him in a circle, leaning back against the force and he grinned, despite the crazy situation. Then she slowed and dropped one hand, leading him as she stepped in a dance, weaving in and out of the stones, all the while singing words he couldn't understand.

The dance was intricate and seemed far more than simple steps she was just making up. A hop here, a delicate spin there as she passed a stone, and singing, all the while the singing. There was a pressure building. Though nothing touched them it was almost as if something pressed against them, like a strong wind. This was smooth though, nothing so ragged as wind. It felt like the pressure you feel when you try and push a wide bowl down into an already full sink, straining against the buoyancy. Eventually he pulled her to a stop, his face red and chest heaving. She stood smiling at him in the moonlight. She didn't even appear to be breathing hard.

"Come on Ma, let's go back now?" he panted. She nodded agreeably and allowed him to lead her from the stones. As they stepped out of the circle, the night seemed to shudder like a sapling shaken by a thoughtless child. Devin looked around in a panic, but there was nothing to see. The sensation ended as suddenly as it had begun, and then the night was still.

Devin managed to navigate his mother back to their little camp without protest. For a short time, it was almost as if he were the parent, and she the child, as he encouraged her to lie down and put a cold wet cloth on her forehead. Eventually, they both slept under the moon. Curled up together to create a little haven against the darkness. She burned with fever but Devin couldn't think of that now. He closed his eyes, and slept.

* * *

The next morning brought harsh realities. Miriam woke mid-morning and made her way to the stream, discovering a host of unexplained scratches and scrapes as she did so. Devin was still sleeping, but decisions had to be made. Whilst there might be water here in the stream, they were not eating enough, nor was it the right kind of food. Her leg was not going to get better by itself. It was time to leave.

She started a fire and soaked her bandages again, before hanging them close to the fire to try and boil the water in them. Looking around she managed to locate a fallen branch that would serve as a crutch or staff. She gathered a few handfuls of mushrooms and ate slowly. They tasted gritty and earthy, but she forced them down and then worked to clean her wound. Her leg seemed swollen and felt hot to the touch. The pus ran freely down her thigh as she worked to clean it with the steaming cloth and the smell was enough to make her gag. The pain was incredible, but she bit her lip and carried on until the wound was clean, and slowly bleeding pure red blood. She bound the wound as best she could, wrapping the still steaming cloth around her thigh and tying it off. Then it was time to wake Devin.

After a small breakfast of the raw forest mushrooms they set off. Devin was telling a tale about his dream, something about her dancing in the moonlight, but she was really only half-listening. Just walking took an enormous amount of effort and concentration, and she was trying hard to not think about the chances of them actually making it out of the woods.

They continued to search for food as they hiked, stopping every time one of them spotted berries or mushrooms. Half of everything they found, they ate, and the rest they bundled into a pouch made from Devin's shirt. The day was warm enough that he could go shirtless with no complaints.

The forest seemed endless, and it was a constant worry that they might be drifting in circles. She tried to keep to a straight line by sighting on a particular tree and walking to it, and then picking another, but there never seemed to be many trees in exactly the direction she picked. Water was another worry, as they had neither seen a pond or heard any other streams and they were both soon dry-mouthed. Berries helped, but for only a second and then the tartness of the berry seemed to create a thirst all of its own.

They came across a shallow pool as the sun touched the tree-tops, and Miriam sank down next to it gratefully. Devin flopped to the ground and immediately drank deeply. She decided that she had never been so tired, or dirty in her life.

"When we get out of here, baby boy, I am never going near another tree!" she announced firmly.

Devin laughed and scooped another double-handful of water from the pool. It was crystal clear and fed from a tiny rivulet, trickling from a trail of rocks up against one side.

Miriam worked to start a fire and they fed on the remains of the mushrooms, before huddling together to ward off the chill of the night. Devin stared silently into the fire as his mother dozed and before long, he heard her snoring as the moon rose.

It had been a fine adventure for a time. Garret had been exciting and the run into the woods, whilst terrifying at the time, was a great tale to tell. Now though, it was just a boring slog and Devin was keen to get out of the trees. As he stared at the fire, he gradually became aware of just how silent the forest had become. Normally there was endless birdsong, the faint rustling of squirrels in the trees and other creatures in the undergrowth, but now it was utterly silent except for the soft snoring made by his mother.

He slowly became aware of an intense feeling of being watched. As a boy in Kavtrin, he had often seen cats stalk their prey. There was a time, just before they pounced, when they simply sat and watched. This was how he felt, as if some predator sat and surveyed their little camp, deciding whether they would make a good meal.

The night had turned cloudy, and so there was little light to be had from the full moon except when it occasionally broke through the clouds. What light there was came from the dying fire.

"Where do you go to, manling?" A voice, soft as velvet, cut through the stillness. Devin leapt up and stared about wildly, his head whipping this way and that as he searched for the speaker.

"Who said that!?" he cried. "Where are you?"

"Where do you go to, and why do you dance? Do you summon with intent?" The voice seemed to come from a different direction. It had an odd accent as if speaking a language unfamiliar to it, the words shaped strangely on its tongue.

"We're just trying to get home," Devin said softly.

"Ahh, home. I understand that. It is bad to be away from your home for too long. Bad to be, *kept* from it." The voice was soft but caught on that word.

Devin jumped again as he caught a hint of movement among the trees. Nothing so definite as catching sight of the owner of the voice, just the merest hint of a passing figure. His eyes caught again on a patch of darkness, and slowly the disparate images coalesced. It was a woman. She stood in the dark calmly, as if it was the most natural thing in the world for her to be there. She stepped towards him slowly out of the shadows, moving with an infinite grace, each step almost a dance in itself. She stopped just outside the tiny circle of light shed by the dying embers of the fire.

The clouds parted to bathe her in moonlight and Devin hissed with a sharp intake of breath. The woman's skin shone with a pale green colour where it was not covered by her simple tunic. It was as if her skin had a sheen all its own that threw back the beams of the moon. Her hair hung long and loose about her shoulders and was as silver as the moonlight. She turned and raised her face to the moon, almost seeming to drink in the light. Then the clouds blew in again and the moment was over.

"Why do you travel?" the creature asked, turning to face him again. Devin had stopped thinking of her as a woman. On some level he knew he ought to be fearful of her but she seemed more curious than threatening.

"We're going to find my grandpa," Devin answered self-importantly, as only a ten year old can.

The creature nodded sagely. "Seeking the elders. A fine task." She stepped towards the fire, another cat-like step that brought her closer to Miriam but yet somehow no closer to Devin. She crouched to her haunches suddenly and sniffed, almost seeming to taste the air in front of Devin's mother, before turning to look at him.

Her eyes shone in the light, and for the first time Devin could see they were a startling shade of amber. It may have been a trick of the poor light but he could see no pupils at all. They were just solid orbs of amber, gazing at him, unblinking in the night.

"This one will not go much further," she said in her strange accent. "Her wound is deep and foulness travels to her centre. When it finds it, she will be ended."

Devin blinked. "Can you help us?"

"Help you?" The creature cocked her head, looking for all the world like a curious bird for a moment. "Why would I do that?" she seemed genuinely perplexed. Devin had no answer to that and gave her a pleading look. "She sang?" she asked curiously. "At the stones? It was she who sang and danced?"

Devin nodded, confused as to how she knew about the stones.

"I suppose I might be able to help, at that." She took one tiny step backwards and suddenly she was gone, between one heartbeat and the next and without seeming to move. The shadows and half-light that made up her form seemed to shift and Devin found himself searching around for her in the darkness. He was breathing heavily, as if he had run a fast sprint uphill, and he turned to his mother still sleeping on the ground. Devin knelt and felt her forehead as he had been taught. It was burning to the touch again.

"As I said, there is a taint that moves to her centre," came the voice again.

He turned to see her stood close to the fire with a small wooden bowl and various implements. She knelt, as he watched in silence, and ground up various leaves mixing them with what smelled like honey and strong red wine. She stirred with one long finger, and seemed to smile as she did so, before taking one crouched step towards Miriam bearing the bowl.

Abruptly she stiffened and sniffed sharply at the recumbent form again. Moving so swiftly Devin wouldn't have thought it possible, she set the bowl down and pushed at Miriam roughly, rolling her over with her foot and revealing Garret's long knife.

The woman leapt backwards and landed in a fighting crouch, hissing savagely at Miriam like a wildcat.

"What's the matter?" cried Devin. The woman started, as if she had forgotten he was there, and bared bright white teeth at him.

"Fie! Fly! Be gone, little manling!" she spat at him. "Take your tainted *She* and be gone!" She drew herself up to her full height and Devin was struck with pure terror as she moved towards him, her steps slow and deliberate. Waves of enmity seemed to roll from her and Devin shied desperately away from her, sinking to the ground beside his mother.

"BEGONE!" the creature snarled and taking two steps backwards, she vanished into the trees.

Devin sank slowly to the ground. His breath was ragged as he looked around in the darkness. The night-calls of birds were slowly returning, and he could once more hear the faint rustling of animals in the undergrowth. He gathered up some of the wood from their pile and stirred the fire into life. The wooden bowl sat just to one side of the fire, and Devin sniffed at it curiously. The mixture had somehow transformed into something closely resembling water, albeit with a faintly oily sheen. The scent of wine had faded and the concoction smelt oddly of moss. He shuffled over to his mother and wormed his way into her arms. Staring out at the darkness, it was a long time before sleep finally claimed him.

Chapter Three

Devin woke the next morning, alone. He sat up on the leaf-covered ground and picked the pine needles and twigs from his hair. Looking around the clearing, he felt the first twinges of panic. The knife and tinderbox lay where they had been left last night, but there was no sign of his mother.

"Ma?" he called out. His voice sounded tiny to himself, the sound almost mocking him.

He made his way over to the pool and knelt, drinking down the sweet water and splashing some over his face. Looking around their small camp one last time, he scooped up the knife, and made his way over to the edge of the clearing.

He almost tripped over the bowl before he saw it. It lay on its side at the base of a holly bush. Devin crouched and picked it up, turning it over in his hands. The events of the previous night had been so bizarre he had almost convinced himself it had been a dream, but the bowl put an end to that. An adult might have been more shocked to see it, but Devin took it in his stride and saw it simply as an indication of the direction his mother might have gone.

It didn't take him long to find her. It looked as though she had got up in the night and blundered on through the dark until she grew tired, then simply slept where she was. Devin felt her head and shook her gently. "Ma?"

She opened her eyes and smiled at him with eyes that weren't quite focused. As she looked around the woods, Devin could feel the heat pouring off her. She was covered in a sheen of sweat, despite the cool of the morning.

"Do you want a drink Ma?" He went off to the pool in response to her nod, and filled the bowl with the cool, clear, water. It seemed to refresh her, but she insisted on setting out straight away without even bothering to search for any food.

Within the hour she was staggering almost aimlessly through the forest. It took all of Devin's efforts to try and keep them on a straight course. He managed to eat some berries as they passed bushes, but he was still desperately hungry. He tried to get her to take some, but she showed no interest.

They reached the ridge around midday. Devin had been following Miriam, trying to keep them travelling straight by sighting on particular trees as she had taught him. Her fever seemed worse than ever, and her skin was dry and burned to the touch. Despite that, she seemed more alert, and was happy enough to be guided by him. They did not stop though. She wouldn't stop to rest, and she became angry when he suggested it.

Between one step and the next, Devin saw the ground fall away in front of them as they passed through the last trees. They stood atop a ridge-line in the forest and, for the first time in what felt like weeks, Devin could see for miles. It actually took a minute or two to sink in that he could see beyond the forest, or that the edge of the trees was in roughly the same direction they had been travelling. The excitement of this was nothing compared to the thrill he felt when he realised that beyond the trees, was a road.

"Ma. Look!" he called, pointing at the brown smudge in the distance. He turned to see her leaning heavily against a tree, murmuring to herself. It didn't look like she had even heard him and after two more attempts, he gave up with a bitter sigh.

The ridge continued for some distance, but sloped downwards to his left. Even if he did manage to navigate through the trees, they wouldn't make it out of the forest before nightfall. Assuming, of course, that his mother would cooperate and walk where he led.

Devin trudged on through the undergrowth, trying to ignore the gnawing of his empty belly. Following the ridge-line proved harder than it looked. They were forced to travel in the wrong direction several times, to avoid bramble thickets, or steep ravines leading in from the ridge. By the time the ground was beginning to level off, indicating that they had made it off the ridge, the sun had almost set and the moon was rising. They had passed another stream some hours earlier so Devin could cope with the thirst, but he didn't think he had ever been this hungry. The berries and mushrooms that had sustained them during the previous few days seemed to have vanished, and with the failing light, it would be almost impossible to spot anything now. As he stumbled along in the near dark, he tried and failed, to keep tears of frustration from falling.

Miriam stopped suddenly, and Devin nearly crashed into her back. She had been leading the last few hours and, whilst still feverish, seemed much more aware of where they were, and what was going on.

She stood with her head cocked on one side, as if listening. Devin froze, listening too. It was too easy to dismiss her behaviour as fever dreams, there had been two or three times now when she'd heard animals he hadn't, and once, she'd saved them from a red-eyed sow with a litter of piglets. Devin was a city boy, but he knew enough not to go near a boar.

He listened carefully, but heard nothing but the sound of the wind in the treetops. "Come on Ma'" he said gently, trying to move her along with his touch. She ignored him, and stood with her head cocked, swaying gently back and forth as if dancing to some distant music.

He ground his teeth in frustration and looked through the murk for somewhere to camp for the night. Finally, with much persuading, he was able to get his mother moving again. Devin dared not move too far from the ridge. The forest seemed to twist in the half-light and he feared they would get turned around and never find it again. The cover given by the forest was reduced by the proximity of the ridge, and the wind tore through the trees, seeming to claw at the ragged remnants of his clothing.

He held Miriam's hand tightly as he led her through the woods, looking for some form of shelter without leaving the ridge. The howl cut through the woods despite the wind. Devin froze in place, eyes wide and his heart pounding painfully in his chest.

"Ma!" His voice suddenly sounded very young, even to himself. "Ma? Was that wolves?"

"Shhh!" came the hissed reply. "Just keep moving. Quietly now." Her voice was focused and clear. She seemed to have come back to herself for the moment.

An answering howl filled the night and suddenly the air was alive with the calls of the wolves. It seemed like they came from every direction at once. Devin looked to his mother for just a second before grasping her hand and running through the woods, his legs driven and ruled by fear. Leaves and branches tore at his hair and face as he fled from the howls, and he darted between the trees heedless of the noise he was making.

He didn't even see the stream, but flew through it, his legs suddenly soaked to the knees as he scrambled up the bank on all fours, grasping at half-seen roots and ferns. He could hear his mother close behind him, her breathing little more panicky gasps, thick with fear.

"Flee little manling," came the spiteful whisper from the trees, so soft that he wasn't sure he hadn't imagined it.

Another howl filled the night, startlingly close and spurring Devin and Miriam to new efforts and they sprinted headlong through the trees. Devin looked around as he ran, searching for movement among the trees over his shoulder. Miriam ignored everything but speed, looking straight ahead as she moved with a lurching gait, using a branch as a crutch.

Devin heard a whimpering noise as he ran and it was several yards before he realised that he was making it himself. He clenched his teeth and tried to concentrate on putting one foot in front of the other. His legs were burning and, despite her leg, his mother was outpacing him. He fancied he could hear snarling, and the crashing of leaves and bushes behind him as the wolves drew closer. Glancing over his shoulder, he saw a flash of silver grey fur in the moonlight, and then something struck his face and chest hard enough to make his vision spin and his ears ring. He slumped to the ground, bark scraping and tearing at his face as his vision swam in crazy circles and slowly faded to darkness.

Miriam jumped at the muffled crash behind her and turned in time to see Devin slide down the tree and collapse to the ground. The cold and the terror seemed to have reduced her fever, and she felt more able to think clearly. The wolves had fallen silent. She didn't know if this was good or bad, but she could hear nothing for the moment other than the wind blowing through the trees.

She flew to Devin in a panic and dropped to the forest floor beside him. Blood ran freely down his face from a nasty gash where he had run into the tree. She cradled his head to her as tears coursed unchecked down her face. "My baby!" she wailed. "Oh Lords and Ladies, Devin!"

Dimly she became aware of a warmth against her arm and realised it was his breath. He was alive at least. She turned this way and that in the moonlight, hoping to get a clearer view of his face but couldn't see much more than the fact he was bleeding.

A light footfall behind her was the only warning she had that she was not alone. She turned fearfully, expecting to face a huge wolf intent on an easy meal. Instead a woman stood there in the moonlight looking at her quizzically.

Miriam had a vague sense of recognition, but panic about Devin overrode any other thoughts. A calmer person would have asked what a woman was doing walking alone through the forest in the middle of the night. A more rational person would have noted the eyes, coloured amber with no visible pupils, or the inhuman grace with which the creature moved. Miriam was neither calm nor rational, and saw nothing other than potential salvation.

"He hit his head. We were running from the wolves, and he ran into a tree," she explained, her voice thick with tears and worry. The woman nodded slightly but made no attempt to move closer. Instead she stood silently, casually surveying the scene.

"He needs help. He's bleeding!" Miriam said, with a plea in her voice.

"He is, as you say, bleeding." Her voice was low and melodic and she almost seemed to sing the words.

"Don't just stand there!" Miriam screamed, fear and anger taking control. "Won't you help us?"

"Why would I want to do that?" the woman asked, seeming genuinely confused by the question.

"I could pay," Miriam said suddenly, her hand going to the purse tied beneath her skirt. The woman smiled a sudden, hard smile and her eyes flashed in the moonlight.

"An exchange then? You would submit to this?"

"An exchange? Yes! I have money, I'll pay whatever you like. Just help him, please?"

* * *

Devin woke to pain. His face felt strange, tight like a bad sunburn. This was overlaid with a throbbing pulse running through his forehead and left cheek, down to his jawline. He tried with some care, to open his eyes and noted only one would open. His hand made its way to his face, and his fingertips encountered what felt like leaves, and something sticky, like mud or honey.

"Do not touch it," a stranger's voice said.

"Devin sweetheart?" came his mother's voice. "It's a kind of medicine. Try not to touch it okay?" Her voice was calm, clear. The clearest she'd sounded in days. Despite the pain that was increasing the more he awoke, Devin felt a relief coupled with a wild exultation. They had found help. They were safe.

"Your manling will need rest. Make him drink this, I will return when the moon rises," the stranger said.

Then his mother was there, holding a wooden bowl to his lips, and encouraging him to drink a thick, sickly-sweet, liquid. It tasted like honey, and strong wine, and something else he couldn't identify. It burned all the way down his throat and the taste seemed to change subtly the more he drank. He didn't even notice himself getting drowsy until he felt his mother gently take the bowl from his lips, and his eyes softly closed.

Devin slept deeply until he was finally roused and they began walking. He was half-awake at best when he first caught sight of her. His head was still groggy from sleep, and whatever it was that he had been made to drink. There was a dreamlike quality to everything which was only exacerbated by the fact that they were travelling by moonlight. Despite this, he was certain that the woman travelling with them was the strange person he had spoken to the night his mother had been dancing around the stones. He squinted and tried to focus his blurry eyes upon her as he staggered along, leaning heavily on his mother.

As his head cleared he used the opportunity to study her more closely, she was definitely the creature from before. At a glance she looked broadly human, two arms, two legs. The similarities stopped there though. Her ears were swept up into points and her skin had a pale greenish cast to it that shone through, even in the moonlight. She was dressed simply in tight fitting clothes of a pale tan colour and though she walked barefoot, she moved with grace, unconcerned by the twigs and pebbles underfoot. As if she felt his eyes upon her, she turned and looked at him sharply, before smiling slowly. The smile said nothing of humour or affection. This was a cold smile that extended no further than the lips, her amber coloured eyes as cold and hard as the gem they resembled.

"What happened to me?" he asked his mother softly, as they made their way between the trees.

"You ran into a tree, knocked yourself senseless."

"Then what happened? I mean, what happened to the wolves?" Devin wondered.

"I don't know. I hadn't thought about it really. I mean, at the time, I was more worried about you." Miriam paused, stopping while she looked up at the sky.

"They stopped as soon as she arrived," she said finally, gesturing at the figure of the woman who was fast disappearing into the night. They hurried to catch up with Miriam supporting Devin with one arm.

"What about your leg?" Devin asked suddenly, realising she was no longer limping or using a crutch.

"She put some stuff on it. Amazing really. I've never seen anything like it, but it was almost completely better overnight." Miriam smiled. "It looks like we are both going to be fine."

Devin grinned at her in the moonlight.

The sky was beginning to brighten by the time the woman finally slowed. She turned and fixed Miriam with a feral look. "Just beyond these oaks lies your path," she said softly.

"Already?" asked Miriam. "It looked so much further away from the ridge earlier."

"You question me?" the woman replied, amber eyes bright and staring.

"No, no," Miriam said hurriedly, her words tripping over each other. "It just passed so quickly. I'm grateful of course..."

"Come." She moved swiftly through the trees, stopping with her hand resting on a huge oak, looking back at the pair of them expectantly.

Miriam hurried after her, eager to be out from under the trees. She stepped past the odd woman and stopped in confusion. The path led into a large clearing, a collection of low stones lay forming a ragged circle with a short monolith standing as a hub to the misshapen wheel. She spun slowly, looking this way and that. The trees were thick around the edges of the clearing and she could see no end to the forest.

"I don't understand," she said slowly. "You said we were here."

"As we are," replied the woman, moving up behind her. "As, everyone always is."

"You said our path was this way!" protested Miriam, her temper beginning to fray.

"As it is, as I have led you. And now you must pay."

"Oh, yes, of course," Miriam said in confusion, rummaging through her skirts to grab the purse given to her by Shalin. "Um, we never discussed an amount?"

"You assume I have any interest in your shiny trinkets," the woman said, moving closer to Miriam. "We agreed an exchange."

As she approached, Miriam wondered how she could ever have mistaken her for human.

"What do you want?" Miriam breathed as she took half a step backwards, away from the creature.

"Foolish *She!* You come and dance among the stones and then you ask what I want? How soon you have all forgotten." With two quick steps she was in front of Miriam and grasping her by the throat.

"Ma!" screamed Devin as the creature dragged her towards the stones with an unearthly strength.

Miriam gasped, her fingers raking ineffectually at the creature's arms.

"Ma!" Devin yelled again, racing after the creature as she moved to the monolith, pulling Miriam along effortlessly. He grabbed at her arm and tried to stop her, but it was like trying to stop the tide.

"Let her go!" he screamed and kicked savagely at the creature's leg. She stopped suddenly and fixed him with an intense gaze and then, as if holding his mother there took no more effort than holding a small child, she struck him with her free hand across the face. Devin flew through the air and landed some five feet away at the edge of the trees. He hauled himself to one knee as his head spun, and turned to face them.

Miriam had been dragged into the circle and was pressed backwards against the small monolith, her hands still clawing at the creature's wrist. The woman raised one hand high towards the moon and between one breath and the next they slipped into the stone as easily as a stick into water. They were gone.

"Ma!" shrieked Devin as he raced at the monolith and fell to his knees, clawing at the rough stone with tears running down his cheeks in the light of the uncaring moon.

* * *

Khorin stepped down from the cart and looped the reins around a dead tree. The horses wouldn't stray far anyway but they might hurt themselves otherwise. He walked through the tall grass easily, making his way under the trees. It was only just dawn and the weak watery light was barely enough to light his way once he was under the dense canopy. He carried a large axe over one shoulder, the haft resting easily on the leather vest covering his simple homespun. He'd spotted a stand of beech in here the other week and it was a good day to bring one or two of them down. He'd come back with Owen from the village later on in the month to have him help with the cutting, but the felling he could manage alone.

He walked slowly but deliberately, wasting no time but not hurrying either. Rushing was for younger men and after thirty years farming these lands, he had just about used up all his rushing. He was not a large man by any means. His hair and beard were shot through with grey and touches of white but his arms showed sinew as he flexed them on his axe handle, which told of a strength that could be called upon when needed.

Whistling rather tunelessly as he walked through the woods he tried to recall exactly where he'd seen the beech trees. Oak tended to burn hotter than beech, but for some reason Khorin had never felt comfortable bringing down an oak tree. Maybe it was something to do with acorns and squirrels. He chuckled quietly to himself at the thought.

He stepped over a small boulder half buried in the ferns, and found his way to the game trail. It wasn't much of a path, meandering this way and that, but it would get him to where he was going. Horses, now they at least would go in a straight line when pressed, but a deer couldn't walk in a straight line if its life depended on it.

He was so caught up in his reverie that he almost missed the boy altogether. He was curled up like a sleeping dormouse at the foot of an ancient willow. The branches and leaves seemed almost to cradle him as he slept. He was also filthy, and as sorry a state of a child that he had ever seen.

Khorin rushed to the boy and knelt down, feeling at his throat. His hair was down to his collar, he could almost have passed for a girl were it not for his sunken features. There was a pulse, but only barely and he almost missed it. He wet his hand in the leaves and held it under the boy's nose, feeling for the feather-light touch of his breath. Frowning he stood back and looked at the lad, there was something very wrong here. The boy was beyond gaunt and soaked through to the skin. The first touches of moss had begun growing on his clothes.

"How long has this child been here?" he whispered to himself.

He knelt down next to the boy, laying his axe down on the ground and gathered him up in his arms. There was ivy growing around the boy's legs but he pulled it free with a sharp tug that somehow failed to wake him. Shaking his head and wondering what could possibly have occurred here, Khorin cradled the child in his arms. A bow lay in the grass and leaves. He scooped it up, grunting at the effort of crouching with the boy. His axe lay forgotten at the base of the tree as he made his way out of the woods.

He made his way back to the farmstead and crashed through the door with one foot whilst crying out for his wife.

"Hannah! Where are you wife?" he bellowed as he rushed down the steps into the kitchen and stopped with the boy near the hearth.

She bustled into the kitchen, a whirlwind of concern and domesticity. "Who's that you have there? Lords and Ladies Khorin! Where did you find him? He's covered in a thousand kinds of dirt. Is that *moss*?"

"I found him in the woods. Sleeping, if you can swallow that. Happy as you please he was. Beneath an old willow, like something out of a tale."

"Why hasn't he woken then?" Hannah replied wringing her apron between two nervous hands.

"Who knows? He breathes, and his heartbeat is strong. Get him warm and let him rest. Questions can wait."

It was rare that Hannah accepted Khorin's lead in such an authoritative fashion but she was so shaken by the state of the child. There was moss growing on his feet. *Moss!* She moved close to him and brushed the long dark hair back from his forehead.

"Set him down in the chair there Khorin, don't just stand about." She knelt and took the boy's cold hand in her own. "What's your story then little man?" she murmured. "Get some water from the pump Khorin and let's put it on the fire. We'll get him clean, and we'll take it from there."

She gave orders and they both bustled about the cottage, heating water and filling a bath. Before too much longer the boy became a bit more skin coloured and the bath water came to resemble a forest floor. Through it all the boy slept on, unconcerned, as two strangers stripped him of his clothes and scrubbed his skin pink.

By midday the child was tucked into a clean bed in the tiny bedroom at the top of the cottage. Hannah stood in the doorway watching the blankets rise and fall over his chest. He was painfully thin, so thin it made him look younger than he really was, but his height suggested he was at least nine or ten.

There was a kind of warped symmetry in it all. It had been ten years almost to the day that their own boy had been taken from them.

Contagion and disease were quite rare, but the flux had swept through the district like a flame in dry grass, carrying off young and old alike. She'd cried for a solid month afterwards and refused to this day to visit the place where Khorin had laid him into the ground. Somehow, knowing where he was buried would make it real. He'd planted an apple tree with the body in the old tradition, but she wasn't interested and refused to take the fruit from him when he'd first brought it to her. The idea was that eating the fruit made the child always stay with you, but she didn't care. He'd been stolen from her, and she didn't want fruit. She wanted her baby back. Now this child appeared from nowhere. And found under a tree no less.

She felt the stairs flex behind her before the hand landed lightly on her shoulder.

"Come away Hannah." Khorin's gentle voice rumbled. "We'll get no more answers just looking at him. Let him rest."

She let him lead her down the stairs and sat silent at the old kitchen table as he pulled the kettle out from over the fire and went about making her tea with a generous dollop of honey. She took the steaming cup from him mutely, her eyes expectant.

"We'll have to wait until he wakes up, Hannah. Boy asleep in the middle of the woods like that? It's like he crawled out of a child's tale. He's bound to have family around here somewhere looking for him."

"Where are they then, Khorin?" she demanded. "How does a boy find himself alone in the woods at his age, with no one looking for him?"

"We wait Hannah. We wait for him to wake, and find out the truth of things. Then we wait for his family to come and get him."

She stared at him, words left unsaid on both sides but both hearing them regardless.

Devin spent three days sleeping whilst Hannah hovered over him, bathed him and fretted. Khorin was back to the farm the next day. There were crops that needed tending and animals to be fed and, at the end of the day, taxes and rents to be paid. Truth be told, he felt he was better off out of the house than in it. Hannah would have driven him crazy.

On the evening of the third day, as they both sat in the long low-beamed kitchen, a tentative creaking down the stairs announced the boy before he appeared in the doorway. He looked confused and a little scared. His cheeks looked more hollow than they had before, but he was awake.

Hannah rushed out of her chair with a low cry and smothered him to her breast.

Bustling him into a chair and setting broth and warm bread before him with a large cup of fresh milk. He inhaled the food like a bear waking in spring and then looked up with fragile eyes. "Where's my mother?"

"I'm sorry lad. I only found you." Khorin managed as Hannah moved over to the table and placed a comforting hand on Devin's shoulder.

"I remember things," he said. His voice was low, almost a whisper. "Things I thought were a dream."

Hannah pulled out a chair and sat next to him, taking his hand. "Do you want to talk about it? It might help." She mothered his story out of him with a skill that would have impressed any noble's inquisitor. Later, once Hannah had fed and mothered him into submission, and encouraged him back into bed, she and Khorin sat and talked long into the night in hushed tones.

"I tell you love, the boy's tale makes no sense!" Khorin puffed on a hand-carved pipe. "Those woods are only half a day's walk from the road. No more than a full day, even for a boy younger than Devin! They're not so dense you could get lost in them and they've not had any wolves in them for decades. You know this as well as I do."

"He believes it all Khorin," Hannah replied with infuriating calm.

"I know he believes it. You can see that on his face, but that don't make it true. I reckon he caught a touch of sickness and wandered away from his Ma at night or something. He was probably walking in circles, fever mad for a day or so."

"Well where is she then?" Hannah retorted, her temper rising. "This is the only village for a good ten miles in any direction and it's older than dirt. Any mother worth the name would have been here by now looking for help. Looking for her boy!"

"I don't know Wife." Khorin trailed off, staring into the fire. "There's something about the whole thing that worries me. Something that's wrong."

Hannah let it drop. The truth was she felt the same way. The story was fantastical, the type of thing you'd tell children at bedtime, or hear from a storyteller or minstrel making his way through the village. Despite all that, there was something about the tale that put a chill on the back of her neck. A feeling that made her walk to put an extra log on the fire and glance at the thick oak door and then up the stairs to where the boy slept.

* * *

On the third day after Devin woke Hannah judged him well enough to be up and walking. She had almost pushed him out of the door with Khorin. The morning was bright and the sun shone on the grass still wet with the morning's dew.

"I expect she wants you filling your lungs with good fresh air," Khorin said with a sly wink as he stepped out behind him. "She's got some funny ideas sometimes. I doubt a walk will do you any harm but I've never known the smell of horse shit to do much for me." He wrinkled his nose and Devin laughed. "Tell you what lad, we'll take a little walk around the farmstead here and you let me know if you feel tired. Then as we walk I can bend your ear and tell you all about this place. How does that sound?"

"That would be nice sir," Devin said, making an effort to be polite.

"Sir?" Khorin laughed again. "I'm a lot of things boy, but I'm definitely not a 'sir'. Khorin will do nicely alright?"

"Khorin it is." Devin agreed smiling sideways at the grey-haired man.

"Widdengate is really a farm that's grown out and turned into a village," Khorin explained as they ambled around the edge of the cottage towards the barn and fields. "There's been a farm here since before my great-grandfather's time. Over time that farm grew and attracted farmhands and workers and the like. They brought families with them of course, and families need homes. Within just a few short years I imagine, the original farmhouse was surrounded by little cottages dotted all over the place." He waved his arm vaguely at the homes Devin could see in the distance.

"All farmhands?" the boy asked.

"No, there were tradesmen too. Coopers, smiths, wainwrights and the like." Khorin replied but Devin seemed to be only half listening as he spun round in a slow circle looking into the distance.

"So where is it then?" Devin asked after a moment.

"Hmm?"

"The farm." Devin explained. "I see the village over that way, and I see little farms like yours, but you made it sound like it was a big place."

"You're a sharp one aren't you?" Khorin looked at the boy with raised eyebrows. "You're right of course, it's long gone. The lands were all sold off or rented. The farmhouse stood empty for years before they finally tore it down. The inn is built where it used to stand, in the centre of what became the village. It's a good thing really. I don't think a village feels complete without an inn. Folk can get by without almost anything else, but a man needs some place to go and tell tales, poke fun at his neighbours and grouse about his wife." He said the last with another sly grin and a look back towards the cottage.

There were other children in the village of course, and word of Devin's appearance and convalescence had spread. In a village as small as Widdengate, with little to do and less to gossip about, a strange boy found in the woods was a tale that would keep tongues wagging for weeks. Khorin had suggested keeping the news to themselves, but Hannah had confided, and so naturally the whole village knew the story.

It took only three more days for two of the village children to come calling. Erinn was a sweet young girl of nine summers. She was pale-skinned with bright flaming hair but also as thin as a rake. Not from any lack of food, she was just one of those girls who seemed destined to be willowy. Willowy, and without a husband, as her father was the blacksmith. A great hulking bear of a man who glowered at anyone who looked at his daughter twice.

Kainen was the innkeeper's son, a friendly faced child who always seemed to be following Erinn around. They were too young for much mischief, but Hannah suspected that before too much longer, Kainen was going to be taken aside by Erinn's father and have a few things explained to him.

She'd hesitated to let Devin out of the house alone just yet, but finally relented when Khorin insisted. "He can't just lay in the bed or sit all day Hannah. It does a body no good. He needs to be out, getting into trouble and getting dirty."

They'd listening with broad grins as Hannah gave strict instructions to walk slowly and not take him too far. Devin's tour of Widdengate wouldn't take long anyway as the village was far from a bustling metropolis. As Devin stepped out of the doorway, dressed in clothes that had once belonged to Hannah's son, he felt a moment's trepidation. He paused on the threshold and gave a long glance back over his shoulder into the cottage. He was only just beginning to feel comfortable with Hannah and Khorin and it felt odd to be moving on so soon, making new friends, almost like he was betraying his mother. He told himself to stop being foolish as Kainen gave him a curious look, and forced himself to follow Erinn out into the sunlight.

Erinn proved to be a fun companion, easy to talk to and happy enough to carry the conversation by herself when she needed to. Devin hadn't had many opportunities to play with other children, and was quite shy to begin with, but he soon found that her ready smile was bringing him out of himself. Kainen was quiet and watchful with his dark eyes never far from Devin's face, taking his measure. So it was Erinn's voice that led them around the village.

She took them through the narrow winding streets filled with tidy cottages and houses with thatched roofs to the smithy. They stood and watched her father and his apprentices beat away at cherry-red steel with huge hammers as the bright sparks flew. The heat, and sheer noise of the place soon chased them out, and she led them through field-lined lanes to the mill, with its great wheel turning ponderously in the slow-moving stream.

They ended up sitting on the front steps of the inn as they talked about this and that. Erinn advised there was an old farmhand named Samen who was the best in the village for telling stories. Her mother said he was a lazy old sot, but he still spun a good tale. If you could catch him on a Setday he would usually tell a story to a small crowd of the village children.

After a time, as if the questions could be held back no longer, Erinn turned to him with curiosity burning in her eyes. "What happened to your mother Devin? There are all sorts of rumours."

"I don't know really," Devin replied hesitantly. "I remember some things but Khorin says I was sick and so it's a bit like dreaming."

"I bet it was a troll!" Kainen burst in with wide eyes. "Did she get eaten by a troll Devin?"

"You shut your hole Kainen," stormed Erinn looking furious as Devin's face paled. "There's no such thing as trolls anyway. Everyone knows that."

"Maybe it was droos then," muttered Kainen. "They'd be coming for you next with your hair like that."

"There aren't droos either, stupid," she retorted. "You need to learn what's a tale and what's true. Just 'cause Samen said it, don't make it real."

Devin looked back and forth at the two of them, clearly this was an argument that had been going on some time. "I don't know what happened to her," he said in an effort to stave off further bickering. "Like I said I don't remember much of it."

"So what about the rest of your family then?" Kainen asked with a defiant look at Erinn. "Ain't you got aunts or uncles, or a grampy that you could go to?"

"We were heading to find my Grandpa in Savarel when the bandits attacked us," Devin explained.

"Real bandits?" exclaimed Kainen with wide awe-struck eyes. "Did you see them? What was it like? Were you scared?"

"Shh!" Erinn scolded as she glared at him. "Let him tell it."

Devin smiled, the story of the bandits didn't seem to bother him as much as talking about the forest and the boy's excitement was infectious. He spun the story of the bandit attack, exaggerating his own part only slightly. He ended with Garret's order for his mother and him to keep going, whilst he dealt with the bandits that followed them.

"Did you really shoot one with a bow?" Kainen asked doubtfully. "I bet you never did. I never even held a bow, and I know I wouldn't dare shoot a man with it. I'd be scared I'd miss or it wouldn't kill him or something."

Erinn looked at the expression on Devin's face as his lips pressed hard together and his face grew pale. "Do you want to head back Devin? You don't look so good."

He looked at her and nodded gratefully. "Maybe that's a good idea."

Much later, as he was sat in front of the warm fire in the cottage, he turned to Khorin who was sat in a comfortable looking armchair. "What do you think happened to my mother Khorin?" He stared into the fire, not meeting the man's eyes.

The grizzled man cleared his throat as he pulled himself upright and exchanged a meaningful glance at Hannah. "Well I can't say Devin, not for sure. If you're old enough to ask the questions though, I reckon you're old enough to hear what I think, and I don't think it's anything good." He carried on quickly as Devin's eyes filled with tears and Hannah rushed across the kitchen to pull him in close, shooting furious looks at her husband.

"She looked after you though boy, and that's something to think about. I reckon the only reason she's gone and you're not, is that she made sure you were okay. That was probably the best gift she could have given you, and that shows love my lad. Deep and powerful love that does."

Devin sniffed and rubbed his eyes as he pulled away from Hannah. "What's going to happen to me now?"

"Well, I think that's up to you," Khorin said as his eyes flicked back and forth between the lad and Hannah. "I do need to go to Savarel at some point. You could come along and we could see if we can find your grandpa. Do you remember his name or anything?"

"No," replied Devin as he plucked at a loose thread on his sleeve, his eyes downcast. "I don't remember anything about him. I don't even know if I ever even met him."

"Well now that might change things a bit." He reached into a pouch at his waist and began filling his pipe as he spoke, tamping down the leaf with his thumb. "You know," he said as if the thought had just occurred to him, "you'd be welcome to stay here with us. I might not be your Da' and Hannah is never going to try and be your Mother, but we could do the job better than some and no worse than most."

Devin looked at the pair of them as they watched him. Khorin met his eyes for a second but then looked down and busied himself with his pipe. Hannah was far less subtle and the hope was clear in her warm brown eyes. "I think I might like to stay for a while, if you really want me to." He cut off as Hannah gathered him up in her arms again and snuffled into his hair in between kisses on his head.

"Glad to have you Devin," Khorin said gruffly. "You stay as long as you like." And then, "Stars above Hannah! Let the boy breathe!"

Devin soon found that Khorin was a practical man who valued hard work and honesty above most things. He and Hannah owned a smallholding which took up a portion of the southern end of Widdengate, and though he didn't have the ability to farm it all himself, he managed to provide for himself and Hannah and remain comfortable. The little cottage had outbuildings across from it in the stone-walled yard that housed the chickens and pigs as well as a small stable which was home to the goats and horses.

Hannah maintained a productive looking vegetable plot which almost overflowed with carrots, beans and potatoes. One of the first things that Devin learned as he became accustomed to living on the farm, was that there was always something that needed doing. That, and the fastest way to be given chores, was to look as though you were bored or had nothing to do.

He was well-treated, though he grew to despise the vegetable plot and the weeds that seemed to spring up there overnight. His favourite chore by far was spending time with the two huge horses that Khorin used to plough the fields. Devin was both terrified and enthralled the first time Khorin took him to meet them. Named Clover and Bramble, they were that odd breed of horse with shaggy hair hanging down over the hooves. A horse is an odd thing, it can be so often reduced to a simple beast of burden in your own mind that you forget just how large they are until you are stood right next to them. Devin's head didn't even reach the horse's shoulder and he had to stand on a wooden stool to help brush them down after a day's ploughing or haying.

When he wasn't helping with chores, he spent more and more time with Erinn and Kainen and the three soon became fast friends. One Setday afternoon Erinn appeared with Kainen in tow and suggested that the three of them go and listen to Samen. The inn was a large stone and timber building with a dark thatched roof which sprouted chimneys like an oversized fungus in a forest's shade.

The well-worn stone front steps gave way to a warm and friendly common room with doors in the back leading to the kitchens and stores. It was almost empty on the warm sunny day, with only a few men talking quietly around tables in the corners. Samen sat alone at a sunlit table sipping slowly from a tankard occasionally. He fixed the trio with a dark stare as they approached.

"Hello Samen," said Erinn with a smile, her red hair catching the sunlight through the well-washed windows.

"What do you three want?" the old man muttered sourly.

"I hoped you might tell us a story?" Erinn replied, ignoring the sour note in Samen's voice.

"Do you think I have nothing better to do than entertain you three brats?" the old man said, grinning and showing his many missing teeth as he caught Devin's shocked expression.

"You've nothing to do old man," called a fat farmer from the corner as his companion laughed. "That's why you sit alone sucking on that mead all afternoon."

Samen shot them a venomous look and turned back to Erinn's smiling face. "I've no time for the bored, untended, spawn of my neighbours' loins. Get on with the lot of you!"

Erinn's eyes turned hard and she reached into a pouch pulling out a single copper penny and watching Samen falter and glance at his nearly empty tankard.

"Well bargained young miss," he said in more friendly tones. "And what was it you were wanting to hear about today? How the stone of the sun was stolen from the firebird's nest and how the thief dropped it as he fled? Leaving it to roll across the skies untended?" he smiled again with a wicked glint in his eyes. "Mayhaps you want to hear about the black-blooded droos ? Wandering the lands searching for red-haired brats to drag across the altar stones and feed their blood to the runes?" he cackled nastily into his tankard as he drained it and wiped his mouth on his sleeve.

"We wanted to hear about the Bjornmen," Erinn said firmly as Kainen and Devin nodded in agreement.

"Ah... the wolves of the sea, come to ravage and burn the homes of, fat. Lazy. Farmers." he said, raising his voice at the last and looking pointedly at the rotund farmer in the corner.

"From their frozen storm-lashed coasts they come, sailing in their galleys with fearsome figureheads the sight of which strikes fear into all that behold them. It's said that the first you know of their coming is the muffled drumbeat of the oarsmaster and then they are among you. Torches fly into thatch and blood runs down the streets as they hew through flesh and bone with their axes and swords. They come to pillage and burn young mistress, and to take pretty little red-haired blacksmiths' daughters back to their ships," he cackled again, joined this time by the farmers from the corner who were clearly listening in.

"Tell us about Frostbeard!" Kainen cried out, already wrapped up in the story.

"Frostbeard? The worst of the lot he is, bastard son of a Bjornmen clan-chief with no respect for life or title. He earned his place by working from a rower upwards, killing every man, woman or child that got in his way. They say he never cleans his blades and that he leaves tracks of blood wherever he steps. He's said to be as cold as his name, burning to the ground every village or town he strikes."

He grinned at the wide-eyed faces of the children in front of him. "Was that what you had in mind young miss?" he asked her nodding face as he held out his cup. "Then get you to the bar and get some more mead in this, and I'll tell you more."

Chapter Four

Selena walked the path through the gardens in silence, her forest green gown trailing behind her and rustling faintly as it dragged the occasional leaf. Her attendants followed some paces behind her, but still she grated at their presence. The grounds were lovely but the high stone wall surrounding them served to remind her of her situation. She was as ornamental as the topiary and the statues in the fountains.

A page approached from the house and walked briskly towards her. She knew without turning that the ladies behind her would have stopped also. They had initially tried to engage her in conversation, but she found them vapid at best.

"The Lady Browntree begs an audience, your grace," the page said, after a tight little bow.

"Mother?" Selena said with some surprise.

"Beg pardon, your grace, but no. The Lady Evelyn Browntree."

"Auntie Evelyn?" she said with genuine pleasure. "Where is she?"

"She is taking some tea in the eastern parlour, your grace."

"Which one is that again? Is that the ghastly pink one?"

The page coughed and she fought to keep a smile from her lips. "The very same, your grace."

"Well, lead the way," she smiled. The page bowed again and turned to escort her back into the house.

"Is Freyton with her?"

"His Grace is... on the hunt, I believe," the page replied as they walked.

Selena caught the pause in the response and wondered at it as they made their way through the hallway.

The parlour was a comfortable, warm room with over-stuffed divans and settees. Selena ignored the page as he tried to announce her and rushed to the tiny old lady who was struggling to rise from the deep armchair in which she was seated, leaning heavily on an ornate cane.

"Auntie Evelyn!" she cried, as she took the old woman's hands and kissed her wrinkled cheek.

"Hello dear," Evelyn replied, her eyes crinkling in genuine affection.

"What are you doing here?"

"I thought I'd check in on you, dear. See how married life is treating you." She looked at Selena's stomach with a mischievous twinkle in her eye. "Oh, and who are your friends?" She looked up over Selena's shoulder.

"Friends?" Selena turned to see her ladies-in-waiting stood just inside the door. "Oh. These are my maids. Freyton, assigned them to me." She dropped her voice to a loud whisper, "They follow me everywhere. I can't get a minute's peace."

Evelyn frowned and looked over at them. "I think that will be all, ladies."

"Begging your pardon, my lady," the dark-haired attendant said. "His Grace, the duke, gave instructions we were to accompany Her Grace at all times."

"Whatever for?" Evelyn asked, as she cocked an eyebrow at Selena.

"I don't really know," Selena admitted. "I've been trying to get rid of them for days."

"Well, I think I would like some privacy with my niece. That will be all." Evelyn told the woman.

"But, His Grace..."

"I said, that *will* be all," the old woman said, pressing her lips tightly together and looking at the maid sternly.

"Yes, my lady." The trio of maids dipped a curtsey together and filed out through the double doors.

"Thank you," Selena said with a heartfelt sigh. "I feel like I'm under constant guard with them always following me around."

"I forget sometimes, that you're not used to having servants and the like," Evelyn said as she eased herself back down into the chair. "You need to keep them in their place, Selena."

"You make it seem so easy." She sat down on the other chair, perching on the edge so as not to rumple her gown overly.

"Well, I suppose I grew up with them dear. We had our own money back then, of course."

"Of course." Selena said. "And now I suppose we will have it again eventually.

Now that you've all sold me off like the family cow."

"Oh Selena," she sighed. "Please do tell me we're not going to go through this again."

"It's just... Well, I don't think I was ready for a husband."

"Oh my dear child!" the old woman laughed. "No woman *wants* a husband! They're a terrible nuisance. Smelly and underfoot the whole time and absolutely no idea of what is proper. They are rather necessary in a marriage though I'm afraid." She picked up her cup and sipped before grimacing. "Cold," she explained and picked up the elegant silver bell on the table. "Hello again dear," she said as the page walked through the door in response to her summons. "Do you suppose you could freshen this up? It's gone cold I'm afraid." She gestured at the ornate tea set on the small table beside the two chairs.

"At once, Your Ladyship." The page bowed and retrieved the tea set, closing the door behind him as he left.

"You see? They do have their uses." She smirked at the young woman and looked around at the room with an expression of disapproval. "Is it all like this?"

Selena laughed. "Yes! This isn't even the worst room. What makes things worse is that most of this is new."

"Newly Lorded and all the money in the world but, somewhat lacking in taste I'd say," Evelyn said with a faintly offended tut. "Now Selena, am I going to have to drag it out of you?"

Selena laughed. "I'm fine. It's fine. Freyton is gone most of the time, hunting and the like. I'm just a bit..."

"A bit what?"

"Bored!" Selena laughed. "It sounds ridiculous I suppose, but I'm bored stiff! I'm trapped in the middle of nowhere with no one for company except those insipid maids and stuttering page boys."

"I'd have thought Freyton would be keeping you busy. Pretty young thing like you. He should be chasing you around the bedroom by now."

"Auntie!" Selena gasped, shocked.

"Oh, come on girl, we're all grown women in here," Evelyn said, with an earthy chuckle.

"I suppose," she said, still fighting the blush from her cheeks. "He doesn't actually seem very interested."

"Well I'm sure that will come with time. It would be nice to have a baby though, to solidify things."

"I am well aware of my responsibilities, Auntie. They were made perfectly clear to me before the signing of the betrothal agreement, if you remember?"

"Yes well, your father was never really one for tact and diplomacy, was he?" She looked towards the door as the chink of fine china came from the hallway and the page struggled through the door with the tea. They sat in silence, as he poured for them both and left.

"You're not really in the middle of nowhere anyway dear. Kavtrin is only a day or so away."

"Kavtrin, Auntie? Really? I want a bit of life and culture, not the smell of old fish."

Selena sipped at her steaming cup, enjoying the heat of the tea as it burned its way down her throat.

"I'll never understand how you can drink it so hot dear. You must be close to scalding your own tongue there."

Selena smiled at her over the rim of her cup.

"As for boredom. Well, if Freyton won't go to you, then perhaps you should go to him? That's the last I'll say of it," she added quickly, holding up her long gloved hand in a placating gesture as she caught Selena's expression. "As for the rest of your time, do as you wish. If Kavtrin is not to your liking then try riding, read, try needlepoint."

Selena pulled a face. "I loathe horses and needlepoint is for women who have lost the right to own their own minds. I would read, but the library is hardly extensive. What little there is in there doesn't often stray from dry histories and philosophy."

"What in all the world would Freyton want with those? Do you think he's trying to appear educated and intellectual?" Evelyn asked in a conspiratorial whisper and then gave a wicked chuckle.

"Auntie, you are awful." Selena gave the door a guilty little look.

"Life is no fun if you play by the rules all the time dear. You should try to remember that."

The visit passed all too quickly and Selena found herself wandering the halls of the mansion. A pointed glare at the ladies-in-waiting soon sent them scurrying when they tried to join her and for want of anything else to do she eventually made her way to the library.

It was a dark-panelled affair, with oil lamps turned low on the walls. She lit a taper from a lamp and touched it to the kindling laid in the fireplace before turning her attention to the bookshelves. The books were leather-bound and dusty, clearly Freyton thought a ducal palace should have a library and so he'd had one put in. Judging by the dust in the room and the impeccable state of the books, the library had been put to little use.

"Decorative," she muttered. "Just like his wife."

She wandered around the room trailing her fingertips along the shelves and tutting at the dust. It was, as she'd said, mostly histories and philosophies. A dark green binding caught her eye and she tugged out the thick book, a history of Eastern Anlan.

"Well if I do have to live here, I might as well learn something about the place," she said quietly to herself and settled back into a deep armchair to read as the fireplace crackled merrily against the far wall.

* * *

The seagull banked with the strong wind and dove towards the slate grey sea that surrounded the small chain of islands. The largest island, closest to where the seagull now flew, was covered in high mountains and rocky terrain. It was a harsh looking place, more suited to seabirds than men. Despite this, and with the tenacity only mankind can exhibit, the inhabitants clung to the island like limpets to a rock. Every tiny green valley was crammed with farms and crops. Towns dotted the coastline and fishing fleets bobbed about in the bays. A fortified city filled the southernmost end of the island, glowering out over the sea like an old man watching unruly children.

The gull cried its ululating call and flew on towards the city. It seemed a cramped place, with narrow streets and tall thin buildings that were nevertheless, sturdy-looking stone structures with dark slate rooftops. The city had few wide roads and avenues. It was criss-crossed with tiny alleyways giving the impression it had been struck a mighty blow, and covered with a thousand cracks. Its thick, granite walls were surmounted with intimidating-looking battlements, liberally dotted with catapults and ballistae.

A rocky islet sat directly opposite the city. It was largely a wind-scoured and inhospitable rock, but towers and small forts had been forced into the surface, which were also bristling with their own weapons. Its presence, so close to the harbour, formed a crescent shaped stretch of water and restricted access to the narrow channels leading between the two. Had the gull cared about such things it would have been left with the impression that the city was almost impervious to attack.

The rain fell gently and was then whipped away by the winds as they clawed at the islands as if seeking to tear them from the sea. The surging waves crashed hard against the dark stone cliffs and the gull banked again, before flying steadily towards the flotilla of small ships making its way around the coast towards the harbour. The vessels were sleek and clearly designed for speed with sharp narrow prows, and long thin beams. Their blood-red sails hung limp and oars sprouted from each side of the boats, driving in unison through the white-capped waves.

Two ships were clearly in competition with each other for the lead position. They were far ahead of the other vessels, but with only a dozen feet separating them. The gull swooped down and settled on the prow of the lead vessel. Carved into the shape of a wolf's head with snarling teeth, the prow was an imposing sight. The gull stamped its webbed feet onto the head of the wolf and settled down to preen.

Klöss swore into his thin beard and hauled back on the oar, trying to keep to the beat of the drum. At fourteen it was his first time on the oars and he needed to prove himself. Had it not been for his size they would never have considered him, but a chance he had been given and so the chance he had. The boat knifed through the waves using both sail and oars for maximum speed but for the moment the sails hung slack and empty as the cliff blocked the wind. Klöss glanced up for a moment across the water towards the other ship. It was a scant fifty yards away, they were catching them.

"Bend your back boy!" cried the oarsmaster and flicked the lash lightly at Klöss's back. Its kiss was as light as a feather but soon turned into a sting of fire and ice. He ignored the pain and hauled on the oar, bracing his feet on the base of the bench in front and leaning back into it. After a time he lost himself in the rhythm of it, the beat of the drum, the spray of the sea in his face and all around the smell of sweat and tar. He heard boots on the deck above him and the roar of the Shipmaster, "faster by the gods!" and then the drumming became frenetic.

"Steersman! Make the turn when you're ready, but make it clean! If you lose my speed on this you'll be swimming home," called the Shipmaster.

Klöss felt the ship begin to turn as it listed to the right, the drumbeat urging him on even as the wind whipped at his hair. He risked another glimpse to the right and saw that their angle was going to cut in front of the other boat, a move that risked them colliding or grinding them both into the rocky cliffs.

"More speed now!" cried the Shipmaster. "Give it all you have!"

The drumbeat increased again and the ship soared towards the rocks. Klöss hauled in time with the others, sweat running freely down his face and neck as he strove to keep pace. They had made the turn smoothly, with little speed lost, and sailed past the cliff face with barely an oar's length distance. Klöss could probably have reached out and brushed his fingers on the cliff, if he dared risk the ire of the oarsmaster.

The sails billowed as the wind filled them again, snapping ropes and canvas tight, and the boat fairly leapt ahead. Klöss felt the shock through his oar and grinned in spite of the torturous labour. He could see the shore now, a glimpse every time he leaned back into the oar. Houses and streets becoming clearer with every stroke.

"Now then my boys, one last push," called the oarsmaster. They were clearly doing well, for the evil-faced man had no good word to say at any other time. They might be "my boys" today, but two days ago they'd been "useless dogs," as he laid about with lash and cudgel.

He could hear the roar of the crowds as they came closer to the harbour, and the drum-beat increased yet again to a ramming speed. Oarsmaster, Shipmaster and Steersman were screaming at the oarsmen in unison now, urging more speed, just one last push. Then they passed the anchored raft with its fire-pot belching oily smoke, and the drums stopped. There was an awful moment of silence. Then cheers and roars erupted in the boat as the oarsmen dropped the oars and flung themselves at each other in congratulations.

Klöss looked over his shoulder and saw the other ship a good three lengths behind them, just now passing the marker. Another fifty ships followed close behind. He slumped down and braced his head in his hands as he laughed through his tears. They'd done it. He'd got the best chance he could.

"Klöss! Stop bawling and get up here!" shouted the oarsmaster, grasping his upper arms and helping him out of the oarpit before moving forward to stand near the prow. Klöss groaned inwardly. He'd received black looks since the first day of training and didn't need this attention.

"You see this lad?" the oarsmaster shouted at the crew over the wind and the still-roaring crowds. "Fourteen summers he has and already man-sized. Frostbeard's blood runs in his veins and it shows. Is he fit to join this crew?" He screamed the last, pointing at Klöss and the crew roared back their affirmation, thrusting fists into the air.

"Oarsman's thirst!" cried out a voice near the stern and it was soon joined by others, forming a ragged chant. Before he could protest, Klöss was hoisted up onto shoulders and passed along the boat towards the oarsmaster, who stood with a wooden keg under his arm. Klöss was positioned level with the feet of the oarsmaster as he broached the keg and began to pour the sweet mead over his face and down his throat. Klöss drank wildly as the cheers rose up again and then, before he really knew it was happening, he was hoisted again. Once, twice and then he was airborne before crashing into the sea and under the waves.

He was met by some of the laughing crew as he hauled himself out of the harbour by way of a small flight of stone steps just in time to see the last trainee hurled overboard. He watched with a grin as they too pulled themselves out of the harbour and then they were marched into the town, still trailing seawater. The Oarsmen bundled the young trainees through the streets and the still clearing crowds, and he was manhandled through a door and down the steps of the closest tavern.

"Let's see if you can handle your drink as well as you handle an oar, my lads," shouted the oarsmaster to a chorus of cheers. Klöss and the others were pushed unceremoniously onto benches and chairs and foamy tankards put in front of them. The ale flowed and he felt his cheeks going numb by the time the drinks were replaced with a huge platter of meat and vegetables.

The rest of the day, and a fair portion of the night, passed in a malty haze for Klöss as he was led from tavern to tavern. He found that as time went on the harsh taste of the ale seemed to mellow. Indeed the drink hardly seemed to be affecting him at all. He had always heard that drink made people act foolishly or lose control, at least that was what his father said, but he seemed to be perfectly fine. He was getting along splendidly with his new crew too, and was increasingly funny he noticed.

* * *

Klöss groaned as the footsteps clumped down the stone steps into the kitchen. He shuddered and attempted to bury his head deeper into his arms as he clenched his eyes tightly shut. His mouth was filled with a foul taste, and his tongue felt hard and dry where he had slept with his lips apart and apparently drooled on his sleeve. He stretched carefully, without lifting himself from the surface of the oaken table and fervently wished he could die.

"Up, boy!" his father's voice boomed. "We need to get that cart loaded and get that shop open. I have a feeling it will be a good day today. The market day always seems to bring them in." His voice faltered and he stooped to take a closer look at Klöss, hunched over the long table.

"Did you sleep in here?" he wondered, mostly to himself. "No matter I suppose. Come on, up, up! There's daylight wasting."

Klöss found himself dragged out of his seat and into the light as his father set about hitching the horse to the large wooden and leather cart he used to haul his new stock to the shop. The day was just dawning and the cobbles in the yard were wet and slick from the light rains of the night. He clung to the wheel of the cart with the look of someone scared they might fall, should it move or it be taken from them. His body felt as if he were wading through deep water. Nothing seemed to work quite as it should. The cart shook as it was loaded, almost but not quite in time with the thumping in his head, and the vibrations were making him feel queasy. He watched his father travel back and forth to the storehouse that filled much of the yard, his limp prominent in the cold early morning air. A pang of guilt almost prompted him to let go of the cart and help, but this was swiftly overcome by another wave of nausea.

"Get up in the front if you're not going to load boy. You're in my way," his father grunted as he hoisted a large bundle up onto the cart.

Nodding carefully at his father's already retreating form, he made his way to the front of the cart and hauled himself up into the seat. He concentrated on wrapping his cloak tightly around him, as if to hide from the clatter of the loading cart and the weak and watery sun just beginning to peek over the slate of the rooftops that mirrored the cold grey sky.

The cart rocked as his father finally climbed aboard and with a cluck at the horse, it was soon clattering through the cobbled streets moving steadily uphill away from the harbour and towards the market square. Klöss sat huddled beside his father in silence and so heard the ringing long before the line of men came into sight.

They were dressed uniformly in black, velvet-soft looking robes, deeply cowled and tied at the waist with a bone-white length of smooth rope that had clearly never had any other use. A man at the rear held a large bell which he swung with every tenth step.

"New Dayers," his father grunted in disgust, and edged the cart as far over to the left of the narrow street as he could. The men, for their part, did not deviate from their path or even deign to look up at the pair until they had almost passed them. The rearmost man offered a smile and nod of thanks as the line wove past them. Klöss's father nodded back curtly and then clucked the horse forward again.

"Why do you hate them so much?" the question left his lips before he had time to think.

"Who? New Dayers?" the older man asked. "Because they came along and decided things were wrong after we'd been living this way for centuries. Who are they to tell us how to live?"

It was ironic, Klöss decided. His father might hate this new religion sweeping through the Barren Isles, and Bresda in particular, because it destroyed the traditions and values he had always held dear. At the same time though, his merchant class was itself considered the lowest of professions, and held in far more contempt than this new priesthood. His father seemed to act oblivious for his part, though it was doubtful that he could be.

The morning grew steadily lighter as they made their way into the narrow alleyway behind the market square and began unloading their wares and hauling them through the back of the shop. Klöss felt his head begin to clear with a combination of the cold air and the hard work. His father, Rhaven, ran a small shop but rather than selling wares he had made himself like other tradesmen, he bought goods from others and then sold them on. As such Klöss never knew what the shop would be selling on any given day, or what wares he would have to haul to and from the cart.

It seemed to be mainly foodstuffs today and he spent the better part of half an hour hauling hams and cheeses from the cart and arranging them to his father's satisfaction on the hooks and counters.

"Ought to be a big crowd today I think," Rhaven said, settling down behind the counter on a wooden stool and stretching out his left leg with a pained grimace.

Klöss ignored him. His head was still not right. Everything felt too bright and too loud. He reached under the counter and drew out a large earthenware bottle, drinking slowly and deliberately in long swallows.

"Slow down there now," called his father. "That has to last us all day you know?"

Klöss wandered over to the front door and looked around at the square as he felt the water begin to work on his dehydrated body. Other merchants and tradesmen were hard at work, setting up stalls and stands. From where he stood leaning against the door frame he could see half a dozen different traders selling everything from knives and weapons to jewellery and clothing.

The problem was that his father didn't actually make anything himself, Klöss decided. There had always been tradespeople of course - rope-makers and sail-makers, shipwrights and blacksmiths. These were all fine and acceptable. Merchant traders didn't really make anything though. They bought from one and sold to another, selling only the act of exchange and the convenience of finding most things in one shop or stall. Anyone who wanted the item badly enough could go and find the tradesman who'd made it to buy it from. Merchant traders were little better than thieves Klöss had decided.

It was not a unique opinion and he knew it. As the merchant class grew, a steady resentment had grown alongside it. Not enough to prevent people from bringing their custom, but enough to lend the merchant a reputation as a swindler at best and a common thief at worst.

The problem was rooted in laziness, Klöss was convinced. People liked the convenience of not having to go to a half dozen different stalls and shops to find their goods. Farmers and tradespeople liked being able to sell two or three cartloads of goods to one person rather than sitting around each market day trying to sell their wares to the public.

He could forgive his father much of it. He had little choice, given his leg. He could hardly become an apprentice and learn a proper trade at his age. He watched sourly as his father sold a loaf of bread and a hunk of ham to a young mother, her children hanging onto her legs through her thick woollen skirts. He ground his teeth together and watched her hand over almost half again what they had paid the farmer for it.

He looked up at the woman's eyes as his father wrapped the food. She was young, little more than twenty summers and, judging by her clothes and the lost look in her eyes, she could barely afford the expense. She was probably raising the small ones alone by the looks of her. The market had filled now and a sea of people made their way past him. He nearly didn't see the hand slip around the front of the woman's dress, gently taking the weight of her purse with one finger, while slicing the strings with a deft flick of the wrist He was so stunned by what he was seeing, that the purse was gone before he could rouse himself.

His cry of "Thief!" was lost in the noise of the market but both his father's and the woman's heads whipped round as he shot from his seat, over the counter, and into the crowd after the face he had caught the barest glimpse of.

Klöss raced after the figure barely four yards ahead of him, as they both weaved in and out of the crowd. The thief was slight, with dirty blonde hair and a nondescript brown cloak. He was also as quick as a weasel. Klöss charged after him, just managing to keep pace in his heavy boots. Whilst the thief might be slight, Klöss was tall for his age and his long legs carried him swiftly through the crowd, though his broad shoulders meant he had to duck and weave more. Thankfully he suffered little of the awkwardness one often finds in boys his age and he ran confidently over the cobbles, still shouting at the top of his lungs.

The crowds were working against him, and he saw the thief making ground as he fought his way through bustling market-goers. Men and women turned and gawked at him as he pushed and shoved his way through.

Hesk was a small city, but it was the largest in the Barren Isles and as the capital of the nation of islands, it made up for in population what it lacked in sheer size. The buildings were close packed and tall with sections often hanging out over the streets. Alleyways snaked throughout the city intersecting with roads and streets and forming a network all their own. Whilst Klöss might only be a few yards behind the thief, he knew full well that if he did not catch him swiftly, or if he lost sight of him, then it would be simple for him to duck into an alley, and once he did that he would be gone. The alleys formed their own rabbit warren and it was not anywhere a man with a purse or one who valued his life would go needlessly.

As he ran he yelled again into the crowd to stop the thief, but they wasted precious seconds turning and looking at him open-mouthed whilst the slight blonde figure slipped past them. Finally his shouting paid off, and he saw an older man in a plain woollen vest manage to grab and catch hold of the thief's cloak, jerking him to a halt. He closed quickly, and was within feet when the thief kicked savagely at the man's shins and tore free once more.

The brown-cloaked figure flung himself at a fishmonger's stall, shoving a barrel over and vaulting over the table. Klöss darted around a fat man laden down with packages. He dashed back behind the thief and then his feet flew skyward as the barrel-load of eels spread further across the cobbles, coiling and wriggling as they searched for seawater.

Cursing and spluttering Klöss climbed back to his feet and raced after the flash of brown as it disappeared into a nearby alleyway. He caught the edge of the building and swung around the corner into a sudden silence.

The alleyway was filled with filth. The stench of fish and rotten rubbish filled the air. If Klöss hadn't seen the thief dash into it he would have sworn no man had stepped foot into the stinking place in some months. Empty doorways to long-since abandoned houses gaped open, and the sides of the street were piled high with rotting refuse. The alley revealed a side of Hesk that Klöss knew little about but now was not the time to ponder it. A scraping sound followed by a muffled curse spurred him to action and he moved carefully down the alleyway trying to avoid both making noise and the worst of the filth. Klöss was prepared to deal with the stink of the eel slime he had over his clothing but there were things on the floor that he couldn't identify and didn't want to.

The alley twisted and turned and he was soon far from the sounds of the street. A soft scrape from behind warned him and he hurled himself to one side as the makeshift club came crashing down where he had stood. He rolled and then climbed to his feet, backing away to give himself some distance as the brown-cloaked figure raised the club again and came after him. The cloak's hood was raised and Klöss caught nothing but wisp of blonde hair and a smooth face as he jumped back to avoid the blow.

With a sudden lunge he grasped the cudgel as it hit the end of its swing and twisted it away from the figure. Rather than being shocked however, the thief simply let go and stamped out at his knee savagely. Klöss hit the ground hard and the thief knelt swiftly on his chest and he felt the blade pressed to his throat.

"What do you want with me rich boy?" hissed the thief in a soft voice.

"You're a girl!" Klöss said in shock as he caught a clear look at her face beneath the hood.

"A girl who has you pinned like a rabbit, with my blade at your throat. Now tell me, rich boy, why do you chase me?" she said smiling coldly.

"The purse. It belonged to that woman," Klöss replied.

"What of it? Now it belongs to me."

"You stole it," Klöss said, a strange combination of wonder and disgust in his voice.

"My my, aren't we the little innocent?" she laughed with a throaty chuckle. "Yes, I stole it, and since we are here, what do you have on you?" Klöss's eyes widened as he caught her meaning and her smile grew as she watched him understand. Her free hand snaked over his body and he gasped at the touch. He might be in the middle of being robbed, but he was still a fourteen-year-old boy with the hormones to match.

"Didn't think being robbed would be so enjoyable, did you rich boy?" She grinned as she found his purse. Coming to his senses he waited until her eyes shot down to examine it and then he struck. Twisting sideways and back away from the blade he bucked with his hips and rolled, quickly, positioning himself on top of the girl with her arms pinned above her head.

"Now who's the little rabbit?" he smiled. Now that he had her pinned he could get his first good look at her. Shoulder-length blonde hair framed a pale and delicate face, but it was the eyes that caught Klöss. They shone. Deep blue and flashing with anger and frustration, as she thrashed and bucked beneath him. Klöss lost all thoughts of retribution as he gazed down at her. The flicker of her eyes was the only hint of warning he had before something slammed into the back of his head and he collapsed into blackness atop her.

* * *

He awoke in a murky darkness with the cold smell of damp and mildew filling his nose. His head ached with that intense throb that only comes from a blow to the skull and his eyes felt gritty. He could see little in the gloom other than the dirty stone floor he lay upon, and the faint suggestion of walls. The floor was covered in damp, musty smelling straw and he could hear water dripping somewhere. As he grew more alert, he became aware of the faint sounds of the street filtering down through the stone. He tried to reach up to his head and discovered his hands were bound and tied loosely to his feet behind him. Panic found him and he thrashed on the floor wildly trying to free his hands, but the rope, whilst rough, seemed to be sound and knotted well.

"Help!" he called experimentally and was rewarded with the sound of a door opening behind him. Candlelight softly filled the room and the slight figure of the girl approached him, dropping to one knee two or three feet from him.

"How do you feel?" she asked in hushed tones.

"How do you think I feel?" he croaked at her, his dry throat making his voice rasp. "Like I've been clubbed in the head."

"I'm sorry about that. They are very protective of me."

"They?"

She twisted her body, turning towards the door and beckoned at the doorway behind her. A small crowd of children approached warily. They looked to range in age from four to roughly nine and were all filthy, dressed in little more than rags and with pale skin, too long from the sun. The youngest ones looked at him curiously, the eldest glared with open animosity. They looked like so many lost ghosts as they clustered close to the girl, half for protection and half to protect her. Klöss pitied the man who ever hurt this girl. Her pack of half-feral street kids would be on them in moments.

"Seth here saw you when you had me pinned and thought you were hurting me." She motioned to the largest boy who stared at him with hate-filled eyes.

"Oh, I'm terribly sorry. I should have just let you rob me," Klöss's voice dripped sarcasm.

"You should have, rich boy. Not everyone is as forgiving as me. The next time you chase someone into an alley you'll probably end up dead."

Klöss ignored that. "So what now? You have me trussed up like a pig here."

"Only because I didn't want you waking up and scaring the children. I don't want them hurt."

"It looks like they can take care of themselves well enough," he replied, nodding towards the eldest children who still carried broken chair legs to serve as improvised cudgels and clubs.

"They have to look after themselves rich boy!" she snapped. "That's why they live huddled in this mouldy cellar. Nobody else will look after them." She produced a slim knife. "Can I trust you not to do anything else stupid?"

Klöss ignored the dig and nodded mutely sitting still as she sliced through the ropes on his wrists and ankles. The knife, he noticed, was horrifically sharp and he shuddered as he thought of how it had been pressed to his throat. He wouldn't have moved a muscle, had he known then.

"Now then," the girl said brightly as she stood up and stepped back. "How about a nice cup of tea?" Klöss was so incredulous that he nodded dumbly and allowed himself to be helped to his feet and shepherded out the door. They passed through several musty smelling corridors to a long low-ceilinged room that looked as if it functioned as a kitchen. Several more children sat at a makeshift table made from planks resting on old barrels, and a large pot hung bubbling on an iron arm over a tidy fireplace set in the far wall.

"Tessa, you go and fill the kettle. Gavin you can fetch a chair for our guest," the blonde girl said pointing into the small crowd of children. Klöss watched them jump to obey without pause or argument.

"Now, I don't believe we were ever properly introduced?" she smiled. Klöss forced a weak grin back as he struggled to catch up. A few short hours ago she had held him at knife-point in the street and now she was inviting him to tea. It was not a situation he felt he was really able to cope with, although he did now understand why the children jumped to obey so quickly. This was not a girl; this was a force of nature. You were so quickly swept up by her that you hardly had time to stop and see what was really going on.

"Um. Klöss" he managed still feeling off balance.

"Klöss," she said, looking up at the ceiling as she considered it. "An interesting name for an interesting fellow. I am Ylsriss." She smiled again and motioned for him to sit in the plain wooden chair that Gavin was just setting by the fire, a surly expression on his young face.

"How did you end up here? Who are all these children?" Klöss countered, trying to take some control of the conversation.

"Well we weren't all born with a silver spoon in our mouth, Klöss," she replied with a tart little edge to her voice. "As for who these children are, well I suppose you could say that they are the little ones who fall through the cracks. When you're at your pretty little shop, exploiting struggling mothers who are too tired to shop around, you might want to remember that." She smiled to diffuse the tension somewhat, and then gave him a wicked look.

"So when you're not chasing young women into dark alleys, what are you usually doing young Klöss?" she asked, mischief dancing in her blue eyes.

"You can't be much older than me!" protested Klöss, avoiding the rather obvious innuendo.

He flushed and drew in his breath sharply to retort when he caught her sly smile. "You're making sport with me," he accused.

Ylsriss laughed and swung the pot to one side to make room for the kettle over the fire. "That doesn't really answer the question though does it?" she said, giving him a sideways look as she busied herself with wooden mugs and jars.

"I'm about to train as an oarsman," Klöss responded, trying not to sound self-important.

"Oh, that was your trial yesterday was it?" She peered into the pot and stirred the bubbling contents with a long wooden spoon before tasting experimentally. She lifted the kettle off the hook with a fire-scarred wad of cloth and poured the water out into the wooden mugs. "It's nettle I'm afraid," she said as she set down the kettle and offered him a mug.

"Aren't you a little young for the trials?" she asked. "I mean you're a big lad, but you've a young look about you."

"I had a sponsor," he said looking into his cup through the steam.

"Oh, I see. Family?"

"My uncle," he admitted in a tone which made it obvious he didn't want to speak about it further.

They sat in silence for a few minutes blowing the tea softly. "Seriously Ylsriss, why are you the one looking after these children? I thought the tithe took care of orphans and the like?"

"Oh Klöss, you truly are an innocent aren't you?" she sighed. "The tithe takes care of those who collect it, first and foremost. Do you really think that it's all dispersed to the children of fallen shipsmen and the poor? Have you actually looked and seen how many people there are in this city who are homeless and hungry?"

He took a sip of the tea savouring the grassy yet smooth taste. "Is that why you..." he trailed off.

"Steal?" she offered. "Yes, that's why I steal. To feed those who depend on me. Is that so wrong?" She laughed at his expression. "Have you ever stopped to think that if you become an oarsman you will be doing exactly the same thing?"

"What?!" he sat up straight, putting the cup down on the table. "How do you figure that?"

"Klöss do you actually think that the people we visit in those pretty little boats are just handing over their food and animals out of generosity?" she asked incredulously.

"That's different!" Klöss protested. "That's taken as spoils of war. Anyway, what about the woman you stole from? How is she less needy than you."

"I would think that was obvious, my innocent little rich boy," Ylsriss replied smoothly. "She had money and I didn't."

* * *

Klöss wandered through the darkening streets towards his home. Flickering lamps were just now being lit every hundred paces or so by a team of men carrying tapers and long poles. Inns and taverns beckoned patrons in with warm candlelight and the sounds of laughter and the smell of freshly cooked food.

She'd called him "rich boy", half an insult and half a joke from the tone of her voice. Klöss had never thought of himself or his family as rich before, but it was all relative. He'd always had a warm bed and food on the table. He'd never owned or worn clothes that were only two steps from rags or sackcloth. Compared to the children in Ylsriss's cellar he supposed he was rich. It was a sobering thought and not one he enjoyed.

He looked around him with fresh eyes as he walked, noting the women standing on the corner and for the first time wondering what their lives were like. What had pushed them to spend their evenings standing under the smoking torches, huddled in their groups of two or three as they called out to passing men with a smile and a wink. He'd assumed they were happy enough. After all they were flirting and calling out weren't they?

His head still throbbed slightly from the blow earlier, but the largest wound was to his pride. He didn't like it but he was forced to admit that not only had Ylsriss had him at her mercy amid the filth of the alleyway, but also that he hadn't heard the child approach before he'd clubbed him. Some raider he would end up to be with instincts like that.

As if the thought had reminded him, though in reality he'd just been avoiding thinking about it, he realised he would have to face his father and tell him about the trials. He'd be furious of course. It seemed he'd been relying on Klöss more and more with each passing year, and Klöss wasn't sure his father was even capable of running the business without him. The oarsmaster had ordered him to report to the training school in one week though, and that gave him only four more days before his training began in earnest. He couldn't really afford to put it off much longer.

The walk through the familiar streets took longer than normal as his feet dragged. It was almost fully dark by the time he crossed the tidy courtyard and stepped down the three steps.

The door flew open as he approached and his father stood there, backlit by the lamps and fire in the kitchen.

"Klöss, thank the gods you're alright!" he gasped and pulled him into a rough hug. His eyes were fierce but worry was etched deep in the lines of his weather-worn face. "What happened to you lad? I've had constables scouring for you all afternoon. Did you ever catch him?"

"Him?" Klöss replied in confusion, trying to decide how to explain the afternoon he'd had. "Oh the thief? It was a girl if you believe that, and yes I caught her. She, ah... She had a few friends and well, it was touch and go for a while."

"Are you okay?" Rhaven asked, looking him over for obvious cuts or bandages.

"A big lump on the head is about all I think."

"You can't afford to go softening your brains lad. Who else am I going to get to run the shop once I'm in my dotage?" his father said with a smile. Klöss's face fell, if possible, even further.

"We need to talk about that, Father," he began softly. "I..." he trailed off.

"You what?" Rhaven asked, his expression darkening.

"I took the trials Father," Klöss blurted, as if scared the words would catch in his throat.

"What trials?" Rhaven asked, the confusion plain on his tired face. "Get in here boy!" He stepped back from the doorway and motioned Klöss into a chair before closing the door against the cool night's breeze. "Now, what are you prattling on about lad?"

"I took the Oarsman trials." Klöss spoke hesitantly, already flinching in anticipation of the reaction.

"What are you talking about?" Rhaven said harshly. "We talked about you taking the trials. I thought we agreed that you would wait a few more years."

"That was what you decided Father, not me." Klöss said in a small voice.

"So you just openly defy me?" Rhaven spat, his temper rising and his eyes dark.

"I did what I thought best Father. That's what you always taught me."

"You'd throw my own words back at me? In my house!" Rhaven was incredulous. "Wait a moment. I didn't support you taking the trials. How did you even enter with no sponsor?"

Klöss flushed and looked guiltily at the tabletop. "I went to Uncle Frostbeard," he admitted.

"Aiden!" Rhaven slammed his palm down on the table. "I should have known it was him filling your head with this nonsense!"

"It's not nonsense, Father!" Klöss found his hands clenched into tight fists as his teeth ground together. "It's who we are. We've had the trials and the reaving for hundreds of years!"

"Aye Son, and what good has it brought us?" Rhaven demanded. "Fatherless children, husbandless wives. Damn it all boy, I was trying to show you that there is another way!"

"What way?" Klöss replied, derision slipping into his voice. "The market place? What life is that for a..." He trailed off quickly.

"For a what?" Rhaven demanded. "For a real man? That's what you were going to say wasn't it?"

Klöss met his father's eyes, his face stricken. "Father I..."

"Don't bother boy. You've made it clear how you feel. Just remember when you're soaked and trying to row with ten men down and the boat full of screaming wounded with their guts at their feet, how you thought it'd all be glory. A life for a real man," his voice was full of scorn. "You think you know it all. How do you think I got this leg? You know nothing boy. Nothing! You think a few hairs on your chin makes you a man? It takes a damned sight more than that!" He turned and stormed out into the night, the door banging hollowly behind him. Klöss sat at the empty table, wondering at himself and listening to the sounds of the wind as he stared into the kitchen fire. He watched the flames grow lower and then slowly turn into sullen embers before he finally realised his father would not be back and he banked the fire, put out the lamps and walked through the dark house to seek his bed.

CHAPTER FIVE

Klöss darted back away from the slash, nearly falling on the sand-covered floor of the training room, as his legs threatened to give way. Sweat soaked his dark leathers and linen undershirt. His hand was slick on the hilt of his blade. He circled warily around Verig, looking for an opening. His training blade was wooden but, after a few minutes, it seemed as heavy as real steel and his arms burned with the strain of keeping Verig's blade from finding his skin.

"Come on, boy! You're supposed to be something special, aren't you? Or are you just some little babe who should still be at his mother's tit?" Verig laughed as Klöss lunged, and idly flicked away the attack with no more effort than it would take to shoo away a fly.

"Really? Is that the best you have?" the man sneered.

Klöss knew he was being baited and shifted backwards to try to give himself time to think. Verig was fast, there was no doubting that. He'd been on the ships for years and trained dozens of men before him. He was small for an oarsman but seemed to have a sinewy strength. His blonde hair was tied at the nape with a leather thong and he went without a helmet, seemingly just to mock his trainees with their inability to get even close to his head.

He was dressed as Klöss was, in dark boiled leathers. Unlike Klöss, of course, he had been wearing his for years and they were well broken in and flexible at the joints. Verig wore his like a second skin, Klöss like a turtle in somebody else's shell.

Klöss shifted awkwardly in his leathers and flexed his grip inside his shield. Holding it before him, he lifted the sword and held it pointed over the edge of the shield, almost in a spearman's stance, ready to thrust. Verig stood silently, watching him, taking his measure as Klöss began to circle anew, trying to mimic the man's cat-like movements.

They'd been in training for three weeks now, drilling daily with sword and shield, learning the basic strikes, stances and blocks for hours at a time until they came without thinking. They had started out in groups but now they'd progressed to fighting one-on-one with a Master.

Klöss stamped his foot on the sand-covered floor, the wooden boards underneath giving a muted thud. An effort to force a reaction, any reaction. Verig stood still watching Klöss, his eyes impassive, only taking the occasional step to match his circling. His sword seemed to be held almost casually in his hand. Perhaps if Klöss could strike hard, close to the hilt, he could drive it from Verig's grasp, or at least loosen his grip and then…

He stopped his thought quickly. Planning led to traps, it was one of the first things he'd learned. Make a plan in a fight and you become dependent on it. Then, when things changed, you'd be left floundering. Act on instinct, he'd been drilled.

He struck, faster and more smoothly than he ever had before. The blade whistled down towards Verig's sword, angled perfectly to cause the maximum impact. Verig's blade, however, was simply not there, as the small man darted backwards and turned Klöss's blow into an uncontrolled lunge.

Verig shifted forward again and closed the distance in one short step. His boots making little or no noise as he moved. Klöss swung wildly as he sought to regain his balance, but Verig didn't even bother to parry or catch it with his shield. Instead, he took a half step to the side and shifted his balance, watching Klöss's practice blade sail past him ineffectually. His shield swung with the blade and caught the back of Klöss's arm, adding to his momentum as he shoved him almost completely around, before planting his foot and shoving hard. Klöss went sprawling to the floor, his sword flying from his grasp, while Verig laughed with a harsh, mocking snigger.

"Again!" the small man ordered, as Klöss clambered back to his feet and snatched up the practice blade.

He shifted back into his stance. It had felt awkward and strange when he'd first been taught it, three weeks ago. His legs had felt like rubber after training. He was beginning to become accustomed to it now, or maybe he was just used to the pain. It was doubtful he would ever feel as comfortable in the stance as Verig obviously did.

He began a patterned step, moving around Verig to the right, his sword held ready in a defensive posture. Let the small man come to him. He was sick of attacking, only to find empty air. He watched the Master's shoulders and upper torso for clues to his movements, trying not to focus on any particular area. Verig, for his part, seemed to be in no hurry and stood, relaxed in the same stance, shifting slightly now and then to stay facing Klöss but making no move to attack.

He clenched his teeth and tried to force himself to be patient but the strain of keeping his sword at guard position and maintaining his stance was growing and his muscles were aching from the abuse of standing in the odd position.

It was very slight, just a tightening of the eyes and a minute shifting of the shoulders as Verig shifted his weight, but it was enough. Klöss stepped to the side, away from the expected thrust. His shield was turned to deflect the thrust at an angle which would allow the sword to scrape along it, diverting rather than blocking the stroke. He waited to feel the impact on the face of the shield and then Klöss turned and thrust hard. The series of moves was intended to leave an attacker off balance and overextended, at which point it would be simple to thrust into the side of the body or the neck. He had performed the manoeuvre perfectly, but Verig simply wasn't where he should be. Klöss gasped as his sword met with no resistance and desperately tried to recover from his lunge, as he saw Verig uncoil like a striking snake in the corner of his vision.

Verig attacked. Once, twice, three times the blade caught Klöss, hitting his arm, back and finally a resounding blow to the helm, making it ring like a bell and dropping him to his knees.

"NEVER, over-extend lad. You put that much force into your blow and you can't recover from it. You as good as threw yourself onto my sword then!"

Klöss dropped his wooden sword and pulled his helmet off with trembling fingers. Turning, he looked at the man with something very close to hatred.

"It was a good attempt, but you need to anticipate a feint too. You threw yourself into it and didn't take the time to see what was really going on." Verig continued.

Klöss blinked the sweat from his eyes and tried to fight back his frustration as he rose to one knee.

"Get up, you useless sack of piss!" the man spat at him at his temper frayed. "What are you going to do? Cry?"

Klöss pulled himself to his feet and waited for the Master to dismiss him. It had been like this almost since the training started. Verig had seemed friendly enough during the initial training for the trials, but now that he and the others were training in earnest, he treated them with contempt. Klöss seemed to fare worse than most, as if Verig had some reason for singling him out. He seemed to dole out seven hands of abuse with every hand of actual training.

"Go on. I'm done with you." Verig said. He spat at Klöss's feet and walked away without another word.

Klöss bent to retrieve his practice blade as his legs trembled, sweat running down his face. He made his way to the water barrel at the side of the training room, and drank down three quick cups as fast as he could dip them out. Verig had yet to break more than a light sweat in their sessions, and had never yet gone near the water. Klöss had no idea how he managed it. The room was low-ceilinged, and lit with reflective lamps and torches. They served to make it hotter, yet somehow didn't seem to really shed enough light. Training was hard enough, without doing it in flickering torchlight that threw dancing shadows around the room. The shadows could make you think your opponent was moving when he wasn't. Klöss couldn't think of a worse place to learn to fight. Perhaps that was the point.

He wiped down the wooden blade with a soft linen cloth, and placed it back in the rack of weapons lining the wall. As he headed out of the doorway, he felt Verig's eyes burning into his back. Twenty minutes later, he was stripped out of his leathers and making his way into the mess. The room was only half-full, with most having already finished their meals. Of the fifteen who had won their trials with him in Frostbeard's reavers, only four were still eating. The remainder sat at the long trestle tables, talking and laughing loudly. The sound served to make Klöss even more bitter as he made his way to the pot. The stew was mostly gone and what remained at the bottom had congealed into an unappetising paste. He took up the long-handled ladle and scraped at the pot, trying to gather up the most identifiable parts. The stew had been left over the fire once it was cooked and had stuck and burnt at the bottom. Klöss grunted sourly as he filled his wooden bowl and moved over to the tables.

"No room," muttered Henrick, as he shovelled stew into his bearded face.

Klöss looked at the almost empty bench. The fat man had thick, hard muscle under the rolls of flab and the soul of a bully. There was no point arguing with him. Klöss found and sat at an empty table.

He wasn't quite sure what he had been expecting. The training before the trials had all been good-natured, and the teams of men had worked well together. Back then of course, they had been working for a common goal. Whilst the final race around the island didn't guarantee acceptance, it didn't hurt and they had all known that. Klöss had been as useful as the next man and there had been no real competition between them. Now, things were different. Not everyone who made it through the schools would be chosen to work the reaving boats. Haulers, the huge warehouses of the seas that served to transport the goods reaped on the raids, needed crews too and the job was not a desirable one.

"Kept late again, Klöss?" Dallan called. "What were you doing this time? Holding the wrong end of the sword?" His jibe was met with scattered laughter, but there was a nervous tinge to it too. Since Klöss had started training three weeks ago, Dallan had dispensed his special brand of misery to almost all of the new recruits at one point or another. He now seemed to have settled on Klöss as his next target. It was odd, as Dallan was not an especially large man. He was perhaps four years older than Klöss, but then so were most of the other trainees. His dark hair hung loosely to his shoulders and his deep-set green eyes glittered as he watched Klöss take his seat.

Klöss knew better than to rise to it and sat on the plain bench as he began to force the stew down. He grimaced as he chewed but managed to swallow it down and take another spoonful. He knew from experience that the first bite was the worst. Your taste buds tended to run and hide after the first mouthful. This was the fifth time Klöss had been one of the last to the pot and this was not the worst it had tasted.

He looked around the room, quickly counting heads, and swore quietly as he realised he was the last to eat. This meant the task of cleaning out the huge pot would be his. It was an effective form of punishment. Those not pleasing their trainers would be kept later and later, ensuring that they not only ate the worst of the food, but also faced the task of cleaning the pot out. As the pot was essentially a huge cauldron this was not a small job. It would take a couple of hours to clean it properly which meant he would miss more training. It was one of the first things they had been taught. They were provided food, but were responsible for cooking it themselves and clearing up. No training would be given to the last man to eat until the pot was clean. Klöss forced the last greasy mouthful down his throat and then made his way over to the pot to begin the miserable task.

He grabbed the long-handled ladle and started scooping out the grisly remnants into a large leather bucket. The pot sides rang with a rasping note as he worked, so he didn't hear anyone approach until the bowl clattered into the pot, spraying stew and half-congealed gravy over his face.

Klöss swore and jumped back from the pot, as the room filled with laughter again. He turned to see Dallan, flanked by Henrick and another smaller man that he'd never caught the name of.

"Surprised a rich boy like you knows how to clean a pot, Klöss." Dallan smirked as he looked him up and down. "Let's hope you make a better scullion than you do a swordsman, hey?"

Klöss felt his jaw clench as he dug his nails painfully into his palms. "Don't you have anything better to do, Dallan?"

"Why yes, scullion, I do." The green eyes glittered. "I came here to train. Not just to clean the pots. We're not all destined for the hauler." He threw a grin over one shoulder to his two companions before turning back, his face suddenly serious and full of mocking concern.

"Listen, Klöss, let me give you some advice. You don't belong here. You're here because you have a famous uncle and that's it. You better leave before you get hurt. It's not a game and it's not all about cleaning pots, you know?" He laughed at his own joke, pushing past Klöss roughly as he headed for the doorway.

Klöss muttered, picking bits of stew from his clothing as a half-dozen witty comebacks came to mind too late. He turned back to the pot and began scraping again.

"Do not let him get to you." The quiet voice came from behind him. Klöss looked over his shoulder to see the huge Tristan looming over him. Mostly silent and keeping to himself, Klöss was not sure what to make of the quiet man. He had a thick accent from the Far Islands and had clearly made his way to Bresda just to train in the schools. "Thanks," he smiled "I…"

"He speaks truth about one thing though." The big man cut him off. "You do not belong here."

Klöss gaped but Tristan was already walking away. He shook his head and turned back to the pot.

The schools worked to rebuild a man from the ground up. Trainees were isolated from their families and lived inside the schools themselves, with only one day every two months to visit. Even this visit must be earned and it was not unheard of for a student to go six months or more without seeing his family.

The oarsman's role was far more than simply rowing a ship through the waves.

An oarsman must be warrior, scout, lookout and guard. When the ships landed, it was the oarsmen who were first through the surf with shield and sword. It was the oarsmen who would fight the villagers who tried to defend their stores. And it was the oarsmen who would help load up the larger hauler ships with the plunder from the raids.

Klöss knew that he would need to prove himself quickly, as it was only once the school's training was complete that it would be decided whether an oarsman was destined for a reaving boat or a hauler. Crewing a hauler was said to be no dishonour but it was not viewed in the same way as working on the reaving boats and, to Klöss's mind, it was little better than driving a cart. If he had to scrape the pot out every night for six months, he was determined to avoid the hauler.

* * *

He woke as the sound of snoring filled the long room mingling with the soft noise of bodies shifting in their sleep. It was still dark and the skies, just visible through the small window, had yet to shift from the inky hue of true night. He shivered in his narrow wooden bunk and pulled the rough woollen blanket more tightly around himself as he tried to identify what had woken him.

The days had settled into a rhythm of weapons training and gruelling physical conditioning which seemed designed to both train the muscles and also cause the maximum discomfort. Yesterday had begun at the crack of dawn when they were awoken and broken into teams of four before being sent on a five mile run carrying long wooden canoes. The boats were large enough to hold five men and were not overly heavy for their size, but they were bulky and unwieldy. By the end of the first mile, all of the men with Klöss were sweating and breathing hard. By the end of the fifth mile, they could barely walk and the upturned canoe dug into their shoulders with every step. They'd come in dead last and the others had all blamed him. He had washed the pot again that night.

He lay in the darkness for a time, but sleep would not come. As the first hint of light began to tint the skies through the tiny window he gave up and dressed silently in the gloom. Carrying his boots, he padded to the doorway and left his bunk-mates to their snores.

He made his way to the mess and made a large pot of porridge, eating it quickly and quietly in the empty room. Despite the fact that he had not a single friend among the trainees, the mess felt strange. Klöss dumped his bowl and spoon into water to soak and made his way through the halls to the training room.

The schools had been established for centuries as a place for the initial training of those joining the ships. Every Shipmaster could use them, although some chose to take a different approach and simply train their new recruits on the ships themselves. Frostbeard was one of the few Seamasters who insisted that everyone who served aboard his ships had worked through the school. There were several of them dotted about the islands, small camps keeping crews separate from each other and only working together occasionally to aid training.

He went to the racks of weapons against the wall and took out a simple steel sword, marvelling at the difference in the weight between it and the wooden swords they had been training with. Glancing around guiltily he replaced the weapon before drawing out the same wooden weapon he had held yesterday.

Moving slowly, Klöss went through a series of stretches to limber up his still waking muscles, before moving through a series of sword strikes and blocks. He did not grunt or posture. He worked slowly making the exercise appear more of a dance than anything else, but moving with glacial slowness. Finally, satisfied with the movements he slowly increased the speed, moving from stroke to stroke, from thrust to strike to block. The sword whistled through the air and sweat began to drip from his face.

A noise behind him caused him to spin in shock and his sword flew from startled fingers to clatter noisily against the wall. Verig raised an eyebrow and then made his way past him without a word to retrieve his own weapon from the racks.

"I didn't expect anyone to be up," Klöss stammered. "I hope I didn't wake you?" Verig ignored him as if he hadn't spoken, and began to work through his own series of stretches and exercises.

Klöss looked at the small man in shock. It is one thing to ignore somebody when in a group. To do so when you are alone together is something quite different, and it bit more deeply than any of the foolish stunts the other trainees had tried in the past few weeks.

Verig continued to ignore him and worked his way through the same series of thrusts, strikes, and blocks as Klöss had. There was a smoothness to the movements that had been lacking with Klöss. Where Verig moved flawlessly from one stroke to another, Klöss had paused. It was more than that though. It was a thousand tiny details. It showed in his balance and the set of his feet, in the line of his shoulders and the snap he put at the end of each stroke. Klöss watched as Verig moved faster and faster until the blade became a whirling curtain of steel, before finishing without flourish or fanfare. Klöss found his heart pounding as Verig turned to face him.

The small man pointed at the ground next to him. A short stabbing motion with one thick digit. "Again."

Two hours later, Klöss sat in the mess, eating another bowl of porridge. He was covered in a thick sweat and his limbs trembled visibly. A light filled his eyes, however, and a grin sprang to his lips between every mouthful. He had vaguely registered the morning gong strike a few minutes ago and trainees were beginning to file into the mess. Some few showed surprise to find the fire lit and porridge steaming but none offered a word of thanks, although Tristan seemed to give him a slight nod as he came in.

"Right lads," came a deep, rumbling voice from the doorway. Klöss looked up from his bowl to see Christoph standing with a vicious grin on his face. "Who's up for a little race this morning?" the Shipmaster asked, with deceptive light-heartedness. The hall erupted with a chorus of groans as the trainees grasped his meaning. They had been informed the night before that a reaver would be at the docks for them the next day. There had been no mention of a race though, and they'd all hoped it would simply be working the ship with full crew.

"Eat up and get to the docks. You have one hour." Christoph smiled thinly. "Oh and let's make it full kit boys." He smirked at the groans, and then was gone.

A race meant working in an undermanned ship. They'd done it on the first day of training. Manoeuvring the huge reaver was hard enough with a full crew, but the Masters split the trainees into two teams, with four seasoned oarsmen with them, just in case things got completely out of hand. In any event, even the smallest reaver held a rowing crew of thirty. Whilst they might be able to move the thing with a crew of ten, it was agonisingly slow and brutal labour. Klöss knew they were trying to get them to work together whilst training their bodies, but this was slim comfort.

He stood and looked around, as the trainees shovelled porridge into themselves. Making his way to the kitchen area, he quickly scrubbed out his bowl. He turned just in time to see Dallan scooping out the last of the porridge. Klöss smiled at him and nodded meaningfully at the pot as he walked past the man whistling cheerfully as Dallan stared daggers into his back.

An hour passes very quickly when you have things to do and Klöss soon found himself on the docks, in his stiff leathers, awkwardly trying to juggle sword and shield, whilst boarding the narrow reaver. The wind whipped at the quay and the harbour water was choppy, despite the high cliffs and the Harbour Island opposite. Klöss struggled onto the pitching boat and made his way to his seat. He secured his sword and shield in one of the racks built into the edge of each bench in the oarpit. Brushing away the wood shavings from his seat, he took his place quickly and looked to the oarsmaster.

The boat rocked gently and strained against the hawsers as more of the trainees climbed aboard. The true oarsmen were easy to spot, their leathers older and scarred thrice over from weather and battles. It was more than just their leathers however, it was the simple way they carried themselves with a casual arrogance, a sureness of purpose. Klöss watched them openly, as awestruck as an eight-year-old watching a juggler with knives.

The Shipmasters chatted idly on the quay, clearly in no particular hurry, as the crews manned the two reavers. The oarsmaster on each boat moved slowly from bow to stern, checking crew and vessel with equal diligence. Finally, the Shipmasters clasped hands formally and stepped aboard. Hawsers were loosed and the two boats moved off slowly towards the narrow channel on the right side of the harbour.

The ship moved ponderously, unlike the sleek creature she had been designed to be. She seemed sluggish to Klöss and the oar felt strange in his hands. The two reavers moved slowly towards the channel and took up positions fifty feet apart, level with a large red buoy. He adjusted his grip on the oar. It was already rubbing at one of his fingers. He glanced across at the other reaver and saw Dallan watching him with a broad grin. The other man waved at him, smiling.

"Okay, lads, we're going for a nice little row around the Harbour Island this morning," the oarsmaster called out. "It's only a little hop, so there'll be no sails. Oh, and you'll be steering by oar too. Stand ready!"

Klöss grasped his oar tightly as he looked across the water at the other reaver. The other oarsmaster stood on the decking between the two oarpits on his reaver, a red flag held high. He looked over at Klöss's boat, catching the eye of the oarsmaster, then nodded and dropped the flag.

"Stroke!" the oarsmaster roared. Klöss hauled back hard on his oar, bracing his feet on the wooden panel in front of him. The drummer started up a slow rhythm and Klöss fought to keep in time with it.

The oarsmen were spread evenly throughout the boat, with three empty benches between each of them. The oarsmaster stood high in the prow with the Shipmaster, looking back over the boat, and the drummer sat below them on the decking. Normally, the Steersman would have stood in the stern and followed the dictates of the Shipmaster, but today the rudder was locked and the navigation would be up to the oarsmen themselves.

Klöss heaved back and tried to adjust his grip on the oar again. Normally, the oars were as smooth as glass, having been crafted smooth and then polished by a thousand hours of hands straining at them. This one, however, seemed to have a nasty little ridge that caught just under the knuckle of his middle finger. It was a small thing, but even after a scant five minutes of rowing, he could feel a blister forming.

They were moving agonisingly slowly through the harbour, ten men were simply not enough to drive it forward at the speed it was designed for, and it pitched and wallowed through the waves. Klöss glanced across at the other boat but they were both moving so slowly it was hard to see if either had lost or gained. He strained at the oars, fighting to contain a hysterical giggle as the image of the snail races he had played as a child came to his mind.

"Are we having fun, Klöss?" The oarsmaster stood on the decking beside him, scowling down. Klöss felt the grin falling from his face like hail from the skies, as he heaved back hard on the oars again.

"If this is too easy for you, I'm sure a couple of the lads would be happy to take a break," the big man suggested, as he knelt and thrust his angry face at him.

"No, sir," Klöss gasped between strokes, fighting the urge to adjust his grip again.

"What do you think, Tristan?" the oarsmaster shouted back over one shoulder to the big man at the rear of the reaver. "Klöss is finding this all too easy. Do you want to take a break?"

"No, sir," Tristan called back.

"And why is that, lad?"

"I want to win, Oarsmaster. We need him," Tristan called.

"That's right! You all need him to win this. And we *are* going to win this, Klöss. So stop pissing about and grinning like a girl who's found her mother's brandy, and damned well ROW!"

"Yes, Oarsmaster," Klöss shouted and pulled hard at the oars, feeling the blister burst as he did so.

After ten minutes, his muscles burned and his hand stung from the seawater in the blister. After thirty minutes his shoulders and back were just a mass of pain. The aching no longer altered, whether he was straining back against the oar or moving forward to set for another stroke. Blood dripped slowly from his hand and he sought a quiet place inside himself.

The wind was picking up and it caught the top of the waves in the choppy waters, blasting spray over the oarsmen as they rowed. They were approaching the turn and the oarsmaster called out instructions over the wind. As they passed the rocky outcrop that marked the far point of Harbour Island, the men on the left of the reaver stopped rowing and quickly shipped their oars. The reaver swung sluggishly into the turn and after a barely a minute, two men began rowing again at the oarsmaster's signal, before the boat lost too much speed.

He strained as he tried to keep to the drummer's rhythm, but his grip was ruined. The ridge on the oar had worn away at his skin and no amount of adjusting his grip had helped. He tried putting more of the strain on his other hand but it made it too hard to keep to the rhythm. With half of the oarsmen waiting for the turn to end, his oar mattered more than ever and he knew he wasn't pulling his weight.

He could almost feel the black looks coming from beside him and behind him, as the other oarsmen felt the extra load and noticed him slipping off the stroke. With the turn complete, he stole a glance at the other reaver as it finished its own turn. Their turn was far tighter, he noticed, as the other boat had two oarsmen on the inside of the turn rowing backwards. It was an awkward thing to attempt. The seats would not allow for a man to brace himself properly and so the oarsmen lacked the power they would normally have. For all that, though, the tactic seemed to work and the other reaver turned far inside of them, gaining maybe three boat lengths on them.

Klöss cursed just a fraction of a second before he heard the oarsmaster stood slightly behind him mutter, "Why that crafty bastard!" and turn to the drummer.

"Right you lot," the oarsmaster called out. "We are not going to be beaten today. I've beaten that whoremonger the last four times and his fancy tricks are not going to change that. I want everything you have now." The drum beat increased and men bent their backs to the task, as the wind lashed them with spray.

"Come on, you Dernish scow. Move!" he roared at the uncaring planks beneath his feet, and darted forwards to stand in the prow, as if he could speed the reaver by force of will alone. He stormed and raged on the decks like a man possessed, laying about with both lash and curse. The trainees and true oarsmen bent their backs to the work and sweat ran freely, as the Shipmaster looked over the crew impassively.

After the final turn, with the docks in sight, Klöss was past the pain. It felt like the oar had cut clear through to the bone on the inside of his knuckle, but he was more afraid of what the oarsmaster might do if they lost the race than he was of his finger falling off at this point. They had closed the distance, though the gods only knew how, and they weren't telling. The lead reaver was a scant handful of yards away, and the oarsmaster stood in the prow hurling abuse and curses at both his own men and the other reaver's crew with equal ferocity. As they came to the final ten yards, Klöss glanced across and saw Dallan watching him openly as he rowed. He risked the wrath of his own oarsmaster to wiggle his fingers at him in an insolent wave and then they passed the buoy and it was over.

Klöss prised his hand from the oar with some effort, and examined the mass of raw and bleeding flesh under his knuckle.

"Has he got a little blister, then?" The oarsmaster sneered down at him. "I don't know how you got it with that piss-poor performance. Your stroke was all over the place. I've seen fishermen's daughters row harder than you just did."

Klöss opened his mouth to protest, but the man thrust a hand in front of his face. "Don't," he advised. "I don't want to hear your excuses. Just get your idle self out of my oarpit!"

There wasn't much he could say to that, so he grabbed his sword and shield from the rack beside his bench and made his way out to the dock. There was a brief congratulation for the crew of the other reaver but Klöss wasn't paying attention. He watched, disinterestedly, as the dock crews secured the boats with massive hawsers, and then, dismissed, he walked dejectedly back to the small compound that housed the school.

"Nice work on the turn there, Klöss," Dallan called mockingly from behind him. "Is keeping to a drumbeat too complex for you? Or this *all* just too much for you?" Klöss ignored him and carried on walking.

"I heard you got a little blister and that's why you couldn't row. Your precious rich-boy hands too soft for real work? Is that it?"

Klöss ignored him and the chorus of sniggers and laughter that accompanied the digs. Dallan was growing in popularity and seemed determined to make his life miserable.

"Leave him, Dallan," Tristan's deep voice rumbled.

"What's it to you?" Dallan turned to face the big man, a feral look on his face and his hand clenching and unclenching, seemingly of its own volition. "He doesn't belong here. You know that. He's barely good enough for a hauler!"

"If that's true, then surely you want him here?" Tristan said calmly. "Some will be chosen for hauler crews. If he leaves, then does this not increase the chance it is you?"

Dallan grinned as he met the big man's eyes. "I like the way you think!" He turned to Henrick, who stood with a smile on his fat, pig-eyed face. "Come on, let's go and make some work for our scullion here!" and he set off, whistling happily.

Tristan caught up with Klöss with no real effort. The big man's strides were half again the length of his own on a good day and Klöss was in no hurry. "You are not as strong as some, Klöss, but I do not understand this?" he said in his thick Far Islanders accent.

Klöss held out his hand to Tristan by way of answer, exposing the raw flesh on his hand.

"That is nasty, but how did you come by it? Not from just rowing?" Tristan shook his head.

"There was something on my oar, a ridge in the wood," Klöss explained slowly.

"How could this be?" Tristan asked. "The oars have been used for many years. They are all smooth."

"He waved at me," Klöss said, half to himself, as his feet first slowed and then stopped.

"What?" replied Tristan, perplexed, as he halted beside him. "Who? And why are we talking about this?"

"Damn him to hell. The damned sawdust!" Klöss spat at his feet, as if something foul had filled his mouth.

"You are making no sense, Klöss. What are you talking about?" Tristan demanded with frustration.

"When I got onto the reaver, there was sawdust on my bench. Not much, but just a few shavings of wood," Klöss explained.

"And what? The boat is made of wood. Some worker had probably been repairing the bench or something," Tristan argued.

"No! You aren't seeing it," Klöss said in frustration.

"Because you are not explaining it!" cried Tristan in equal frustration.

"When we were racing, I saw Dallan wave at me," Klöss explained. Tristan nodded and motioned with his big hands for him to carry on. "You felt how hard it was to move the reaver, how heavy the boat was? It took all of our efforts to get the thing going, didn't it? Why would you take the time to wave at someone on the other reaver? Especially someone you hate," Klöss said, his face animated as he spoke.

"It does seem odd," Tristan admitted, confusion clouding his face.

"It's more than odd, it's bloody stupid," insisted Klöss. "We were close. Really close! Would you have risked the oarsmaster seeing you take a hand off to wave? No, of course you wouldn't. He wasn't even waving normally, he was wiggling his fingers at me, like a little girl would. No, now I think about it, he was making a point. His fingers were working fine. He knew! He damn well did it!"

"What are you suggesting? That Dallan sneaked out, got to the reaver and carved up your oar?" Tristan asked doubtfully. "How would he know where you sat? Or which oar? Or even which reaver?"

"I still think he did it." Klöss shook his head. "Somehow he knew."

"And how do you know it was not just a rough patch on the oar?" Tristan asked. "It is a big thing you suggest. A serious thing."

"It was more than that. Anyway, what about the wood shavings? It's all too convenient," Klöss insisted. Tristan shook his head doubtfully, clearly not convinced.

"Look, come and look at the oar yourself." Klöss said as inspiration struck him.

"We are expected back at the school. We are late as it is," Tristan objected.

"Tomorrow then?" Klöss pleaded. "Early, before training?"

"I suppose," Tristan agreed and turned towards the school. Klöss walked slowly behind him, silently seething as he stared at his hand.

The mess hall was quiet by the time Klöss made his way to it. His freshly bandaged hand felt strange and now the race was finished and he'd had time to calm down, the pain was intense. He made his way into the room and found it empty except for Tristan who was scraping away at the inside of the pot with a long wooden tool. He turned at the sound of Klöss's footsteps and glowered at him before turning back to the pot.

"Why?" Klöss floundered. "I mean, I'm the last one here. I've not even eaten yet. Why are you stuck with this?"

"Your hand," Tristan muttered. "You are not to get it wet, they said. So I get the pot, as I was the last to eat before you."

"But that's not fair!" Klöss objected.

Tristan shrugged. "Fair or not, it is what was decided."

"Well, let me help you with it at least."

"You can't," Tristan said flatly. "Your bandage. You must not get it wet."

"I don't care about the bandage," Klöss said, his temper rising. "I'm not going to stand here and let you scrape out the pot just because I hurt my hand."

"No," Tristan replied flatly. "We will need your hand for group training. You must not get it wet."

"Oh," said Klöss in a small voice. "I'm sorry. I didn't understand."

"Sometimes speaking your language is not so simple for me," Tristan explained.

"You don't speak Islik on the Far Isles?"

"Yes, we do," explained Tristan. "It is just older there, purer. Islik is much changed over the years. It is not so similar now." He turned back to the pot and handed Klöss a wooden bowl with some cold potato soup and a heel of bread. "I save this for you."

Klöss nodded his thanks and began to spoon down the soup. It wasn't bad, despite being cold.

* * *

He awoke in a panic as a hand closed over his mouth. Kicking and thrashing out wildly, he felt his foot connect hard and was rewarded with a muffled grunt of pain.

"Is me, you stupid man," grunted Tristan in the dark. "You wanted we should look at the oars, yes?"

Klöss nodded in the darkness, before realising how stupid that was. "Yes. Sorry."

He threw his clothes on and they left as silently as they could, picking their way between the bunks.

The streets of Hesk were dark and a light drizzle misted down from the still, black sky, as they warily crept out of the doors to the school. The courtyard was deserted and the heavy, tar-smeared gates were barred shut against the night. Klöss spun around in a slow circle and then turned to face Tristan in the dark.

"I never really even looked at this place in the daytime," he admitted in a whisper. "How are we going to get out?"

Tristan sighed, and motioned for Klöss to follow him, as he trotted between two buildings towards the tall stone walls surrounding the courtyard. He stopped in the darker shadows of the wall where it passed behind one of the storehouses. "Climb here," the big man whispered, gesturing to the old stone wall. Klöss turned to examine the wall and reached up for a hand-hold. The wall was made of huge limestone blocks, set close together and well-mortared. His hand scrabbled vainly for purchase until he heard Tristan's despairing sigh again.

"Not like that. Here, watch." He planted his feet firmly against the wall of the storehouse and braced his back against the courtyard wall, working his way up the wall with small steps and then shifting his back. Klöss grinned and followed.

They climbed down the other side of the wall using a worn rope that Tristan pulled from over one shoulder, and then made their way quietly through the pre-dawn murk towards the docks. Hesk was a different city at this time of night. Usually, the place was alive with the sounds of the street hawkers and the bustle of city life. Now the streets were almost silent, the only noise the faint hiss of the rain on the slate rooftops and a dog somewhere, barking at the night.

The docks were not far away and the two made their way through the alleyways easily. There was no need for concealment, as nobody would have been able to see them in the darkness. The torches and lanterns had long been snuffed or allowed to burn out, and the city was wreathed in an almost inky blackness, the starlight held back by a heavy blanket of clouds.

The reavers were still tied up at the school's docks. Usually the docks stood empty, reaving boats were simply too valuable to leave unused. They were borrowed, when available, from the various Seamasters and Shipmasters who used the schools to train their own crews.

Klöss crouched down in the shadows of a building, noticing that the skies were starting to lighten. They wouldn't have much time. The boats appeared to be unguarded, which was an odd but happy turn of events. Motioning Tristan to follow, he moved quickly and silently to the first reaver. It was hard to tell which was which in the dark.

"You check this one, I'll go to the other," he whispered to Tristan, gesturing at the closest reaver. "Check the oar on the left-hand side, six rows back." Tristan nodded and bent to shift the heavy gangplank into place from where it lay on the dock.

The planks were heavy and it was hard work to move them alone. Klöss eventually managed his and it locked into place with a heavy thud. He stepped across it easily and onto the gently swaying reaver, moving swiftly back past the rows of benches. As he stepped down into the oarpit, a soft noise suddenly froze him. Any noise sounds deafening in the night and Klöss was impressed he hadn't jumped and made noise himself. As it was he crouched by the bench, his heart pounding as he strained his ears. Being caught out of the school would be bad enough, but being caught on the reaver would raise questions he couldn't yet answer.

Slowly Klöss raised his head so he could see over the side of the boat. Dawn was fast approaching. He could make out the docks easily, but there was no sign of movement, or of Tristan. He sank back into a crouch and turned to examine the oar. It was drawn in and lashed to the bench, the blade protruding two or three feet out the side of the boat. The handle extended through the oarpit and the supports of the wooden deckway that ran the length of the ship.

Klöss worked the ropes holding it in place and began to slide the oar slowly out. He worked quickly but as quietly as he could, extending the oar out and feeling for the sharp, ridged section. He winced at the soft scraping noise the oar made and searched frantically with his fingertips as he went. Finally, he conceded he must be on the wrong reaver. This oar was as smooth as a river stone. He swore under his breath and began to move the oar back into its stored position, before moving down the gangplank and shifting it back onto the docks.

The docks were silent but faint noises were now coming from the city, as people began to rise and begin their day. He moved quickly over to the other reaver, searching for Tristan but the big man was nowhere in sight. Klöss went to the gangplank and stepped silently aboard.

"Did you find it?" he called softly.

"No, he didn't," a voice said from behind him. Klöss spun like a startled cat. Verig stood on the end of the gangplank, and he did not look amused.

"Can you tell me, young Klöss, why you have snuck out of the school and crept about this reaver in the middle of the night?" The man's eyes were black holes in the darkness but the greater darkness was in his voice. An anger lurked there, like a great sleeping wolf, and Klöss felt as if he had just jabbed it with a pointed stick.

An hour later, Klöss sat waiting on his bunk in the school. The room was empty, the other trainees having already eaten and gone to train, and the silence only seemed to make the wait worse. He'd not had a chance to speak to Tristan, as Verig marched them back to the school and through the now unbarred gates. Verig had insisted on silence and cut off his explanations, saying only that the seamaster would speak to them himself.

Klöss was more than a little worried. Some children and nephews would consider it a reprieve to be dealt with by their uncle, but he knew he faced serious repercussions. Frostbeard had not wanted to sponsor him when he'd first sought him out, almost a year ago. It had taken several months of long conversations and blatant pleading to even get him to consider the idea. Since taking the trials, and then finally admitting he had done so to his father, Klöss had avoided his uncle as much as possible.

He sat up quickly as the door opened and Tristan came into the room, his face drawn and tired. "You are to go and see him now." His deep voice held none of the camaraderie of yesterday or the gently mocking humour of that morning. Klöss sighed and made his way through the doorway.

Frostbeard was only in the school once in a blue moon. He was simply too busy to pay much attention to his newest recruits, so the day to day running of the school was left to the Training Masters. It was just Klöss's bad luck that he happened to be in the school at the moment. Had he known, he would never have attempted going near the reavers.

He forced himself through the cold stone corridors and stopped outside a solid mahogany door, intricately carved and varnished to a deep rich shine. In a nation with little or no woodlands, which was dependent on raiding for anything that could not be gleaned from the sea, the door spoke volumes as to the wealth of its owner. Klöss steeled himself and knocked. He might look older, but he was still only fourteen, and right now he was keenly aware of just how young he was.

"Come," came a firm, gravelly voice.

Klöss entered boldly. He was not going to be the timid mouse here. He had crept out of the school, but he was the one who had been wronged, after all.

His uncle sat in a large chair, behind a cluttered but beautiful desk. His eyes looked tired as he surveyed the young man in the doorway and he sighed visibly as he motioned Klöss into the room and pointed at a straight-backed chair opposite him at the desk.

"Sit," he muttered. He had piercing blue eyes that looked out from under heavy, steel grey eyebrows. His mouth was a tight line buried in a thick beard. There had been a time when his beard had been black as coal and his name earned from his taming of the Vorstelv. Now his beard was more a deep grey with fleck of white in it, and a person could have been forgiven for thinking this was the reason.

"Explain yourself," he said flatly and glared over the desk at him.

"My oar had been tampered with before the training race yesterday, sir," Klöss began. "Someone had worked a ridge into the wood, so it would grind against my hand and make it impossible to row properly."

Frostbeard grunted and motioned for him to continue.

"I wanted to show someone and ask their advice before I brought it to a Master's attention," Klöss admitted. "I wasn't sure if I should just let it go."

"So you convinced Tristan to sneak out of the training compound in the middle of the night and visit the reaver," Frostbeard finished for him. "And did you find your damaged oar?"

Klöss shook his head mutely.

"No, neither did Tristan," Frostbeard said quickly, holding up a hand against Klöss's startled outburst. "I have heard the reports of your injury and I have no doubt that the oar was tampered with. Whoever did it had no doubt switched the oar with one from stores by this time."

"It was Dallan, I am sure of it," Klöss blurted, his anger mixed with relief.

"Perhaps or perhaps not," his uncle continued. "I suppose you think he should be brought in and questions asked?"

He slammed his hand down onto the desk, scattering papers and spilling ink that poured unheeded across the polished surface. "You think you are the victim here? Let me ask you, boy, did you check your weapon and shield before you boarded that boat?" He continued, without waiting for an answer. "You think your oar is not just as important? You should have checked it the second you sat down. There was space on that boat to have moved you or you could simply have swapped oars but no, you didn't even think to look until it was too late, did you?"

Klöss was scrambling to keep up. He had come into the room full of righteous indignation and this had caught him as unprepared as one of Verig's strikes.

"Damn it all, boy. I already have half the Masters thinking I let you in here just because you're my nephew. That you're too young, too soft. Then you go and pull this stupid stunt, sneaking out of the school, like a girl climbing from her bedroom window to meet a lover."

Klöss took a deep breath. "You are right, Seamaster," he began respectfully. "I should have checked the oar and brought it to the oarsmaster's attention before we sailed. But the oar itself should have been fine. I neglected my duty to check, but this does not alter the fact that it was tampered with."

"And was your reaver not guarded?" Frostbeard said, with deceptive mildness.

Klöss swallowed carefully. They hadn't even discussed guarding the reaver when they'd been informed it would be at dock for them the night before.

"Of course it wasn't," the old man said scathingly. "Go on, boy. Get out and find your Masters. Perhaps they can teach you something."

Klöss turned to the door, his hands clenched tight and shaking. He left quickly, before his mouth betrayed him, but the colour of his cheeks already told the tale of his anger.

Chapter Six

Klöss slammed the gate hard behind himself and swore. The afternoon was warm and it was too nice a day to waste, but he was furious. It had been a full three months since he entered training and he had finally been allowed a day off, to visit his father. After the incident with the oar and the reaver, he'd been expecting to be denied it again, but things seemed to have blown over. He hadn't expected his father to welcome him with open arms, but it had been three months. He should have calmed down by now.

He turned down the cobbled streets, letting his feet guide him whilst his head was elsewhere. The man had barely let him into the house before he'd started on him about shirking his responsibilities, leaving him to scramble whilst he went off to play with boats. When he'd started about how disappointed his mother would have been, Klöss could take no more and had stormed out.

He took a deep breath and exhaled slowly, trying to force himself to calm down. The day was sunny and bright, he had money in his purse, it was too good to waste worrying about the old goat. He muttered to himself darkly as he wandered towards the market and tried to shake off his mood. The city was alive with a thousand scents and colours. Klöss knew this was only because he'd been locked away from it for a time, but he revelled in the sights and sounds. He stopped at a street vendor and bought some hot pork in flatbread. He'd been living on porridge and fish stew for so long, it felt good to have some real meat between his teeth.

A cart trundled down the street laden with sacks of grain, he stepped aside easily, and wandered aimlessly for a time.

"For these are the New Days!" a deep voice cried, from a set of stone steps. "Cast off your old pagan ways, for they are the shackles of the past. The Lord of New Days will show you a better way!"

Klöss glanced at the priest, clad in his dark robes with bell in hand. The church steps were half full with a small crowd of onlookers. The religion was growing with leaps and bounds. He wondered for a brief moment where they were getting the money for the churches. A young woman stepping past the priest caught his eye and his breath caught in his throat. In three quick steps, he was behind her as she hurried down a side street.

"Ylsriss?" he called out. She stopped and glanced back, catching his eye and raising an eyebrow with a smile.

"Well, hello rich boy," she smiled, as he caught up. "I didn't think I'd be seeing you again. Aren't you supposed to be on a reaver somewhere, stealing some poor farmer's crops?"

"Aren't you supposed to be robbing a young man in a dark alley?" he grinned back.

She pointed to a narrow passageway behind them. "Well, I was in a hurry, but I suppose I could fit you in if you have the time." They both laughed.

"What are you doing here? I thought they locked you all away while you were in training?" she said.

"They do," Klöss replied, nodding. "They let us out once every five weeks or so for family visits, if we earn it."

"So why aren't you with Daddy dearest then?" She brushed her long hair away from her face and then caught the expression that flickered across his features. "Never mind," and then, "Oh! Is that pork?" He offered the bread across to her and she reached in to take a chunk quickly, popping it into her mouth. He studied her while she ate. She hadn't changed. She was wearing a pale green dress today, that was little more than rags. On her though, it seemed to flow and she looked like she'd just stepped out of a meadow.

He shook himself. "So, New Dayers? You don't strike me as the religious type."

"Still my innocent rich boy," she said. "Everyone with a hungry belly is religious. At least, until they stop handing out bread to the poor."

"Faithful until the kitchen runs empty then?" He scratched at one bearded cheek.

"Yes," she said, serious in the face of his joke. "It's more or less that way with everything, isn't it?" Klöss didn't know what to say to that and so they walked in silence for a minute or two.

"*Are* you busy?" he asked finally. "You said you were in a rush."

"No, not really. The children will be fine for a while." She licked the grease from her fingers and then dusted her hands together.

"Well, I have until sundown until I need to be back so..." he said, drawing out the last word and raising an eyebrow.

"Are you asking me on a date, rich boy?" she laughed, mocking him gently, and then laughed again as his face reddened, a genuine and delighted sound. "I have nowhere I really need to be. It would be nice to spend some time away from the cellar for an afternoon."

He couldn't help grinning, and she reached in and linked arms with him in one smooth motion.

Ylsriss walked Klöss around the city and he felt like a young child stepping out into a strange place. He'd lived his whole life in Hesk, but she showed him things he'd managed to never quite see. They walked to the fishing docks, a place he was more than familiar with, having visited with his father many times to buy fish for the shop. He pointed out the vessels he knew and she pointed out the beggars he'd never noticed. Her education was harsh and brutal, but it was tempered by her company. She was a cool breeze on a hot day. She was the first taste of summer's mead. She was the thief who had held a blade to his throat and he realised he was smitten.

As they walked, he found his gaze drifting more and more often to the smooth skin of her neck. She had an unconscious grace that one so often sees with dancers and acrobats that carried across as she walked. Each step deliberate and careful yet with no more attention than one takes to blink or to take a breath. She was dressed in little more than rags, her clothing patched and scuffed to the point of ruin. On her however it didn't seem to matter. She took no notice of her clothing and her grace eclipsed it anyway. She had a ready smile and a gently mocking humour that she shared freely with him, herself, and anything else that fell under her gaze. She was never cruel however. Her humour was a gentle dig but never too harsh and never intended to hurt.

He bought a bottle of honey mead and they sat on steps by the docks, idly watching the labourers unloading the massive haulers, as they passed the bottle back and forth.

She drew her feet up under her, smoothing her dress down over herself. "Did you know that the New Dayers are saying we should stop the reaving?"

He shook his head. "They'll never stop the reaving. There are just too many of us on these islands now for us all to live on fish."

“That’s not what they’re saying,” she protested. “They say it would be better for us to trade or something.”

“Trade what, Ylsriss?” he laughed. “We have nothing anyone wants. We stand alone, we always have.”

“I’m just repeating what I heard,” she said. “I’m not saying I agree with it.”

He shook his head. “No, I can’t see it happening,” he said slowly, chewing over the idea. “It’s probably not a very clever thing for them to be saying either. It’s not going to make them very popular.”

“Do you think they care?” She nodded up towards the palace in the distance. It was an imposing building, built high upon the hillside, gloating greedily over the city as it glared out to sea.

“The Lords or the Thane?” he asked, and then answered his own question. “I don’t suppose it matters. The Sealord and the First of Merchants wouldn’t be too happy. They’ve always been allies of a sort. The merchants would have to function in a completely different way if we managed to find a way to trade with other nations.”

“I had no idea you were so political,” she teased with a lopsided smile. “What about the Thane?”

“I don’t think he really has all that much power anymore. He’s more of a figurehead than anything else.” He reached over and took the bottle back, taking a sip. “I don’t expect he wants anything upsetting the way of things though.”

“So when do they set you loose on the seas, then?” she said, stealing a sideways glance at him.

“I’m not sure,” he admitted. “I doubt it will be too much longer. We’ve learned just about all we can without actually taking part in a raid.”

“Are you really sure this is what you want to do, Klöss?” Ylsriss asked, with serious eyes. “It won’t be much of a life, you know? It’s not all like the tales, I’m sure. The last fleet that came back had lost two-thirds of its oarsmen.”

He started at that and looked at her sharply. “I hadn’t heard that.”

“No, I didn’t imagine you would have. They wouldn’t want you to know, would they?” She reached out and took his hand in both of hers. “These are not simple, unprotected farmers anymore. I suspect they haven’t been in some time.”

Dropping his hand, she hopped down from the steps. “Come on. I want to feel the grass under my feet for a change, instead of this lifeless stone. Take me to the park." She took his arm again and tugged, until he relented and climbed down.

Hesk was divided by a river running through its centre which parted to flow around a sizeable island in the middle of the city. Bridges arched over the river at four points leading onto the island which was the only green area of any size. An island in the river, and an island of green in a sea of grey stone. Klöss had been there many times as a child but since his mother had died, some years ago, he could count the number of times he'd entered the place on the fingers of one hand. Even then, it had simply been as a means to cut through.

He followed Ylsriss gladly, his calloused hand held in her tiny grip as she pulled him, laughing, through the city. They paused on the bridge while he showed her the tiny carvings of men on each of the white stones that made up the sides. In turn, she pointed out the family, huddled in rags, living under it.

They wandered easily around the garden for a time, pausing only so she could remove her shoes. "I like the feel of grass in between my toes," she said, with an embarrassed smile. Eventually, they came to the old standing stones and sat in the grass, leaning back against them. The stones had been fashioned at some point so long lost in history that nobody could say who built them or for what purpose. Fashioned from two massive standing stones with another lying flat across the lintel, they seemed to create a doorway of sorts. It was a popular spot for picnics and lovers, and Ylsriss raised an eyebrow as he pulled her down to sit on the grass beside him.

"And is this where you bring all your conquests?" she asked, archly.

"Only those who hold a knife to my throat in a back alley," he grinned.

"How long are you going to hold that against me?"

"Funny, that's more or less what I was thinking at the time." He laughed and batted her hands away as she made to swat at him.

They passed the remains of the mead back and forth and Klöss could feel his cheeks become slightly numb as the potent wine took effect.

"How long have you been there?" he asked, watching the swifts swoop and dive after insects as the sun began to sink behind the tallest buildings.

"Where?" She drew her knees up and wrapped her arms around them. "With the children?"

He grunted his agreement.

"Two years or so. I don't really keep track."

He sat up from where he was lying in the grass. "Will you always stay with them?"

"Why are we talking about this now?" She twisted towards him and fixed him with her eyes. "Why are we talking at all?" He froze like a startled deer and his heart started to pound. Her arms snaked around his neck and she kissed him lightly. Her lips tasted of honey mead, as she pulled him down into the grass.

* * *

Rhaven sipped at his whiskey and stared into the fire, watching the glow of the embers. He slumped in his deep armchair, his leg propped up on a beaten stool to allow the heat to soak into his knee. The sun was long gone and rain lashed at the windows, but he couldn't bring himself to care enough to close the shutters.

He took a deep drink of the whiskey and sighed as it warmed his throat, the burn running down inside his chest. The bang at the door made him jump and his leg dropped from the stool, slamming down onto the hard stone floor.

"Gods damn it!" he roared in pain, as he fumbled for his crutch and hauled himself across the room. He tore back the steel bolt and ripped the door open. "What!" he snapped out, into the night.

The old man standing on the doorstep recoiled a little and then grinned. "You've still got that temper, Rhaven," he said mildly.

Rhaven glared at the man. "What do *you* want, Aiden? Isn't it enough that you've taken my son?"

"I thought you might like to know how he's doing," Frostbeard replied, as he leaned in to escape the drips from the roof.

"Hmm, you might as well come in then," he muttered, as he turned awkwardly and walked inside to sink gratefully into the chair again. He bent to lift his leg onto the stool and picked up his glass. "Close the door, you're letting all heat out," he barked. "You can fill this too," he said, waving his empty glass in the air.

Aiden took the glass and went to the tall cabinet against one wall, busying himself with bottle and glasses. He found a seat and handed a glass to Rhaven.

"So, how is he doing then?" Rhaven asked, eyeing the glass in Aiden's hand sourly.

"Quite well, actually, despite his age," the old Seamaster replied.

"He's too young," muttered Rhaven.

Aiden smiled broadly, the expression at odds with his fierce face. "That's not what Verig says."

"Verig? Is that whoremonger still with you?"

"He says the lad has a natural talent. One of the best he's seen."

"I'd wager he doesn't say that to Klöss though," Rhaven said, a smile cracking his face for the first time in what felt like days.

"Gods, no!" Aiden laughed. "The seas would boil dry before he paid a compliment. You know that!"

"I'd worried that the other lads... well, you know how it was with us." Rhaven said, softly.

"I'm not saying he's having the easiest ride of it," Aiden admitted. "He had his oar messed with the other day. A lad cut an edge into the handle for him, made a mess of his hand." Rhaven sat up at that and drew a breath to speak, but stopped as Aiden held a hand up. "He's fine, it'll heal. Besides, you won't believe what the little bastard did!"

"What?" Rhaven said, his expression darkening.

"He only snuck out of the damned compound in the middle of the night to go and get proof."

"What?" Rhaven blurted. "How did he get out?"

"He chimney-climbed the wall behind the eastern storehouse," Aiden laughed.

"What, you mean..."

"Yes! Right where we used to sneak out to go to the tavern." Aiden pounded the arm of the chair with laughter. "They even used the same place to tie the rope. Honestly, I had to talk to the boy and it was all I could do to keep my face straight!" He watched, as Rhaven convulsed with laughter and drained his glass.

Rhaven waved his brother over to the cabinet. "Bring back the bottle," he said with a grin.

Aiden turned with a serious expression on his face as he examined the bottle. "Listen, there is something I need to talk to you about."

"I knew this wasn't simply a social call," Rhaven said, as his eyes narrowed. "What do you want this time?"

"What do you know about the reaving lands?" Aiden asked, curious. "I mean, really know?"

"What do you mean?" Rhaven replied. "I know the same as everyone and better than most. It's where we go to raid. The Islands, the Storm Coast, Dern and now your route to the Farmed Lands."

"It's the Farmed Lands I was talking about, really." Aiden explained. "Most have stopped bothering with anything else these days."

"Well then, not much. You know full well I never made it there before..." He looked meaningfully at his leg.

"Hmm, I suppose that's true." Aiden grunted. "Well, they've started resisting. Not enough for it to matter but it's strange behaviour. We always thought of them as ignorant peasants, but maybe there is something more to it."

"Like what?" Rhaven said.

"I don't know. I'm starting to question just how far those lands stretch though," Aiden replied. "I assume you've heard about Kieron's fleet?" He raised his eyebrows as Rhaven shook his head. "He's done a better job of keeping things quiet than I thought, then. Well, he limped back into the Stormport about a week ago. Only sixteen reavers out of thirty, and most of them were full of dead and dying."

"What the hell happened?" Rhaven demanded, his whiskey forgotten.

"He won't tell me all the details, but apparently he'd lined up raids on five villages that he'd hit a few years back. Anyway, a bell was ringing as they landed and they thought nothing of it. They hit their first village hard and were loading up the haulers when they were attacked." He grimaced and refilled his glass hurriedly. "Not just twenty farmers with pitchforks, either. I'm talking five hundred men, armed, trained and half of them on horses."

"Lords of Blood, Sea and Sky!" Rhaven breathed "Those that got away were lucky to have lived." Aiden said, looking down into his glass and swirling the whiskey.

"So, what's your point?" Rhaven said, as he took a deep swallow.

"My point is that we don't know how many of the bastards there are or how big this land is." Aiden said. "Why are we sat huddled on this damned rock when the sodding land of plenty is right there?"

"Now you sound like a New Dayer," Rhaven laughed. "Shake off your shackles of mindless tradition," he intoned. "What do you want to do? Trade with them?"

"Gods, no!" Aiden laughed. "What have we got that they'd trade for? No. I want to invade the bastards," and his face split with a long cold smile.

"So why come to me with this?" Rhaven asked after a long silence.

"Because I need you to take it to the merchant's council," Aiden replied. "If we can take enough land, then this will create new towns and villages. Whole new areas of opportunity will open up."

"Why not simply take it to the Thane?"

"Because he's a puppet, Rhaven," Aiden spat. "He's a puppet who hasn't much more sense than the marionette he reminds me of."

"Unless you happened to be the one holding the strings?"

"Which I am not." Aiden said, wearily.

"I thought you were the great favourite?" Rhaven asked, curiously. "You certainly used to be."

"Ah, that's because Frostbeard, the discoverer of new lands, was of use," the old man said with a wry smile. "I distracted the people of these islands, Rhaven. I brought in luxuries we'd not seen in a generation, and filled young minds with the thoughts of great deeds in far-off lands. It was useful, and it kept them from realising the truth."

"The truth?" Rhaven prompted, setting his foot back down onto the floor and holding his glass between his legs as he leant forwards.

"The truth," Aiden repeated, his voice heavy and quiet. "The truth is that these islands are dying. We soak the seas in blood each year for nothing."

"How do you mean?"

"We are dying as a people, Rhaven," Aiden said sadly. "We do a wonderful job of pretending otherwise. We muddle along, fishing and farming where we can, supplementing this with the reavings, but it's not enough. Too many people in too small a place and simply not enough food to go around. Take a walk around the docks some morning and look. I mean *really* look. There are three times as many beggars as there ever used to be."

"And you think this plan of yours is the answer?"

"It's *an* answer," Aiden said, with heat. "It's better than sitting here with our head under our wing like a sleeping bird. We have to do *something*."

"You'll need to give me a more complete plan than this, Aiden," Rhaven said in exasperation. "These are serious people. I can't go in there with a half-hatched scheme."

"So you'll do it?" Aiden asked, a sudden light shining in his ice blue eyes.

"Yes, I'll do it, fool that I am! If not for you, then for Klöss." Rhaven sighed. "If you're lucky, we can take it to the First of Merchants. What about the Sealord, though? You know you'll need to get them both on side for this to go anywhere?"

Aiden nodded. "The Sealord is as worried as I am. He's been convinced for years that it's only a matter of time before some sea captain in the Farmed Lands figures out the trick of the Vorstelv and finds us."

"I never took him for a coward."

"He's not scared, Rhaven. Don't underestimate him. He just thinks that the time of reavings will eventually come to an end."

"Fine. I'll see what I can do." He fixed Aiden with a steely glare. "But you look after my boy, Aiden. I hold you responsible for him."

* * *

They stood in lines, silent as he walked in. For some of them, he was a figure out of legend come to life and, though they'd all seen him more than once, he was something quite different when dressed in furs, armour, and cloak. He had a breastplate worked onto his leathers, with golden scrollwork and elaborate etching. A man could have been forgiven for thinking he was a self-indulgent old man, until he stood before him and really looked at him. He would easily measure six foot in his bare feet and his frame was undiminished by his age. His ice-blue eyes were fierce as they stared from above his grey and white beard, and they missed nothing as he walked slowly down the line.

Klöss stood with the others, dressed for raid in full leathers and furs. His helmet felt heavy upon his brow and his shield hung loose from one arm, as the morning breeze stroked his cheek. The sun was just starting to rise and long shadows stretched across the docks. They all knew why they were here. It had been explained to them all the night before by the school's Masters. They were to participate in their first reaving. Admittedly, they would be surrounded by seasoned men with many years of experience but this did little to diminish the thrill. Not only was it to be their first reaving, they would be crossing the Frozen Sea, travelling directly through the Vorstelv, the icy current that passed through the centre of the seas.

Three great galley reavers rocked gently by the docks, like they were eager to be loosed their hawser, and plough through the seas. Beyond them, two huge haulers sat at anchor, their crews already aboard and the great red sails furled for the moment.

Frostbeard spoke quietly to each of the Masters. It seemed to Klöss that his eyes sought him out for just a moment, before he turned to address the group.

"This will be your first reaving," he said. His voice was deep and sonorous as it flowed over the docks. "An easy task to test the skills you have developed here under your Masters. This reaving will determine who of you will man my reavers, and who is better suited to work my haulers, but I expect you all to work as you were trained. We work together and anyone who thinks they work better alone will be given the honour of swimming home." He paused and let that sink in for a moment. "You all know your jobs and you'll get no flowery speeches from me. I am no Lord. I am your seamaster. Do your jobs and earn your places. To your ships!" He ended with a roar, which was taken up by the men as they ran to the reavers, and thundered up the gangplanks.

Klöss followed Tristan onto the ship and then down into the hold to stow his weapons and shield, before making his way to the oarpit. This was a deep-water ship and he'd not need arms or armour until they landed. He made his way to his bench and checked the oar carefully before looking around and taking in the huge vessel. It wasn't his first time on a galley reaver, as they'd trained on them several times over the past three months, but he was honest enough with himself to admit that all he'd really learned was how much there was left to learn. Rowing was rowing, when you got right down to it, but the galley reaver had a hundred ropes snaking this way and that. They led to the sails, and down this mast and that, tied off to rings set in the hull or twined round themselves. He couldn't even begin to understand them but knew enough to stay well away from them, and to mind the sailmen and the Sailmaster.

He waited in his bench and took in the vastness of the vessel. The galley reavers were four times the size of a standard reaver and had been created at Frostbeard's insistence, after he'd discovered the Farmed Lands. Able to hold more than a hundred and fifty oarsmen, and bearing mighty sails, they dwarfed anything else in the harbour, save the massive haulers. Where a standard reaver had little space below the deck, barely enough room for hammocks to be slung in three shifts, the galley reavers had a complete hold. They sat low in the water, with evil-looking rams attached to the prow and extending down below the waterline. Archers' platforms sat high on each side of the deck, and large ballistae were mounted in the prow and stern. They were far more a weapon of war than the standard reaver.

Klöss watched, as the oarsmaster and Shipmaster spoke briefly with the Steersman and Sailmaster, and then made their way to the prow. The Steersman walked to the rear of the massive reaver. The drummer struck two hard blows on the drum, signalling them to make ready, and Klöss took up the oar, noting again that it was far thicker than those on the standard reavers. With a quick grin at Tristan, who sat behind him, he focused all his attention on the oarsmaster and saw him nod to both Steersman and Drummer as he called for the first stroke.

The huge galley reavers moved ponderously away from the docks and towards the channel leading out of the harbour. The drummer held them to an easy rhythm and, in less than half an hour, they had cleared the narrow channel. They took up a position in the choppy swells whilst they waited for the haulers to come up behind the three evil-looking ships. Once they were in place, the drums signalled again and they began the row in earnest, out to deeper waters.

The sails were hoisted after the first hour and oarsmen divided into three shifts. Once the reavers caught a good wind, the oars would be of little use anyway, as they would only slow the ship down, but until then they would split the duty. Months of training had hardened Klöss's muscles and given him strong powerful shoulders, but he had no desire to row for the whole three weeks it would take them to sail to the Farmed Lands.

The first day was a mixture of excitement at being aboard the galley reaver and actually being part of a reaving, combined with hours of rowing. The oars were slightly larger around than any others they had used for any real length of time and Klöss found they made his hands ache. It was odd, the pain in his hands seemed worse than the pain in his arms and back.

When they weren't rowing, they were expected to be out of the way, so he found himself spending many hours below decks, drilling with his sword, eating the rough fare that was served up in the ship's galley or lounging in his hammock.

By the end of the first week, the boredom was interminable. This ended abruptly midway through the second week. Klöss woke with a chill penetrating to his bones, shivering uncontrollably in his hammock. He cursed and managed to roll himself out onto his feet, before stumbling to the galley in search of heat. He found the room crammed with men dressed in full furs, thick fur-lined gloves and heavy boots. He looked around in confusion, sleep slowing his brain, until he caught on. They had reached the Vorstelv.

He made his way to the tiny stove and huddled as close to it as he reasonably could, gratefully taking a hot mug of tea and hunching over it, as if he could leach the heat from it with his hands.

"Cold weather gear, Klöss," came Verig's gruff voice, from deep inside a mound of fur beside him. "In the chest against the wall, by your hammock." Klöss nodded gratefully and made his way back to his hammock, tin mug in hand. He pulled out a collection of fur and climbed into it quickly. It took a while to find boots and gloves that fitted properly. By the time he was done, he could barely bend his arms and legs, but at least he was warm.

"Hot food! Three days of this, Klöss," Tristan enthused, by way of greeting, as he came into the galley again. Klöss grinned at him and went back to the stove to grab a large bowl of steaming porridge. As he spooned it down, he felt the warmth spread from his core and it wasn't until he stopped shivering that he realised he still had been.

The oarsmaster worked his way through the ship, rousing the shivering trainees and thrusting furs at them, before calling them all together. He didn't seem overly affected by the cold. He stood with the hood of his furs thrown back, holding his gloves in one hand as he spoke.

"This is the Vorstelv. You've heard of it, but there's no point talking about it until you get here. People just don't understand," he began brusquely. "It's an icy current in the ocean. I can't explain it; it's just how it is. The water goes from a normal temperature to freezing within the space of three boat lengths. We will be rowing in two shifts, half on, half off. When you are not rowing, you eat and then you sleep. You do not take your furs off, even to piss. We're only just on the edges here and it's going to get a damned sight colder."

Klöss's eyes widened in wonder and shock at the words. He could see a similar impact on the faces of the others.

"It will take three days of solid rowing and that's if we have a good wind. Ropes will freeze, sails will shatter and fingers, lives and the occasional cock have been lost here. I wasn't joking about the pissing." The man spoke plainly, and there was no humour or enjoyment on his face as he spoke. The sudden change away from the veiled threats and bravado served to highlight just how serious he was.

"You will be cold. You will bloody freeze. But understand this, it *can* be done and you *will* get through it," he said. "Keep an eye on both yourself and the man in front of you. If you stop shivering, or you start to feel warm all of a sudden, then you damned well tell me or the man closest to you. The cold tells you you're still alive. When you stop shivering, it's your body giving up." With that he turned and strode out onto deck, as if this was all the most natural thing in the world.

Klöss was in the first shift. He ate quickly and made his way out onto the deck. His breath came in great clouds in front of him as he walked, and the deck and lines were already white with frost. He made his way to his bench and tapped the oarsman there on the shoulder. The man wasted no time. He quickly shipped the oar and climbed out of the oarpit. He didn't speak, and did nothing that would delay his passage to warmth.

Klöss sat quickly before the bench could cool and took up the oar. The gloves were thick but were well used to the girth of the oar and Klöss found they gripped it better than he had expected. He braced his feet and took up the drummer's rhythm.

The air was cold. So cold that it hurt to breathe in. Klöss tried breathing through the edges of his thick fur hood but found it left a sheen of moisture in his short beard, which quickly froze in the icy air. In the end, he gave up and tried to lose himself in the rhythm. It wasn't so bad after a while. The act of rowing itself was keeping his body warm, though his hands felt cold, despite the gloves. He took to clenching and unclenching his fingers tight around the oar as he worked, in an effort to keep the blood flowing.

It was three days of hell, broken only by moments of terror. The frigid seas gave off mists and it was impossible to see any further than another ship length ahead most of the time. Five watchmen were posted at the prow and on the archers' platforms, switching in and out every half hour because of the cold. Klöss wondered what they were watching for. Then the first cry came out.

He was lost in the rhythm of the drum, working at a steady but gruelling pace, when the watchmen at one of the archer's platforms screamed out, "Sea Mountain!! Starboard!"

The response was immediate as the oarsmaster yelled, "Stern-stroke!" ordering every oarsman to row backwards as best he could. Klöss stood up on his bench and turned around as fast as he could, bracing his feet on the bench now in front of him rather than the brace-board, and hauling back on the oar. The drumbeat slowed to allow for the unnatural stroke and the galley reaver shuddered as it slowed. Men dashed to the stern and began shouting to the other reavers, whilst a red flag was hoisted. The sailmen worked desperately to furl the frozen sails, moving as fast as they dared to without cracking the canvas.

Klöss struggled with the unnatural stroke, pulling as hard as he could, but he didn't have the space to lean fully into it or anything to truly brace himself against. He felt them slow and then he saw it. A colossal white mountain, moving with the current and heading directly for the reaver.

"Port side! Double-man!" the oarsmaster screamed. Klöss turned back to the normal position, shifting over as far as he could to allow room for the other oarsman to sit beside him. The drumbeat increased and they worked together, straining with all their might against the oar. Sweat, born of equal parts labour and terror, ran down Klöss's face and joined the frost in his beard. The mountain moved closer and closer, made even more terrifying by the total silence.

"What *is* it?" he muttered, half to himself, as they worked to turn the reaver.

"Ice!" His partner said shortly. "A damned mountain of ice."

The icy behemoth drifted silently past them. Less than two oar lengths lay between Klöss and the icy cliffs, and he found himself holding his breath. They backed off another fifty feet and then sat, silent as the iceberg slowly drifted into the mist.

The days passed slowly but, at the same time, shifts would fly past when the call to stern-stroke came through. Klöss learned that crossing the Vorstelv was a gamble. It had to be tackled at breakneck speed, before the men succumbed to frostbite or the sails and lines perished in the cold. At the same time, utmost caution and alertness was required to watch for sea ice.

It was with a combination of relief and exhaustion that Klöss collapsed over his oar as the call came out that they had cleared the Vorstelv, and made their way into warmer waters. From the corners of his eyes he could see other oarsmen doing the same thing, but at that point he wouldn't have cared if he were the only one. They travelled on for another hour. Then all oars were shipped, the sea anchors dropped and the men sent to their hammocks, with only a skeleton watch left on deck.

After only two days beyond the Vorstelv, the trip transformed back into boring drudgery. Klöss learned two things during his three weeks at sea. Firstly, that gambling with someone who has a strong accent is never a good idea. It's almost impossible to tell when they are bluffing. Secondly, that the galley reavers whilst huge, seemed to shrink each day and it was never possible to find time alone. Klöss was not overly solitary by nature, but he was not popular in the training school. Dallan might have eased off a little, with his sick little games, but a week did not go by without some form of dig or petty attack. Klöss had taken to training early in the morning to gain some respite. The exercise was a good way to hone his skills and also to vent frustration. He was denied this on the ship, and there was always someone awake. A sleeping ship is a sunken ship.

The land began as the faintest smudge on the horizon. For a good hour, Klöss was convinced that it was a cloud bank, though Tristan was insistent that it was land. Then the smudge slowly grew features: a cliff face, tiny trees and surf. All hands were at oar. The reavers had to close with the shore as quickly as possible, to allow the canoe-like longboats to be lowered and men put ashore. The haulers would stay at anchor in the deep water, protected by the reavers once they had unloaded all but a defensive crew.

He glanced at his sword, shield and helm again, despite the fact he had checked they were there three times already. He could see the land clearly now. It was lush and green, and a yellow sand beach awaited them. It was markedly different to the Barren Isles. The only sand there was coarse and dark, and what few trees did grow tended to be tall pines. He could see broader, bushy trees here, unlike anything he'd ever seen at home. A large fire burned on a clifftop next to the bay they were about to enter, but for what purpose, Klöss could only guess.

The oarsmaster called out orders and Klöss shipped his oar, pulling it into the reaver and lashing it tightly to the bench as he'd been taught. He grabbed up his sword and shield, and set the helm on his head before stepping up onto the deck and lining up with the others.

The canoe-like longboat felt tiny after being on the massive reaver, and it pitched and bobbed alarmingly as they paddled madly through the surf. It was with no small sense of relief that Klöss felt the sand crunch against the bottom of the boat. He leapt out, grabbing the side and hauling it up onto the beach out of the reach of the tide, before drawing his sword and looking around for Verig. The fire on the cliff was belching great clouds of white smoke. Green wood, he surmised.

He stood with the others as Verig explained that the village was less than an hour away by foot. They were to be split into three groups, the smallest of which would proceed to the village, whilst the larger groups would be sent with felling crews from the haulers to harvest trees or left to defend the boats. Klöss glanced behind him to see a number of longboats making for the shore from the haulers with the felling crews.

The raiders were swiftly split into the three groups with all of the trainees in the group making for the village. Supplemented by experienced reaving crews, they numbered sixty men in all. Verig split them again, into groups of fifteen. The felling crews from the hauler were landing and the escort crews were already making their way over to them. With one last look at the galley reavers and haulers sitting at anchor, Klöss followed Verig and his team into the trees.

Klöss had spent all of his life in Hesk and so had only a very limited experience of anything outside the city. The Barren Isles were rocky and what limited green space there was tended to be dominated by farms. There were very few trees on the islands at all, and he found being surrounded by so many to be awe-inspiring and a little unnerving. They stretched up to fill the skies, their leaves creating dancing shadows as the sunlight filtered through the canopy. He found it was also almost impossible to be stealthy, and they crunched and cracked as they snapped twigs and crushed fallen leaves underfoot.

Verig's path took them through the woods and then up a steep incline, to skirt around the edge of the village. Through the gaps in the tree-line, Klöss could make out a small farming community of perhaps two hundred souls, with a small river meandering its way past a watermill. A number of houses dotted the area and Klöss could see three or four farms scattered about the village. Verig motioned the team close and sank down to his haunches in the ferns.

"Listen up, then," he began, in a low voice that carried no further than the trees. "You can see how small this place is, but that's no reason to get cocky. Stay close to each other and remember your training." He brushed a clear space in the dirt and scratched at it with a stick. "We're all going to come in at once, from these four directions. I don't expect much resistance. These are farmers, not warriors. If they surrender, that's fine but if not, well..." He shrugged. "We're here for lumber and food this time. This does not include women. Understood?"

"We're going to run into the village from here. I'll set the pace, so don't pass me. I don't want anyone too winded to fight." He looked around at the trainees and experienced raiders. "Any questions?" When none were forthcoming he stood, and made a point of checking his weapons and armour.

They strung out in a long line at the edge of the trees, just barely concealed by the bushes and thick leaves, but probably visible to anyone who really chose to look. Klöss drew his sword, and checked his shield and helm for the hundredth time. Then Verig charged. He was silent as he ran and the sudden movement caught Klöss by surprise. He'd been expecting a shout or yell. For a second, he froze. Then he caught hold of himself and hurtled down the slope towards the village.

Klöss kept pace, with Tristan at his side. The big man was carrying an ugly-looking axe with both hands, his shield slung on his back. The hill passed in a blur and Verig finally let out a scream as they approached. The cry was taken up by the others and they howled as they flew past the first building and into the village proper.

The shout faltered and the men came to a halt in confusion. The village was empty. The Islanders spun slowly as they looked around but there was not a villager in sight. The three other groups of raiders charged in, and they met in confusion in the village square.

"What the hell?" Dallan swore, as he looked about.

"Quiet!" Verig barked, as he made his way to the other team leaders.

"I don't like this," Klöss muttered to Tristan.

"No. You are right, something is wrong here." The big man murmured, as he fingered his axe.

"Can you hear what they're saying?" Klöss nodded to where Verig was speaking with the three other leaders.

Tristan shook his head and continued to look about him with a worried frown.

Verig turned and struck his sword on the rim of his shield, calling for silence. "It looks like this place is deserted. I don't like it, but we're already here, so we might as well have a look about.

"Klöss and Tristan, go and look in the large barn and see what you can find. Dallan," he said, turning to the smaller man, "Go to the mill and see what there is in terms of flour. I'm going with some of the others to check out these farms."

Klöss looked to Tristan, who met his gaze calmly and nodded towards the large barn on the outskirts of the village. It was a two-storey, sturdy-looking structure, with a loading platform and winch on the upper floor. They walked through the village and then circled the barn once, to be sure. Klöss went to the large wooden door and found it wouldn't budge. He looked inquiringly at Tristan, who shoved it hard. A clatter came from inside and Tristan raised an eyebrow at Klöss before pushing the door open. A pitchfork lay across the doorway, fallen from its position against the door. Tristan stepped over it without comment, and into the gloom of the barn.

The barn was silent and seemed dark after the bright light of the morning. Shafts of sunlight filtered down through small gaps in the planking, picking out motes of dust that danced and spun in the air. Empty stalls showed where livestock was usually penned and traces hung from the walls, demonstrating that at least one horse was missing. The hayloft appeared well-stocked from where they were standing and a ladder stood propped against it to give access.

The two made their way further into the barn and slowly around the edges by the walls. A faint rustling made Klöss think of rats. It made his skin crawl. Fighting another man and spilling his blood was one thing, but rats had always made him squeamish.

"Klöss, those are barrels in the loft, yes?" Tristan said, in his sing-song accent. He turned and saw where the big man pointed. It did appear to be a stack of small barrels.

"Toss one down and we'll have a look?" he suggested. Tristan shrugged and, laying his axe on the floor, began to climb the ladder. It bounced and shook as he made his way up. He had just placed a knee on the floor at the top, when a boy erupted from the piled hay. Screaming and armed with a pitchfork, he charged at Tristan, burying the fork in his shoulder and sending him toppling from the loft. Klöss watched in shock as the big man fell and landed on the floor with a resounding crash. The boy, his balance spent by his furious charge, fought to keep his footing. He teetered at the edge of the loft for a second and then fell, arms pin-wheeling

Tristan cursed and rolled, scrambling to his feet. He took two quick steps and spun to face the boy, his huge axe raised and ready to strike. The child lay on his back, eyes wide with terror as the huge man advanced.

"Damned fool boy!" he raged, and lowered his axe slightly. Klöss suddenly found he could breathe again. He heard a muted squeak from the loft and glanced up to see three young girls peering over the edge.

"Pere, tash velen cur?" called down the oldest of the three, with fear clear in her voice. Klöss didn't understand the words but the tone was clear enough. She was blonde and couldn't be more than ten summers, by Klöss's guess. He sighed and turned to the child. "Get back up the damned ladder and be silent boy!" The lad looked at him in confusion. He looked at Tristan, who was fingering the hole poked almost through his armour where the fork hadn't quite penetrated, and muttered to himself. He crouched and grabbed at the child, dragging him to his feet in one swift motion. The child's eyes grew wide in terror. Gritting his teeth, Klöss propelled the boy to the ladder and pointed upwards, before pressing his finger to his lips. The boy nodded mutely and scurried up the ladder.

"We'd better find Verig and tell him. There might be others hiding." Klöss said. Then both their heads shot round towards the open door, as the call of a hunting horn sounded clear and sharp in the village.

Tristan dashed to the front of the barn and peered around the corner, before waving Klöss closer. The village was a scene of chaos. Uniformed men in blue and bright steel were charging into the streets to meet the oarsmen, who seemed hopelessly outnumbered. Dallan stood closest to them, alone beside the smithy, his back to the wall as two men with long-swords advanced.

Klöss didn't hesitate. He threw himself into the fight. He charged without battle-cry and ran up behind the closest of the two men. The man heard his approach and turned in time to have Klöss's sword slice into his neck, just underneath the reach of his tall, conical helmet. The sword bit deeply and blood geysered out as the man collapsed, gurgling, to the grass. Dallan took advantage of the other man's distraction and thrust deep into his back.

Their eyes met briefly and Dallan gave a small, grudging nod, before they turned to survey the scene. The oarsmen were fighting a retreat out of the village, passing up opportunities to strike in favour of chances to move back towards the trees. Tristan, Dallan and he seemed to be behind the line of battle and Klöss realised that, unless they acted soon, they would be cut off and left behind.

He led them along the side of the smithy and a small row of cottages, running low in an awkward hunched position to keep below the edge of the wall. The oarsmen were only fifty or sixty feet away now, but were outnumbered by almost two to one. As Klöss watched he saw Henrick go down, a bloody rent in his leather chest plate.

He glanced behind him and could see more soldiers marching into the village and past their position with more men on horseback behind them. They were going to be slaughtered to a man unless he acted. He looked carefully at the scene in front of him again, taking note of how the men were bunched, and then turned to Dallan and Tristan.

"We're going to have to make our own way out," he said. "We're cut off."

"Well, we can't stay here!" Dallan objected. His face was pale and his eyes looked a little wild to Klöss. The man was on the verge of panic.

"No one is staying anywhere," he said, in what he hoped was a calming tone. "Let's head for the river."

He led the three of them out from the cover of the wall and they ran towards the small river. The ringing clash of steel on steel filled the air and Klöss grimaced at the sounds of screaming. The bank was low and he slid down on his side into the thick reeds. The water was shockingly cold, but he forced himself to crouch low in the shallows, bringing the water up to his shoulders as the murk at the bottom sucked at his boots.

"Great, now we're trapped *and* wet," Dallan said, as he slipped into the water next to him.

"Shut up, Dallan," Klöss muttered back at him as he peered out through the reeds. He turned slowly, so as not to disturb them and reveal their location, and looked across the river. It was not a great expanse of water. The slow current and muddy colour hinted at a shallow depth, or he hoped it did. Beyond the gently sloping bank lay open ground leading to the woods in the distance. It was not exactly the right direction, as it would take them more south-easterly than south, but it was still away from the enemy and towards the ships.

He could no longer see any of his own men and the sounds of fighting were growing fainter.

"We're going to have to swim across and then break for the trees, I think." He pointed at the edge of the woods in the distance.

"That's a lot of open ground, Klöss," Tristan said, in a low voice.

"I don't like it either, but I don't see we have much of a choice," he admitted.

"Sounds like a great plan, Klöss," Dallan said scathingly. "First you get us wet, then you get us killed."

"Shut up, Dallan," Klöss and Tristan said in unison, both looking out across the far bank.

They made their way across the sluggish river, half-swimming and half-walking along the shallow bottom, allowing them to keep their weapons and shields, which Klöss had feared they might need to drop.

The bank was another gentle slope and, within moments, they were climbing out through the reeds and running low towards the distant trees.

The first signs they'd been spotted were the arrows hissing past them. Klöss risked a glimpse over his shoulder and saw half a dozen archers lining up on the far bank of the river, along with two men on horseback. With little to do but run, they doubled their efforts and ducked their heads down as they sprinted for the trees.

Dallan screamed out, as an arrow glanced off his helm with a loud clang. He faltered for a moment and Klöss looked back at him as they ran. Within another fifty feet, the arrows were falling short and the trees were growing closer, but then he heard the hoof beats.

They turned to see the two horsemen bearing down upon them. Both men were heavily armoured in an all-over steel plate that Klöss had never seen the like of. If it were not for the horses bearing them, he doubted the men would be able to stand under the weight of it.

"Scatter!" he roared, leaping to one side, as the first horseman thundered past, swinging down with an odd hammer-axe but finding only empty air. Klöss rolled, as he'd been taught and sprang back to his feet, readying his sword and shield as the horses wheeled and began the charge back to them.

Dallan, he saw, had not been so lucky and lay face down on the grass. Tristan stood over him, his fearsome axe in hand.

"Go for the horses," Klöss called across, and saw Tristan nod in response.

They spread apart, wide enough to force the horsemen to split up, and then set themselves. Klöss planted his feet firmly in a low stance, his shield held up and slightly to the side of him. The mounted man was coming in at the perfect angle, his weapon raised as he leaned slightly into the stroke.

Klöss caught the axe on the way down. His shield was angled and the hammer-axe scraped along the wooden face, before biting and almost tearing it from his grasp. He used the force of the blow to turn himself and hacked hard as the horseman passed. The horse screamed as his heavy blade hacked into its rear leg, before falling heavily to the ground and throwing its rider, who landed with a metallic crash.

Klöss wasted no time and ran past the flailing horse that rolled screaming in the grass. The rider was on hands and knees, struggling to stand in his heavy plate. Klöss dropped his shield and swung his sword with two hands at the base of the man's helmet. The thick steel stopped most of the force, but Klöss's sword was well made and sheared through, cutting deeply into the neck. The man dropped like a stone, pulling the sword from Klöss's hand.

Klöss stooped and pressed hard with one boot, as he yanked the sword from where it was caught in the armour. He heard Tristan finish the other horseman with a sickening crunch. A quick check on Dallan revealed a sizeable dent in his helmet, but he seemed to still be breathing. Tristan threw him over one shoulder, like a sack of grain, and they made their way into the trees.

Dallan came to after a few more moments and was able to walk, though his eyes looked glazed and Tristan doubted he could be trusted if it came to a fight. The distant sound of combat was easy to follow and they caught up quickly as they ran through the trees.

It was hard to see how many of the raiders were left, but Klöss could see enough to see they were outnumbered. The oarsmen flowed easily around the trees, while the soldiers were clearly more used to fighting in ranks. It was probably a matter of training, Klöss thought, as he readied himself. The oarsmen were taught to fight individually. These men were clearly trained to be part of a unit.

The three of them charged silently, weapons at the ready. Some might say there is something dishonourable in stabbing a man in the back, but these are not the men who are in danger of being slaughtered to a man. Klöss and the others tore into the packed mass of men like a tornado into a wheat field and the effect was instant. The oarsmen moved easily, not holding to a unit and taking advantage of the gaps as they fought with sword and axe, but still just holding their own. Klöss had evened the score but the fight was far from won.

Then Verig was there. He flew into the fight like a man intent on suicide, spinning and striking, with axe in one hand and sword in the other. To the layman, he looked like a lunatic but to a swordsman, there was a beauty in his movements. He never overextended or took more effort than necessary. Where Klöss and the others hacked, he would slash lightly. Cutting just deep enough to do the damage required and no more. Where they buried their weapon into the enemy up to half its length, Verig dipped his sword into his foe almost delicately. Around him, men fell gently to the earth with tired sighs and, almost between one breath and the next, the tide was turned.

The oarsmen went to with vigour and, within moments, the last of the enemy lay screaming between the trees. Verig pointed through the woods with his bloody sword, "Go!" he gasped, his arm pressed tight against his chest.

To say it was an orderly retreat would have been a gross overstatement. They numbered fewer than twenty now, and Klöss couldn't see any of the trainees, other than Dallan and Tristan, as they lurched between the trunks. In the distance behind them, a line of fires burned on hilltops leading into the distance. As he ran, he wondered how they hadn't noticed them on the way into the village. Verig swore and cursed beside him, as they fled for the beach.

* * *

Aiden stood on the stone steps and waited. The cold wind caught his long black cloak, tossing and whipping it behind him. He reached back, absently, and caught an edge with one gloved hand.

"A little fine for a reaving, isn't it?" Rhavin called out to him, as he approached the steps, leaning heavily on a polished oak staff.

"What?" Aiden replied, confused.

"Look at you, you're as well preened as a girl at her first dance." Rhaven gestured at Aiden's clothes and laughed a rough laugh.

Aiden looked down at his freshly oiled, black leathers, which had been buffed until they shone. His chest and forearms were covered in a polished steel plate, inlaid with gold scrollwork.

"It's expected, I suppose." He shrugged. "Are we prepared?"

"It's as I told you," Rhaven replied. "The merchant's council met last week. It was touch and go but, broadly speaking, the First of Merchants will support you in this."

"Broadly speaking?"

"There was some opposition," Rhaven admitted. "There were those that said we should try simply trading with the Farmed Lands and other nations like Dern."

"Do they suggest what we might trade?" Aiden scoffed. "I'd not like to try and haul iron through the Vorstelv, and that's the only thing we have in any quantity. As for Dern, they have more than enough of their own iron."

Rhaven smiled. "These are the kind of merchants you despise, Aiden. They know little of the Vorstelv, let alone the problems of shipping goods through it."

Aiden grunted and looked up at the huge stone building, surmounted by a dome and spires. "Shall we, then?"

Rhaven left him at the door and made his own way through the maze of hallways to his seat at the back of the merchant's circle. Aiden paused for a long moment by the glowing brazier inside the main door and held a hand out, as he tucked his gloves under his belt with the other. It wouldn't do to appear cold and shivering before the council.

Finally, he drew in a deep breath and let it out slowly, before making his way along the short corridor, with its plush red carpet, towards the double doors at the end. He had been in the Thane's palace a thousand times for council meetings. This was one of the few times, however, that he would be speaking as a petitioner, and he found himself oddly nervous. The doors were swung open without a word by the guardsmen posted there, and Aiden stepped into the antechamber and stood by the black and gold clad guardsmen at attention with their long halberds before the two massive gold-inlaid doors.

"Seamaster Aiden Kurikson, to address the Thane's council," he said, unnecessarily, to the black-robed attendant behind the long desk that filled one side of the chamber.

"Not Frostbeard this time then?" the attendant said with a small smile.

"Not this time, no."

"Very well then, Seamaster, if you'll follow me? I will announce you."

The attendant joined him in front of the guards and nodded to one, signalling them to pull the doors open. Frostbeard followed him into the massive chamber. The doors led onto a gently sloping path that led upwards, towards the centre of the hall. On either side of the path sloped walls revealed rows of benches rising towards the back of the room.

Aiden glanced to his left, knowing Rhaven would normally be seated far at the back of the chamber, with those of little influence, before remembering he would more likely be with the First of Merchant's this time. Both Rhaven's and his own reputation would rest on the outcome of this petition. The thought did little to calm his nerves.

The attendant touched his arm softly and bade him wait, while he stepped forward into the circle of light at the centre of the room, which was formed by cunningly-wrought lamps positioned around the raised platform.

"Seamaster Aiden Kurikson begs permission to address your council, my Lord Thane," his deep voice made thunderous by the acoustics of the large room.

"Then let him approach and he will be heard," the ritual response was returned. Aiden knew the voice was not that of the Thane. It was just a servant, positioned close to the throne. The Thane was probably asleep by now.

He walked forward into the light, as the attendant stepped to the side and melted into the gloom. The chamber was designed to impress and overawe. The rows of benches were all filled with council members. Aiden could see red-robed merchants and the First sat in the centre row, his gold chain of office glinting in the faint lamplight. To his right, the Sealord sat, surrounded by his fellow Seamasters. Behind him would be the rows of the Keeper's council, formed of farmers, fishermen and miners. Aiden nodded minutely at the Sealord, turned his attention to the end of the chamber and gave a deep bow.

The throne was raised upon a stepped dais covered in thick red rugs and bordered with tall scarlet drapes climbing up into the darkness towards the roof of the chamber. The Thane himself appeared to be an old man, though Aiden knew him to be little older than himself. A succession of illnesses had aged him prematurely and he was a pale shadow of the vigorous man Aiden had once known. He sat, dressed in a simple white woollen robe with a plain iron circlet about his forehead. Peering down at Aiden with uncharacteristic interest in his pale eyes, he leaned against one side of the throne.

"My Thane, Lords and members of this council," he began, his deep voice spreading easily to fill the chamber. "I come before you to discuss the reaving. For more than two hundred years, we have survived on these Barren Isles by eking out an existence using the skills of our farmers and fishermen," he said, gesturing towards the Lord Keeper, "and the reavings." He said the last with a nod towards the Sealord.

"The times are changing. It is time we changed with them. Our people grow hungry as the reavings begin to fail. Our docks and alleyways groan with beggars, whores and thieves. Our farmers and fishermen struggle to feed us all. It is only a matter of time, my Lords, before we outgrow our islands, if not in terms of land then in terms of their ability to feed us." He saw eyes narrow in thought as they shifted nervously. He was touching on truths that they all had considered, but that none spoke of openly.

"Thirty years ago, I stood as the Shipmaster aboard the first vessel to face the Vorstelv and return. The reavings of the Farmed Lands have provided for us, given us new sources of food and riches. Some, including myself, have prospered. I tell you now, this will not last much longer. Already our reavings face greater opposition. More and more boats return to our isles with empty places in the oarpits. Are we to constrain ourselves, then? To limit our growth when our nation touches the edges of its true strength? I say no! I say we travel to these lands, not to reave, but to conquer. To take new lands for ourselves and to settle them. Why do we live crammed into our isles when there are lush green lands, ripe for the taking? Where our farmers can work to their potential and our children need not go hungry?"

He paused to draw breath and a voice from the darkened benches took advantage of the silence. "So you suggest we stop the reavings? Turn our back on centuries of tradition and honour to become simple farmers? Has your blood grown so thin, Frostbeard? Where is your honour?"

Aiden turned, seeking the speaker but the bright light he was surrounded by made it impossible. "I do not *suggest* we stop the reavings. I tell you that they are failing. We face opposition in the Farmed Lands, enough to question whether the reaving is worthwhile. The Storm Coast and Dern are poor alternatives." He paused again and took a long breath before continuing.

"There is one other thing also that I would ask my Lords and council members to consider. The Vorstelv itself is the only thing that prevents ships from the Farmed Lands from following our reavers back to our own islands. We face increasing opposition with every reaving. How long do you imagine it will be before these people discover for themselves the technique to passing through the icy waters? How long before we must face them in our own waters? On our own shores?" He fell silent. The quiet filled the chamber for the length of a long breath, before it erupted in chaos.

He stood in silence as council members shouted from bench to bench, even as the Sealord and Lord Keeper stood to call for order. A clashing of steel on steel brought silence and wide eyes. The Thane handed the sword back to his guards and stood leaning heavily on a polished oaken staff.

"I would know your meaning, Frostbeard." His voice was weak but in the sudden hush it easily carried to the farthest edges of the hall. "Is it your intention to conquer these people and bring them under my rule? I fail to see how adding more mouths will solve the problems you have presented here."

Aiden took a moment before replying. The Thane rarely spoke up in council meetings and the power rested in unstable alliances between the factions. "My Lord Thane," he began in a respectful tone. "I do not suggest we conquer the people themselves. Rather that we drive them westwards, taking their lands for our own, where we can build settlements and farms."

"And what honour is there in that?" a voice shouted from the benches.

"Silence!" roared the Thane, drawing to his full height and showing a light in his eyes that Aiden had not seen in thirty years. "I will not have our future decided by squabbling children in the guise of farmerfolk and shopboys!" He lifted the iron circlet from his brow and waved it in the air above his head. "I am Thane here. The rule is mine!"

A black-robed advisor stepped close to whisper into the old man's ear, but the Thane turned and glared at him so furiously that he faltered and stepped back, muttering apologies.

"This session is at an end. The council will have no vote on this matter. I will receive the Sealord and the Lord Keeper in my chambers, along with the petitioner." Howls of protest followed his announcement, but the man was clearly unmoved. He stepped down from the dais and moved around it, towards the back of the chamber, flanked by his guards. Aiden stood, stunned, for a moment before he was ushered along by the Sealord towards the doors and the Thane's private chambers.

Aiden raised his eyebrows at the Sealord as they entered the chambers and saw his own surprise mirrored back at him. Whilst the Thane still had the power to rule as he wished, he had handed more and more decision-making powers to the council. In recent years, almost the entirety of the governance of the Barren Isles had been conducted by the three Lords and the council.

The Thane's chambers were surprisingly plain and utilitarian. Where the council chambers and the anterooms were dripping with opulence, these rooms were comparatively spartan. Aiden found himself ushered along into a simple room with a large, well-polished table in the centre. The Thane lowered himself down into a wooden chair and fixed his pale eyes upon him "Talk," he said, as Frostbeard and the others were settled into seats by a trio of servants.

"My Thane," he began, but stopped as the old man held up his palm.

"None of that. That's fine for out there but in here, we're just men." He eyed Frostbeard until the man nodded. "Now, tell me your plan and what you think you would need."

"It would need to be a sizeable force," Frostbeard began, cautiously, as the others at the table leaned in to listen.

Chapter Seven

The goat bleated again, loud and insistent. This time, the door to the cottage opened and a man stepped out into the daylight.

"I'm coming!" he called out, as he made his way gingerly across the grass to the small barn that housed the animals. He walked slowly, like a man not far from his dotage but he wasn't old, not in the normal sense. His was an age born of endless fatigue and it showed in his pale blue eyes, his frequent heartfelt sighs and the lines on his face. His was the kind of face that comes from bearing an endless, relentless responsibility that knows nothing of respite.

He made his way into the barn and climbed in with the animal, reaching a stool and pail in with him, and settling down to milk her.

"All that fuss, hey?" he said, soothingly. "I was barely awake when you started all that noise. You'll wake the neighbours!" He chuckled at his own joke.

He hummed as he worked and the milking was soon finished. He moved mechanically, then set the pail aside and moved around to the side of the barn, opening the doorway to the fenced in paddock and letting the animals out to graze.

"Do you think I can have some breakfast myself now?" he asked the animals, as he tossed a scattering of grain out for the chickens.

"Never a word of thanks, either," he tutted, as he made his way back through the barn and out into the clearing. It was simply a hole in the forest. No visible paths led into it or to the cottage. The paddock sat next to a well-worked square of land with vegetables growing in orderly rows.

He walked back to the cottage and set about putting some water on to boil over the iron woodstove. The building could have been mistaken for a ruin from the outside. It looked like nothing more than a pile of branches and twigs that had somehow combined to form walls and a roof. Moss and ivy grew freely over the structure, and it seemed far more like a part of the forest than any form of dwelling.

Inside, it was orderly but plain. A simple cot to sleep upon and a serviceable kitchen took up much of the space. A chair by the small fireplace and a corner filled with a cluttered desk and bookshelf were the only home comforts.

He waited until the water began to boil before dumping in a double-handful of oats and a splash of the goat's milk from the pail. As he stirred the porridge, he stared out of the window, his thoughts far away.

He could feel it again. The Wyrde fluttered in his mind, like a minnow caught between two cupped palms in the shallows. His brow furrowed as he bore down and clenched around it, forcing it onwards.

His eyes drifted to the centre of the clearing and the great stone circle that stood there. He sighed and lifted the pot from the stove, leaving it on the burn-scarred table and making his way outside. The porridge would finish itself off now, anyway.

A rust-encrusted pole leant against the side of the cottage. It was fashioned from iron and utterly unadorned, though it was so pitted it would have been impossible to tell. The rust had bubbled and formed nodules along the length of the staff. It resembled a long orange candle which had been allowed to burn and collect rivulets of wax along its length.

Taking up the staff, he began to shuffle around the clearing. A keen observer would have noted that his path took him along a clearly marked trail. Not so much one that had been cleared, but rather one that had been worn and marked out by the fall of endless footsteps.

The stones were irregular, showing no signs of tool marks, and formed the roughest of circles. They were not especially large, the tallest being no higher than the man's thighs. Despite the moss growing freely on the earth between them, none had taken hold on the stones themselves. In fact, a small bare circle surrounded each of them, as if the plant life feared to come too close.

The centre of the circle held a monolith, roughly seven feet in height, and deeply scored and stained on the sides with rust. Two more lay on their sides nearby, as if they had once formed some manner of structure which had long since toppled.

His shuffling steps covered the path surprisingly quickly, moving him in and out of the stones. They formed a square here, a triangle there and then some nameless shape that was, nonetheless, clearly defined. He tapped the staff sporadically as he went, but the taps seemed to have nothing to do with balance. He moved in silence, his eyes unfocused and his mind somewhere else. His dance was mechanical and nothing he needed to pay attention to. In his mind, the Wyrde calmed, ceased its writhing and then flowed on, maintaining.

As the resistance faded, he allowed himself to relax, and think of other things, though a portion of his mind was always focused on the Wyrde. There should be others, he thought, for the thousandth time. The task was possible with just one, but only just barely. Others had been with his master long ago. He could still vaguely remember them. There had been visitors arriving in a panic, men and women talking late into the night. He'd been just a boy then. It suddenly all seemed such a terribly long time ago.

He sighed in resignation as he shuffled the last length of the path, performing the final steps of the ritual only to begin again. His was the spider's web against the hurricane, the hands holding back the tide. His was the task that would fail. He would be swept away eventually, that was a certainty. First though, he would hold, and perhaps just long enough for another to be sent as he had, and trained.

* * *

Lady Selena Freyton read the dispatch again with care, before crumpling it into a ball and hurling it across the opulently appointed room.

"When did this arrive?" she demanded as she turned to face the page.

"Just this hour, my lady," the young man stuttered, still kneeling with the silver tray held out in front of him.

Selena took a deep breath and wished she had something else to throw. "Get up, boy! You look ridiculous down there on the floor." The blonde boy scrambled to his feet, trying to straighten his blue and green livery without it appearing too obvious.

"Fetch me Hanris," her green were eyes lost in thought.

"The chamberlain, my lady?" the page replied, frowning.

"Unless you know another Hanris in my household's employ?" Her eyes snapped back into focus and she glared at the boy. "Of course, the chamberlain! Oh, and bring me Captain Rhenkin as well." The boy bowed quickly and fled the room.

She paced while she waited, from one end of the parlour to the other and then back again. Rain lashed against the expensive windows and the dark skies seemed to reflect her mood. She moved across the room again to retrieve the report, smoothing it out against her leg through the teal gown she wore. She read it again, as she went over to the hearth and warmed herself by the fire, holding her hands out in front of the gleaming brass fireguard.

A knock at the dark-panelled door preceded its opening. The young page stepped in and to one side as he announced "Chamberlain Hanris, my lady."

Hanris was a small, bird-like man, with thinning black hair and brass-rimmed spectacles perched on the end of a long nose. He walked in odd little steps towards her and gave a perfunctory bow.

"You sent for me, Your Ladyship?"

She waved the paper at his face as she stepped closer. "Have you seen this, Hanris?"

He recoiled from the report slightly, before collecting himself. "I have not, as yet, had the pleasure, Your Ladyship."

She pressed her lips together tightly and closed her eyes, as she took a deep breath. "It's from Squire Thorpes, he..." She broke off and thrust the paper at the little man's chest. "Just read it."

Hanris smoothed it out, frowning with unconscious disapproval and examined the message, reading slowly and meticulously.

"He reports that those thrice-damned raiders have attacked again," Selena fumed, before he could read more than the first line.

"That is most unfortunate, Your Ladyship," Hanris said, cautiously.

"I'd say it's a little more than *unfortunate*! That inbred idiot has allowed three villages to be razed to the ground."

"The Bjornmen are reputed to be most savage, Your Ladyship," Hanris murmured.

"He reports that tax collectors left empty-handed from Fallows Deep and Heston," Selena said, watching for his reaction.

A crimson flush spread up Hanris's neck, creeping above his tight collar and cravat. "What?" he spluttered. "I mean, that is simply not acceptable, my lady. The King's tithe is due in a matter of months."

"I am quite aware of that," she said, in an icy tone which was lost on him.

A soft knock at the door interrupted them and the page entered again. "Captain Rhenkin, my lady," he announced in a firm voice, before withdrawing.

Rhenkin was everything that Hanris was not. Tall, confident and resplendent in his grey and green uniform, he bowed slightly at the door before striding across the carpet. "my lady." He spoke in a firm, serious tone, making it both a greeting and a query, before offering a nod to Hanris. "My Lord Chamberlain."

"Rhenkin," she said, her voice softening. "How familiar are you with the Eastern Reaches?"

"Passing fair, your grace," he admitted, silently rebuking himself as the flicker of annoyance touched her green eyes.

"What about defences, garrisons and the like?"

"It has a number of small garrisons," he advised. "Nothing of any consequence. There is nothing to really defend against."

"Except the Bjornmen raiders," she finished for him, biting off the words.

"Except the Bjornmen," he agreed. "An inconvenience, at most."

"If I may, Your Ladyship?" Hanris said quickly, noting the colour rise in her long elegant neck. At her sharp nod, he turned to Rhenkin. "The... ahem...situation appears to have changed somewhat, Captain. The raids are interfering with tax collection and this has an obvious financial implication."

"What he means," grated Selena, "is that my incompetent and deficient husband, your duke, has squandered funds right, left and centre, and now we have to scramble to find every copper penny. We can ill-afford to be losing money to raids."

If Rhenkin was fazed by her outburst, he didn't show it. "As you say, my lady. I gather you have some manner of remedy in mind?"

"I was under the impression that the uniform indicates some form of military training?" She moved closer and plucked at the epaulettes on his shoulder. "However, not enough to venture military advice, it would seem." She glanced at Hanris. "Perhaps we should find a Lieutenant worthy of promotion, Hanris?"

"I'm sure you are aware that the issue with the Bjornmen has always been the speed with which they strike," Rhenkin said quickly. "By the time any alarm has been raised, they are already gone."

"Then, clearly, we will need to raise the alarm faster." She turned abruptly and moved towards the far end of the room. The entire wall was painted with a map of the known world. She'd always hated the thing, ostentatious and gauche. How funny that now it would become useful.

"Show me where the garrisons are." She pointed vaguely towards the Eastern Reaches, at the very edge of the map.

"From memory, we have several in the area." He moved to the corner. "This is also not the best map but I believe we have three within reach."

"So the issue is purely the speed with which the alarm is raised?"

"Precisely, my lady." He nodded.

"Tell me, Captain," she turned to him, tapping her lips with the now folded report. "How would we raise the alarm if we were to be invaded from the south?"

"From the south?" He frowned. "Baron Rentrew's lands stand between us and the border, my lady."

"How does he do it then?" she snapped.

Rhenkin flushed and moved to a different area of the wall. "He has signal towers along his southern border, Your Ladyship. They light a fire when invasion or troops threaten and..."

"Yes, I am quite aware of what a signal chain is, Captain," she cut him off. "I believe he has also been visited by the Bjornmen on occasion, has he not? Why can't we implement the same system in the Eastern Reaches?"

"The principle is sound, my lady," Rhenkin replied smoothly. "The garrisons, however, are undermanned and too small to support the necessary troops."

"So expand them." Her eyes flashed.

"There...um...is the issue of cost, my lady," Hanris interjected, apologetically. She whirled to face him. "Cost is precisely why it must be done," she bit the words off. "Draft something, Hanris. I want signal towers running inland to these three forts."

"Garrisons, my lady," Rhenkin corrected, in a soft apologetic voice.

"No. Forts," she said firmly. "They need to be expanded and the muster increased."

"Now, Hanris." She pointed to the desk in the corner of the room.

"Of course, my lady," the chamberlain agreed, seating himself at the desk and readying pen and paper. "It will, of course, require the duke's signature."

Selena grunted and tapped her foot as she watched the little man scratch the pen across the page. Slippers and carpet were simply not designed for tapping one's feet. There was no point in acting impatient if nobody noticed. She sighed and cast sideways glances at the window and at Rhenkin's rather impressive physique in equal measure, until the little man finally offered up the sheet.

Grasping the folded document firmly, she stalked through the halls of the ducal palace, silently wishing again that she was wearing proper shoes. She could stalk perfectly adequately and her teal gown was more than suited to the task, but padding silently was simply not the same as heralding her arrival with the clack of decent heels.

She made a mental note to remedy this, as she turned the corner and approached the double doors to the formal dining room. Two men-at-arms stood to attention as she approached, drawing their halberds across themselves.

"Is my husband in there?"

"He is, indisposed, your grace," the taller of the two advised, with a faintly pained expression.

"He's drunk, you mean," she retorted. "And do not address me by that title. My family had land and title three hundred years before this idiot's ancestors crawled out from their cattle shed."

"Yes, my lady," the guard managed.

"Were you planning on opening the door?" she asked sweetly.

"At once, my lady," he said, and stepped inside to announce her. She didn't wait and swept past him in a flurry of silks.

The formal dining room was dominated by an enormous oak dining table and was richly appointed, with thick, red, velvet curtains on the windows and heavy tapestries on the walls. A cavernous hearth in the centre of the wall was filled with a roaring fire and, directly opposite it, sat Duke Freyton, Lord of Druel, The Wash and the Eastern Reaches.

Freyton was a fat, bald man in his mid to late forties. His jowls hung heavy below his cheeks and down to his double chin, and his skin glistened with sweat in the light of the fire. His collar was undone, as were the uppermost fastenings of his shirt, and pink flesh strained at his remaining clothes in a bid for freedom.

His head lolled slightly to one side and he was snoring loudly. A large meal lay mostly untouched before him and a silver goblet listed precariously to one side, held in one pudgy hand as it rested on his belly.

"Freyton!" Her voice cracked like a whip as she slapped her hand down on the table beside him.

"Wassat?" the fat man jumped. The wine in his goblet sloshed over the side and onto his shirt and garish yellow pantaloons. He sat up and tried to brush the wine from himself before it soaked in. "Damn it, woman, am I never to have any rest from you?"

"If only you could!" She stepped away from the table to avoid any drips from the wine. "I need you to sign this." She waved the paper at him from a safe distance.

"What is it?"

"Provisions for the expansion of the defences in the Eastern Reaches and measures against the Bjornmen."

"Foolishness," he snorted. "I won't sign," he said, as he lurched to his feet unsteadily and blinked at her owlishly.

Selena stood her ground before the fat man and suddenly realised how ridiculous he looked. To think she had allowed this idiot to run their affairs for so long! "Listen to me, you revolting little toad." It took an effort not to laugh at the foolish creature, as his face coloured. "You may be my husband but we both know that is only for the convenience of both of our families. You are a paper duke with no more pedigree than the hounds of your huntsmaster."

"Now just you see here!" Freyton protested as his temper rose visibly, his face now a brilliant scarlet against the grey and white of his moustache and sideburns.

"No," she said, in a dreadfully quiet voice. "You have run the affairs of our estates and lands since we were married two years ago. Oh, that someone could take *that* day from my memories! Since you laid your drunken hands to the reins of our estates, the ledger has been bled dry on one foolish excess after another. Now we will do things my way!"

"By the Lord of New Days, we will not!" he shouted again, and staggered to the side slightly. "Get out of my chambers and return to your parlour. You ought to be sewing or something. Women do not possess the intellect required for statecraft and the managing of estates."

"Listen well, little man. You will sign this provision and anything else I bring to you from now on. You will do this and more. And then, perhaps, I will allow you to sit here and drink yourself into insensibility and eat yourself even more stupid."

"And why, foolish woman, would I do that?"

"Because if you don't," she replied, allowing a cruel little smile to show on her lips, "I will inform my father of your drunken excesses, your inability to get me with child, and your unwholesome inclinations towards some of the younger pages. Our marriage is of no use to my family if the line dies with me."

"What are you talking about, woman? I've never so much as..."

"It doesn't matter what you've done, idiot!" she snapped, interrupting him. "It matters what my father and the King believe." She stood and watched his reaction, fighting the smug smile which fought to show on her lips. He drew back. First shock, then anger and finally affronted resignation passed across his sweaty features.

"Give me the paper," he finally sighed.

"Not there!" She batted his hands away. "You're all covered in wine and food. Honestly, Freyton, you look like a drunk in a tavern's gutter." She moved to a small serving table at the edge of the room and set the paper down. "Send for pen and ink," she instructed, without bothering to turn.

"Why do we need extra defences there, anyway?" he asked, returning from the door. "There's nothing there to defend. Small villages, at most." She moved adroitly away from the stench of stale wine on his breath and faced him.

"Not now, no, but we need more revenue. I have plans for this land. We could have five score more farming villages here without even scratching the surface of the land's potential. The only reason it's never been done before is the threat of the raiders." Her eyes were filled with ambition and almost as unfocused as his.

"Why bother? One village of peasants or a thousand. They do little but complain," he protested.

"Because, you fool, peasants produce revenue." She shook her head wearily. "We could have the taxes on the homes, the farms, the revenue from the sheep. Lords of Midwinter, Blood and Sky, do you truly not understand? You cannot honestly be this stupid, surely?"

He flushed again. "Stop your pagan blathering, woman. I understand well enough, but this will cost a small fortune. How do you plan to raise the funds for it all?"

"How else?" she smiled. "Taxes. If we need to bleed the peasants a little more now to make this estate work in the future, then that's what we'll have to do." She turned away, as a servant arrived with pen and ink on a silver tray, which she took with a self-satisfied smile. Motioning Freyton towards the paper with one hand, she handed him the pen, her smile fading. "Now, sign."

* * *

Devin leaned back against the broad trunk of the elm tree and sighed in contentment. The woods were still, with just a faint breeze rustling the leaves and gently caressing his face. The sunlight danced and weaved through the ever-changing gaps in the canopy. It was the beginning of autumn, when summer has not yet truly given in and there are still more warm days than crisp, and Devin was hiding. It wasn't so much that he was avoiding the work itself, more that he was avoiding the boredom and drudgery of it. It helped assuage his guilt somewhat if he justified it in those terms. That said, the guilt was not strong enough to stir him from the woods and bring him back to the village in time to help with the harvesting. Crops were for girls and men too old to hunt, Devin had decided, the numerous young farmhands in the village and his own adopted father not being strong enough evidence to the contrary.

He ought to be hunting. He would catch an earful from Hannah regardless, but he had more chance of avoiding the worst if he came back with a deer or a brace of pheasants. Groaning wearily, he rose to his feet and took up his hunting bow. It wasn't the greatest weapon, by any means, but it was one of the few things that Devin truly owned and he loved it with a fierce pride. Checking his pack to make sure all was still in order, he set off at a light pace deeper into the woods.

He'd gone into the woods to the north of the village. It was only a day's walk at most from here to the road to Savarel, but there were some nice game trails to be had. Besides, if he'd headed to the south, he'd have had to pass half a dozen people who would have remarked on it to Hannah. Devin was arguably lazy, but he was no fool.

He cut a slight figure. At a little less than five and a half feet, and slender along with it, he could and had, been mistaken for a young girl on more than one occasion. His fair features did little to help this and Devin longed for the day when his beard would finally begin to sprout in earnest. He was dressed simply, in green homespun and a sturdy travelling cloak, hardly the ideal clothing for trying to find a deer. At least they were a few days on him and wouldn't carry the scent of soap.

Devin had always been at ease in the woods. They felt more like home to him than Widdengate itself. The village had taken him in when he'd needed it to, and Khorin and Hannah had cared for him as if he were truly their own, but he'd always be the outsider. Even five years later, he still felt the eyes on him and the hushed words. In the woods, he was free.

Amongst these trees, he had been the greatest hunter. He had fought off ravaging Bjornmen. He had battled dragons and barrow revenants. He was not a child though, not any longer. That child had died shortly after his mother.

It was small wonder then that Devin's woodscraft was mostly self-taught. Who had there really been to teach him? Khorin knew his way around the woods in terms of what mushrooms not to eat, and the difference between an oak and a beech, but little more. Devin had learned through trial and error. How to move quietly through the woods, by seeking out soft earth, moss or hard tree roots to step on. How to place his foot down flat instead of rolling it when there were no other alternatives. How to make sure he was upwind of his quarry. Most importantly, he'd learned how not to be quiet when there was no other choice. The woods were full of sounds. Animals that moved through the brush were not entirely silent themselves. The trick was to make the right kinds of noises.

He smiled to himself as he reached a small game trail meandering into the woods. Setting down his pack, Devin reached into a pouch and then strung his bow in one smooth motion, bracing one end against the soft forest floor. He ran his hands through his dark hair, sweeping it back from his forehead, and nocked an arrow to the string. He set off slowly along the game trail, his eyes alert now and showing none of the glaze they had during his last half an hour or so of daydreaming.

He walked in an odd half-crouched stalk that would have looked ridiculous to anyone watching, his eyes and head tracking slowly back and forth but not settling on anything. The woods were oddly quiet today. Normally, he'd have spotted a game bird or two by now, but so far he'd seen nothing. He skipped lightly over a shallow stream, his feet finding large stones that extended above the rushing water easily. The bank was steep and he had to hold his arrow along the length of his bow, using his free hand to grasp at bushes to assist him.

It was as he made it to the top that he spotted the stag. It was a truly beautiful creature, fully sixteen points on its antlers, and easily as tall as he was. It stood proud and tall at the edge of a small clearing. He was so captured by the scene that he almost didn't think of his bow. Swearing silently and praying the breeze didn't carry his scent, he nocked an arrow and pulled back to just past his eye. He carefully sighted along the shaft and took a deep breath, holding it. Before he could release, the deer tensed and sprang out of the clearing to the north.

Devin cursed quietly and made his way slowly across the clearing in the hopes that the creature had not gone too far. An old and winding trail led northwards.

From the look of the leaves, it hadn't been used by man or beast in some time. The stag's tracks were plain to see in the disturbed leaves and soft earth beneath them. The animal itself, however, was gone.

More from idle curiosity than anything else, he followed the path. He knew he had little chance of finding anything, given the pristine state of it. For whatever reason, animals seemed to be avoiding it. He largely ignored the trail itself, concentrating his attention on the trees in the hopes of seeing a pheasant at roost. The path meandered for a time and then opened out into a small clearing. Devin looked around in confusion, not really sure what he was looking at. It felt familiar somehow, yet he could have sworn he'd never set foot in it before. The ground was covered in a thick blanket of leaves, blown free by the autumn winds. He walked towards the centre of the clearing, turning to scan the trees as he did so, and caught his heel on the edge of something. He fell hard and landed on his backside in the brown leaves. Devin muttered a curse and pulled himself up, relieved that no one was around to see. "Can't even walk across a clearing without falling over!" he chided himself. He picked up his fallen bow, thankful he hadn't had the string pulled back.

He chuckled at his own foolishness and kicked at the leaf-covered log he'd tripped over. He spun in a slow circle noting the humps buried by the fallen leaves. They formed a circle of sorts. He shivered, despite the warm day and wondered at himself. What was this place? Why did he have this reaction to it? He took a cautious step towards the centre of the clearing and a scream cut through the silence of the forest.

Devin jumped violently and muttered a curse that would have turned Hannah's face white. He turned towards the sound, the strange reaction he'd had to the clearing forgotten. It was definitely a woman's scream and Devin set off towards it at a dead run. He knew the woods like the back of his hand up to about three or four miles radius from Widdengate, this odd clearing aside. He'd travelled about two miles into the forest today and so knew roughly where he was. There was little ahead of him but woods, aside from a pretty clearing with a stream in it. A good place to catch trout if the weather was right, but no use for anything else.

He slowed as he heard voices and, without really thinking about it, began to move as quietly as possible.

"I told you, no!" a woman's voice snapped. Devin peered from behind a tree to see Erinn and Artor from the village. They lay beside the stream on a checked picnic blanket, the remains of a meal scattered about them. Well, Artor lay. Lounged would be closer to it. Erinn sat bolt upright, her arms clasped around her knees over her pale yellow dress, with a look of embarrassed outrage on her face.

"You know what you are, Erinn?" Artor said. "You're a damned tease, is what you are. You lead a man on, flirting an' kissing, and then when it's time to do more, you blush and run like some nervous maid."

"I *am* a nervous maid, you fool!" she spat at him.

"Of course you are," Artor said, his voice heavy with sarcasm. He was a big man, about three years older than Devin. Working with his father in the watermill had given him a strong physique and his dark hair, blue eyes and chiselled features tended to attract girls like moths to a candle flame. Devin privately despised him.

"What do you think I am? Some kind of slattern?" Erinn's voice rose with her temper and she climbed up from the blanket, dusting off her dress. "Some bitch in heat you can just pounce upon?"

"Well, what did you think we were going to be doing? Why do you think I asked you out here?" Artor said, disbelievingly. "Come on, you know you want to."

"I most certainly do not!" Erinn flushed and her lips pressed together in a thin pale line as she folded her arms over her breasts.

"You may as well. I'll tell all the other lads you did, anyway," he smiled a sickly-sweet smile.

Her temper snapped at that and the sound of the slap filled the clearing. Her face went from angry to smug to scared in the space of two breaths, as Artor's face rocked back from the blow, and he turned back to her with anger in his eyes.

"Maybe I should just take what I want anyway?" he said, in a low, dangerous voice.

"You wouldn't dare!" Shock swept over Erinn's face and she backed away slowly.

Devin had been preparing to move back through the trees, as this was clearly a private moment, but Artor's words stopped him cold. He hadn't been particularly close to Erinn for a few years now, but he wasn't about to let this happen. He reached for his quiver again and set his arrow in place by feel, his eyes never once leaving the scene.

Artor lunged for her and she backed away again, just out of his reach. She turned to run and he grabbed her long, red hair in one fist, twisting it around his hand for a better grip. "Now, let's just see if you're as sweet as you look," he said softly into her ear.

"My father will kill you, if you do," she hissed through clenched teeth, her eyes watering as he pulled her hair.

"Why would he do that? When I was working in the mill all afternoon?" He pulled hard and forced her down onto the blanket.

Devin stepped out from between the trees, his bow taut and aimed squarely at Artor's rump. "I think she said no, Artor," he said, with a calm he definitely did not feel. The boy's head shot round in a way that would have been funny if it had been in any other circumstances, and his eyes narrowed in recognition.

"What are you doing here, boy?" he said with contempt. "Peeking at your betters, you little pervert?"

"Let her go," Devin said, trying to control the trembling in his knees.

"Or what? You'll poke me with your little squirrel killer?" Artor released Erinn and she slumped down, as he got to his feet to face Devin. They stood only thirty or forty feet apart and, all at once, Devin was keenly aware of just how big the miller's son was. He had six inches and easily two stone of muscle on him. If it came to a fistfight, Devin would not only lose, he'd be lucky to be alive.

Devin nodded towards the trees. "Good. Now, I think you'd better go."

"If anyone is going, it'll be you." Artor laughed, incredulously. "Honestly, sneaking around the woods, so you can catch a glimpse at a couple. You little pervert, you ought to be ashamed of yourself."

"We didn't, Devin," cried Erinn, her face a mixture of outrage and shame. "I mean, I wouldn't!"

"Shut up, girl!" Artor snapped, before turning back to face Devin. "I'll tell you what, boy. You leave right now and get back to hunting for hedgehogs, or squirrels, or whatever it is you do with that little toy of yours and I won't mention this to anyone."

"I don't think so, Artor," Devin said, hoping no one could hear the tremor in his voice. "I think you better put your little weed away. Nobody is interested in playing with it today."

"Why, you little..." Artor began, and came at him with fists high. The shock that came over his face was priceless, as the arrow buried itself in the earth, not six inches from his foot. He froze, looking aghast, as Devin smoothly nocked a second arrow. "You *shot* at me!" he cried, incredulous.

"No, Artor. I shot at the ground." Devin replied slowly, as if explaining things to small child. The shock on Artor's face had robbed him of any menace, and Devin was finding it hard to keep a straight face. "If I'd shot at you, I'd have hit you."

He nodded towards the trees again. "Go!" he snapped, trying to put some menace into his voice.

"This isn't over." Artor glared at Devin, then at Erinn and stalked off into the woods. Devin watched until he was out of sight and then relaxed the bow. "Well, shit..." he murmured and leant heavily against a tree. He looked up to see Erinn's eyes upon him, an unreadable expression on her face.

"Are you okay?" he asked, trying to read her face.

"I'm fine," she snapped. And then, "I'm sorry, Devin. I'm not being short with you. I'm cross with myself."

"With yourself?" Devin wondered. "I can't see that you did anything wrong. He was the one like a stag in rut."

"I went to the woods. For a picnic. Alone." Erinn said, wondering at her own stupidity. "With Artor!" she laughed a helpless little laugh. Devin smiled, unsure just which part of this it was that was so funny.

"Oh, stars above and all the droos -scarred altars. What a fool I am!" she cried, still laughing. The laughter had a touch of hysteria about it that spurred Devin forward. He went to pull her close but she flinched away.

"Devin," she said, sniffing and rubbing at her eyes, "if you hadn't come along..." She left it hanging.

"You'd probably have slapped his face and sent him off with his tail between his legs," he finished for her. They smiled at the image, both knowing it wouldn't have played out like that.

"What *were* you doing out here, anyway?" she asked, with a shaky smile.

"Well, it wasn't because I was hoping I'd catch a glimpse of Artor's bare arse, I can tell you that!" snorted Devin. She laughed with him and, for a moment, it was like they were both children again.

"I suppose we better gather these things up." He moved about the clearing, gathering up the bowls and empty bottle. Erinn watched wordlessly for a moment, before shaking out the blanket and folding it up.

"Come on," Devin smiled. "I'll walk you back to the village."

She pulled the arrow from the soft earth with an odd expression and handed it to him, before walking away towards the village without another word. Devin replaced the arrow in his quiver and followed her.

It was mid-afternoon by the time they made it back to the village and Devin was ravenous. He left Erinn with vague promises to spend more time together and catch up, but they both knew it probably wouldn't happen. He walked quickly through the long grass, as he made his way toward the road and home, replaying the day's events in his head. He vaguely noted a heavily laden wagon coming along the road towards him, heading in the direction of the inn. A middle-aged man held the reins loosely. Devin was immediately struck by the soft black robes the man wore and the bone white rope about his waist.

"Boy!" called the black-robed man in a condescending tone. "Hey, boy!" Devin stopped and looked over at the man expectantly.

"Is there an inn in this village?" he asked, a smile upon his face. It was the type of smile that a childless man uses with a friend's children. Patronising and tolerant.

"Along the path you are following, sir," he replied, Hannah's manners coming out before he had a chance to realise it. "Another five minutes or so."

"Blessings of the Lord be on you, my son," the black-robed man said pompously, and clucked his horse on. Devin stepped to the side of the path to allow the wagon to pass. He watched for a moment, before his stomach spoke to him again and he headed on to the cottage.

"Any luck?" Hannah said, as he came down the steps into the kitchen.

"Luck?" Devin replied, his brow twisting into a tight frown.

"Your bow. I assumed you were hunting," she replied, with an edge in her voice. "At least, I assume that's why you left before sun up, without saying a word to anyone?"

"I...umm," he fumbled.

"You what?" She wiped her dough-covered hands on her white apron and frowned at him. "You know Khorin wanted your help today? Honestly, Devin, sometimes I don't know what to do with you." She sighed, obviously biting back harsher words. "Did you at least manage to bring anything back for the pot?"

"I nearly did," he replied, moving on quickly as he saw her expression fall. "I had a deer, but it was spooked by Erinn screaming."

"Erinn? What was Erinn doing there?" Devin stalled for a minute, kicking himself for his own stupidity. He hadn't planned on talking about this with anyone.

"Devin?" She drew out the word, managing to make it both a question and a threat. He gave in and, before he knew it, had recounted the entire tale, right down to shooting the arrow at Artor's feet.

"That damned fool girl," Hannah sighed. "She's going to get herself into all manner of trouble if she doesn't start thinking a little more." She sat back at the table and began working the bread dough she'd been kneading.

"She's hardly the one at fault, Hannah," Devin said.

"You sound like Khorin," she said, over her shoulder. "That's exactly the type of innocent nonsense he would come out with." She laughed again at his nonplussed expression. "Yes, Devin, Artor is the one at fault, but Erinn should know better than that. A girl as pretty as she is needs to be careful, especially with men like Artor."

"So she's at fault for going on a picnic with him?"

"For going alone, with a man like Artor, miles from anywhere? Yes! And she knows it!" she said, jabbing a flour-covered finger at his chest. "She carries on like that, she'll be travelling to Cobton to find a priest to marry them both before the year's out."

"Looks like she wouldn't need to go to Cobton, at least not today," Devin replied. "There's one at the inn."

"Oh, my stars!" Hannah said, with a gasp. "Maryanne mentioned a pastor was coming when I had lunch with her last week, but you know how she is. Running that inn has put gossip so far into her mind that she spouts it whether it's true or not!" She spun on her heel and dashed out of the room without another word. Devin watched in amusement, as she hurried halfway up the stairs, only to stop and run down again.

"Be a dear and sweep up in here for me, would you?" She waved an arm vaguely at the kitchen.

Laughing quietly to himself, Devin took up the soft broom and began sweeping the floor. He was only just finishing the first corner when Hannah bustled back into the room. She had changed into a bright flowery dress and twisted her hair up into a complex arrangement. "Now then, dear, would you please run and fetch Khorin out of the fields and tell him to wash up, while I go and invite the pastor over for some tea?" She climbed up the three stone steps and was out of the door before Devin had a chance to answer. For a short woman, she could move deceptively swiftly.

By the time Devin had found Khorin and they had made their way back to the cottage, Hannah was already outside with the dark-robed priest. As they approached, Devin could see that the man wasn't as old as he'd first thought. His hair was fully grey, but his face was young. He was barely out of his twenties, by the looks of things.

"It's not much," she demurred, "but we like to call it home."

"It's lovely," the robed man said, with that condescending smile again.

"Oh and here they are!" Hannah said, as she noticed them both approaching. "Khorin, Devin, this is Father Trallen." She gestured as she spoke. "Father, this is Khorin, my husband, and our son, Devin. Father Trallen is going to be building a church here in Widdengate, Khorin," Hannah gushed.

"A church?" Khorin gave the robed man a frank and appraising look.

"Well, a chapel," Trallen clarified. "And it will be workmen building it, not me." He laughed a small little laugh. "For now, at Mistress Maryanne's insistence, I'll be lodging at the inn and holding regular services on the green beside it."

"Well, you must come over for tea whenever you need to escape," Hannah said, smiling. "She's an awful gossip, you know," she confided, as Devin and Khorin exchanged a glance and fought to keep their faces straight.

The priest coughed and cleared his throat. "Yes, well, I am sure that would be lovely."

"And, of course, you'll be attending the harvest festival? It's only a week away," she enthused.

"Ah well, I'm not sure," the robed man said hurriedly, with a halting gesture. "Sometimes these things don't go very well with the teachings of our Lord of the New Days, you know? Old pagan ways, and dances and the like."

"Oh," she said, in a small voice, and her face fell. "It would have been such a nice way to introduce you to our little community, as well."

"Well, we will see," Trallen said, in a mollifying tone. "It's just as I will be speaking about tomorrow in my sermon. People sometimes find it too hard to let go of the old ways. Things like that horseshoe over your barn door," he continued, somehow not noticing Hannah's stricken expression. "Some people put them up for luck. Really though, it's a symbol, meant to keep away those things that we fear in the night. These are the things that shackle us to the past, you see? How can we grow as people, when we hide in fear of the ghosts and goblins from children's tales?"

Hannah nodded, smiling. "It's a silly old thing. Been up there for years, I'll have Khorin take it down this afternoon."

"My grandfather and I put that up!" Khorin protested, in a hoarse whisper, as Hannah made frantic flapping motions at him behind the priest's back. Devin coughed into his hand and turned his face away.

"Anyway, let's go inside for some tea, shall we? Listen to me, gossiping on the doorstep!" She laughed a silly little laugh and led the robed man down the steps into the cottage, leaving Khorin and Devin on the doorstep.

"The woman's as giddy as a young girl at the Midwinter's dance!" Khorin muttered in a low voice to Devin. "She's not been this bad since we had that messenger here, who'd had a tumble and had to spend the night. Cooing and gushing all evening, she was. To think, she dragged me back here for this. I've half the field left to do." He gave Devin a pointed look. "Tomorrow," he said, firmly.

* * *

The following day, Devin was woken by Hannah at dawn. She forced him into a shockingly cold bath to scrub himself until she was satisfied with his pink and slightly sore skin. He and Khorin sat out of the way, at the kitchen table, in freshly laundered shirts whilst Hannah busied herself with getting ready. They waited in silence. The woman had disturbingly good hearing. Devin could tell that Khorin was not happy. There was a definite atmosphere in the kitchen, as if the harsh words that hadn't been spoken were still fighting to be heard.

Eventually, she descended the stairs and marched them off to the green beside the inn. Neither Khorin nor Hannah had shown the slightest interest in religion in the years Devin had lived with them. They made a bow to the Lord of Midwinter when the snows first fell and at the Midwinter's dance, but that was really as far as it went.

Trallen had arranged things simply beside the inn, with a semicircle of benches and chairs, and then an empty patch of grass next to an old stump for himself. Devin sat with Khorin and Hannah, curious as to what the mysterious new figure would have to say.

The villagers filed in quietly, driven by curiosity more than anything else. Less than ten families attended, though Devin noticed that many of the womenfolk were wearing dresses which were definitely not for everyday use. His was also not the only pink, well-scrubbed face in attendance. He hadn't been to a religious service before and wasn't quite sure what to expect. He jumped as Hannah poked him in the ribs, without seeming to have moved, to draw his attention back to the priest, who had moved to the centre of the patch of grass, ready to begin.

"Welcome all," began Trallen, "and thank you for such a wonderful welcome to your village. The Lord bless you and keep you safe always." He looked up from his folded hands with a broad smile, "I wanted to start by asking what you have heard of the Lord of New Days, and see if there are any questions I can answer?" He looked over the small crowd expectantly, but was faced only with silence.

"Come now, someone must have heard something. It doesn't matter if it's wrong or even insulting. I promise not to be offended." He said the last with a smile.

"I heard how he don't like holidays, and you're forbidden from dancing and the like," Kainen said from the back row, while his mother, scarlet-faced, tried to hush him.

Trallen laughed and replied, "That's a new one, I must confess. I hear all sorts of stories and it's nice to be able to set the record straight. I quite like holidays. Some festivals can be a great deal of fun. I'll confess, I'm not much of a dancer, but the only thing stopping me is my two left feet." He chuckled at his own bad joke, as a nervous ripple of laughter went through the small crowd.

"The Book of New Days," he said, pointing to a large, leather-bound book he'd set on the stump beside him, "tells us that the Lord loves us and protects us. He created everything around us and He wants us to prosper. Some things hold us back, but dancing isn't one of them."

"I heard you New Dayers don't hold with old beliefs and traditions, and you work to stamp 'em all out." The crowd turned as one, to see Samen leaning on his stick behind them. The old man was still hale and hearty, despite his advancing years, but age had done nothing to tame his cantankerous nature or to blunt his tongue.

"I think that 'stamp out' might be a little harsh," Trallen replied, mildly. "We simply want our Lord's children to progress as He intended." He turned to Erinn's father. "You, sir, unless I am mistaken, are the blacksmith in this lovely village, aren't you?" The large man nodded. "Now, let me ask you something. If you were making a new plough, would you use iron or steel?"

"Given the choice, I suppose I'd use steel. It's stronger," the bear-like man said, slowly.

"But years ago, we used iron or even wood, didn't we?" Trallen said, smiling indulgently at the man's nod. "Now, should we continue to use iron or wood, just because tradition tells us so? Of course not, that would be foolish. This is the heart of the Lord's message. He wants us to progress and to be the best we can be. To achieve the future He has planned for us."

"So why not just give us steel to begin with?" Samen called out, earning himself a glare from both Hannah and Maryanne, who had arrived late and now stood beside him.

"Well, let's ask one of the mothers here something. If you have a child who wants something, is it better to just give it to them or to make then earn it in some way?"

"Earn it," said Hannah firmly. "That way, they value it more."

"Exactly," the priest said with a warm smile.

"Don't see what that has to do with stamping out the old ways," Samen muttered, loud enough for everyone to hear. He clamped his lips shut, as Maryanne whispered furiously into his ear.

The rest of the service passed quickly with a short sermon and, finally, a brief prayer. The new pastor was clearly no fool and realised that a short, successful sermon would be much better than a long-winded failure. His choice of location was obviously not just by chance either. As the service finished, the men drifted into the inn while most of the women stopped to chat to the new priest.

Devin wandered towards the inn, hoping to catch Kainen for a short time. It felt like months since they had really spent any time together. It seemed the older they got, the more chores they were given.

He walked through the door of the inn and made for the bar, spotting Kainen polishing glasses. A large hand came down on his shoulder and he turned to find Harlen, the blacksmith, looking down at him over his thick red beard. "I heard what you did for Erinn," the big man said simply.

"What? How?" Devin replied, caught flat-footed.

"Parents do speak to each other sometimes, Devin," Harlen rumbled with a smile. The expression looked odd on his usually dour face. "Artor, his father and I, we will be having a conversation." He managed to make the word 'conversation' sound like a dire threat and Devin nodded quickly, not wanting to aggravate the man.

"Anyway, I wanted to say thank you. I owe a debt to you." He squeezed Devin's shoulder, in what was supposed to be a comradely fashion but was one which very nearly sent the boy to his knees. He walked back to his table before Devin could protest.

Devin made his way quickly to the bar, leaning over it and grinning at his old friend. "Did you get an earful for asking questions then, Kainen?" he said.

"Too right!" the pale lad replied. "You've never seen such a simpering and carrying on. Between her and your Ma, there's enough calf eyes and scraping to please any priest."

"You'd not say that within earshot, though," Devin laughed.

"I'm no more fool than you," Kainen grinned back, before casting a guilty glance along the bar. The once sickly-faced lad had sprouted like a new tree once he hit thirteen. Now, at fifteen, he was already almost taller than his father. He'd grown tall but not broad and so had the gangly, over-stretched look of some young men his age. An overly prominent Adam's apple did little to improve his appearance.

"So what did you think of it all?" Devin asked, in a conspiratorial whisper.

"I don't know, really," Kainen replied, seriously. "It's things I've never really thought about. I mean, some of it made sense. Like the thing with the plough and there being no point in holding onto things just for the sake of tradition."

"Not all tradition is bad though, is it?" Devin argued. "I mean what about Midwinter? We have the feast, and the dance and presents. Everyone has a good time. Where's the harm?"

"Would he have a problem with that, then?" Kainen wondered.

"Of course he would," Devin snorted. "There's the bow to the Lord of Midwinter, isn't there? I can't see him putting up with that."

"It's only a bow," Kainen protested.

"True, but then it was only a horseshoe on our barn, and he made it clear that it ought to come down too," Devin pointed out.

"You'd better get a drink," Kainen advised, as he watched his father pulling drinks. "You know how Father hates to see sleeves polishing his bar with empty hands."

"I'll have a cider then." Devin looked over at the innkeeper. The man could be welcoming and jovial to his customers, but he'd brook no nonsense from Kainen and his friends. It was more than once that he'd been chased from the inn with harsh words.

"He's in a foul mood, anyway," Kainen said, just softly enough for Devin to hear. "Mother's made him cancel the morris, both for the harvest and Midwinter."

"Why?"

"It's this priest again," the gangly man admitted. "He said it was a relic of a pagan past, honouring false and forgotten gods. Or something like that."

"I bet your father didn't like it, though," Devin said.

Kainen shook his head vigorously. "Bloody droos, no! You've never heard such a row. I mean, they argue a lot anyway, but this was nothing like that. Father was calling Trallen every name under the sun. He must have heard it all too. He's only one floor down from them. She gave as good as Father did though." His voice took on a high-pitched, nagging tone, "Owen Taplock, I'll not have you offending Father Trallen with your silly dance! He's only just arrived!"

"He's never really had enough men for it anyway though, has he?" Devin said, laughing at the image of the tiny Maryanne berating her husband.

"I don't think that's the way he feels about it, though." Kainen shook his head slowly. His eyes brightened suddenly. "Hey, I hear you're best friends with Artor now though?"

"What are you talking about?" Devin asked, with a suspicious look, as he set his cider back onto the bar.

"Your little conversation yesterday. Got a little *pointed*, did it?" Kainen grinned.

"Is there anyone who hasn't heard about this?" Devin muttered despairingly, as his head sank into his hands.

"I doubt it. You know what this place is." Kainen grinned, enjoying his friend's misery. "So, did you really threaten to shoot him?"

"I wouldn't have done it really. Well, probably not," Devin whispered.

"You really did it?" Kainen giggled madly. "I thought she was making it up or exaggerating."

"Wait a minute," Devin said, as he fixed his friend with a suspicious look. "Just who are we talking about here?"

"Karren." He grinned at Devin's blank expression. "You know, the cooper's daughter?"

"Karren!" Devin exclaimed, his voice breaking and coming out as a girlish squeal.

He cursed and cleared his throat. "Karren?" he repeated, in a normal voice. "How does she know?"

"I expect she was there when your mother was telling her father and Samen," Kainen gave a wicked chuckle, having saved this bit until last.

"Samen?" Devin moaned. "I might as well scream it from the rooftops then."

"I shouldn't bother," Kainen advised, smiling. "Telling Samen is much faster."

* * *

The harvest was always a busy time in the village. Devin found himself torn in two directions, as Khorin demanded more of his time to help bringing in the crops and Hannah made him help with preparations for the festival. Secretly, Devin was pleased to be busy, as it gave him fewer opportunities to run into Artor. He'd been reasonably certain that the incident in the woods would quietly blow over, until he'd discovered that half the village knew about it. He'd avoided Artor as much as he could during his childhood in Widdengate. The boy was a prime example of an only child, pampered, indulged and someone who gave little thought to others. Devin had secretly despised him for years but had usually managed to stay out of his way. After the incident in the forest, this would probably be impossible.

The days trundled by. Harvest was an awful time of year and Devin hated it openly. It meant hours of backbreaking labour in the fields, working from sun up until almost dark, reaping and threshing. To make matters worse, Hannah had offered his assistance to Father Trallen too.

Devin made his way reluctantly into the village. Although the cottage he lived in with Khorin and Hannah was technically inside Widdengate, there was a goodly distance between them and the nearest structure. He found the priest beside the inn, speaking to a number of burly-looking men. Five large wagons stood next to them, weighted down with building materials and large stone blocks. He stood quietly, not wishing to interrupt, and watched three of the youngest village children skipping, and singing a song as old as time.

"*I'm to keep a fairer way,*
With horses' shoes and miller's weigh,
From wax to waning moon, we pray

Keep us warm 'til light of day."

He watched the children disinterestedly, his mind working over the issue with Artor and how best to avoid another confrontation. He worried at it like a dog with a piece of meat, but couldn't see a way through it and his mood grew darker as he waited.

"Deep thoughts this close to a festival, young man?" Trallen's deep voice startled Devin. He spun in shock and then flushed at the grey man's smile. He truly was a grey man. It extended from his hair, of course, but his eyes were a pale grey and his skin held no trace of tan. It was as if the colour had been leached out of him.

"Not really, Father," the young man said, politely. "Just wool gathering, really."

"Artor?" the priest asked pointedly. Devin felt his mouth fall open and closed it with a snap. Even the priest?

"I just don't want any more trouble with him," he said, in a low voice, looking down at his shoes.

"You don't know what trouble is!" Trallen laughed. "But I know what you mean." Devin cocked an eyebrow at that.

"What? You think I was born a priest?" The grey man laughed again, a deep infectious laugh and Devin smiled a true smile for the first time in days.

"Your mother generously offered your assistance," Trallen smiled. "It's not much really. I need to travel away for a day or two and I have these men here to work. I wonder if you could show them to the site I have picked out for the church and school."

"School?" Devin asked quickly.

"Yes, for the little ones." Trallen replied in an offhand manner. "There are so many here who don't even have their letters." Devin flushed slightly, remembering the years it had taken Hannah to drill the skill into him.

"Anyway, I must be away or I'll never make it back in time for your festival," Trallen said. "There'll be another four or five deliveries in the coming days. If you could make sure they get to where they are supposed to be, I'd be in your debt."

Devin nodded easily. It wasn't a great task. Trallen shook his hand firmly in thanks and turned to go back into the inn.

The site the priest had picked out was on the other side of the village, but only about five minutes' walk from the inn. A large area had already been staked out and marked with string. Devin led the workmen over to the site, listening openly as they chatted about local gossip.

"I heard Baron Rentrew got sick of Bjornmen raids." A short, thick-bodied man confided. "He built signal fires."

"What, to let him know when his villages were burning?" laughed Lorn, the foreman of the crew.

"No, fool. So they could send warning when they saw the boats coming," the short man said scathingly. "My cousin Jasper worked on 'em. He said they stretch over a hundred miles, going this way an' that."

"So now he gets to know they've burnt down, just faster than he used to?" Lorn laughed again.

The short worker's face flushed. "Why do you think they've stopped raiding so much then, hey?" he demanded. "The fires worked, is why. Couple of year ago, they got men there from the garrison in Holt and nearly wiped a whole load of the thieving bastards out."

"I hadn't heard that. You serious?" Lorn said, his laughter gone.

"Almost to a man, Jasper reckons," the man said, seriously. "He reckons Old Freyton caught word of it and he's so impressed, he's going to build forts."

"I can't see that, Len," Lorn replied. "Not enough villages to make it worth his while, is there?"

"Just what I heard, is all," Len said, sourly.

Devin left them bickering at the site, as they started to unload the stones and supplies, and walked slowly back towards the farmstead, his head reeling. The Bjornmen had always been a thing of myth and legend to him. They'd never penetrated that far in from the coast and Widdengate, being three days from the closest shore, had never been touched by them. They'd always been like a force of nature to him, a storm that struck and devastated farms and families alike. Hearing they'd been forced back gave them a human element he'd never considered before. For the first time, he wondered what sort of people they were. Did they have homes and families? He supposed they must have. What could drive a people to inflict such suffering on others? The thought kept him going all the way back to the farmstead.

Chapter Eight

Samen leaned back in the chair with a satisfied sigh and admired the colour of the glass of red wine, holding it up and watching the glow of the firelight through the blood red liquid. There had been a time when you would have been hard-pressed to find any wine this far east, at least anything worth drinking. The cask of wine had travelled further in the last few months than he had during his whole life, from the vineyards of southern Surama, through Feldane and then into Anlan, before finally being transported east, to his tiny corner of the world. He savoured the aftertaste, before turning back to the small crowd of expectant eyes at his feet.

"A story, then?" he said musing. "Do I even have any stories left that you haven't already heard?"

"You know all the stories in the world, Samen!" cried a young girl.

His eyes crinkled at that and the ghost of a smile played over his lips. "I know one or two, it's true, Daisy."

He glanced around the inn, noting the farmers pretending not to listen, and Owen and Harlen at the bar with more than half an ear cocked his way. Khorin's foundling, at least, was more honest and sat at a table with his father, listening openly. His dark eyes were fixed upon Samen, his mug of ale sitting untouched before him.

A glance at the windows showed the snowflakes dancing against the glass panes as the wind howled. It was late, but none of the people in the inn seemed inclined to brave the weather to return home to cold cottages. He was in a whimsical mood and, when the children had approached him for a story, he'd barely bothered to put up a fight.

"A winter's night calls for an old tale, wouldn't you say? Winter is the oldest season, after all. The world was born on a winter's night just like this." The eyes at his feet grew wide and glittered in the firelight, as he leaned in towards them. "A story, then. *The* story, you might say. I'll tell you the story of the beginning and of the droos." The inn was silent as Samen took a sip of his wine. The blood red colour of the vintage was not lost on him or his audience, both young and old.

"Well, now, the droos," Samen began. "This world is old, older than most people imagine. Its countries and empires are children when compared to the history of the droos, though. Their tale stretches back into the farthest misty reaches." He looked up at his audience. Even Owen and Harlen were no longer bothering to hide the fact they were listening. His mouth twitched with a tight smile, as he watched Father Trallen come in through the doorway, kicking snow from his boots before making his way to the bar.

"The world was spun out of the darkness by the Master of All Skies and the Lady of Deepest Night, or created by the Lord of New Days, depending on which version you want to believe. I doubt any man really knows the truth of how our world came to be, but it matters little. It's enough that you realise it is old and that few men, if any, know the truth of its beginnings. We have always sought the truth, however, and it is this search for the truth, and maybe for meanings which aren't there, that lead us to search in dark places. We raised churches and gods, when perhaps they had best been left alone." He stopped suddenly, as Trallen stormed to his feet, knocking his chair over in his haste. The priest marched over to Samen, white-faced with fury.

"I think that will be *quite* enough!" he hissed.

"You just get back to your sherry, Father," Samen said mildly, not bothering to stand.

"I don't think so," Trallen spat. "I'll not have you filling the children's minds with that sort of nonsense. Or the minds of the good people of this village, either!"

Samen climbed to his feet, leaning heavily on his stick. He squinted up at the priest and poked him hard in the chest with one gnarled finger. "You listen here. You've done a lot in this village since you arrived. Some of it good and some of it bad. You can make people stop the morris, and maybe talk them into getting rid of horseshoes and luck charms, which never did anyone any harm. One thing you can't do, though, is stop a story."

Trallen gaped open-mouthed at the old man. "It's a load of old nonsense and it…"

"It's older than you or I put together, young man," Samen said, with a hint of steel in his voice. "It's older than the pages of that book you wave around and call the sole source of true knowledge. I'll tell you this for free, young man. If you think all the knowledge of the world comes from a book scarcely five years old, then you're a bigger fool than I thought you were."

The inn was silent, and the children and customers watched on in amazement, as the gnarled old man, who barely came up level with the priest's shoulders, dressed him down before young and old alike.

"Now, just you see here!" Trallen tried again.

"No!" Samen cut him off, raising his voice for the first time. "You just close your yap for a minute." Trallen closed his mouth slowly, as the wizened old man went on. "It's a story. Maybe there's a grain of truth in it, maybe there isn't. Thing is, it brings a bit of joy to these children and I'll not have you taking it from them just because of the scratchings in that book of yours." He moved closer and his voice dropped to little more than a whisper. "Or maybe I need to be having a chat with our good miller about just what it is you've been teaching his lady wife in those meetings of yours? She makes some very strange noises for a lady studying scripture. I could hear her clear outside the window. I'll wager the miller could work a way to fit more than wheat between the stones of that mill." He looked down meaningfully before giving the priest a pointed look.

Trallen swallowed hard and took a step back. "How did you...? Who else..?" He stopped himself and looked around guiltily, before turning on his heel and marching out of the inn without another word.

* * *

The clearing was silent. A light covering of snow dusted over the fallen leaves and twigs. It was the last night of the full moon and the ground was bathed in a light almost as bright as day. A hand slowly reached out to touch the monolith at the centre of the clearing. It was gnarled and thick-fingered, the long thick nails more than halfway to being claws. Coarse hair covered the back of it, extending as far as the middle knuckles in wisps and tufts. The hand extended, not from an arm, but from empty air, which rippled gently around the wrist like the waters of a still pond. It hesitated, as if fearing the stone would burn, or feel as sharp as the blade of a knife. It jerked back suddenly but then reached again. It grasped the stone firmly, as a laugh, high and wild, filled the glade.

The few leaves that the wind had not tossed to the edge of the clearing crunched lightly as the feet stepped through the snow and frost. Cloven hooves leaped high and landed lightly, as the laughter carried around the stones. The creature cavorted in and around the circle, with a delight few men ever have the luck to experience. There was a brief trill on a wooden flute as it danced in the moonlight, and then it froze, head on one side like a bird, though no sound disturbed the stillness of the night.

It stood only as high as a tall child and was naked, other than two leather straps which came down from each shoulder and crossed over its chest, before looping around its waist. The dark leather mirrored the colour of the short horns jutting from the thick hair atop its head and the short beard sprouting from its chin. The bottom edge of its belt was lost in the dense wool-like fur that covered the creature's legs and haunches. A fierce grin split its face, bright white teeth catching the moonlight as it stood up straight, as if it had just finished listening. It turned abruptly and shifted into a run, making its way into the trees.

It moved with a hircine grace as it darted through the woods, giggling quietly to itself as it glanced around at the trees, the stars, the moon. It sprang easily over the small stream, weaving its way through the tightly packed beech trees. The woods were silent in the wake of its passage. Animals which had never seen the like huddled down into burrows or lay quiet under bushes, as ancestral memories bubbled to the surface, warning that this, more so than any other creature, was a thing to be feared and avoided. Its eyes burned with a cold amber fire whenever the moonlight caught them and the grin never left its face. At last, it burst free from the trees and stopped, chest moving lightly as its breath misted away in the cold winter night. It gazed down the hillside towards the lights of the village, its own eyes mirroring the warm light shining from the lanterns in the windows.

A small collection of buildings and barns stood close to the edge of the trees. The satyr moved silently through the long grass, towards them. A dim light shone from an upstairs window of the cottage, but it was otherwise dark. It reached behind its back to pull a long horn knife from where it lay tucked under the back of the broad belt, as it moved slowly towards the quiet house.

It stopped at the gate, as if expecting something. Its black tongue flicked out for a second, almost seeming to taste the air, and it giggled madly again, as if overcome with some unexpected delight. Slowly now, it moved closer to the buildings, its head darting this way and that, stopping every few steps to listen to the silence in the darkness.

It glanced up at the large barn. The large doors caught the light of the moon fully, and the old wood appeared silvery. Above the doors was a dark horseshoe shape, formed from flakes of rust and wood that had been covered for a generation and protected from the elements. The satyr grinned at the shape formed by the darker wood and sneered at the few flakes of rust, though it made no move to go closer. Instead, it skirted around the barn, seeking another entrance.

The side door opened easily beneath its gnarled hands and it stepped lightly inside. The darkness within was almost absolute but it moved easily, clearly having no problem picking out a path. The barn was rich with the smell of animals, and they shifted uneasily from a scent that was both new to them but also sparked instinctive warnings. It stared through the gloom into the goat's pen for a moment through the gloom. The goat stared back into the pitch darkness. It could see nothing, but the scent was tantalising its nose and its nostrils quivered.

The satyr laughed and danced in a tiny circle as it gazed at the goat. The animals shifted nervously at the sound and the cows let out a worried lowing. Smiling to itself, the satyr went out the way it had come and continued on through the night.

* * *

Samen muttered spitefully to himself for a minute as he lowered himself into his chair, wincing as his old joints protested. "Where was I?" he said softly, more to himself than to anyone else.

"The droos," a red-haired girl breathed in a carrying whisper.

"Yes, yes," Samen said into his glass, as he drank down the last of the wine. He waved it at the bar, catching the eye of Owen and noting, with satisfaction, that no other conversation stirred the air of the inn.

"So, this quest for knowledge was probably best left alone." he began again. "The droos began as one such people. A people driven by the quest for understanding, to discover their place in this world and the starry skies above. They had no temples, no churches. They gave no Setday services, unlike our good priest." He nodded towards the door Trallen had so recently stormed out of. "They spent their time, instead, in the study of all things, and of the secret workings of the world. The unseen flows of power that turn the seasons and lift the tides. Some say they succeeded in finding answers. Some say they discovered dark and terrible things, and this is how they shattered the moon."

"You've seen how the moon changes its face as it moves across the skies?" He smiled as the children nodded as one. All traces of the sour-faced old man had been wiped away by the telling of the story. "Only for the shortest time each month does the moon hold itself together. Too soon, do its parts fall away and drift, all unseen, into the darkness. This is the legacy of the droos, of a magics gone so terribly awry that they destroyed the face of their own silvery mistress. For, you see, they loved and revered the moon. Some say that was where they drew their power from and, when this disaster happened, then they were left as helpless as a child in the snow on a winter's night. So there they were, this wise and ancient order, suddenly as powerless as the lowliest peasant."

He stopped for a second to take the full glass of wine from Owen, who had picked his way silently through the crowd. Nodding his thanks, he took a sip and cradled the glass to his chest.

"So, where now were they to draw their power? The order crumbled and splintered. Many simply faded away, living simple lives the same as anyone here. Others, though, they clung to their lost power like drowning man clings to a plank of wood. They travelled the lands and sought out new ways to draw it to themselves. They constructed circles of stone and carved their dark runes into the cold slabs, even as they hunted down those who had a fire in their blood. A fire that shone through to the very roots of their hair," Samen stopped and looked pointedly at Daisy, smiling a cold smile as realisation dawned, and her hand flew to her red hair as the other covered her mouth in shock.

"Have you never wondered why there are so few people with hair like yours, Daisy?" The girl let loose a terrified sob and she fled to the comfort of her mother at a nearby table. The woman shot a look like daggers at the cackling old man, but Samen had been on the receiving end of far worse than a mother's glare over the years.

"So they hunted for those with the most fiery hair and dragged them screaming across the altar stones of their circles. Children were highly prized and yielded the most power. And, for a time, their power grew and they became a force close to what they had once been." He trailed off and stared into the fire for a time, as if reliving painful memories, his old face twisted into a grimace. Despite the silence, no child complained. No conversations struck up in the shadowed corners. The inn waited, almost holding its breath.

"This was a time before the empire had fallen, almost before it had risen. Feldane was just a collection of squabbling duchies and Anlan, our fair land," he said the last with a sarcastic lilt, "was a tiny fraction of what it is today. The man who would become our first emperor was a vicious-minded wastrel by the name of Caltus. Whatever else you might hear about Caltus is almost certainly wrong. The man was little more than a thug who happened to be in the right place at the right time. However, he managed it. Caltus became a force and took it upon himself to oppose the droos. These were not two nations at war, though. The droos never built fortresses or cities. They lived solitary lives, coming together in the light of their wounded moon to work their magics and feed the runes of their stones. Warring with a group like this was like trying to fight the wind. They were here and then gone, striking a village in the night and then vanishing, leaving little trace of their passing. No, the greatest victory Caltus could claim was in raising the people against the very idea of the droos, driving them even further into the shadows. It was probably this common cause that allowed him to seize power the way he did and build the foundations of the empire.

Caltus became Emperor Caltus the First, also known as Caltus the Bloody-Handed, Caltus the Red-Eyed, and Caltus the Priest-Killer. It's said that Caltus became completely obsessed with the droos and this eventually tipped him over the edge into madness. Some say the droos cursed him with his madness, but I think it's more likely that he was just terrified by them. He saw them in every shadowed corner, every quiet room. His very name Caltus the Red-Eyed comes from the fact that he was too terrified to sleep. This fear drove him to madness. He was convinced that the droos were behind all religion, that they controlled all of them from the shadows, and so he declared war on every one within his reach. For ten years, churches burned from one end of the empire to the other. Priests were hunted down with as much glee as the droos had been themselves.

Finally, after years of searching, his men rooted the droos out. A small gathering of tired old men and women hiding in huts in the woods. A greedy farmer with an empty purse had been supplying them with grain for their animals and he sold information about their whereabouts to Caltus's agents.

It was a dark business, but they were butchered almost to a man one night, under the full moon, while Caltus hid in his fortress and huddled under his blankets.

Only one of the droos was allowed to live and he was dragged back to Caltus and thrown before him in chains. Caltus sat quivering on his gilded throne, staring at this bedraggled old man, who wore only a thin, grey robe and the chains he'd been bound in. Caltus's men demanded to know the location of the treasures of the droos, because none would believe that over centuries of power that they'd hoarded nothing. The old man lay on the cold stones and said nothing, though they beat him and kicked at him with savage blows.

Finally, Caltus gave the order. and they dragged the droos to chambers far below and had at him with glowing coals and spikes of iron, until he screamed out into the night. Not a word about their treasures did he utter, though. In disgust, Caltus had him brought before his throne one last time and demanded himself to know the nature of their treasure.

The droos pulled himself up onto his knees and stared Caltus in the eye, shaking slightly from his pains, but showing no fear or deference. "You wish to know the nature of the treasure of the droos, small king?" He cackled, as blood ran from his wounds and his eyes fought to close.

"Yes!" cried Caltus. "I demand it!"

"You sit upon it, foolish man." The droos laughed, and then bent double with a hacking cough, as Caltus screamed at him to make his meaning clear.

"This whole world was our treasure, you fool," the droos wheezed, as he lay upon the stone floor. "The treasure of all mankind. We guarded it against a foe more terrible than you."

Caltus was enraged. He grabbed a sword from one of his guardsmen and drove it down into the old man's back, twisting and wrenching the blade to force the droos to speak. The droos didn't seem to even notice the pain though, and laughed and howled on the floor. "Spent your life searching for a treasure you already had, and then worked to hand it to an enemy you never knew," cackled the pitiful man. Then, bright blood boiled from his mouth and he dropped dead at Red-Eye's feet."

Samen looked around slowly, meeting each pair of eyes briefly before moving on and catching another. "Some say that was the end of the droos right there. Others say they never existed, that they are just creatures from a tale. That they're stories designed to scare children in the night, like the tales of the fae. But then, there are others who say the droos had a terrible secret, and that they are out there still, hidden away in the dark places of the world, watching, and waiting."

He drained his glass in one slow, deliberate motion and rose to his feet, his hand grasping at his stick. Weaving amongst the tables, Samen fought the urge to smile, as questions flew at him like stones, as he made his way to the door and out into the night. The inn came slowly back to life in his wake, conversations starting slowly and quietly, as if its patrons were waking from a deep sleep.

"He may be a miserable old sot, but he does spin a good tale," Khorin offered to Devin, as he lifted his drink and peered mournfully in at the dregs. He looked at the young man's tankard. "You going to drink that? We ought to be heading back soon."

Devin looked at his ale and was surprised to find it almost untouched. He was not a big drinker, mostly through lack of opportunity, but when Khorin bought him a drink, it didn't usually sit in the cup for long. He took a long drink, savouring the malty taste as his eyes roamed around the, now noisy, taproom.

"She's grown into a pretty one, I'll give you that. I'd not want to take on her father, though," Khorin said to him softly. Devin realised he'd been staring unseeing at Erinn, who sat with her father across the room. "I wasn't. I mean, I don't think of her like that. We're just friends. Really," Devin protested, as Khorin smiled at him, clearly not believing a word of it. Devin drank deeply, hoping the tankard would hide the deep blush on his cheeks, and then caught Erinn smiling back at him from across the room.

"Are you sure she knows that?" Khorin asked slyly, and laughed as Devin coughed and spluttered into his cup.

* * *

It moved with caution now, on its graceful hooves, as it stalked towards the farmstead. The satyr stopped and sniffed the air every few steps, licking its lips often with its long, dark tongue before moving on. It moved in a curious fashion, inspecting the windows and the brass door hinges, and looking closely at the lintel above the doorway. It circled the cottage three times, still grinning wildly, before returning to the front door. An old iron ring set into the dark oak served as a knocker and the creature hissed at it, as if fearing it might bite. It grasped hold of it with both hands and wrenched at it forcefully. Its face twisted in pain, as a bright blue light flared from between its hands, accompanied by a faint hissing noise. With a tortured squeal, the nails tore out of the wood and the knocker came free. The sudden force was enough to bowl the creature over backwards, and the knocker came down and landed on its chest.

With a scream of pain and fury, it batted the iron ring aside, for once heedless of the noise it was making. The cry was high and visceral, like the cry of an owl in the night or a cat fighting. There was another element to it, however, something primeval which spoke eloquently of fury and blood and hurt. The sound carried well in the still night and the animals, still penned in the barn, began to panic at the noise, crashing against their pens and crying out in the inky blackness inside the barn.

* * *

Hannah didn't mind when Khorin and Devin went to the inn together of an evening. It was nice to see them spending some time together. Devin had changed as he'd grown older, all boys do. He'd changed in different ways, though. He'd always had a guarded way about him, ever since Khorin had first brought him home. It was as if he was never quite sure how what he said would be taken, and if there might be consequences. As he'd become a young man, he'd become more sullen, but then this was the way of boys the world over. He'd also become adept at avoiding his chores and helping Khorin with the farm work, but this also was no different to any of the lads in the village.

No, it was something almost indefinable. He looked at people just that little bit too long, gauged their reactions just that little bit too carefully. It wasn't that he seemed to be scared of the responses to anything he said, it was more as if he simply didn't understand how people would take things. As if he didn't truly understand people at all.

So it was nice when they went off to the inn together. She could have gone along of course, but that wouldn't have been the same for them and this way, they could both be that little bit more foolish and free. That said, it was definitely time they were back now. It had been dark outside for a good few hours and the snow was coming down hard. She'd sat for a time in her favourite chair in the corner, sewing in the light of the fire, but it had mostly died down now. She felt little inclined to put more wood on it this late at night.

She looked around the darkened room and decided it was high time she went off to bed. If the fool men wanted to traipse home through the snow in the middle of the night, then let them! She laughed to herself at the image of them trying to get into the house and up the stairs whilst being quiet. They never drank too much, but they were incapable of not waking her. She was a light sleeper anyway, but the whispered conversations on the stairs were enough to make her split her sides as she lay under the blankets, pretending to still be asleep.

She left the fire to die on its own and lit a small hand lamp. Little more than stub of candle on a mounting really, but it would light her way. She could have made her way around the cottage with her eyes closed, of course, but she'd never been fond of the dark. Not that she'd ever have admitted that to either Khorin or Devin. Give them something to tease you about and they were on you like a terrier on a rat. She went up the stairs, stopping after two or three steps. A cup of tea might be just the thing. She smiled as she made her way down into the kitchen, lighting the lamps from her candle's flame. The stove was still hot, not hot enough to boil a kettle full, but enough that she would be able to boil a cup's worth. She busied herself with cup, water and kettle and went into the pantry for the tea leaves.

A sudden noise from the barn stopped her. The animals were hardly ever this loud. The goat, in particular, was making a frantic bleating. She muttered to herself and glanced through the window. The snow was still coming down hard. Fetching a thick fur-lined cloak from a peg by the door, she lit a large, heavy oil lantern and opened the door to the darkness. The barn was only a two minute walk from the house but it always felt longer at night. She huddled against the snow and cursed herself for not putting on boots. Her slippers were covered in snow already and, really, what was the point in grabbing a cloak if you walked out in felt slippers? She scuttled to the barn quickly and wrenched open the side door, hanging up the lantern on the hook and shutting the door against the weather.

"What's all this noise about, then?" she asked, in a soothing tone. She didn't feel like soothing, she felt like bed. Shouting at animals rarely soothes them though, so she worked to keep her voice calm, low and even. She looked quickly around the barn but could see nothing amiss. She popped some oats in for the horses, and made sure the goats and sheep had plenty of hay. She even tossed some food to the ducks. "No reason you should miss out is, there?" she said softly, then wondered why she was almost whispering. "Right, you lot, no more noise tonight. Understood?" With that, she stepped out into the snow.

* * *

The satyr shrunk back against the wall, as the human slipped and slid her way to the barn. Even under the covering of snow and the heavy cloak, there was no mistaking the scent of human female. The smell almost overwhelmed it for a moment. It had been so long since it had touched the flesh of a woman. It shook its head violently, dislodging snow from the thick hair on its head, and fought down the urge to chase after the woman and take her where she stood. It moved up to the side of the cottage and pushed open the door. The smell of iron was stronger in here, but not as strong as it remembered. The kitchen stank of it, the stench of iron and fire grating at its nose. It could spot the hateful items from the small hallway.

Forcing itself, it moved into the long, low kitchen. The firebox was solid iron and hot, at that. The satyr grimaced and muttered. There was a counter against one wall, under the window and a rack of knives stood close to the sink with its simple pump. The smell was less. The satyr cocked its head, confused. Knives, but not the stench of iron. It moved quickly to the rack and plucked out a long carving knife, the steel shining brightly in the lamplight. The satyr stared at the metal. Gingerly, it reached out a finger and touched the steel, flinching in anticipation. The hard, dark nail scraped down the length of the knife and the satyr laughed in delight. It reached out and licked the blade and then laughed even harder, tossing the knife away. Playing a trill on its flute, it danced and twirled in a joyful caper.

The barn door slammed in the wind and the sound brought the creature to attention. Fixing its gaze on the window, it cocked its head and turned its ear to the glass. A slow smile spread over its lips, as it tucked the flute back into its belt next to the long bone knives.

* * *

Hannah pushed the barn door shut and scurried to the house, eager to be inside and warm. That cup of tea was even more appealing now. She stumbled in through the door, a tangle of cloak and lantern. Kicking off her frozen slippers, she danced her feet on the rug by the door, trying to force some heat into her toes from the friction.

The smell hit her like a wave. An overwhelming scent of musk. She smiled a wicked smile. Khorin must have got back while she was in the barn. She hoped Devin was already in bed. The scent was giving her ideas already. Tossing her cloak carelessly on the floor and primping her hair with one hand, she went in search of him.

She made her way into the kitchen and stopped dead. The man was tall, dark-haired and definitely not Khorin. Other than that, the features were indistinct but the sheer *presence* of him was intense. She didn't scream, she didn't start at the sight of him. She couldn't care less who he was. He was here and Khorin was not.

He smiled broadly and walked confidently towards her. *By all that is holy, even the way he moves is sensual!* She smiled a shy smile, but there was nothing shy about the way she moved to meet him. He gathered her up in strong arms and she met his kiss fiercely, gasping for air.

"We must be quick. My husband," she managed to gasp, before his mouth found her lips again. She buried her hand in his dark hair, caressing the horns on his head. She stiffened in his arms. *Horns?* He nibbled on her neck lightly, painting a portrait of lust with his lips, and she was lost again.

They stumbled about the kitchen, crashing from one surface to another in a drunken dance of passion. He threw her back against the work surface, strong hands roaming over her body and tearing at her dress. She grinned and gasped with equal measure, as he ran a calloused hand up her thigh, and they sank sideways to the hard stone floor in front of the stove.

"Please!" she gasped. It was half request, half order, her mind lost in the passion, in the *scent!* He moved above her and they rolled slightly towards the stove. A violent shudder ran through his body and he screamed, a shockingly animalistic sound, as he threw himself away from her. A stink of scorched fur suddenly filled the kitchen. He frantically brushed blue sparks from his arm, where it had touched the base of the iron woodstove. Hannah shook her head as if waking, pressed her hands to her cheeks and screamed.

The man was gone and in his place stood a creature out of legend and nightmare. Slightly shorter than Devin, it had the hooves and legs of a goat, and a thin covering of fur. A dark beard covered its chin and two small horns peeked out from the curly hair atop its head. It glared at her as she screamed and made a strange motion with one hand. A look of confusion crossed its face as nothing happened.

Hannah stood paralysed with shock until the creature reached behind it and pulled out a long, intricately carved knife from the leather belt that crossed its chest. The weapon was a dull yellow colour and she would have wondered at it, had she not been so terrified. She looked wildly from side to side for anything she could use as a weapon, but she was pressed almost up against the stove and all of the knives were on the counter by the window. She felt down and behind her blindly, her eyes fixed on the creature as it moved slowly towards her, grinning.

Her fingertips touched a rod of some kind and her hand closed around it even as the monster sprang at her. She grabbed and swung blindly, and the poker slammed into the side of the creature's face. She would have screamed anyway from the sheer terror of the situation, but she was not expecting the explosion of blue sparks that came from the side of the beast's face. It flew across the kitchen, smashing to the floor, as if she'd stuck it with a sledgehammer rather than an iron poker.

The poker was shaking in her trembling hands, but she clung to it desperately with both fists. The creature rolled slowly and came to its feet. Its face was charred on one side, but its eyes were ablaze with hate, glowing amber in the lamplight. It raised the knife again and she lifted the poker in response. Its swarthy face paled at that, and it turned and bolted for the door, its hooves clattering on the flagstone floor.

She followed, slowly enough to maintain a distance, but fast enough to watch it flee through the door and into the night. Then, and only then, did she allow herself to sink to the floor, wrap her arms around her knees and sob like a broken child.

Chapter Nine

Winter hit the village hard, leaping from the shadows whilst some were lulled into complacency by the gentle embrace of autumn. It seemed that hardly had the golden autumn apples been harvested when the first snows fell. The wind howled down from the hills and the little collection of cottages seemed to huddle together against the cold.

Devin shuffled through the snow, bundled down in thick, heavy furs, as he dragged the sled towards the door of the cottage. It was heavily loaded with wood and, though he'd tried to move smoothly, he already knew he'd have to make another trip to retrieve the logs that had fallen off on the journey from the barn.

The day was bright but the sun seemed to do nothing about the cold. It seemed cruel that the light provided no heat, but yet reflected so blindingly off the snow. The snow had frozen overnight and hadn't softened during the day at all. A thin crust of ice crystals lying on top of the frosty crust tore loose in the wind, flying at his face like a thousand tiny daggers. He cursed into the scarf covering his mouth and held up one mitten-clad hand against the wind, as he unloaded the wood into the bin, and began to trek back for the rest of the logs.

Thankfully, the snow wasn't deep, just four or five inches. Widdengate only ever seemed to receive either a light dusting, like this one, or a foot or more in one night. In either event, it was a rare thing and Devin was usually glad to see it, until he had to go out into it.

He was thoroughly frozen by the time he had stomped his way down the steps and into the cottage. He paused only long enough to kick the worst of the snow from his boots, before slamming the door hard behind him. He stripped off the furs, soaking in the heat from the woodstove. Water was already pooling around his feet and he looked around for a cloth to wipe it up with. He had just walked across the kitchen towards the sink and pump when shouting from above froze him in his tracks.

"It was *not* a dream, Khorin!" Hannah's voice, harsh and brittle, filtered down the stairs. "You don't wake up from a dream huddled in the hallway with half your clothes torn off, as your husband comes in."

He couldn't make out Khorin's response, but his tone was clear enough, frustration and helplessness. Devin silently rebuked himself for listening in. He wrenched open the inside door of the woodbin to pull out a single log and then slammed it closed. The voices above stopped immediately. He stripped the rest of his furs off in silence, listening as the footsteps crossed the room and made their way down the stairs.

He stood beside the woodstove awkwardly as he listened to Khorin approach. He'd spent too many years for him not to know the man's footfall in the little cottage.

"You heard?" Khorin said, in a soft voice. It was not a question really, just words to fill the silence. Devin turned and shrugged awkwardly, meeting his eyes fleetingly before his gaze slipped away. There was too much hurt and confusion in those eyes.

"She's going to take a nap," Khorin said, but they both knew it was a lie. Hannah hadn't really left the bedroom in days. She came down long enough to do what was required, but soon drifted away, back to the room that she seemed to regard as her refuge.

"Is she going to come to the festival?" Devin looked at the man who had become his father, and really saw him. Saw through the front that Khorin put on for the sake of those around him. He looked old and tired. Helpless.

"I doubt it, lad. She's not much in the mood for dances and music." Khorin sighed as he moved to put the kettle over the stove.

"Will you?" Devin asked, with a lump in his throat. The whole cottage felt strained at the moment.

Khorin was silent as he put the heavy kettle in place. "I'm not really much in the mood for it myself, Devin," he said finally, in an odd voice.

"I think you ought to, Khorin. You need a break, even if she won't come. Give her some space and get out yourself." He spoke firmly, not really thinking about where the advice was coming from.

Khorin gave him a quick appraising look. "I forget how big you're getting sometimes." He gave a sad little laugh. "Life is passing me by while I'm busy fretting about things I can't fix." He looked Devin in the eyes. "You're right. It's good advice and I will try. It'll probably be later than most, but I'll be there, lad."

"I'm going to head over early." Devin advised. "Kainen wants me to give him a hand with the fires to get the place warm enough."

Khorin gave him a confused look. "The inn's never been cold that I've noticed?"

"It's not at the inn, Khorin." He shot older man a concerned look. "It's in the church hall, where Trallen runs the school. It's been the talk of the village for a week or more."

"Yes, well, I suppose I've had other things on my mind." Khorin grunted, his gaze flickering to the stairs and then back to Devin. "Well, you go on then. I'll find my own way there a bit later on."

The church had taken months to build, but the hall beside it seemed to have sprung up almost overnight. It was an odd fusion of a building, built with excess stone from the church, and finished off with sturdy timbers and thatch. Devin and Kainen came to a stop beside the large building, each grabbing an armful of wood before hurrying in out of the cold.

The hall was busy with children working to hang holly boughs and decorations fashioned from pine cones. Maryanne stood in the centre of the hall like a tiny general, as she directed children and men alike. Her breath steamed from her lips in the cold air.

She turned as they crashed in through the doors. "Oh, finally!" she said, with obvious relief. "Get the main fire going first and then we'll see about the others."

The hall had an open fireplace, which was easier to light than a woodstove, if less effective at heating the place. They set to work, with Kainen splitting off kindling while Devin carried in the rest of the logs. Within ten minutes, a large fire was burning and the room was beginning to warm.

Maryanne worked them all mercilessly, ignoring most of the calls for breaks or drinks, as she arranged the decorations, tables and food. Lanterns were strung from the beams in the ceiling and the cold, shadowy hall was transformed under her direction.

The food began to arrive soon after, and it seemed every time Devin and Kainen returned with more wood to stack in the corner, another delicious smell filled the chamber. A clattering outside announced the arrival of Owen with casks of ale and wine, and the two lads were again pressed into service, rolling the large barrels into the hall as Owen gossiped in the doorway.

A whole ox was set to roast over a large iron trough, filled with glowing coals from the fire, and a host of children took it in turn to be in charge of working the handle to the spit. In spite of the strange atmosphere at home, Devin started to relax and the excitement of the festival began to build in him. Winter was a miserable season and the folk in the village had little or nothing to do but endure it. It was more than just the cold, although that was bad enough. It was the endless slog of making sure there was enough dry, split wood for the fire. It was the sheer effort of dressing in enough furs to keep the cold at bay while you worked. It was the dark evenings that seemed to start almost before the day was half over, and countless other small things that combined to make life hard work. Everyone looked forward to the Midwinter dance. It was more than just a recognition that half of the winter had passed. It was a day to forget the strain of the season and allow yourself to relax.

Devin flopped down into a chair and grinned at Kainen across the table. "I reckon your Ma is busy enough now not to notice if we take a few minutes."

"I don't think she ever gets busy enough not to notice, but I'm sitting down anyway," Kainen laughed. He looked around at the transformed hall. "It does look good though, doesn't it?"

Devin admired the hall. "It does. It feels a bit weird with it being in here instead of at your place, though."

"Don't let Da' hear you saying that." Kainen glanced about quickly. "He's been grousing for a week about how much of a pain it's going to be to drag all the ale over and everything else. Says it won't be the same."

"It wasn't really all that much bother, though, was it?" Devin looked over at the barrels piled in the corner next to the table, which was already covered in cups. The innkeeper stood behind the table, handing drinks to villagers thirsty from a day's work under his wife's direction.

"I don't think so, no. He's still sore about the morris, I think," Kainen replied, in a soft voice.

"Where is Trallen, anyway?" Devin asked, as his eyes searched over the hall.

"Bothering his Lord still, I expect," Kainen muttered darkly.

"Still not his biggest fan, then?" Devin asked, his eyes still wandering over the growing crowd. The hall was filling quickly, as more and more villagers stamped their way in from the cold, brushing off the snow, and piling their cloaks and furs on chairs near the doorway.

"It's alright for you. The shine soon wore off for your Ma. I get dragged along every Setday to listen to him ramble on." His face twisted into a sour expression. "They've started singing now. Did you know that? Singing!"

Devin knew better than to laugh, but Kainen was not making it easy. He stifled what they both knew was not a cough, and made a show of looking around the hall.

"There are some things different though," Kainen said. "The Midwinter's Wreath is missing, for one."

Devin turned to look where his friend pointed. He hadn't even noticed the easternmost wall was bare where the huge wreath fashioned of fir, holly and pine cones should have been hanging. "What are the girls going to bow to then?" he wondered aloud.

"Don't know if they even will." Kainen muttered. "Trallen's been all over Ma about this. Look, there he is now." He pointed through the growing crowd at the black-robed priest, who was speaking earnestly to Maryanne with a concerned expression.

Devin chuckled. "At least someone else is getting an earful this time. I think it's about time we got a drink, don't you? This place is starting to fill up."

The table that served as a bar was busy and it took some time for them to both get a drink. They settled back down at their table just as the music started. Samen was perched on a stool at the end of the hall, working his fiddle, with two other villagers on flute and bodhran, and the music soared.

Devin watched, grinning as the doors opened at the end of the hall and the girls filed in. The village girls were dressed identically in dresses which flared at the waist. Their close-fitting black and green tops should have been enough to draw the eye, but instead your eye was drawn to the dark woodland green skirts with the flash of berry red. Whirling around in the complex dance, they resembled nothing more than boughs of holly whisking about the room.

The girls' dance carried on for three or four minutes when the music paused and they stopped as one to bow to the empty eastern wall, though more than one of them shot a confused look at Samen. Then the tune started up again and the girls took another turn around the room, before spinning off into the crowd and searching for partners to pull in.

Devin sat grinning at the spectacle and almost missed Erinn in her midwinter's gown twirling towards him. She flashed him a mischievous smile and he stood uncertainly, before reaching out for the hand she offered. Suddenly, a large body shoved its way rudely between the two of them and Artor took her hand.

"I think the lady needs a man tonight, not a little squirrel hunter." He laughed and led Erinn onto the floor. She shot him an apologetic glance and then was gone.

"Utter bastard!" Devin exploded, in a combination of shock and anger, as he sank back into the chair. He turned to look at Kainen, but the chair was empty. Then, he caught a glimpse of him being whirled around the floor by Karren. Kainen wore a slightly startled expression, but was clearly enjoying himself. Devin swore and finished his drink in two long swallows. He glanced over at Kainen again, muttered to himself and then finished his friend's cup too.

Trallen was furious about something by the looks of things, red-faced and gesticulating wildly as he spoke with Kainen's mother. It was only then that Devin realised that the morris had indeed been cut out of the festivities. The girls should have danced around the four men in the centre of the room, who would be dancing their own steps and clashing the large iron staves. He was surprised to find that he did actually miss it. Tipping the last drips of Kainen's ale into his mouth, he made his way to the bar. The line was long and the music had stopped by the time he made it to the front and refilled the wooden cups.

He weaved his way through the crowd, heading back to their table. He was looking more at the level of the ale than where he was going, in an effort not to spill it, so he didn't spot her until he was almost on top of her.

"Sorry about that, Devin," Erinn said with a smile. "He's hard to say no to sometimes, but I promise to come and find you before the night is out." She was truly stunning. The dark forest green of her dress served to make her hair stand out even more. He gaped at her for a second, until her wry smile forced him to speak before she laughed.

"I was surprised to see you with him after...well...you know?" Now what had made him say that? He silently kicked himself for spoiling the opportunity, as the smile slipped from her face.

"Well, he's just a little jealous, I think. It wasn't anything I couldn't handle, you know?" she replied as her face coloured at the memory.

Devin certainly did not know, and doubted Artor would have stopped if he hadn't come along, but he had successfully killed the moment. He muttered a meaningless goodbye as Erinn nodded at him, and slipped away into the throng. He doubted he'd be dancing with her at all now.

"Stupid bloody fool," he whispered to himself, as he made his way through to the table. Kainen sat with Karren on his knee, her arms wrapped around his neck. Devin caught the pointed look Kainen shot him as he approached and he set his friend's ale on the edge of the table, before making his way back into the crowd. The night was not working out at all as he had expected. The fire and the sheer number of people in the hall had made it uncomfortably warm, and he was suddenly desperate for some fresh air. He fought through the crowd and stepped out into the night air with relief.

There was a small group of men outside. Samen and the musicians drank ale and laughed loudly, as they sucked smoke through hand-whittled pipes. The night was clear and the stars shone brightly over the snow, lending a cold light that showed the village in shades of midnight blue and grey.

He stood and enjoyed the cold as he drank his ale in silence, ignoring the door as people came and went. It was with some surprise that he noticed that Samen and his men had gone back inside, and he was alone. He drank down the last of the malty ale and was about to go back in, when the door opened and Artor stepped out. He stopped as he saw Devin and an arrogant smile spread over his face.

"Sorry about taking her away from you like that," the dark-haired man said, with a smile which showed very plainly that he wasn't sorry at all.

Devin grunted and moved to step past him, but Artor stopped him with a hand on his chest. "You need to stay away from her though, boy." The arrogant sneer was back on his face and Devin clenched his fist tightly. That look had always made him want to smash it off the miller's son's face.

"Why is that, then?" he said, feigning ignorance.

"Because she's mine and you'd do well to remember that." Artor took a half step towards him, so he towered over him.

"She's not a sheep, Artor," Devin said, putting as much scorn into his voice as he could muster. "Though that might be more your type." He barely had time to realise just how stupid that remark was, when Artor's fist drove into his stomach. Devin staggered back from the blow into the side of the porch and doubled over, wheezing as he tried to force his lungs to work. The next blow caught him high on the cheek and his head crashed back into the wooden beam supporting the side of the porch. He slumped to the ground, as his head spun and the taste of blood filled his mouth.

"You're nothing but a child." The distant voice was scathing, but Devin couldn't focus on it. By the time he had come to, he was alone. The snow underneath him was starting to melt and soak through his clothes and his face felt three times its usual size. He pulled himself to his feet and probed at his face, his fingertips coming away smeared with blood. He wasn't about to let anyone see him in this condition. He spat blood into the snow and prodded his teeth with the tip of his tongue. Scooping up a handful of fresh snow to press to his face, he lurched off into the dark towards the edge of the village and the path home.

* * *

The morning was cold and a thick frost lay on the ground. The pale, winter sun shone onto the grass and leaves, throwing a thousand sparkles back. It was a beautiful sight in its own way, if there had been anyone to see it. The frost covered the stones too, highlighting designs and whirls in them which would probably have been invisible otherwise. Even then it would be obvious to any observer that the marks were ancient. That once they had been carved deep into the stone, and that hundreds of generations of wind, rain and ice had scoured them down to make them this faint.

Inside the cottage the old man sat staring into the fire. The fireplace had been stacked high with wood at one point, but this had burned down to ruddy embers and a few stubborn chunks of charred wood, with the flame licking tiredly at the ends. He sat in a well-worn wooden rocker, possibly the only thing in the cottage that could have been classed as a luxury by even the most generous of observers.

A long clay pipe poked from his mouth and the man sucked on it sporadically, not noticing that it had either gone out some time ago, or had never been lit in the first place.

"Footprints," he muttered quietly to himself.

He'd felt the weakening, of course. How could he not have? The ritual was such a part of his life now, after a lifetime of walking the path, that he felt every ripple and push. He'd felt it weaken with every passing year, even as he'd felt his own body age. There was a perverse symmetry in that, but it had increased over the past few years. He pulled himself to his feet and threw a thick woollen cloak over his rust-stained robes. Stamping out of the door, he decided to forego the frost-covered iron staff and he made his way out to the centre of the stone circle, following his own footprints in the frost.

He stared at the ground with a sour expression and chewed the errant wisps of his white-streaked beard. Kneeling, despite the cold, he brought his face closer to the footprint and sniffed at it gently. It was as clear as if it had been made in potter's clay. A perfect footprint. A single cloven hoof print.

He stood again and moved back to view the whole scene. The footprints began beside the hubstone, that was the rub. He'd had a hundred deer in here over the years, but their prints didn't look quite the same. His own goat had even got loose one time and the shock had nearly killed him when he had seen a thousand hoof prints leading back and forth across the glade.

The prints started about a foot from the stone and made their way directly to the cottage, circling it two or three times. Here and there, he could see faint scorch marks on the now frost-covered ground, where iron spikes protruded from the dirt. Hard enough to see in the day, they'd be almost impossible to spot in the dark, even for one of that kind.

He wasn't overly concerned. The Wyrde wasn't perfect and never had been. There had always been the odd one or two slip through between full and new moons. They'd never approached the cottage before, though. The staff beside the door was usually enough to deter them. In all his time at the glade, it'd only happened half a dozen times. He laughed a mirthless chuckle as the memory of the first time bubbled up from the hidden corners of his mind. He'd sat huddled in the cottage, *feeling* it move back and forth around the clearing before it dashed into the woods.

Inside his head, a pressure was growing as the Wyrde continued to fail. He'd felt it weaken over the years, though he had no idea why. The pressure increased at every full moon and he could almost feel them pushing, pressing, fighting to get free. It only lasted from the full moon until the new and then it ebbed, until the moon grew full and it began again.

The piteous bleating of the goat stirred him to action, and he opened the door to the barn and made his way inside. Tossing hay into the goat's pen, he looked into the animal's black eyes. "You saw it, didn't you, girl?" he said softly. "You saw our little visitor, hmm?" The goat didn't answer. She was far too busy with the hay and, in truth, she seldom had much to say anyway.

He went about his business in the barn mechanically, feeding the animals and giving them fresh water from the barrel in the corner. It wasn't until he turned to leave that he noticed the knife embedded in the door.

He moved towards it, holding his breath despite himself. It was made from horn, but then it would be. Beautifully carved, with a long curved blade and a hilt fashioned into the shape of intertwined roses, it had been rammed in with terrific force, sticking a full two inches into the thick wood of the door. He touched it briefly with his fingertips and felt the cold suck the heat from his hand. For just the faintest second, he could smell the rich red wine and hear the wild flutes. He tore his hand away, biting down hard onto his lip.

He paced back and forth, ignoring the occasional stares from the animals. "We'd tell someone, wouldn't we?" he asked the goat. "But who is there left to tell?"

Finally, he pushed his way out of the barn and made his way back to the cottage, where he rummaged through cupboards until he found parchment and ink. The ink was solid, of course. It hadn't been touched in a decade. The man swore and poked at the crumbling remnants with the end of a quill for a moment. He sighed and fetched a small bowl and knife, setting them on the table. He made a quick cut in one forearm, hissing at the pain, and held the small wound over the bowl as the blood began to drip. Then, dipping the pen in the fresh blood, he began to write in a tiny, cramped hand.

An hour later, he stood out in the glade once more. His arm freshly bandaged and hanging loosely by his side, as he watched the speck that was all that was visible of the bird fly out over the trees. He sighed a forlorn sigh and made his way over to retrieve the iron staff. Then, with a meticulous care he hadn't shown in years, he began to trace the path around the stones that formed the core of the ritual.

* * *

Winter passed uneventfully and gave way to an early spring. The ground began to thaw weeks before anyone really expected it. The river rose and lapped teasingly at its banks, but the light snows meant the spring thaw was not enough for it to burst them.

Devin hacked again at the ground with the pick and swore. The ground was still half-frozen and he was having a hard time making much of a dent in it. Hannah had insisted that it be done, however, and so he stood in the vegetable garden, vainly trying to turn the earth. He wasn't, it must be said, trying especially hard. The ground also wasn't, if he was honest, really all that frozen. He wanted to make the point though and he'd felt her eyes on him several times from the windows of the cottage.

It wasn't that he was deliberately deceitful. He just firmly believed that effort ought to be recognised, and if that meant slightly exaggerating the levels of effort required for a task, then that is what he would do. He'd never dream of trying it with Khorin, however. The grizzled farmer would laugh in his face and tell him to stop being so wet. Devin had learned the hard way that, given the choice, a day spent working at Hannah's chores was infinitely preferable to a day spent working with Khorin. Unless it was in the woods, of course. Some things never changed and he would still find any excuse to be under the trees.

He cast the pick aside and took up the spade, stabbing down hard and ramming the blade home with his booted foot, before turning the earth over. The wind was picking up and he decided it was time to start putting some effort in. He stabbed it down into the earth again and then turned, as the voice came over the fieldstone wall.

"What did that patch ever do to you?" Kainen asked. Winter had been good to him and he'd finally started to fill out. His gangly appearance had been muted slightly by the addition of five or six pounds.

"It's not the dirt I'm worried about," Devin said, with a nod towards the kitchen window.

Kainen nodded in understanding. "Do you think you can sneak away for a time?"

"Sneak?" Devin laughed. "From Hannah? Are you serious?"

"Good point. There's not much chance of it, is there?" Kainen leaned heavily against the wall and looked over the vegetable plot. "It looks like you've a fair amount of work here to do. I hope the soldiers haven't moved on by the time you've finished."

"Soldiers? What are you talking about?"

"Oh, didn't I mention it?" Kainen said, with feigned innocence. "There's a great troop of soldiers making their way along the road."

"What would they want to come here for?" Devin looked across the fields towards the village, as if he could see through the slight hill that blocked his view.

"Who knows? But they've got men on horseback, as well as walking troops."

"You mean infantry and cavalry," Devin corrected him.

"Whatever." Kainen dismissed him with a waved hand. "Mounted troops, infantry, and huge carts of tools and stone. Wherever they're going, they're building something big there. In the meantime, though, they're coming here." He looked meaningfully at the vegetable plot and grinned evilly. "Shame you're tied up here."

"Bastard," Devin muttered.

"Well, I can't stand around here talking to you all day." Kainen gave him a calculating look. "I wanted someone to talk to, but then I'm sure Erinn will be there, alone, looking at all the soldiers. Did I mention she'd be alone?"

Devin cursed and dropped the spade. "A real friend would have just helped me dig the garden out, you know?"

"You're right. You know, you really ought to see if you can find one of those," Kainen called back over his shoulder, as he walked away. Devin swore again and hopped over the wall.

The soldiers were visible from the top of the small rise near Devin's cottage. Though Widdengate proper was a good twenty minutes away, the line of men and carts was easily visible. Kainen and Devin walked towards the village, speculating about where the troops were heading, and then watched as they established a large camp just outside of the village itself.

Erinn wasn't easy to miss. Her red hair stood out like a beacon against the dark green grass of the freshly born spring. The tall man behind her, with his arms wrapped possessively around her, was also hard to miss but for different reasons.

Devin stopped in his tracks and looked at Kainen. "That's never Artor with her?" His words were both an incredulous question and a disbelieving statement.

"Apparently," muttered Kainen, busy looking at the soldiers. Devin shook his head silently and began walking again into the village.

"You're not truly still sweet on her?" Kainen gave his friend a calculating look.

"No!" Devin's face coloured as he glowered. "Just don't see what she sees in the dumb lummox."

"No, I know what you mean. He's not my type either," Kainen said, shooting a grin at the boy beside him, but the smile dropped from his face when Devin ignored it. "Look, Devin, she made herself clear at Midwinter, didn't she?"

"How's that, then?" Devin replied sourly.

"She's made her choice, is all," Kainen said with a shrug.

"He's not good enough for her." Devin said, with a rough edge to his voice.

"Probably not," Kainen admitted, with an honesty that he wouldn't have shown had there been anyone else there to listen. "I expect he'll fall foul of Harlen soon enough, anyway."

Devin grinned as he imagined what the barrel-chested smith would do to the arrogant miller's son if he caught him hurting his only daughter.

The soldiers were dressed in the dark blue and green of Duke Freyton. Devin gawked as they marched past in an orderly fashion. Rank after rank of men clad in hard boiled leather, and shining plate on their arms, legs and chests. A sword or spear, shield and gleaming helm finished off each uniform and Devin couldn't help but be impressed. He watched for a while, as they moved in groups of fifty or so and were directed to a clear area to make camp. He and Kainen ambled closer, looking on as the arriving men quickly stacked their weapons and worked together to erect white tents. Another group of men was busy digging latrines and the boys faltered as they were met with flat, unfriendly stares from the men.

"Hoy, you boys!" a tall man, with a slightly different uniform, called. "Be off with you!"

Turning quickly, the two made their way back to the road where they could gawk in peace.

"None too friendly, are they?" a deep voice rumbled from behind them, and they turned to find Harlen approaching the village green. "I expect they're just busy and don't want curious lads underfoot is all it is, though."

"Why are they here? Who are they?" Devin asked, glancing back to the road, as a company of cavalry arrived in a flurry of hooves.

"Freyton's men," Harlen grunted, folding his thick arms over his burn-scarred leather apron. "They're just passing through. I expect Samen would know more. He usually does. Would you two like a closer look, then?" He chuckled at their open mouths. "I ought to go and see if they need any work doing while they're here. You two can tag along, so long as you behave yourselves." He held their gaze until they both nodded.

They followed in the red-bearded smith's wake, as he made his way through the growing encampment. Harlen led them to the long line of wagons being secured at the edge of the camp, in search of the quartermaster. The man wore a slightly more embellished uniform, with green flashes on his cloak and upper sleeves, to show his higher rank. He stood directing the wagons with one hand, whilst speaking from the corner of his mouth to two sergeants. He broke off as the trio approached and looked at Harlen appraisingly. "You'd be the village smith then," he said, in greeting. "I'll probably have an order or two for you before the day's through, I expect."

"Fair enough," Harlen replied, reasonably. "Just don't leave it to the last minute. I don't like putting other things off, and I don't do rush jobs."

"A man that does things properly. That's a rare thing, these days," the quartermaster said, with approval. "Do you have a mayor or village council? The commander's going to want to talk to them later."

"Not as such," Harlen replied. "There's a council of sorts, which is the miller, the innkeeper, me, and one or two others. We make any decisions which need to be made. Why?"

"Orders from Freyton." He pulled the helm from his head and scrubbed a hand through his black hair. Despite his young face, his hair was shot through with grey. "Do you think you could gather your council together for noon-hour?"

"I expect that could be arranged, if it's important enough," Harlen grunted.

"Good man." He held out his hand and Harlen engulfed it in his burn-scarred paw. "The name's Danner," he said, as he gave a firm shake.

"Well met, Danner," Harlen replied, a rare smile cracking his red-bearded face. "Harlen," he added.

"Where shall we find you?"

"I reckon the inn's as good a place as any." Harlen nodded towards the large building. Danner's smile looked odd on his hard-bitten face, as if it wasn't quite at home there. "That's an excuse I can work with. Noon-hour, then."

"We'll be there. The innkeeper has a back room we can use." Harlen nodded once and led the boys out of the camp. "Kainen, you go and let your father know we'll be needing his room," he said, as they stopped by the inn. "Devin, you go down to the mill and let Cedril know what's going on too, would you?" With that the big man was gone without waiting for their replies.

Kainen watched the man walk away and turned to Devin. "Sounds like something major is happening."

"I'd give a lot to be in this meeting," Devin agreed, his eyes bright.

"That could be arranged, you know?" The innkeeper's son had a sly glint in his eye as a slow smile grew on his face.

"How?"

"Well, you run down to that mill and see Cedril. Assuming Artor doesn't find another excuse to pound on you, I'll let you know how when you get back."

"Artor!" Devin's face showed his dismay at the prospect.

"Haven't you two made nice yet?" Kainen spat in disgust. "It's been two months now."

"I haven't really been around him," Devin said, trying to hide his embarrassment at being caught in childish behaviour.

"Of course you haven't." Kainen didn't bother to soften his scathing tone. "It's too easy to sit and hate him from a distance, isn't it? What if he and Erinn end up together? What if they get married? Are you going to hate him then? She's one of your oldest friends, Devin."

Devin kicked at the ground and tried hard to avoid the gangly man's eyes. "You're right. I know you're right. It's just..."

"Just what?"

"I don't know. It's just...does he have to be such a massive prick?" Devin asked plaintively. Kainen stared at him for a full five seconds before bursting into laughter. "I would recommend you don't mention that if you run into him."

"I'll bear that in mind," Devin said, dryly.

The mill was on the far side of the village due to the river. Wide and slow-moving, the waterway provided a strong, steady current, but it had burst its banks during more than one spring thaw. Whilst the mill itself was unlikely to be affected by this, the village was set back a ways from it for this very reason.

The great creaking mill wheel had always been a source of fascination and Devin reflected back on the numerous afternoons the three of them had sat watching it turn ponderously as the current drove it. It took him twenty minutes to walk there, his speed not especially helped by his lack of enthusiasm.

Millers don't tend to be a popular people and Cedril fulfilled every stereotype. Devin found the fat man shaking out sacks beside the set of wooden stairs that led up into the structure. He was drenched in sweat, despite the chill in the air. There was a broad, moist line down the back of the thin shirt he wore and large damp patches under his arms. The cloth was sticking to his skin and the fat pink flesh was clearly visible through the wet fabric. He jumped slightly as Devin approached, and scowled at being surprised.

"You're Khorin's foundling, aren't you? What do you want here, boy?" He scraped his thinning, mousy hair back from his forehead with one hand.

"Harlen sent me, sir," Devin replied, as politely as he could, whilst trying not to openly grit his teeth.

"And?" The man had a whining, nasal tone to his voice that grated on Devin's nerves. Even if it weren't for his half insults and rude manner, Devin would have found it hard to like the man, based on his voice alone.

"There is a division of soldiers in the village. The commander wants to meet with the council at noon-hour at the inn," Devin explained, wishing he wasn't quite so close to the sweaty man. "Harlen sent me to fetch you."

"To *fetch* me?" Cedril's eyebrows rose. "What am I? A sheep wandered out from pasture? Fetch me indeed!"

"I apologize, sir. It was a poor choice of words on my part," Devin backtracked. "I meant to say he sent me to let you know."

"Hmmm," the fat man frowned, trying to find something wrong with that. "I see. Well, you scurry back and let them know I'll be there." He stomped his way up the wooden stairs, wheezing with each step.

Devin watched him go. The fat little man had annoyed him so much, he'd almost forgotten Kainen's plan to get them into the council meeting, although he had no idea how he would manage it.

"Devin?" a voice came from the long grass behind him, and he turned to see Artor walking towards him from the path to the village. He felt himself flush. Despite the fact that the fight they'd had at Midwinter had not been started by him, he still felt guilty for some reason. "What?" he managed, as evenly as he could.

"Did I hear you say something about a council meeting?"

"You might've done," he grunted. Where his father was short and fat, Artor was dark and tall with a strong physique. Devin had speculated on his parentage more than once.

"Where are they holding it?" Artor asked, excitement shining in his dark eyes.

His enthusiasm was contagious, and Devin forgot his awkwardness and surly attitude as he answered.

"At the inn," he offered.

"I'd give a lot to be in that." Artor grunted. "He's not likely to tell me anything." He nodded towards the mill with a grimace. Devin smiled despite himself.

"I'm sure you'll find out soon enough," he replied, unable to keep the smugness from his voice.

"What do you know?" Artor asked, suspiciously.

"Nothing," Devin's face was a picture of innocence.

"Look, Devin, I know I was a bit of a swine to you at Midwinter," Artor began. "I know we've never been friends really, but..." He walked down the steps to stand in front of Devin. "Erinn really likes you and maybe it's time we just moved past all this, hey?"

Devin looked up at the larger man and bit back a dozen responses. His hands fought to curl into fists. The miller's son was everything he despised. "Don't think I can help you there," he said meeting Artor's eyes, and walked away towards the inn.

Kainen met him behind the main building of the inn and ushered him over to a quiet corner filled with barrels where the inn met the outbuildings. "They've all gone in already," he advised, in hushed tones.

"So, what's this big secret then? How are we going to get in?" Devin said, in a hoarse whisper.

"We're not getting in," Kainen explained. "We're getting under." He grabbed one of the barrels and rolled it on its rim to move it to one side, motioning to Devin to do likewise. In a few short minutes, a low wooden hatch was revealed.

"We stopped using this a few years ago. It's too damp these days to store barrels in it for long," he explained, as he struggled with the hatch. "It does go right under the back room though, so if we're quiet, we should be able to hear a bit."

The cellar was low and Devin had to duck down to fit through the narrow hatch. He slid down the wooden ramp designed to accommodate the barrels of ale and into the darkness. Kainen followed, pulling the hatch closed behind him.

There was a soft scraping noise and a burst of sparks, as Kainen lit a small lantern, turning the flame low. It provided just enough light to show his face. He pressed his finger to his lips, calling for silence, and led the way through the cellar.

The damp was evident as they made their way through the gloom. A chill in the air and a slippery feel to the stones of the walls and wooden beams, which were enough to make them place their feet with extra caution. Noises filtered down from above, the footsteps loud enough to make Devin realise that a single noise made at the wrong time would have the two of them discovered.

Kainen led the way through the cellar, past disused racks that had once housed barrels and shaped shelves designed for wine bottles. He stopped close to the wall and pointed upwards, before cupping his ear.

They sat on the damp floor for a while and Devin began to wonder if they had wasted their time as he tried not to think about the possibility of rats. A loud set of footsteps made both of them look up and they came silently to their feet.

"Thank you all for coming together so quickly," an unknown voice carried down through the floorboards. "I won't keep you for long. I just need to inform you of our orders from Duke Freyton."

"It's no trouble, Commander," Father Trallen said, his pompous voice carrying just as clearly.

"Why don't we all take a seat?" Owen said and a scraping of chairs and muted thumps accompanied their seating themselves around the large table. Devin had been around the rooms of the inn enough times to be able to picture the room they sat in. A simple chamber, dominated by a large circular table able to seat ten or twelve, it was probably originally intended for private functions, but it had little use beyond the council meetings these days.

"To business, then," Harlen growled, as glass clinked and a liquid gurgled.

"As you probably know, the Bjornmen raids have worsened in recent years," the commander began, to a rumble of assent. "The duke has ordered that we put in a relay of beacons leading in from the coast. They've proven effective to the south in Baron Rentrew's lands, so we've been sent to put them in place here, along with forts."

"What does this have to do with us?" Cedril's voice was harsh and bordering on outright rudeness.

"That's hardly civil, Master Miller," Father Trallen said, with a reproachful tone.

"Civil or not, this is building up to something and I doubt we'll like the smell of it," Cedril snapped.

"Gentlemen, please!" Owen staved off the developing bickering. "Commander, please carry on."

"We've been ordered to put in a beacon tower on the hill near your village," the commander explained. "We're also looking for some good young men to help man it."

"It'd keep some of them out of trouble," growled Harlen.

"For a proper wage, I trust?" Cedril asked.

"Wage, uniform and training," the commander said, reassuringly. "It's not the most glamorous job in the world, but it is important and we need responsible lads for it."

"Alright. What else?" Owen sighed.

"His Grace has ordered us to fortify all of the villages within twenty leagues of the coast."

"Fortify?" asked Owen softly, in the silence that followed. "How?"

"A stone wall or wooden palisade is the usual method," the commander advised. "Widdengate is hardly ideal, however. You're a little spread out for my liking."

"We're built the way we're built." Cedril said. "Mill near the river, farms near the fields. How do you put a fence around that?"

"The only thing I can suggest is that we leave some of the outlying structures outside of the palisade," admitted the commander. "We'll have to set up some form of warning signal calling people into the village."

"The bell tower on the church might suffice," Trallen said.

"I can't say I see the need for all of this," Cedril said, scraping his chair back. "Widdengate is miles from the coast. It must be close to twenty leagues away, as it is."

"I'm just informing you of my orders," the commander said, in a tone that left no room for argument.

"Yes, but it's not you having to scurry through the dark to the village every time a boy gets drunk and sneaks in to play in the church, is it?" snapped the miller.

A silence fell for a moment, as both the men above and the boys below absorbed the information. Finally, Harlen spoke. "Who will pay for all this?"

"You're a wise man, Master Smith," the commander said. "Nothing comes for free in this life. I've not heard anything about it, but if I were you, I'd expect an extra visit from the tax collectors this year."

Harlen grunted and his chair scraped against the wooden floorboards above Devin's head. "Is there anything else?"

"I think that covers everything," the commander said, briskly. "I will place notices in the village about the recruitment. Any lad interested should come and see my sergeants before sunset this Noonday."

Devin hunched low without thinking, as the scraping of chairs indicated the end of the meeting. Dust fell from the beams above their heads and long-abandoned spider webs shook in the light of Kainen's lantern.

The sunlight burned Devin's eyes as he pushed the hatch open, but he ignored it and clambered out of the cellar. The smell of dust and damp still filled his nose and he took deep breaths of the fresh spring air to try and clear it. Kainen closed the hatch and pushed barrels back into place.

"So, it looks like we're getting our own beacon tower," Devin said with a broad grin.

"You going to try for one of the jobs?" Kainen asked, as he brushed the cobwebs from his hair.

"I'm not sure," Devin said, as he picked dust and dirt from his clothes. "It sounds good and all, but I bet it'd get awful boring before long."

"I'd wager you our friendly miller's son is one of the first in line, though," Kainen said, with a knowing smile.

"If he wants to stand guard over a bonfire, he's welcome to it." Devin spat. "That's if anyone's stupid enough to trust him with an open flame."

Chapter Ten

Klöss leaned against the tree and looked out over the bay. Ships at anchor filled the waters and the shore itself was packed with crews working on the new vessels that would become the fleet. Keels, sprouting ribs, extended out as far as he could see along the bay in either direction, and another five camps just like this dotted the shores of the surrounding islands. The morning was grey and menacing clouds hung low in the sky. The weather was a good match for his scarred and bearded face and he seemed to reflect the mood of the skies, as he glowered down at the ships. He scratched at his thick beard and rolled his shoulders inside his well-worn leathers. The wind grabbed at his long, black cloak, whipping and tossing it as it tugged at his shoulders. He grabbed at it irritably and made his way down the hillside towards the camp.

The camp was surrounded by a high wall, made of thick, sharpened poles, and a deep ditch filled with short, vicious stakes. He grunted at the guards on the gate as he strode through without challenge, and made for a long, low building at the edge of the camp. The smells of cooking food filled the air, mingling with the ever-present smell of sawdust and pitch.

The streets were not paved and the spring rains had turned them to into an oozing mess. Wooden walkways had been laid down to try and help, but they seemed to make little difference. They didn't cover everywhere, the lay of the land prevented that. Sooner or later, a man needed to cross the street and this meant trudging through the thick, clay-like mud. This, in turn, was tracked onto the walkways and by mid-morning, on any given day, the walkways were only marginally better than the streets.

The camp was busy. He didn't know why he even still thought of it as a camp. It was closer to being a small town now, with men and women bustling through the mucky streets, dressed in thick, practical clothing. There were subtle differences, though. The camp had no hawkers on the streets selling this and that. No one stopped to chat idly with friends. There were few children and those there were worked as hard as their parents. This was a camp preparing for war and it showed in a thousand tiny ways.

He stamped up a set of wooden steps and stopped to scrape the mud from his boots on an iron scraper set into the wood beside the top step, before going inside.

"Klöss!" Verig said, opening his arms wide. He was sitting at a long table, behind a huge platter of food. The man had changed in five years, turning greyer and harder. "How is my Lord of the Mud Camps, this morning?" He belched hard and wiped his mouth on his dark, leather-clad sleeve before returning to the plate in front of him.

Klöss grunted in response and went to the fireplace, lifting the kettle from its hook and shaking it experimentally to listen to the water slosh. "As well as any other day in this god-forsaken place," he muttered. He swung the kettle over the fire on the bent iron rod set into the stone fireplace.

"How do things look?" the old trainer asked, more for something to say than from any real curiosity.

"Bad. The same," Klöss said, without looking around. He rested his forearm on the stones of the chimney. "We're still behind schedule. We will only have two-thirds of the ships ready in time, at this rate. It's all I need."

"You wanted it, Klöss," Verig reminded him, drinking deeply from a tankard.

Klöss grunted again and then looked curiously at the man. "What is that? Mead?" The older man nodded and smiled. "It's barely past sun up, man!"

"You sound like you have a point, Klöss," Verig said, with dark eyes. "Were you planning on making it?"

"Just don't let it interfere with the training, is all," Klöss said quickly. "My uncle is due here today to inspect things and, given the state of the fleet, the last thing I need is men who aren't ready either."

"Listen to yourself, man. You're whining like a petulant child," Verig said, his voice stern. "You asked for this post. Badgered him for a month or more, if I recall rightly. Though why you'd want to give up a decent reaver and crew to sit in a muddy camp is beyond me."

"Because, Verig, here in this muddy camp, he has me. On the reaver, all he has is sweaty men," a soft voice carried in from the doorway.

"That's a good reason to go to a muddy camp, Ylsriss," Verig said, unruffled by her nearly silent entrance. "Not a good reason to stay there, though."

"You have too little soul in you, Verig," the willowy blonde said, as she moved behind Klöss to wrap her arms around him. The thin, grey dress clung to her body beneath the thick fur-lined cloak she wore and the swell of her belly was just starting to show. It wouldn't have done, if the dress had been slightly less clingy. Verig was almost glad when she pressed herself to Klöss's back. Some things you shouldn't be caught looking at.

"You're not the first to say that, Ylsriss," the small man said easily. "The New Dayers seem to say it all the time." He turned back to Klöss. "Are you sure letting them in the camp was a good idea? I mean, I understand bringing the women, but priests? Really?"

"She's right, Verig," said Klöss, with a dry chuckle "You do have too little soul in you." He disentangled himself from Ylsriss gently and went to the fireplace to pull the hissing kettle from the fire. "Luckily, you have the finest sword skills I've ever seen. I'll take that and let the priests worry about your soul." He busied himself with kettle, ground leaves and cups for a moment, before handing a steaming mug to Ylsriss. "Nettle, I'm afraid," he said, with a wink. "As for the priests, Verig," he said, blowing on his own cup, "the men need something to take their minds off where we are and what we do. Not every man is as lucky as I am, or as soulless as you."

Verig grunted and drank deeply from his tankard, before thumping it down on the table and pushing his chair back as he stood. "Well, I suppose I ought to be turning these downy-faced lads into something more than walking targets," he said.

"As a once downy-faced lad, I know they'll appreciate it some day," Klöss said, with a tired grin. "Just probably not today."

"Definitely not today," Verig said, with an evil glint in his eye, and left.

"He's a bad man, rich boy," Ylsriss said, in a low voice.

"You haven't called me that in years," he chuckled. "As for bad men, sometimes I think we all are." He turned to her as a thought struck him. "What are you doing this morning?"

"I'll have to check my calendar," Ylsriss replied, with a straight face. "There is so much to occupy a lady's time here."

Klöss ignored that. "I need to walk through the shipyards and speak to the work crews. Would you like to come?"

"And miss the opportunity to wade through all that sludge?" She smiled her crooked smile. "Not for all the stars in the sky!"

He set his half-empty cup down on the table and moved towards the door. "What? Now?" she said, as he laughed and held the door open for her.

The sun was bright, but carried little heat, as it peeked through the hazy clouds, and the breeze coming in from the sea brought a wet chill along with it. It was a welcome breeze, however, as the camp always seemed to have the lingering stink of burning pitch about it. They huddled into their cloaks, as they walked along the wooden walkways towards the edge of the camp. The distant noises of the shipyard drifted up to them, mingling with the ever-present ringing from the smithy.

"Was what Verig said true?" Ylsriss asked, after a few minutes.

"About what?" Klöss replied, in a distracted fashion, as he scowled out at the distant waves.

"About you asking to come here." Ylsriss replied, with a dangerous lilt in her voice.

"Oh. That."

"Yes. That."

"Yes, I did." Klöss replied, shortly. "It's a big thing Uncle Aiden intends to do. I want to be a part of it."

"And you will be," Ylsriss said firmly. "He'd not likely leave his most successful Shipmaster out of his scheme. But why this?" She waved her hand vaguely at the camp and distant shipyard.

He looked around and frowned.

"What's wrong, Klöss? You've been in a foul mood for days," she demanded.

"It's just not possible!" he burst out, stabbing a finger at the shipyards. "We're falling further and further behind, and I just can't see a solution. Frostbeard wants the ships and men to be ready in three months, and he just doesn't seem to see a problem with that. I had to build the camp from nothing, harvest the lumber and get Gareth to design the landers. There simply wasn't enough time."

"Why don't you just tell him, then?" Ylsriss replied, reasonably.

"Because he doesn't damned well listen!" Klöss exploded. "He doesn't see it. I only have so many men. I needed them all to harvest the lumber and build the camp. Then I needed to get the ships built as fast as possible. I couldn't have them harvesting lumber and training to be halfway decent oarsmen at the same time."

"So what have you done?" she asked, in a small voice.

"I've let the ships suffer," he admitted. "We're only going to have two in three of them ready in time."

He stepped off the end of the walkway and led her along a shingle path running alongside the beach. Almost the entire shoreline of the bay had been transformed into a shipyard, with space only spared for the docks. The huge boats were in various stages of construction. Some were waiting to be moved down towards the sea on the massive log rollers. Others were little more than skeletons, with just the keel and bare ribs completed.

Workmen scurried around the bones of the ships like so many ants. Massive cranes worked to move the huge beams into place, while ponies walked docilely inside the large wooden wheels that drove the winches.

Klöss spotted a grey-haired man standing high on the deck of one of the ships that looked close to completion. He held his arm high as he hailed him. "Gareth!"

The man looked across and raised a hand in greeting, before turning back to the men he was talking to. Some of his long, grey hair was tied at the nape with a simple leather thong, but most of it had come loose and whipped wildly about his face in the wind.

As they drew closer, Gareth waved his arms at the men, his whole air one of frustration. His shouts could be heard through the wind, though the words could not. He climbed nimbly down one of several ladders leaning against the sides of the hulking ship and made his way over to meet them, adjusting the large rolls of parchment he carried under one arm.

"My Lord Campmaster," he said formally, offering a slight nod of the head that could have grown up to become a bow, had it had slightly more ambition. He turned to Ylsriss and the bow bucked its ideas up as he greeted her. "my lady."

"I'm not a lady, Gareth," Ylsriss said, with a wicked smile. "And I'm certainly not yours." She placed a hand on her stomach and gave Klöss a meaningful look.

"Gareth, I've asked you not to do that," Klöss muttered. "I'm no more a lord than you are. If you must call me something, call me Shipmaster. At least that implies I go somewhere. This camp seems to be going nowhere!"

The grey-haired man responded with a tight grin.

"Tell me you have some good news for me, old man," Klöss said, his eyes showed his worry and plead more urgently than his voice.

"Nothing's changed, Shipmaster," Gareth said, without apology. "I told you six weeks ago that we needed more men."

"And I explained to you then that you couldn't have them," Klöss said, as his face grew hard. "I told you to find a way to get the work done with what you had."

"I can't work miracles, Klöss," the man said firmly. "I've done the best I could with what I was given and if that's not good enough for you or your uncle, you need to find another wright."

"Is that a threat, Gareth?" Klöss said, his eyes turning flat and hard. "You'd walk out on me and on this?"

"No. I'm just saying you need to tell Frostbeard to be more realistic."

"You can tell him yourself," Klöss snapped. "He'll be here in a few hours."

"He's coming here?" The old man's face paled visibly.

"Yes, so I hope you can understand why I might be a little short." Klöss ran a hand through his hair and swore under his breath.

"Children, please. Can't you play nicely?" Ylsriss said, cheerfully, drawing dark looks from both of them and smiling a sunny smile back.

Klöss sucked air in through his teeth as he turned back to the old shipwright. "Alright," he breathed out explosively. "Tell me what we do have."

It was nearing sunset as the ship came into sight. Klöss stood on the end of the docks with Ylsriss beside him. Gareth stood slightly behind them as they waited. The reaver was still some distance away, but the man stood in the prow was still recognisable over the water. The years pressed down upon him but Frostbeard stood tall, resplendent in his leathers and shining breastplate, his blue cloak streaming out behind him.

"Bloody old poser," muttered Verig behind him and Klöss had to fight to keep from laughing as the reaver came in to dock.

The old raider leapt onto the dock before the first hawser had been tied, and grabbed Klöss up in a rough embrace. "You're getting more of your uncle's good looks the older you get, my boy," Aiden laughed as he stepped back to look at him. "You've a lovely collection of sticks on this beach, Klöss." He waved expansively towards the shipyard. "I have to tell you though, I was hoping for some ships."

Klöss gave a sick smile and ushered his uncle towards the camp. "Let's go somewhere we can talk."

Klöss's quarters were nothing extravagant. Other men in his position might have insisted on grander accommodation, but the log cabin he shared with Ylsriss was simple, at best. It consisted of just a living area and a bedroom, and the main room was taken up by a long, wooden table, which was half-covered in maps and parchments. He ushered the seamaster inside and quickly filled a tankard with strong honey mead, passing it to him before getting one for himself.

"I don't think I know you, do I?" Aiden said, looking curiously at Ylsriss, as he sat back in a wooden chair at the table. She stared in shock at the white-bearded man and then at Klöss.

"You didn't *tell* him?" she asked, through clenched teeth.

"I've been a little busy, Ylsriss" Klöss said.

"Obviously," Aiden said, looking admiringly at Ylsriss and then pointedly at her swelling midriff.

"I'm Ylsriss," she said, with a warm smile, before Klöss could make introductions. "Your nephew has told me a great deal about you. It's interesting to finally see the man. It brings a different side to the stories you hear in taverns and the like."

"And you frequent taverns a lot, do you?" Aiden replied, with a grin.

"Not so as much as I'd like," she replied. unabashed.

Aiden laughed uproariously. "You've picked a fine one here, Klöss," he grinned and raised his tankard to Ylsriss in mock salute.

"What makes you think *he* picked *me*?" Ylsriss said with a wicked smile. Aiden's eyes widened and he lurched from the table as he fought to keep from spraying his mouthful across the room. Klöss groaned and ran his hands through his hair.

Aiden walked across to the window as he chuckled, wiping mead from his beard. He stared in silence out of the window for a moment. When he turned back to the table, all traces of humour had gone. The man that walked back to the table was not the friendly uncle, laughing and flirting with Ylsriss. This man was all business, and his eyes were ice as he sat again.

"Send your woman away, Klöss. We need to talk." His voice was flat. Hard. Klöss felt Ylsriss stiffen beside him, but she stood without a word and walked quickly to the door. Aiden waited until she had closed it behind her before he began.

"So. You're behind, that much is obvious. How bad is it?" His voice was level, calm. The lack of emotion was even more disturbing than if he'd been slamming his fist on the table and screaming into Klöss's face.

"I'd say we're going to hit two in every three, Seamaster," Klöss said firmly, refusing to let himself be cowed.

"Two in three," the old man muttered. "Both ships and men?" He grunted as Klöss nodded and gazed across the room to the small window in silence.

"You assured me you could handle this task, Klöss," he said, in a quiet voice. "I passed over several men in favour of you, because you sought me out and pursued it. You made it clear that you wanted this."

"I did," Klöss said, simply.

"I sent you here with the best men I could offer you. You had engineers, carpenters and shipwrights. I even sent you Verig." His voice was still low and even. "What do you have to say for yourself, boy?"

"You asked for the impossible, Shipmaster." Klöss said, fighting to maintain his calm. "To establish this camp, work on the ships and get the men trained in the time you allowed was simply not possible. I needed either more men or more time, and you've given me neither." He grabbed the bench below the level of the table and squeezed, trying to hold his temper in check.

"I sent you reports, Frostbeard. Hell, I sent you letters directly with the supply ships, explaining what the issues were. You never replied, not once."

Aiden sat silently, his eyes locked on Klöss's face. The only sign of emotion was a slight twitching of his lip, as Klöss's voice began to rise.

"You knew I was falling behind and still you ignored my messages. Damn it, old man, you've set me up to fail!" He slammed his hand down onto the table at the last, three months of frustration forced into a single blow. Klöss sat slowly. He hadn't even realised he had stood until he'd found himself leaning over the table. His heart was racing and his chest heaved. He forced himself to meet Frostbeard's eyes, waiting for the tirade. The man's gaze dropped to the table, and the reports and piles of parchment, then a dry chuckle slipped past his lips.

Klöss looked on in confusion, as the old man's shoulders shook and tears began to roll down his cheeks. Eventually, as Frostbeard began to pound on the table, he snapped.

"What?" Klöss roared. "What is so damned funny about all of this?"

"Two in three," Aiden wheezed. "You've managed two in three." He grabbed up his mead and took a drink, clearing his throat. "I never expected anybody could achieve more than one in two!"

"What?" Klöss frowned, confusion plain on his scarred face. "You expected me to fail? Well, why the hell didn't you send more men?"

"You've got it all wrong, Klöss, you haven't failed. You've performed better than I could ever have hoped." He laughed as the confusion on Klöss's face deepened. "I knew you'd strive for this. You chased me for a good two months, badgering me for this command. I knew you were hungry for it." He smiled a cold smile. "So I decided to see just how far you could go when pushed."

"You mean..." He cut off as understanding dawned.

"You probably passed what I expected you to achieve a month ago," Frostbeard admitted.

"You miserable old bastard!" Klöss breathed.

"Well, yes," the old seamaster admitted. "Frostbeard isn't the only thing I've been called over the years." He grinned again. This time, Klöss managed to crack a smile himself.

"Why don't you run and find that woman of yours." Aiden suggested. "I owe her an apology for being so rude and it looks like we have a few things to celebrate. Drag Verig out of the training halls as well, if you've a mind to."

* * *

Klöss was breaking his fast on cheese and the remnants of the last night's chicken when Aiden thumped on his door. The sun was just barely over the horizon and the sea had that silvery sheen it gets in the early morning light. He opened the door quietly, so as not to wake Ylsriss, and saw his uncle on the step. Despite the early hour, the man looked fresh and had clearly been awake for some time.

"It's time to talk about the next steps," Aiden said, not bothering with a greeting. Klöss glanced into the cabin without thinking and Aiden nodded in understanding. "Get your cloak, we'll go for a walk."

The shipyards were quiet, the only sounds the mournful calls of sea birds and the crunching of the pebbles under their feet.

"I've still not forgiven you," Klöss said, as they stopped beside the hull of a ship.

"I imagine you'll get over it in time," Aiden replied, smiling slightly as he patted the thick beams. "Besides, it worked. You'd never have got these results if I'd told you the real targets."

Klöss grunted, unconvinced.

"Do you remember your first raid?" the old man asked, suddenly.

"It's not something I'm likely to forget," Klöss replied. "It was a bloodbath. We lost fifty men or more on that reaving. The soldiers came from nowhere."

"Not nowhere," Aiden corrected. "They were warned."

"Warned by who?" Klöss asked, sharply. "Who could have known we were coming?"

"We've been reaving those lands for twenty years, since I first found them. We've never run into anything close to that level of defence," Aiden said, a faraway look in his eyes. "We can't continue in the face of that. There hasn't been a proper reaving in the Farmed Lands for two years now."

"So that's why?"

"That's why we need the fleet. We're not going to raid, we're going to take the lands ourselves. But you're no fool, Klöss, you knew that."

Klöss nodded. "It's obvious you planned something on a large scale. The landers alone..."

"We were caught with our britches down on that raid of yours. We'd never had to face more of a defence than a handful of farmers with pitchforks, so why would we expect beacons? We can't let that happen again," Aiden said, as he met Klöss's eyes.

"So what are you saying?" Klöss asked, scratching his beard.

"We need to scout the landing area and the lands surrounding it." Aiden admitted.

"Scout?" Klöss turned to face him, his eyes wide. "It's a damned long way to send a small party like that. Getting through the Vorstelv alone means you'd need a larger ship."

"I know. We'd need to send a galley reaver. That's not the worst of it, either."

"Tell me," Klöss said, with a resigned sigh.

"A reaver couldn't sit at anchor waiting for a team to return. It'd be seen." Aiden said. "It couldn't sit further out either. There's too much risk of a fishing boat or something passing, and it'd need too many supplies."

"So what would it do?"

"It would need to go through the Vorstelv, leave the scouts and then return."

Aiden looked out over the bay.

"Leave them there?" Klöss was aghast. There was something about the prospect of being cut off in a foreign land that repelled him at the deepest level.

"And then return for them in a month or two, yes," Aiden said.

"Who were you thinking of?" Klöss knelt and picked up a handful of stones and walked towards the distant surf.

"I was hoping you might have a few ideas," Aiden called, as he watched the younger man walk off.

Klöss turned to face the seamaster, walking backwards over the pebbles. "No, you weren't. You were hoping I'd volunteer."

"Well, would you really trust it to anyone else?" Aiden said, with a grin.

"Ylsriss would kill me, you realise." Klöss warned, as he turned and threw a stone out into the surf.

"One of the reasons I've never married," the old man laughed, following his nephew. "Look, I'm not going to force you to go. We could pick someone else."

"I can sense a but..?" Klöss leaned into the next throw, whipping it out, skimming the stone across the waves.

"Well, there are very few I'd trust with this, Klöss. You, Verig. A handful of others." Aiden came to stand beside the man. They watched as the small waves broke over the shingle.

"So you plan to send us all," Klöss finished for him. He paused and threw the rest of the stones into the surf. "When?"

"In a week or so. For now, continue to prepare the troops and ships. We need to be ready in three months. A month after you get back, I want to be ready to sail."

* * *

"You're doing *what*?" Ylsriss said, folding her arms over the sheet she had wrapped around herself.

"It's the only way, Ylsriss," Klöss explained. "We have to scout the landing site if there is to be any chance of success."

"I understand that, you fool." She climbed out of the bed and stormed into the small kitchen. "What I don't understand is why it has to be you."

"There are only a few people that he trusts to get the job done properly." Klöss stood and followed her across the small cabin. He reached out and grasped her shoulder gently, but she jerked herself away.

"Don't touch me!" she hissed, and moved away from him to face the wall.

"What?" His voice was incredulous. "You knew this was going to happen, Ylsriss. There's a war coming! You know that better than most."

"That's different," her voice was strange, tight.

"How is it different?"

"I don't know!" She spun round and he was shocked to see tears on her cheeks. In the years he'd known her, she'd always been the fierce, controlled woman who had once held him down with a knife to his throat. He'd never seen her lose control, seen emotion like this.

"Are you crying?" he asked, regretting it instantly.

"Of course I'm crying, you great damned idiot," she snapped. "You've gone and gotten me with child, and now I cry all the time. You needn't think I'm crying about you!"

"Oh." He didn't know how to respond to that and was suddenly acutely aware of his nakedness. For some reason, being naked in the kitchen with a woman in tears seemed very wrong.

"Klöss, yesterday I cried because I dropped butter." She threw her arms in the air, pulling the sheet tight against her body.

"I'll be back before you get used to having me gone," he said, rubbing her arms.

"What makes you think I want you back?" She sniffed and rubbed her eyes. "You get in the way and mess up the place."

"Is that how it is?" he said, playfully.

"Just because you're naked in the kitchen doesn't mean you can charm me, rich boy." She stepped back away from his growing smile. "You just keep your distance, I've learned what happens when you get too close." She gestured towards her stomach through the sheet.

"You weren't complaining at the time," he said with a smile.

"You just keep telling yourself that," she shot back. "When do you leave?"

"In a few days." He moved back to the bed and pulled back the furs. The cabin was definitely too cold to be naked in for long. "Time enough to get provisions, and make plans with Verig and Tristan."

"Verig and Tristan," she muttered. "At least you should stay in one piece, provided you can avoid the ale barrel. Who else are you taking?"

"I'm not sure. That's why I need to talk to Verig," he admitted.

"So why are you still here, then?" she asked, cocking an eyebrow.

"Well," he replied, drawing the word out and shooting a less than subtle glance at the bed. "I was hoping that..." He left it hanging.

"Oh no, rich boy!" she smiled sweetly. "You're far too busy for that. You have planning to do. Off you go now." She made shooing motions towards the door, then grabbed his clothes from the floor and tossed them at his chest.

* * *

The small boat cut through the waves in the darkness. The night held just the barest sliver of moon, and the light it shed was only just enough to turn the darkness from pitch-black, despite the faint reflection in the water. Klöss hauled at his oar, reaching forward to tap the back of the man in front, before leaning back into the next stroke. He was gratified to feel the tap on his own back was less than a second out from his own motion. Rowing at night was difficult and rowing in silence made it worse, but it could be managed.

The surf was a silvery line in the distance, the moonlight catching the white foam as it hit the beach. The cliffs, oddly, didn't reflect the faint light and appeared as a dark wall in the night. The boat finally crunched softly into the small pebbles and he leapt out with the others to haul the ship up out of the waves.

They'd scouted the coast carefully, in a small boat dressed with nets and fishing gear, several times over the last few days, before picking this beach. Working as silently as possible, they carried the boat up to the cliffs, pressing it hard up against the rock face, and covering it with a tarpaulin, sand and bushes. It would never pass close inspection and it was doubly hard to be sure that it was well-concealed in the dark, but the boat would be hidden from a casual glance.

The six men took up their packs and weapons, and Klöss led them along the base of the cliffs towards the path they had spotted days earlier. He stopped at the top of the path and motioned the men closer, hunkering down and speaking softly. "You all know the plan and our purpose. We will meet here on the second full moon. Work to avoid any contact but also make sure no word of our presence survives. If it comes to it, remember no one must be taken alive." The men nodded in the gloom and split into two groups of three, one heading north over the clifftop, the other inland to the west.

Klöss, Verig and Tristan travelled through the darkness, until they found a tight copse of beech trees to make camp in.

"We'll rest here for a few hours and then move on," Klöss said, sighing as he sank down to the dirt.

"He's getting old," Verig muttered to Tristan. "Tired out after a little row in the evening. That woman must have worn him out before his time."

"A sad thing," Tristan replied, ignoring the look Klöss was giving him.

"If you two are quite finished?" Klöss said, shortly. "I'll watch for an hour, then you, Verig."

Tristan and Verig wrapped their cloaks about them and were soon dozing, with their heads on their packs. Klöss sat listening to the wind in the leaves and thinking how different it was to be back in this place. They'd landed far to the north this time, but it was the same land where he'd watched his training class being decimated by soldiers. It had been a long time ago and he wondered if the place had changed as much as he had. Before long, he found himself nodding off and forced himself to stand up in the blackness. He moved out of the copse, so as not to awaken the others and began to pace quietly.

It felt odd to be among so many trees and so much grass. The Barren Isles were a rocky place and so there was little grass to be found. All arable land was already used for farming and so any place grass would grow was either used for crops or pasture for sheep and goats. He'd had little cause to travel outside of Hesk much. There were any number of small towns but they tended to be mostly fishing villages or the occasional farming community. His only real experience of woodlands and greenery came from reavings.

He wondered idly what life would be like for those that came to settle here. Would Ylsriss want to come to this new land? Would he? His thoughts were disturbed by the sound of Verig rousing himself and crunching through the bushes towards him.

"Your turn to get some sleep, Klöss," his old trainer whispered.

"I expected to have to kick you," Klöss replied, in a soft voice.

"I didn't sleep. Not really," Verig muttered.

"Nerves?" Klöss's eyes widened. "You? I'd have thought that after all this time…"

"No. I still get nervous. You should too," Verig advised. "It's your body's way of telling you that what you're doing is a damned stupid idea, so you better pay attention."

Klöss chuckled quietly and squeezed the man's shoulder, before seeking his own pack to lay his head on.

Morning came too quickly, and Klöss woke to the sound of Tristan and Verig packing up and making ready to leave. He drank quickly from the skin, and grabbed a quick bite of dried fruits and ship's biscuit before grabbing his pack and making his way out of the copse.

The dawn had just passed, and the early spring air was crisp enough to clear his head and chase away the cobwebs. Still, it was a shock when he saw the tower in the distance. It was a small squat thing, positioned close to the edge of the cliffs where they jutted out into the sea. From where he stood, he could just make out the surrounding wall, clearly still under construction.

"How, in the name of all that's holy, did we miss that?" He pointed at the tower and looked across at the other two.

"It was dark," Tristan shrugged. "They had no lights."

Klöss bit back choice words and turned back to the tower. It was set back from the edge of the cliff just enough that it would be hard to see from the sea itself. The ground rose immediately before it, on an incline ending at the cliff's edge. It would be hidden from anyone aboard a ship.

"Verig, you remember the fire on the cliff during my first training raid?" he said slowly, receiving a confused nod in response. "I think they've gone a bit further than that here."

"Signal tower." Verig nodded. "Yeah, that makes sense. It's in a good position." He scanned the horizon inland for a few moments, before pointing sharply. "There! There's the next one. It's a chain."

"A chain?" Tristan said, clearly confused.

"A signal chain," Verig said, and then sighed at the blank look. "A beacon. The tower here will have men keeping watch over the sea. They see invaders coming and light their beacon." He turned and pointed again. "The men in that one see the fire and light their own, and so it goes on. It could stretch for miles."

"There must be a garrison not too far off, or a fort or something, though," Klöss mused.

"Probably in a central location so they can respond to other beacons. I doubt they are that close." Verig chewed at his lip as he stared at the tower. "That thing would be burning long before the landers ever got near the beach. I'd bet they have a spyglass or something, as well. They can probably see for miles."

Klöss looked more closely at the tower, paying attention to the details. It was not that large, just a small stone building, really, with a platform on top, presumably for the signal fire. He couldn't see it from where he was standing. The entrance must be on another side, but the stone walls looked new and well made. The approach itself was either by means of a thin and winding road that snaked back and forth as it rose up the hill, or over steep but open ground.

"I'd not want to attack it, though," Tristan said, echoing Klöss's unspoken thoughts.

"It doesn't matter anyway," Verig said, pointing at the distant tower on the horizon. "That's the one we want. That or one beyond it. We've no chance of taking this place by ourselves and any ships would be spotted on the way to land if we left it until the fleet attacked." His face was grim as he faced the others. "We need to leave this one alone. Let them light their fire as we land. If the chain is broken further on, the signal goes nowhere. I say, we follow the line of beacons and see if we can find one that's less well protected."

Klöss nodded and shrugged his pack into a more comfortable position. "We may as well get started then."

The clifftop tower had a road built for its approach but it travelled in the wrong direction so they were forced to hike across country. The terrain looked fairly flat, but the long grass was deceptive and the way was full of hidden ditches and mounds. After a few hours, Klöss could feel his legs burning and his head ached from lurching unexpectedly into holes. Tristan was offering an almost constant stream of complaints. Verig, Klöss noticed, was neither suffering nor complaining.

The small copse of trees they had slept within the previous night was one of the few sheltered places on the broad plain, although a dense wood stood some distance away to the south. Klöss gave the wood more than one passing glance as they travelled, remembering a different time here. A time when he was fleeing through the trees with Tristan and Dallan in tow. A time when the blood rushed in his ears as he battled not to give in to terror, and the temptation to just stop and hide.

The plain eventually gave way to woodland and, before night fell, they had made camp amongst the trees, not far from a small stream. Tristan surprised them all by producing fish hooks and line and, after a time, fresh fish to eat, which he cooked on sticks positioned over the well-concealed firepit. Verig scouted through the trees, returning with large forest mushrooms which he baked on stones beside the fire. Supplemented with some of the dried fruit from their packs, it proved to be a pleasant meal and not something Klöss had expected.

Verig eyed him and gave a small smile. "The trick is to take the small pleasures when you can find them, Klöss." He sighed and picked at his teeth with a vicious-looking dagger.

"We will reach the next tower tomorrow, most likely," Tristan said, as he pawed through his pack. He pulled out a folded square of parchment and a thin charcoal stick, and began tracing their progress. Klöss watched him curiously, before pointing to the coastline. "Did you do this from the boat?"

Tristan didn't bother to look up but nodded. "Whilst you were admiring the pretty cliffs and looking for a beach to play on." He folded the map carefully and tucked it into his pack, before squinting up at the darkening sky. "I will do first watch. We move at first light, yes?"

Klöss looked to Verig but the small man was already tucked into his cloak and bedroll. He turned back to Tristan and nodded curtly, before rolling into his cloak himself.

The morning brought a drizzle that woke Klöss long before Verig could wake him for the final watch. The soft rain misted onto the leaves of the trees and collected there, before dripping down. Klöss started awake when a very fat and very cold raindrop splashed onto the small part of his neck that was exposed. Enough of it ran down his neck to make him shiver and twist to swat at his neck as he lurched up into a seated position. Across the small clearing, Verig laughed softly as he oiled his sword with a linen cloth.

Klöss moved over to him. Verig had hung his cloak and blanket between two branches to make an effective shelter against the rain. It was not yet light but not entirely dark either and Klöss reasoned it was shortly before dawn. "You ought to have woken me sooner."

Verig shrugged in the half-light. "I didn't feel like sleeping. You might as well get the rest, if I'm not going to."

"Something bothering you?" Klöss said, as he pulled out his own sword and held his hand out for Verig's oil-soaked rag.

"Something, but I couldn't say what." Verig grunted, passing the rag across. "You up for good now?"

Klöss stretched his neck, rolling his head around in a circle to work the kinks out of his shoulders. "I expect so. Tristan is the only one likely to sleep in this." He held his hand up, as if to catch the raindrops.

"Well, I'll be buggered if I'm going to sit in the wet while he snores." Verig snorted and pulled himself to his feet. He marched over to Tristan, who was wrapped in his cloak and blankets close to the base of a thick fir tree, and planted his foot firmly in his side. "Wake up, princess."

Tristan mumbled something indecipherable. The words were indistinct but the tone made it clear that it whatever he had said was not flattering. "Yours is not the face I want to see waking me up in the morning, Verig," he finally managed, as he wiped his face and ground his eyes with the heels of his hands.

"I'm crushed." Verig said, shaking out his blanket and rolling it up into his pack. "Next time, I'll get Klöss to kick you."

Tristan sniggered as he loaded his pack. He unhooked the large arbelest from the back of it and Klöss gave him a quizzical look as they set off.

"I am sick of this dried stuff," he said, holding up a chunk of dried fruit. "If I am lucky, we can eat some meat tonight." He hefted the large weapon with one hand.

"Anything you shoot with that thing will be in too many pieces to eat!" Verig scoffed, as they set off through the trees.

Their pace was slow as they made their way through the woods, but by the second day, they had joined the road and moved steadily inland. They were forced to flee the path several times, as travellers passed. Whilst Verig knew a smattering of the language, possibly enough to get by, they were clearly not from this land.

The second signal beacon proved to be surrounded by a small garrison. They spent several tense hours skirting around the area, as Tristan marked their route on his map. The terrain became steep and rugged beyond the beacon, and the trees fell away as they made their way into the foothills. The next signal tower was just visible on the horizon, perched on a barren hilltop protruding from the woods.

Klöss trudged over the rocky ground in silence. His stomach was gnawing at him again and he was in a foul humour. The tower seemed no closer to him, although he could now see that, unlike the first two beacons, it was not made from stone.

"Klöss!" Tristan called again, his irritation thick and clear in his voice.

"Hmm? What?" He stopped and turned. Tristan had stopped some distance behind him and was crouched down, sketching, his map braced on the back of his pack.

"I do not think there is profit in this."

"What are you talking about?" He stared at him.

"He means 'benefit', I think," Verig said. "He's right, there's no need to get any closer. We only came to scout and we've done that. Frostbeard will need a way to stop this signal and we've mapped it out for him."

"Shouldn't we check to see how many troops are there?" Klöss objected.

Verig shook his head quickly. "No. Absolutely not. Our job now is to get out of here as quickly and safely as possible. This map is more important than anything else."

"I don't know, Verig. I don't like leaving the job half-done."

"It's done," The small man said, firmly. "We're leaving. Besides Ylsriss is going to kill you, anyway. You don't need more danger out here. You have enough at home."

"Fine," Klöss sighed and turned, walking down the rocky hillside towards home and the fleet that waited for them.

* * *

He sat in the cottage, on a simple wooden chair, and watched the sun through the window, as it went down over the clearing. It was the last night before the new moon, but he knew they would come again. They had come every night for the past week and a half, and so, with a growing sense of dread, he sat, and watched, and waited.

The sun sank beneath the treetops and all too soon the moon began to rise, casting a thin, pale light over the ground that seemed to leech the colour from everything it touched. The first few nights, he'd sat in the gloom, not wanting to attract undue attention. He'd since learned that this didn't make a difference and he refused to huddle in the darkness, so now every lamp was burning and the fire was built high. And he watched. And he waited.

They came as soon as the moonlight finally filled the glade, when the sliver of moon was high in the sky. They stepped out of nothingness, close to the monolith at the centre of the circle. He watched from the window, sucking in his breath through clenched teeth as he saw not one, but three of them, arrive. The first was tall and pale, the second darker, shorter and with a hateful glint in its eyes. The last was darker still with fur that looked black, even in the moonlight, and a long curled beard.

They danced in delight around the stones and one trilled a tune on his pipes that he could hear clearly inside the cottage. Then their heads turned as one, as if he'd made some noise and their eyes met through the glass. In a flash they had drawn long horn knives and hurled themselves at the cottage. The ground had been well prepared with tiny spikes and iron filings. He'd made a special point of doing it during the previous week. They screeched as they got close, blue fire exploding from under their hooves, and leapt backwards, screaming hate at him in their strange lyrical tongue.

He watched for a time, flinching whenever they flung themselves towards the cottage, but never once did they get any closer than three good, man-sized strides away. His fear faded after a while and he gazed openly through the window at them. They circled this way and that, the lightest-coloured one capering in a mad dance and occasionally singing, its voice a rich tenor. He lost sight of the short one after the first five minutes. The darkest one, though, stood stock-still, facing the window, and glaring at him with eyes full of hate as it stroked its beard in thought.

It stepped forward slowly, probing at the ground with its hoof as it moved. It hissed in pain as the blue fire flared, but did not move back. Instead, it crouched down and examined the ground, poking at it lightly with a gnarled finger to make it flare again. Looking up, it caught his eye in the window and smiled.

The man shivered and drew back from the window. "It's okay. It's fine. They can't step on that ground. They can't get in," he muttered, reassuring himself. He forced himself to leave the window and made his way to the tiny kitchen, putting the black iron kettle onto the woodstove to boil. "A nice drink will help," he whispered. "Why am I whispering?" he whispered again and burst into laughter. After a moment, he stopped abruptly as he heard himself. His laugh had been high and hysterical. "Control in all things," he said in a low voice. "Who am I trying to fool?" he snorted and went to a small cupboard against the wall and rummaged around until he pulled out a dusty, dark brown bottle. It was two-thirds full and hadn't been touched in a decade. The corked top came free easily enough though, and the strong aroma of the spirit filled the little cabin instantly.

"Medicinal," he whispered and took a gulp.

For a while, he was able to shut it out. There was no way to actually tell the time in the cottage. He'd had a mechanical timepiece years ago, but it had never been consistent anyway. He'd kept it mostly for the tick. All he could hear now was the occasional flare of the iron, as the satyr got too close to the cottage. He'd give anything to hear that tick right now.

He had just tipped the bottle up for another long swallow when a massive crash filled the cottage. The wall shook and he dropped the bottle to the floor, where it bounced on the wooden floorboards, spinning and spilling the rich brandy out. He let loose a whimper of pure terror and scurried to the window. He peered through it, his eyes slowly adjusting to the darkness. A large branch lay close to the window. If he pressed his face to the glass, he could just see the mark on it, where it had struck the wall. He scanned his limited view for the satyrs, but he couldn't find them in the darkness. He raced to the other window and peered out, but the clearing was still.

"Damn them," he muttered and moved back to his chair. A spreading pool of brandy lay under it and the cottage was thick with the smell. He swore again and went to the kitchen to fetch a cloth. Then the scream came.

It was high-pitched and piteous, a scream of absolute agony, but clearly not human. He thought for just long enough to hope that it might be one of the satyrs themselves, and then he heard the frantic sounds of the other animals. The panicked screeching of the chickens joining with the sounds of the other animals in a sickening harmony of terror and pain.

Without really thinking about it, he rushed to the door of the cabin and wrenched it open. At the last second, he caught the frame and held himself, one foot hanging across the threshold, as three dark figures raced across the clearing towards him. The satyrs launched themselves into the air, throwing themselves at the doorway, their eyes glowing in the moonlight and their teeth bared.

He scrambled back into the cabin, losing his balance and landing hard on his rump, as he slammed the door with one desperate kick. Bright blue fire flared outside, and he could see the light shining through the gap in the door frame. He scurried backwards, crab fashion, until he felt the wooden wall pressing hard against his back.

The screams of the satyrs filled his ears and then there was silence.

He forced himself to leave the wall and step over to the window again. He was six feet from it when the glass shattered. An object smashed through it, crashing to the floor, and spraying liquid and glass everywhere. Screaming, he threw his arms up against the flying glass to protect himself. A moment later, he dropped them and saw it. The severed head of his goat lay on the floor, blood still running from the hacked and jagged remnants of its neck.

Broken for the moment, he sank to the ground and wrapped his arms around his knees. Silent tears ran down his wrinkled cheeks and were lost in his tangled grey beard as he rocked back and forth. Outside, he heard the high, wild laughter of the satyrs and he huddled and wept.

Morning came eventually, or at least the sky began to lighten. He couldn't have said when the satyrs vanished, but he stood at the window looking over the clearing for hours until he saw the sun finally climb above the trees.

"New moon," he breathed and with an effort, forced himself to leave the cottage. Two steps took him to the iron staff and he held it across his body as a shield, rather than the instrument of a failing ritual. He could feel the Wyrde slipping faster from his grasp. It was like trying to cling onto the hand of someone hanging from a cliff. Moment by moment, day by day, he felt more of it slip away from him.

The clearing was silent, save for the faint rustling of the leaves in the morning breeze. Blood and feathers were scattered everywhere and scorch marks covered the ground around the cottage. Silently, he thanked the one who'd been paranoid enough to riddle the ground with iron rods, and stud the walls and door.

A foolish impulse forced him towards the barn. The door hung from one hinge, battered inwards and the smell of blood carried even in the morning breeze. The silence was telling, but he forced himself inside, regardless. His eyes took a moment to adjust to the dim light. Then he bolted from the building, crashing through the wildly swinging door, and falling to his hands and knees as his stomach heaved. The sight filled his mind and he heaved, spat, and retched again.

Eventually, he pulled himself up onto his knees, spitting the foul taste onto the grass. He stared blankly at the hoof-turned earth in front of him, tears running unnoticed from his face, until the flutter of wings disturbed him. The dove settled down on the roof of the barn and began to preen its feathers. He looked at it disinterestedly, almost unseeing. His eyes followed the bird as it hopped across the rooftop, until he finally registered what he was seeing. A small leather tube was attached to its leg.

A wild hope seized him and gave him the strength to go into the barn. He retrieved a handful of seed to coax the bird down from the roof. It flew to his hand easily and he quickly removed the leather canister. Hands trembling, he pulled the message free and unfolded it, his old eyes straining to read the faded script. Then it hit him. The script had faded because it hadn't been written in ink. It had been written in blood. The message was his own. The dove, unable to deliver its message, had simply returned as it had been trained to. His sigh was heartfelt, the final resignation of a broken man.

Chapter Eleven

Klöss stood at the stern of the great reaver, the massive ship rocking gently in the calm seas. Dawn was still two hours away and the dark waters reflected the lights of a thousand lamps. He watched the lights of the closest ships as they moved into position, and unconsciously shifted his weight to feel for his weapons. He wondered idly what Ylsriss was doing right now. Probably tucked into bed like anyone else with any sense. Then he remembered that she would be travelling too, heading back to Hesk, and to his father. He smiled at himself and went over the sections of the plan again in his head. So much hinged on the beacons being brought down.

A light footfall behind him alerted him before the man spoke. "Almost time, Klöss," Aiden said, as he joined the younger man at the rail. "Is everything ready?"

"As ready as it can be, Seamaster," he shrugged.

"An awful lot depends on Dallan and his team," Frostbeard said, echoing his own thoughts. "You're sure we've given them enough time to get there?"

"More than enough, really," Klöss replied. "They're travelling light, so they don't have a lot of supplies. He can't afford to sit around once the job is done."

"Why Dallan, anyway? You never told me," The old man asked.

"He came to me, shortly after we returned from the scout," Klöss explained. "Asked for it. Much like I was with you, when I wanted the camps."

"I remember," Aiden said, with a smile. "You were like a dog with a bone, wouldn't leave it alone."

Klöss chuckled. "Well, Dallan was much the same. Said he needed to prove himself, make something of himself. He has a good team with him, though."

"Fair enough," the old man grunted. He slammed his hand down on the rail in frustration. "I hate this, you know?"

"Waiting?" Klöss ventured.

"No! Though the waiting beforehand is bad enough, you're right." He stared out at the ships as he spoke. "I hate sitting on-board like some old woman while younger men fight and die."

"You're too important to risk, Uncle. The whole plan is yours. It'll fall apart without you."

"I know, I know," the old man sighed. "You're quite important yourself, you know?"

"I'm just an oarsman with a famous uncle who had a few lucky reavings, hadn't you heard?" Klöss glanced sideways at him.

"I hadn't heard that one," Aiden smiled. "Be careful. Your father would never forgive me if you did something stupid, like dying. The Sealord is quite interested in you as well."

"I'll do my best," Klöss said, dryly. "Besides, if I died, you'd have to deal with Ylsriss too."

"There is that," Aiden admitted. "You know, you ought to do something about that woman."

He shook his head. "Not now Uncle. Not before the battle."

"You're right, of course." The seamaster looked over at the position of the closest ships. "You're clear about the plan?"

"We've been over this, Uncle." Klöss sighed.

"And we'll go over it again. And again and again," Frostbeard snapped, "until I am certain that you have it."

"The first wave goes with the landers." Klöss recited from memory. "We attack the signal tower and establish a beachhead."

"And the other towers?" Aiden quizzed.

"We only know of the one signal chain." Klöss explained. "Dallan's team will move inland ahead of our strike, find a weak link and destroy it."

"And then?"

"Then we fortify our position and land the rest of the troops."

"What about ships?" Frostbeard asked, a smile on his lips.

"We've not encountered anything larger than a fishing boat. I don't know if they have any, but there are enough great reavers here to handle just about anything. They'll patrol up and down the coast, keeping within sight of each other." Klöss looked over at the ships. "I know the plan, Uncle. Trust me."

The old man sighed. It felt unnatural to be playing such a small role in his own campaign. He glanced out over the water and realised he could delay no longer. "It looks like they're about ready," he said. "You'd better get over to the lander."

Klöss grasped his uncle's forearm formally and gave it a firm squeeze. "Luck," he said and headed for the steps leading down to the deck. The wind was picking up, he noted, and the waves growing taller. He glanced up at the skies. There was no sign of the moon and the stars were hidden by clouds. Tiny raindrops pricked at his face and he smiled grimly to himself. A good cold spring rain. Just the thing to keep a sentry inside in the warm. He climbed down the rope ladder strung from the deck and stepped lightly into the small boat that would ferry him to the odd-shaped Lander.

He hardly noticed the short trip pass. The two oarsmen manoeuvred the craft alongside the lander and he clambered up the ladder onto the deck.

"Shipmaster aboard!" called out the guard posted by the ladder, but Klöss didn't hear him. His mind was deep in the plan and the events of the next several hours. He looked across the water at his uncle standing in the lamplight, then took the lantern from the guard, raising it high and moving it back and forth. He watched as the old man turned and a second later the horns began to sound. The noise started on Frostbeard's craft and spread out from ship to ship, until it seemed the very ocean should tremble at the sound. The beating of the drums soon followed and slowly, ponderously, the fleet began to move towards the unseen coast.

* * *

Stefan blew into his cupped hands and rubbed them vigorously together, as he silently cursed himself for not bringing his gloves out with him. It was supposed to be spring, wasn't it? The light rain had been falling for hours, but he'd learned the hard way that there was no such thing as a light rain here. The wind caught it and hurled it at you, somehow finding all the tiny gaps in a man's armour and clothing and forcing the wet through, until you were as soaked as if you'd stood in a torrential downpour. He drew his blue and green cloak tighter about his shoulders, and turned to the guardsman at the other side of the tower platform.

"Jeron?"

"What?" the lean man answered, huddling down against the cold stones at the corner of the platform in an effort to stay out of the wind.

"You ever think this is a bit stupid?"

"How do you mean," Jeron replied, cautiously.

"Well, here we are, right? It's as cold as a witch's tit, and we're stood next to a bloody great bonfire, freezing our arses off!" Stefan laughed, waving at the mound of oil-soaked wood under the treated tarpaulin.

"You're a card, Stefan," laughed the lean man.

"I'm bloody freezing is what I am!" Stefan stamped his boots. "You feel like getting us a cuppa?"

"Corporal'd go nuts if he caught me!" Jeron hissed. "You know that."

"So be quick then?" Stefan suggested, with a wink. "I'll stay here and freeze while you go into the warm for a few minutes, eh?" Jeron gave a worried smile but nodded in response to Stefan's shooing motion, and made his way down the spiral stairs to the guardroom below.

The sun was just starting to come up, though Stefan could barely see it through the clouds. He strolled around the platform to look out at the trees in the distance. When you spend your life staring at the sea, it's nice to look at something green once in a while. He could just make out the distant hilltop which was home to the next beacon, though he couldn't see the tower itself for the rain.

He looked down over the side of the stone wall at the new fort, half constructed beside his tower. It would soon be home to three times its present number. He wondered, for a moment, what that meant in terms of promotion opportunities and then laughed at his own naivety. New troops meant new officers, and new corporals to go along with them. He was doomed to being a lowly guardsman for a good while longer.

The site looked a mess to his eyes, with building supplies, timber and freshly quarried stones piled with no apparent order. The tower and its beacon were the only things that were really complete. A defensive wall had been staked out along the clifftop, with trenches half dug for the foundations. Two lonely ballistae and a catapult glistened in the morning's rain.

His breath steamed in the dim light and he walked to the stairwell. "Jeron, stop fiddling with yourself and get your bony arse up here with that tea!" He stamped his feet again and muttered to himself. "Bastard's probably stood drinking his at the fire." He glanced out to sea for a moment but the waves mirrored the slate grey sky, both as miserable as his mood.

"Lords and Ladies, keep your voice down, will you?" Jeron swore, as he climbed out of the stairwell with two steaming mugs. "You'll have the corporal up here, for sure!"

"Don't be daft. He's tucked up in a warm bunk," Stefan scoffed. "It's only us idiots up at this hour." He shook the rain from his cloak in an attempt to keep it from soaking through, and took the tin mug from Jeron's outstretched hand.

"Oh damn, that's good!" He savoured the heat from the tea, feeling the warmth spread all the way down.

"It's hot, is all it is," Jeron argued, as he held the cup tight, warming his hands. "I'd take hot ditch-water right now." He followed Stefan's gaze towards the newly built defensive wall, the ballistae perched behind it like malevolent insects. "That'll give 'em a bloody surprise next time they try an' raid, eh?"

"Bit late though, isn't it?" Stefan said.

"How d'ya mean?"

"Well, this fort an' the beacon an' all." The blonde man waved his hand vaguely at the half-finished construction. "It's all well an' good, but it don't help those people in Fallows Deep who nearly starved three winters back, does it?"

"Stops it happening again though, don't it?" Jeron said, plainly disapproving. "You talking like that's going to get you in the shit, Stefan."

"Yeah, you're right. I wouldn't want to get put on a night shift in the rain on this bloody tower now, would I?" He stared out at the sea morosely. The rain was easing as the unseen sun lightened the eastern skies. The distant waves cast odd shadows against the rising light and he enjoyed the sight for a moment. "Sorry mate, I'm just a miserable sod this morning."

"You're just missing your woman, I expect." Jeron waved his apology off.

"Yeah, well, she smells better'n you." He forced a smile. "Makes a better cup of tea too!" He spat and poured the remainder of the now cold tea over the edge of the stone wall.

"Ungrateful sod," Jeron muttered. "You know it'd have been my balls on the block if I'd been caught down there. You can bloody well go yourself next time!" He frowned at Stefan, who hadn't bothered to turn.

"Lords of Blood, Sea and Sky, preserve us," the guardsman breathed.

"Enough of that too!" hissed Jeron. "You'll have that damned New Dayer up here with us."

Stefan turned to him, his face pale and drawn. "We need to light the beacon," he said in a quiet, urgent voice.

"What?" Jeron said, confused.

"Light the gods-be-damned beacon!" Stefan screamed, pointing desperately out to sea. Jeron turned and the blood drained from his own face. The ocean was stained dark in the distance before the rising sun. Dark from the shadows of hundreds upon hundreds of ships.

Jeron's cup fell to the floor and clattered about, spraying tea across the icy stones, as the two men wrestled with the tarpaulin. Stefan ran for the large lantern and touched a pitch-coated torch against the wick, before he thrust it into the oil-soaked wood. It caught hesitantly for a moment, blue-tinted flames hungrily consuming the oil, and then the fire shot heavenwards. The two men staggered back from the sudden onslaught of heat, and then Jeron dashed to the corner of the platform and took up the bell. As the inky stain that was the Bjornmen fleet spread further across the sea, the fire crackled to tune of the desperate clang of the watch bell.

Stefan went to landward side of the platform, barely even aware of the heat from the fire. He clutched at the stones, his eyes desperately scanning the horizon. Long minutes passed before finally a flame shot up as the beacon was lit in the distant tower. "Gods above and below, let it be enough," he breathed, as men began boiling out of the barracks and up the stairwell in response to Jeron's frantic ringing.

The fleet closed with shocking speed, as the fort came frantically to life. Crossbowmen lined the short sections of completed wall, and the ballistae and catapult were manned and made ready.

Stefan half heard orders being barked, but stood frozen on the tower, watching in horror as the ships coursed towards the shore. The lead vessels had a strange design, their hulls splitting into three sections at the prow, almost as if the ships had runners like those of a sled. Oily smoke rose from prows of the ships, and men clad in leather and furs scurried around the long-armed catapults mounted at the foremost portion of each ship. He stood frozen to the parapet as the first ballistae hurled its massive spear towards the oncoming fleet, lurching forwards on its ties and tearing a hole through the deck of a Bjornmen vessel. He could hear the drums clearly despite the distance, and they somehow sounded clearer than the screamed orders of his officers.

The lead ships crunched into the surf, the split hulls acting as supports as the vessels drove themselves onto the beach, holding them secure and level. Stefan flinched, as the catapults on the ships lurched as one and hurled pots streaking fire through the sky. He vaguely heard the command to get down but stood, rooted to the spot, as the ball of flame came closer and closer.

"Stefan! Move!" Jeron yelled, grabbing him by the arm, and hurling him down the steps, into the tower.

The flaming beacon was eclipsed, as the pitch struck the tower and exploded, transforming the building into a pillar of fire far larger than the beacon had ever been. Men screamed and ran in a mindless panic as the flames consumed them, collapsing like broken toys.

The uppermost portions of the prows on the split-hulled ships slammed down onto the beach, forming a ramp. Men boiled forth roaring as they sped to the narrow path leading to the stricken fort. Crossbow bolts hissed into the fur-clad mass, as the defenders fired their weapons and struggled to reload the awkward devices, working with a speed born of terror, as the howling raiders surged closer and closer.

Stefan found himself being dragged along through the darkened tower by Jeron. Finally, they staggered, drunk with smoke and terror, out of the entrance. The fort was a scene of chaos. Men still lined the walls, firing bolts at the mass of Bjornmen as fast as they could, while others ran forward with drawn swords. Bodies lay everywhere, and the stench of burning flesh and pitch filled the air. The slope leading to the beach was littered with the dead and dying, as the guardsmen found themselves pushed back as fast as they could form a line.

"Stefan! Get over here!" the corporal yelled from the walls. Blood ran freely from a gash on his forehead, and chips of stone and dust clung to the wound. He wiped the blood from his eye with the back of his hand, and dropped the crossbow as they approached.

"I want you and Jeron to grab horses and go to the Abbot's Hill tower," he said, quickly.

"What and just leave?" Jeron said, aghast. "Can't just leave the men."

"Stupid prat!" Stefan said roughly, shoving at the small man who fell to one knee. "This place will be gone in an hour."

"He's right," the corporal said, giving Stefan a black look. "This tower was built for raids. This is far more than that. You need to get to Abbot's Hill and warn them. Don't let them send the garrison. It'll be a bloodbath!"

"Come on, you fool! Time for me to return the favour" Stefan pulled Jeron to his feet. "Take a few of the bastards with you, sir," he said to the corporal, but the man was already turning back to the wall.

"Come on!" Stefan shook Jeron roughly and ran, almost dragging the man, to the stables. The building was smouldering on one corner from bits of pitch that had fallen from the tower. Inside, the horses were screaming and kicking at their stalls. He wrenched open the door and smoke billowed out past the terrified horses. Thanking whatever gods might be listening that someone had either had the sense to saddle the beasts or had been too lazy to strip them down, he grabbed a bridle and led one of the horses out through the smoke.

It was a trained warhorse, but any animal will go mad with panic in a smoke-filled building, and it took all his strength to keep the creature from bolting. He threw himself into the saddle and, glancing back to make sure Jeron had followed his lead, he gave the horse its head, letting it charge across the fort, and out past the building supplies which lay forgotten in the smoke.

They stopped and looked back, as the road started to turn. The screams and sounds of steel on steel carried this far, but they couldn't see men through the smoke. As more pitch fell upon the fort and exploded in flame, they kicked the horses into a canter, and headed for the next tower, with its flame burning bright on the horizon.

* * *

Dallan crouched down beside the tree and looked out at the hill. The woods ended at this point and the rest of the hillside was wide open. White rocks poked through the long grass that had fought through the stony ground in search of the sun.

The tower was little more than a wooden watchtower with a platform on top. It had been hastily built and Dallan didn't need to move any closer to see it was not the sturdiest of constructs. A flat platform, surrounded by a low rail, topped it. From where he crouched Dallan could clearly see the beacon fire. It was just a massive pile of wood, covered with some form of tarpaulin. He briefly wondered if the tower itself would burn down if they ever lit the beacon.

A small cabin stood beside the tower, smoke rising from its chimney. It also was new but showed more care in its construction. A woodpile was stacked up against the side of it, the eaves of the roof sheltering it from the rain. It was little more than a hut, really, and Dallan doubted it could hold more than two men in comfort.

They'd arrived three hours ago, approaching slowly through the trees and working hard to remain silent. As it turned out, they needn't have bothered. The cabin had been silent since their arrival and the smoke from the chimney was the only sign of life.

"What do you think?" Dallan said, over his shoulder, twisting a leaf between his fingers.

"Hard to say," Scoth replied. "Can't see there being more than three in that cottage, but I can't see the top of the tower from here. Can you?"

"Not really." Dallan replied. "Could be someone up there."

"Better to wait for nightfall," Khel interjected. "We take it at night, then they can't see us coming over this ground."

"Unless the other beacons go up between now and then," Dallan said, turning awkwardly, so he could face the others without standing.

"It's a risk," Khel admitted. "But then so is charging over this ground in broad daylight. Bet they've got orders to fire the beacon if they're attacked. That's how I'd do it."

Dallan nodded at the two men. Both had more experience than he did and he'd wondered why they were deferring to him. He glanced at Khel, who was squatting down in the dirt, toying with his dagger. Dressed entirely in black leather, the man was a fearsome sight. His long, black hair was caught in a thong at the base of his neck and, unlike most men from the Black Isles, he was clean-shaven. Dark stubble covered his cheeks, testament to their time spent travelling, and a long silvery scar ran down one side of his face, extending from just below his eye to the side of his lips. The scar and the puckered skin around it were hairless, Dallan noted. It was probably why he didn't grow a beard.

"You want to take the tower?" Dallan said, seriously. "When it's time?" The scar-faced man looked past him, towards the structure in the distance, his eyes squinting as he went through the exercise in his mind. It was no small task. Climbing the narrow, winding stairs in the near darkness, at full speed, whilst trying to be quiet would be difficult. If he alerted the man at the top, the beacon would almost certainly be lit, and if he moved too slowly, he may well be seen before he even reached it.

The darkness would help, of course, but the tower was only a stone's throw from the cottage itself.

"I'll do it." he said, after a long moment. Khel was a man of few words. Dallan could count the conversations they'd had on the trip from the coast with the fingers of one hand.

"That leaves you and me with the cottage, then," Dallan said to Scoth. Scoth was everything Khel was not. Where Khel looked like a man better suited to a dark alley, Scoth was bright and fair, with an open and friendly face. His weapons looked out of place strapped to his body and his smile was never far from his lips.

"We wait until dark, then?" the blonde man asked.

Dallan nodded, inwardly chafing at the delay. "If the fire is lit, we'll rush the tower and kick it off the edge, or put it out somehow. If we're lucky, we can stop it being seen by the next tower."

"It's not much of a hope," Scoth said, with a glance at the tower platform. "But then, we wouldn't have much choice by then. If we do manage to take the tower, though, we should see if we can destroy it."

"How? Why?" Dallan asked, confused.

"We don't know how often supplies come in," Khel said, still playing with his dagger. "It doesn't do us much good to kill this crew, only to have the tower lit the day after we've left."

"I hadn't thought of that," Dallan admitted. He felt a fool in front of these two, like a child playing at being soldier. "What do you think would be the best way to destroy it? It's not like we can just burn it down."

"It doesn't look too sturdy. Looks almost temporary, like it was thrown up in a hurry." Khel replied, examining the distant tower. "I bet if you were to just chop through one of the supporting legs, it'd go over. Even if it didn't, two would definitely topple it."

"That's a lot of work to do with a sword." Dallan objected.

"I doubt the squirrels piled that wood there, boy," Khel replied, with a sardonic smile, pointing at the side of the cabin.

"Oh, yeah." He looked away for a moment, forcing the flush from his cheeks. "We wait for nightfall then."

The men nodded and settled down to wait. The day was grey but dry, and the woods were full of the sounds of small animals. Dallan found it hard to relax, jumping with every little noise. He had noticed that his two companions seemed to have no such problems. Khel was working over his weapons, a curved sword and a nasty-looking dagger. Scoth was lying back in the leaves with his head on his pack, his regular breathing enough to show he was already dozing. It wasn't a bad idea. They'd been travelling hard for the last few days but, despite this, he found it hard to sleep at night. The need to keep a watch meant what little sleep he did get was inevitably disturbed.

Dallan met Khel's eyes and gestured towards the ground, wordlessly, cocking an eyebrow. The silent man nodded once in understanding. Dallan lay down in the leaves, closed his eyes and tried to sleep, the odd harmony of Scoth's breathing and the regular rasp of the stone against Khel's already razor-sharp blades strangely comforting.

He woke to find Khel's hand pressed over his mouth. "It's time," the man said, in a hoarse whisper through the twilight. Dallan sat up and tried to force his heart to slow down. The man was clearly good for the mission, but he was definitely not the sort you wanted waking you up like that.

"Scared the shit out of me," he muttered, with a grin. Khel looked at him, his face impassive.

"He doesn't do humour," Scoth advised quietly, from where he sat with his back against a tree.

Dallan looked around, assessing the light. The dark ground was already a stark contrast to the light sky, and the shadows were long and growing longer by the minute. He looked through the trees towards the clearing and was pleased to note he couldn't see more than thirty feet ahead of him. Turning back to the others he nodded and said softly, "Let's go."

They made the short trip through the woods in silence and dropped to the ground at the edge of the trees. Lamplight was shining through the windows of the cottage, but the clearing itself was still. The night calls of birds and the occasional rustle of small animals in the bushes were the only sounds to be heard.

"Any movement while I was sleeping?" Dallan whispered to Khel.

"Three men, I think," the man whispered. "Two have climbed the tower and come down again. One, I suspect, is still in the cottage."

"What were they wearing?"

"Looked like some kind of uniform. They don't look to be farmers, if that's what you're asking," Khel replied.

They moved over the rocky ground, keeping low but not crawling. Moving smoothly they closed the distance in minutes. Dallan stopped, facing the windowless side of the cottage. The edge of the tower was just visible around the corner.

He pressed his face to Khel's ear and whispered more quietly than was probably necessary. "We'll circle to the door, while you go to the tower. When you're halfway up, we'll go in." The man gave a silent nod, and dropped to his hands and knees to work his way around the cottage.

Now that they were close, Dallan could hear sounds coming from inside the building and make out different voices, though the language was strange to him. He didn't know if Khel or Scoth could speak any of it, he'd never thought to ask.

He crawled under the window until he was level with the door, then drew himself up and pushed his back up against the wall. He watched Scoth lean in and press his ear to the wood to try and determine where people were in the cottage.

Khel made his way quickly to the tower and drew his weapons without flourish or noise, moving silently up the stairs. He concentrated on staying on the very inside of the narrow stairway, to try and blend into the structure in the darkness. The stairs were new, as was the whole tower, but some still creaked softly under his light steps. As he reached the halfway point, he waved down to the watching Scoth and the blonde man kicked in hard at the door as Khel began to sprint up the steps.

* * *

Khel dashed up the final steps and threw himself to one side, expecting an attack. He rolled easily to his feet as none came and moved quickly around the platform. A shadow moved on the other side of the mound of logs, giving him the only warning he had as a crossbow bolt flew past his arm. The twanging report of the weapon was impossibly loud in the darkness and he grinned to himself.

"That was stupid," he said, conversationally, as he darted round the beacon to attack. He saw the figure drop to the ground, crossbow in front of him, and he raised his weapon to strike. At the last second, he realised the man was not reloading the weapon but picking another up. He twisted to the side in desperation, but it was too late, there was just no way to miss at this range and the bolt slammed into his ribs as he crashed into the beacon's guardian.

The guard was not expecting Khel's sudden weight, and Khel used this to his advantage as he grabbed the man and rolled. The pain was excruciating and the edges of his vision were growing dark. In desperation, he slammed the guard over him and into the railing. The wood splintered loudly in the darkness. He heaved with one arm and the guard toppled off the platform, into the night. Too late, he realised his own balance was gone and he screamed as he too dropped off the edge.

* * *

Scoth kicked hard and the door flew inwards on its hinges, he followed it in, his weapons drawn and ready. A young man, little more than a boy really, in a simple white shirt, sat at a plain wooden table holding the lamp. His eyes were wide with surprise but Scoth didn't slow. He lunged and the dark-haired boy gasped, making no attempt to defend himself. Scoth drove both swords into his chest, twisting the weapons savagely to ensure the job was done. The boy groaned and lurched backwards as a bloody froth poured from his mouth.

Dallan stood at the doorway. There was no room to move past Scoth, but he saw the thrust as he killed the guardsman. He relaxed for a fraction of a second as the blonde man twisted the weapons he had rammed into the boy's chest and then, from nowhere, Dallan saw the blade sweep through the air from one side.

Scoth never saw the strike that took his head and his body collapsed to the side, driven by the force of the blow. Dallan screamed out involuntarily and took a step backwards as the third man filled the doorway. His eyes widened as he saw Dallan and he raised his blade again to strike.

The figure was wearing blue and green over his armour but the chainmail didn't appear to slow him down as he struck out at Dallan. The lamplight filled the doorway and the backlit man was a creature of darkness as the sword swung down towards him. The silence of the hilltop was shattered by the sound of steel on steel, as Dallan met the strike with his own sword and tried to bring his own blade to bear.

He realised within seconds that he was hopelessly outmatched, as the soldier flicked his blade away and thrust savagely at his belly. Dallan lurched backwards to avoid the thrust and buy himself time, but the guardsman simply followed the movement of his weapon, smoothly stepping in behind the thrust and turning it into a deft flick towards Dallan's eyes.

Desperately, Dallan brought his sword up to block the blow and, like a snake, the man struck. Bringing a dagger up with his other hand, he thrust it under Dallan's arm, the blade biting deep into the oarsman's side. He gasped in pain and staggered back against the side of the tower, dropping his sword as he bent against the wood, and waited for the guard to raise his weapons and finish him.

The man moved in for the kill, anger and contempt plain on his clean-shaven face. Dallan had no doubt he was about to die. He looked on in terror, as the soldier began the thrust that would kill him and felt a hot wetness spreading between his legs. He tried to close his eyes but couldn't seem to make his body respond. Then he watched in amazement, as Khel and another guard fell, screaming, a mass of tangled limbs, swords and armour, onto the guard with a resounding crash. The three men crumpled to the ground and lay still.

Dallan scrambled backwards, crab-like, away from the tower. Searing pain shot through his side, but he couldn't bring himself to care right now.

Shit!" he cried to himself. "Just... Shit!"

His chest ached from breathing so hard and his throat burned, but his eyes were wild and terrible. With an effort, he managed to uncurl from the semi-foetal position he'd hunched into and drag himself to his feet. A low moan came from the mound of limbs and he lunged forwards, grabbing up a sword and stabbing wildly into the pile of bodies, thrusting over and over as the tears poured down his cheeks.

"Just die! Just die! Just fucking die!" he screamed, until his voice failed him and he collapsed to the ground and sobbed hot tears of panic.

It was some hours before he came back to himself. He couldn't bring himself to pull the bodies apart to look for weapons, so instead, he went into the cottage and searched until he found a woodcutter's axe. Dallan was small, but years on the reavers had piled the muscle on where he needed it. The axe was well-maintained and the sharp head cut deeply into the wood. Within the space of half an hour, Dallan was sprinting out of the line of the tower as it fell crashing to the ground. "Light your damned beacon now!" he laughed and then stopped suddenly. He didn't like the way he sounded, high and hysterical. Casting guilty looks about the clearing, he half ran, half staggered to the trees, making his way back to the place where they had sheltered while waiting for nightfall. It was hard to find in the dark, and he found himself stumbling over fallen limbs and protruding roots.

Eventually, he found the packs by falling over them. He slung his onto his back, leaving the others where they lay out of guilt or panic, and staggered through the trees. Finally, exhaustion claimed him and he collapsed by a shining, silver birch. He stared into the darkness, the silence of the forest a counterpoint to the thundering tumult inside his head.

* * *

The sun rose over the clearing slowly, as if it feared to reveal the contents. As slants of sunlight came through the ruined window, the man woke and threw back the blanket he'd used to cover himself in the chair. For some reason, it hadn't seemed right to sleep in the bed.

The light picked out the pile of things he'd put together the night before. He'd packed hurriedly, more a general throwing of things into a travel sack than packing, really, but then in truth, he didn't have much to take.

"Not much point in waiting around, I suppose," he said to himself.

He ate quickly, a simple porridge made with the last of the goat's milk. He ought to have butchered the remains of the animals, but he couldn't bear to go into the barn. Somewhere in the back of his mind, a small voice informed him he was being stupid and would regret his wastefulness, but he paid it no heed.

When he was done, he stood at the entrance to the glade and stared at the circle. If he had to go, then this would be the time. It was the first day of the new moon. He looked at the battered barn which had housed his animals, now surrounded by buzzing flies. A sigh escaped his lips and he turned to face the path. He hadn't left the glade in more than twenty years and now that the time came to actually leave, it was hard to make himself take the first step. He glanced over at the monolith at the centre of the circle and his resolve hardened. Leaning lightly on the iron staff, he made his way down the track in search of civilisation.

He made good time, despite the overgrown track. The woods had mostly reclaimed it, but he was spry despite his age, and managed to negotiate the undergrowth and roots that sought to trip him with ease.

He reached the bottom of the track and looked about for a moment, trying to get his bearings and to remember landmarks. There had been a time when he'd had a map of the area, but he'd long since stopped caring about such things and hadn't managed to find it as he packed.

His eyes fell on a distant hill protruding from the trees. If he could get up there, he would have a better chance of finding a proper path or a road.

It took the better part of three hours before he stumbled upon the road. It was little more than a worn, muddy track but it ran in the right direction and showed signs of recent use. He clambered his way down the bank and onto the road itself, a feat which required some less than elegant sliding on his rump.

The road made for much easier travel and he caught himself almost enjoying it. "Stupid fool," he berated himself out loud. He clenched his grasp upon the Wyrde, feeling its oily texture slip under his grip in his mind. He relaxed his grip slightly. The slipping had been enough to remind him of what he was about. This was not a happy jaunt through the woods.

He was drawing level with the hill when he saw the track. It turned off the road he was on and led directly to the hill. From the cart tracks that turned also, he could tell it was in more or less frequent use and he made the turn himself gladly. It would be good to see past the trees for once. He paused to take a drink from his skin before trudging up the hill.

A crack from the bushes was the only warning he had before the man tumbled from the bush and down the slope onto the road. He was short, little more than shoulder height as compared to himself and dressed in boiled leather armour covered with furs. He carried a long sword in one hand and a pack on his back but what caught his attention was the man's eyes, wide and terrible. Filled with horror and self-loathing.

He held a hand out. "Are you okay?" he asked gently and flinched back as the man crouched into a defensive posture, raising his sword.

"K'rak hu talaad!" the man barked at him. "Su vetesh?"

It was obviously a question, but the language was like nothing he'd ever heard. Then he noticed the gash in the man's side and the blood covering the hand that was pressed to it.

"I'm sorry. I can't speak that tongue," he said slowly, calmly. "Your side, can I help you with that?" He gestured to the man's injury.

"Suranum ka latutha!" the man barked again, brandishing the sword and lifting his bloody hand away from his side to point at the ground.

He moved back a step cautiously. The strange man was becoming more and more agitated. He didn't have time for this. He stepped to the side, keeping his eyes on the man, his iron staff held between them.

"Look, I think I'm just going to go, my friend," he said carefully, easing his way around the man.

"K'rak harlan su revek larn!" the leather-clad man screamed, pointing at the ground again.

"I don't understand you!" he snapped, growing exasperated himself.

The man suddenly flung himself forward and thrust with his sword as he kicked the staff away. The old man gasped as the blade bit deeply into his side and he tumbled into the mud. The pain was excruciating. He clenched his eyes tight and fought to keep control, but it was just all too much. The Wyrde flailed in his grasp, slipped. He clenched his grip convulsively but it twisted like an eel and then it was gone, escaping like the last breath of a drowning man. His eyes flew open and he glared at the strange foreign man "You fool!" he gasped as he slumped back in the mud. The man looked at him with an odd mixture of fear and anger and turned. As his eyes slowly closed he heard him run off towards the road with the frantic pace of naughty child.

He couldn't say how long he lay in the dirt. His side burned and throbbed with each pulse, but the pain told him he was still alive. Gingerly, he probed at it with one hand, keeping the rest of himself still. His robe seemed to be soaked with blood but the wound itself didn't appear too deep. Pressing down hard on it, he found his way to his feet and looked around at the empty track.

"You're worried about your modesty? Now?" He wheezed a painful laugh, as he pulled open the robe to get a better look. The blade had skidded along one rib before stabbing deep into his right side. He swore and cut a makeshift bandage from his robe, wadding it up against the wound and binding it tight.

Bending awkwardly against the pain and hooking it with one foot, he managed to retrieve his staff and he leant on it heavily as he staggered up the small path towards the hilltop. He silently thanked the fact that the main road had been rising for some time, so this side track wasn't overly steep. He was gasping as it was and the pain in his side threatened to overwhelm him with each step.

After what felt like hours, but which was probably no more than half an hour, he reached the end of the path. His heart sank as he took in the wreckage. A mass of splintered timber was all that remained of what had clearly been some form of tower. A small cabin sat near the wreckage but the violence that had occurred here was visible even from the edge of the muddy track.

"Hello?" he called cautiously. His side prevented him from taking too deep a breath and so the shout he'd intended came out weak and querulous. His only answer was silence and as he staggered closer to the cabin, he realised that the odd pile beside the doorway was a collection of bodies. He muttered to himself as he drew closer, there would be no salvation here. Perhaps inside at least, he might find something to better tend his wound.

The ground was slick with blood as he reached the doorway, and he held on tight to the frame as he pushed the door further open and stepped quickly inside, away from the blood-spattered grass. Letting go of the doorway, he turned swiftly to find a lamp, and his foot skidded out from under him in the pool of blood that covered the floor of the cabin. He slammed hard against the table and cried out. As the light faded from his vision, he saw the young man sat at the table with two swords embedded in his chest. He had just enough time to wonder what he had blundered into, when the darkness took him.

Chapter Twelve

Selena strolled through the gardens towards what had become her wing of the palace. The sun was bright this morning but the air was still crisp. Spring was definitely here, she decided, as she examined the buds on the roses. She was alone for once, having sent away her ladies-in-waiting and the ever-present pages.

She breathed deeply, enjoying the crispness of the air and the solitude of the gardens. It was so nice not to be surrounded by toadies and hangers-on. The power structure in the palace had changed and everyone was aware of it, from the chambermaids to the guards. It was nothing official, of course. The world wasn't even close to being ready for that. Everyone knew, however, that it was she who now held the reins and the sycophants already trailed in her wake.

She sat in the gazebo for a time, and admired the tintias vines that ran up the side of the trellis, their fiery orange blooms already out and basking in the sunlight. The flaming blossoms matched her hair. Closing her eyes for a moment, she enjoyed the silence. The sun felt nice on her face. She was not one to sit still, however. Had she been content to do that, she would never have worked to seize effective control of the duchy. She stood and brushed her gown with the backs of her hands, as if wiping away the peace of the garden to make room for other things. It was time for business.

She made her way inside, through the decorative patio doors and her chambers, until she reached the parlour. As she entered the room, her manner became sharp and businesslike. She strode to her favourite chair by the window and made herself comfortable, positioning her gown just so and pulling the little table closer.

"Mikel?" she called. The page, who had been waiting attentively by the door, stepped forward. "my lady?" he replied, with a small bow.

"Be so good as to invite Chamberlain Hanris to attend me with the accounts at his convenience," she said. At his convenience would, of course, be interpreted as an immediate summons.

"At once, my lady." The page bowed again and stepped back three paces before turning and moving swiftly to the door.

She looked out the window as she waited, enjoying the view as the light wind blew the puffy clouds across the sky. The sound of distant running brought a slight smile to her lips and she glanced expectantly at the door as she imagined Hanris puffing and blowing in the hallway and trying to put himself in order.

The door opened and the page entered, slightly ahead of Hanris who, remarkably, had managed to get his breathing under control.

"Chamberlain Hanris, my lady," the page announced unnecessarily, as both he and the bird-like Hanris gave small bows.

"So good of you to come, Hanris." She flashed a warm smile. "You needn't have come immediately you know?" He was wearing another of those black coats and ruffled white shirts. She briefly wondered how many of those outfits he had. He seemed to regard it almost as a uniform.

"It's no bother, my lady," he replied. He was clutching a thick, leather-bound ledger under one arm.

"Why don't we have Mikel bring over a chair and you can talk me through the accounts?" she suggested, with a smile that made it clear it was nothing remotely like a suggestion.

"Of course, my lady," Hanris said, in a defeated tone as the page struggled with a heavy wooden chair.

"Now then," she said brightly, as he sat. "Why don't you dazzle me with how well our new estates are doing in the Eastern Reaches?"

"We've had, some success," Hanris said cautiously without releasing the ledger from his grip. "The new villages of Frenton's Cross, Shayton and Selene are well-established now, and they should be planting fields as we speak."

"Selene?" She cocked an eyebrow but sounded pleased, almost girlishly so.

"The villagers named it themselves, my lady." Hanris coughed, apologetically.

"It's an...*interesting* name for a village, I suppose," she mused, and tapped her elegantly painted nails on the deeply polished rosewood table. "And the tithe?"

"We have sent collectors throughout the duchy, my lady."

"What a delightful way of avoiding the question!" She clapped her hands in a giddy fashion and then fixed the little man with a piercing look. "I had assumed that much, unless you were planning to totally ignore my order. How much success are we having?"

"Moderate at best, I'm afraid," he sighed. "I've given instructions to the collectors to take no more than the village can afford to spare without causing hardship, as per your instructions."

"And?" She leaned forward, one finger tapping out a staccato rhythm onto the tabletop.

"And we are bringing in revenue, my lady. Of course, it will be more in years to come, when the new villages and farms have had a fruitful season or two." He smiled a thin smile that didn't reach his eyes.

"What aren't you telling me here, Hanris?" she asked, suspiciously, as she stared into his eyes through the spectacles perched on his beak-like nose.

"Whilst the revenues have increased, my lady, our position is unchanged." He sighed and suddenly looked very old and tired. She wondered how she'd never noticed before, but the man had to be at least in his late forties. "The expenditure on the forts and beacons has been enormous, and frankly your husband's donations are exacerbating our situation." He winced apologetically.

Selena sat back and composed herself carefully before she spoke. "What exactly are these donations, Hanris?" She watched as the chamberlain's composure cracked for the first time in the five years she'd known him.

"I…I'm sorry, my lady," he sputtered. "I assumed you knew!"

"Knew what, exactly?" She folded her hands in her lap and fought to remain calm as she held his gaze.

"I really can't say, my lady," Hanris was like a startled bird in a cage, flapping to try and escape danger despite the knowledge that there is nowhere to go.

"I'm afraid I really must insist, Hanris." Her green eyes turned as hard as her tone.

"Your Ladyship, you must understand my position," he pleaded, wringing his hands.

"I understand your position perfectly, Hanris," Selena said, in a soft, calm voice. "Your position is one in the employ of the ducal household. Now, much as I usually try to deny it, at present it is advantageous to me to accept that I am your duchess and, as such, your employer. It would seem to me, Hanris, this it is you who does not understand his position."

"my lady..." She brought her hand up with a snap and made a short, shushing noise. He froze mid-sentence and closed his mouth with an audible clacking of teeth.

"Hanris," she said, smoothly. "I understand your problem. You are caught between your duty to my husband and your common sense, which informs you that denying me would be extremely foolish." She stood and walked over to the window, continuing to speak as she looked out into the gardens. "Now, whilst I understand your problem, and can even sympathise, it is *your* problem." She turned to face him as he sat slack-jawed in the chair. "Now, are you going to answer my question? Or shall we see how long it takes Freyton to notice his chamberlain has been dismissed? Personally, I would wager it would take a good few weeks. You know how he can be." She smiled sweetly at him and settled down behind the little table again, waiting.

Hanris gaped at her for a long minute before removing his glasses and cleaning them on a handkerchief he pulled from an inner pocket. "I see you leave me little choice, my lady," he sighed. "In truth, I thought you knew." He gave a sad little smile. "The duke has been meeting with a priest from the Church of New Days for some years now."

"A priest?" She didn't bother to conceal her shock. "What on earth would Freyton want with a priest?"

"Honestly? I have no idea, my lady. The meetings are kept strictly private." Hanris pushed his gleaming glasses back onto his nose. They completed his face, somehow, and he looked odd without them. "In any event, the donations have been quite sizeable."

She pursed her lips in thought. "Show me."

A noise outside the door diverted her attention for the moment and the page slipped out to see what the commotion was. She turned back to the thick ledger that Hanris had spread out over the table.

"I don't care if she's with the King himself!" The shouting penetrated the heavy door. "You open this door now or I'll do it myself, you jumped up little piss-ant!" Selena raised an eyebrow at Hanris who looked back over his shoulder at the door.

The page entered, looking decidedly flustered. "Captain Rhenkin insists on seeing you immediately, my lady." He gave Hanris an embarrassed look. "I did inform him that your meeting was private and not to be disturbed, but he is quite insistent."

"My, my. An insistent man in uniform," Selena purred and burst out laughing as she caught the look on Hanris's face. "Show him in, then. By the sounds of things, he's likely to do something painful to you if you don't."

Rhenkin pushed his way past the outraged page with a dishevelled guardsman in tow. He gave the briefest of bows. "my lady, I apologize for this interruption but I felt this needed your urgent attention." Selena motioned for him to go on. "It seems the Bjornmen raiders have invaded."

She shot to her feet. "Why weren't we informed? If there has been a raid, why weren't the beacons lit?" She clenched her fists by her sides.

"It seems this is far more than a raid," Rhenkin replied. "This is Guardsman Stefan. He rode all the way from Tibbets Shore to bring the news."

She fought to calm herself. "That is a goodly way, Guardsman, but why were the beacons not lit?"

Stefan's uniform was covered in mud and dust from the roads, and his face was unshaven. He cleared his throat, and twisted his tabard in his hands as he spoke.

"Beg your pardon, M'Lady, but it was lit." He plunged on, as her eyebrows rose, "I lit the first one m'self when I saw the bas... beg pardon, M'Lady. When I saw the ships arriving."

She ignored the almost profanity. "If you lit the beacon, then why are we only just now hearing about this?" Stefan flushed and looked down at his mud-spattered boots.

Rhenkin interjected smoothly. "It seems that the chain has been interrupted, my lady. Stefan saw the second beacon had been lit from his position on the tower. The chain must have been broken farther inland."

She paused, digesting the information. "You mentioned this was more than just a simple raid?"

"Yes, my lady." He turned to the nervous guardsman. "Tell her."

"There were thousands of them, Your Ladyship," Stefan blurted. "They overran the tower an' the fort in minutes."

"Thousands?" she scoffed. "Come now, the ships don't hold that many, surely?"

"Beggin' your pardon Ma'am, but yes thousands," Stefan said, holding his head high. "I saw easily four or five hundred ships, with more in the distance behind them."

"Five hundred," she gasped, reaching blindly for the back of her chair. She sank into the seat and for a moment stared blankly into space. "The garrisons?" she asked, weakly.

"Ordered to stay where they are, for the moment, my lady," Rhenkin advised. He stood at attention, shoulders back. It was probably his way of coping, she realised.

"Has anyone informed Freyton?"

"Not as of yet, my lady." Rhenkin cast an embarrassed glance in the direction of the formal dining room.

She sighed. Her idiot husband was simply too much for her to cope with right now. Drawing herself up, she looked Rhenkin squarely in the eyes. "What do you suggest?" He seemed surprised by the question, as if he didn't expect her to ask for an opinion.

"We need to understand their forces and their intentions, my lady. For this, we will need to send scouts into the area. We will also need troops." He gestured towards Stefan, who seemed to have calmed a little and was listening attentively. "If half of what Stefan says is true, then we simply do not have the troops or resources required to meet this threat alone."

She nodded and turned to Hanris. "I want you to draft an urgent message to the King advising him of the situation. Send it by the fastest possible means." She looked back to Rhenkin, as Hanris walked swiftly to the door without stopping to bow. "What of the villages?"

"Tebbits Shore and the next closest village to the tower are almost certainly in enemy hands," the captain said, frankly. "I cannot predict the condition of the others."

"Are you proposing we simply leave them to their own devices?"

"I propose nothing, my lady." His retort was curt, the first sign of his fraying nerves. "Whatever course of action we take places them in danger. Evacuation is possible but who could take them in? It also places them at considerable risk of attack during the process."

"I refuse to just leave them to these savages, Rhenkin," she burst out, slamming her hand down upon the table.

"I am afraid we have little choice at this point, my lady. By the time any evacuation order reached them, they would most likely have already been overrun." Rhenkin stepped closer. "May I speak frankly, my lady?"

"I wish somebody would!" she complained.

"We were not prepared for this. We planned for raiders and we've been met with an invasion. The best we can do is send word to the King and seek information ourselves."

"Fine," she snapped. "Send word to our garrisons to withdraw to a central location, whichever you see fit. We may as well establish a forward staging post."

Rhenkin nodded, approvingly. "A very good idea, my lady. We can make further decisions when we hear back from the scouts."

Hanris returned and gave a small bow. "I've drafted the note, Ma'am, and had it sent by bird and messenger. The birds will probably arrive first, but I thought it best to send a messenger too."

"Agreed," she said. "I don't believe there is anything further for the moment, Rhenkin?" He shook his head, his eyes distant as his mind worked through the problems of troop positions and supplies. "I trust you will reward this guardsman for his exemplary service," she continued. "For now, Hanris and I have other matters to discuss." She waved Hanris back into the chair, and nodded in response to Rhenkin's bow as Rhenkin and Stefan withdrew.

"Now," Selena drew herself up in the chair. "As to the matter of these donations, and indeed my husband in general, Hanris, something must be done."

"I quite understand, my lady, though it is a somewhat delicate situation," the chamberlain replied.

"It occurs that over these past few years, I have made somewhat of a fool of myself," she said as she stared up at a point on the ceiling.

"I'm not quite sure what you refer to, my lady." Hanris spoke cautiously, as if looking for the trap.

"I've avoided thinking of myself as a duchess," she explained. "I've even made a point of avoiding the title."

"You have been, quite clear, about your feelings on the matter," Hanris offered.

Selena gave a small smile at that. Perhaps the bookish little man wasn't entirely devoid of humour. "In doing so however, I have neglected to note that the title carries its own authority. Not so much as that of my husband's perhaps, but authority nonetheless. Certainly over my own household."

"I would have to agree, my lady, but I am not quite sure…"

She smiled broadly. "It's quite simple, Hanris. Since my husband has seen fit to squander the contents of our coffers on donations and his own gluttonous excesses, we will simply have to tighten our belts. You will inform the Master of the Kitchens that we will no longer be needing to restock the wine cellar." She carried on as Hanris's eyes grew wide behind his spectacles. "I would also like to liquidate our holdings in this area, and so perhaps you can inform the owners of the local hostelries and dining rooms that we would be open to receiving offers for the contents of cellars."

"my lady, the duke will be incensed!" Hanris appeared genuinely dismayed at the notion.

"Are you denying that, as duchess, I have this authority?" She folded her hands in her lap and looked at him sternly.

"No, my lady." Hanris shook his head vigorously. "No, the running of the household has traditionally always fallen within the remit of the duchess. But..."

"Good, so then it's settled," she said. "Now, as to this priest and these donations. I am afraid, Hanris, that you are simply going to have to try and reclaim them."

"my lady, that is highly irregular!" Hanris seemed to be fluctuating between being genuinely appalled and shocked to his core.

"I think we'll dispense with the 'my lady' as well, Hanris. I am Selena Freyton, Duchess of Druel, The Wash, and the Eastern Reaches, and I *will* be obeyed."

"Yes, your grace," Hanris stuttered.

* * *

Erinn clucked the horses on through the wooden gates, smiling at the guards in their bright new uniforms as she passed out onto the road. The cart was heavily loaded with supplies and moved sluggishly through the soft mud, giving her the chance to take in the changes made to her little village.

A tall wall, fashioned from sharpened wooden stakes, now surrounded the village, with only the mill and a few scattered cottages left outside. The thick gates were the only way in or out, and these were guarded day and night by village boys who'd jumped at the chance to wear uniform and play with swords, though most were armed with long cudgels instead. The long shadow cast by one of the four watchtowers spread over the road as she trundled on in the early morning light, and she almost missed the shouting from behind her, due to the creaking of the wagon. She glanced over one shoulder and smiled as she saw Kainen running after her.

"The inn's back the other way," she teased, as she pulled back on the reins. The cart slowed to a halt. He wheezed as he caught up to it, holding onto the side and blowing like a bellows. "Thought you...might like...some company" he managed, with two words between each gasped breath.

"Well, I can't very well send you back in this state, can I?" She looked him up and down. "Seriously Kainen, you look like you've run a day solid. Look at the state of you!" He ignored her and clambered up into the seat beside her, still breathing hard.

She fixed him with a suspicious look, narrowing her eyes as a thought occurred to her. "Did my father put you up to this?"

Kainen squirmed for a moment, before nodding.

"Honestly!" She raised her eyes heavenward. "I'm going to bring supplies to Artor and two other men, and he thinks I need a chaperone? What does he think is going to happen?"

Kainen shrugged, clearly uncomfortable, and looked back over his shoulder at the village. "It hardly looks the same at all, does it?"

She smiled at his obvious attempt to change the subject. He'd never managed confrontation well. "I know what you mean," she replied, looking back herself. "It's changed so much in such a short time."

The beacon was only about three hours away with a good horse, but the cart was well loaded with supplies and would take the better part of the day to make it there. Truthfully, Erinn was glad of the company, as she hadn't relished the thought of travelling back alone in the dark.

"Kainen? Umm, you know how Artor can be about me sometimes?" she said.

"A complete jealous fool with less sense than a stag in rut? Yes." He laughed as she glared at him.

"Would you mind, waiting, when we arrive. You know..." She could feel her cheeks burning as she struggled to force the words out.

"Out of sight? So Artor doesn't get the wrong idea?" Kainen finished for her. "Fine, but only if you tell me that you know you shouldn't have to do things like this."

"I know," she said, her eyes downcast.

"Right, then. Good enough." He looked around at the budding trees and then gave her a conspiratorial grin. "Did you hear that Father Trallen got so drunk at Midwinter that he asked three men to dance?" She laughed and the mood brightened. Widdengate might have changed, but she could always rely on Kainen to bring a smile to her lips and salacious gossip to her ears.

It was quite a bit past the noon hour when they finally arrived at the small track that led to the hilltop. The track was new and had been cut by the workers when they built the tower. Despite the efforts of the spring sunshine, the ground was still wet and the roads still soft. The cart made slow progress towards the summit.

"I'll go for a wander in the woods while you two canoodle then, shall I?" Kainen said, with a leer, as he hopped off the side of the cart. Erinn gave him a withering look and clucked the horses onwards.

It took less than fifteen minutes to reach the top of the hill. As she turned the last corner, her fingers went limp and the reins fell into her lap. She fumbled for them, and reined in the horses with one hand whilst the other flew to her mouth. The tower was in pieces. It had fallen across the hilltop, narrowly missing the cottage and shattering as it fell, by the looks of things. She clambered down from the cart and began to run, her legs trembling, towards the cottage, but then stopped dead before she'd travelled ten steps.

"Stupid, Erinn," she whispered to herself. "Very, very stupid." She hunched down without thinking and scanned the clearing. Seeing no movement, she turned and ran past the cart, back to the trail.

Kainen was not hard to find and the two of them soon stood at the top of the trail, peering past a stand of birch towards the cottage and the wreckage of the tower.

"Did you hear anything?" Kainen asked, his gaze still fixed on the cottage.

"No," she replied. "But then, I wasn't listening for anything, either."

"There's no smoke or anything. I don't think anyone's here." He turned to look at her. "I think maybe we should just get the cart and go back," he said. "If there is still anyone here, we really don't want to run into them."

She shook her head violently, her red hair flying free of her green, hooded cloak. "No. No, I won't just go. Artor could be in there, wounded, for all we know. He could have been taken. Anything could have happened. We can't just leave."

Kainen put his hands on her shoulders and held her facing him. "Erinn, this tower didn't just fall down on its own. It's a beacon tower. You know what must have happened here…"

"No!" She shook her head again, her dark green eyes serious and intent. "No, I won't just go. We need to go and look, Kainen."

"This is not a good idea, Erinn," he said.

"Well, I'm going to look. Are you going to come with me or are you going to hide in the woods?" Her eyes flashed with anger and hurt. She pulled back away from him as he reached for her, and pushed out of the woods to the hilltop. Kainen cursed in a loud whisper and followed her.

They made their way over the rock-strewn ground in silence, crouching low in the long grasses, although it would help them little if anyone happened to look their way. The clouds were scudding across the sky before the stiff breeze, and the hilltop alternated between being bathed in sunlight and cast into deep shade every few moments.

The cottage stood about four hundred yards from the end of the trail. The debris from the tower obscured their view, and they were more than halfway there before Kainen saw the bodies. He reached out and pulled Erinn to a stop. She shot him a cross look, thinking he wanted her to leave again, but then she saw the expression on his face.

"What is it?" she said, in a hoarse whisper.

"Why don't you stay here and let me check ahead?" he said, thinking out loud. "If there is someone here, one of us needs to be able to run and get word out."

She looked at him suspiciously. "Why are you saying this now?"

He gave up and tossed his hands in the air in frustration. Sometimes there was simply no point in being subtle. "Because there might be things in there you won't want to see, Erinn," he said. "Just let me check ahead, then I'll come and get you, okay?"

"Oh!" Her eyes grew wide as she considered it, but then she saw the tangle of bodies beside the cottage. "Artor!" she cried and ran, jerking her arm away from Kainen as he grabbed at her. She lifted her plain, grey skirts and sprinted towards the pile of men, her green cloak billowing behind her as the wind caught it. She was dimly aware of Kainen shouting for her to stop, but she was past hearing him. She came to a stop as she drew close. The men were caught in a tangle of arms, legs and armour. Swords lay on the ground and flies were thick on the bodies, buzzing this way and that. The wind shifted and then the smell found her. It wasn't the stench of rotten meat or something decomposing, but the iron-rich smell of blood. It was a smell she'd always associated with violence. She covered her mouth and nose with the end of her cloak and turned away.

Kainen stepped past her and moved closer to the bodies. "He's not here," he said simply, as he looked back over one shoulder. She drew up to his arm. "Who are they?" Her voice was muffled by the cloak.

"Soldiers, by the looks of them." He pointed. "These two anyway. This one looks different though." The man was dark-haired and wearing close-fitting, leather armour. "They don't look like they've been here that long, though." He glanced at her. Her skin, pale enough at the best of times, looked paper-white and her eyes were huge over the cloak she held pressed to her mouth and nose.

"I'm going into the cottage. Stay here." For once, she didn't argue.

The cottage was silent and Kainen felt his heart pounding as he took in the broken door hanging on one hinge. He pushed it and the bottom corner dug into the floor, jamming after an inch or two. Grabbing the top corner, he lifted and walked it open.

The cottage was dark and thick with flies. The smell of blood filled the air. Kainen pulled his own cloak to his mouth and worked his way around the door. Only the fact that he was still clinging onto it saved him, as he tripped over the leg. There was blood everywhere, and he gagged as he took in the headless corpse at his feet. Then he saw Artor.

The man sat in the wooden chair, his face frozen in a grimace of pain and shock. The swords looked to have been driven through him, pinning him to the wall. Kainen gagged again and stepped backwards. The scream that flew from his throat, as the hand grabbed his ankle, was high-pitched and girlish, not the manly cry of surprise he might later claim it to have been. He jerked away, spinning around to face the body.

The man lay in a pool of congealed blood, his face and robes covered in gore. He looked up at Kainen with pain-filled eyes. "Help me." His voice was little more than a whispered gasp, but it carried a depth of pain that brought Kainen to his senses.

Erinn jumped as the scream came from the cottage, and she moved cautiously closer, ignoring Kainen's implied instruction to run. The door scraped as someone dragged it inwards and she flinched. Kainen's back filled the doorway as he dragged a body out of the cottage. She prepared herself for it to be Artor, but instead it was an old man she'd never seen before. He was dressed in robes that might once have been grey, but which were now stained a rust colour and half-covered with blood.

Kainen turned and caught her eye. "Don't go inside, Erinn."

"Is he...?"

"Yes," he said. "There are others too. You don't want to see it, trust me. Can you give me a hand, here?" He lay the old man down on the grass. She knelt down beside him and took a closer look. The man looked dead, but his wispy, grey beard was moving where the whiskers hung over his lips. A darker stain on his robes led her to the gash in his side.

"Oh, Lords and Ladies," she swore, as she took in the wound. "Get me a knife," she ordered Kainen, suddenly all business.

"From where?" he demanded, looking about.

"Get me a sword, if you have to." She leaned in peering closely at the wound. He ran to the pile of bodies and returned quickly with a bloody knife. She took it without comment and cut away the dirty robe around the wound. Whoever he was, he'd put a bandage of sorts over it, but he'd almost have been better off leaving it open. The rag he'd bound over it was soaked in blood and the few areas that weren't were filthy.

"There's not much we can do for him here. We'll have to get him onto the cart and back to the village. Can you go and bring it closer, while I try and clean this up?" She cut strips of material from the bottom of the man's robe and wadded one up, pressing it over the bloody bandage already in place, before binding another over the top.

It took both of them to clear enough of the supplies from the cart and lift him onto it. For a thin man, he was shockingly heavy. He gasped in pain once as they hauled him up, but then his eyelids fluttered and he lay still.

"You drive. I'll stay with him," Erinn said, as she knelt down with the man.

"What about them?" Kainen nodded towards the cottage.

"We can't do anything for them. This man needs our help now," she said, biting her lip as her eyes flicked to the cottage.

Kainen knew when to stop talking and shook the reins lightly to get the horses moving. They were eager to get away from scent of blood and the cart fairly bounded down the track. He reined them in as they reached the bottom of the trail.

"Why've you stopped?" Erinn asked, speaking back over her shoulder. She turned at the lack of response and her jaw dropped. The road was filled with people. Some were lucky enough to have carts and they were piled high with salvaged possessions, their families curled up in what little space remained. Others trudged wearily through the mud. Mothers carried crying babies and pulled young children along. They all had same expression in their eyes, a look of fear and exhaustion.

A young woman in mud-spattered clothes ran to them from the crowd. "Is there a town nearby? We've young 'uns that can't go much further."

"Widdengate," Kainen replied. "It's some miles away but we can lead you there."

"Who are all you people?" Erinn managed, as an older man drew closer. "Where have you all come from?"

"We're from all over the east," the man answered, as the young woman stretched her hand out to two young children. "I'm from Frenton's Cross. That fellow there was in Tebbits Shore when they came," he said. "Bjornmen, burnt it to the ground."

Bjornmen?" Kainen asked. "I thought they just raided the coast?"

"If this is a raid, young man, then I'm a mother of four." He spat into the mud beside the road. "There were thousands of them. I think this is far more than that."

It was nightfall by the time they came within sight of the walls. The torches were lit, and children and adults alike found new strength at the thought of warmth and shelter. A cry to "halt and be recognised" came up from the walls and Erinn stood up in the back of the cart.

"Don't be an arse, Gavin Treadler! You can see these people need help. Now, stop playing soldier and open the damned gates!" She folded her arms across her chest and fixed the boy in the tower with a stern glare until he began climbing down to pull the gates open himself.

The gates creaked as they opened, despite the fact they were less than a month old. Erinn jumped down from the cart, and dashed between them as they were still moving. People attracted to the shouting were already gathering to gawk and doors were opening in the small street as the word spread.

Erinn dashed along the street until she spotted Maryanne. "Mother Taplock!" she gasped, her chest heaving.

"Erinn!" the woman cried, looking her up and down. "Look at the state of you, girl. Whatever's happened?"

"The tower's been attacked. Artor's dead!" As she said it, the enormity of it crashed down upon her and she felt the burning of tears welling up in her eyes. She dashed them away. There simply wasn't time to be that girl now.

Maryanne was gaping like a landed fish, as she stared first at Erinn and then at the ever-growing crowd of strangers moving through the gates. "What? How? Who are all these people?" she asked, the questions tripping over each other in their haste to get out.

"Villagers from the east, seeking refuge. The Bjornmen have attacked."

"Bjornmen!" The woman was fast becoming hysterical, her voice rising in pitch with every word.

"Listen, we don't have time for this. Where's Trallen?" she demanded.

"Don't you take that tone with me, young lady!" Maryanne snapped.

Erinn gave the woman an appraising look. "I'm sorry," she said. "It's just...I need help with all this."

"Well of course you do, dear!" the woman gushed. "Why didn't you just say so? Leave these people to me for a little while. You go and get something warm to eat and get yourself cleaned up. You look all done in!" With that, she waded into the chaos, snapping orders and giving directions.

Erinn turned to find Kainen beside her. "Your mother," Erinn said, "is possibly the most infuriating woman I have ever met!"

"I know," Kainen replied. "Try living with her."

The refugees were settled in the church hall and the wounded were taken into the cottages of those who could accommodate them. Erinn and Kainen were pulled into the inn and sat before steaming plates of food, whilst first Owen and then Harlen peppered them with questions.

"How long ago would you say it happened?"

"How many bodies were there?"

"What was the old man doing there?"

The door flew open, cutting off the stream of questions in mid-flow. "There she is!" Cedril shouted, as he stormed in. "There's the harlot that got my Artor killed."

Erinn drew back into the chair as Harlen rose to his feet. "Don't you talk that way about my daughter," he growled, curling his hands into fists.

"Now gentlemen, please," Maryanne said, moving to stand between the two and placing her hand on Harlen's chest. "We're all upset and we all want to know what's happened. Let's just try to stay calm."

"Calm? My son lies dead, according to this young strumpet," Cedril yelled, his fat face red with anger and grief.

"I can't see how it could be her fault," Maryanne said, in a reasonable tone, while shooting pleading looks at Harlen.

"She's the one who encouraged him to take up this ridiculous soldier idea," Cedril said. "If it weren't for her, filling his head with chaff and nonsense, he'd be home now. Safe as stone."

"He didn't need encouraging!" Erinn said, rising to her feet. "He hates the mill and everything to do with it. You're always nagging at him, putting more work on him there and all he wants is away from it. The beacon guard was his idea. I didn't even know he'd gone for it until he had it." Her face was red with grief and anger, and tears began to fall down her cheeks.

"Now then, lass, pay him no mind." Harlen engulfed the girl in his huge arms and looked squarely over her head at the miller. "I know you've had a shock. I know what it is to lose someone. But I'll tell you now, Cedril, you stop badgering my girl or we will have a reckoning." He spoke quietly and the threat hung cold in the silence that followed.

Cedril froze, his mouth open and the thoughts were clear on his red face. He looked at the crying girl in Harlen's arms and then at the smith's stony face, then closed his mouth with an audible clack of teeth. Owen came out from behind the bar and pulled the miller away. "You need a drink, Cedril, after a shock like this. I'll get you a nice brandy. It's on the house, this time." He stepped back behind the bar and poured a generous measure.

"Now, then, what are we going to do about this?" Maryanne breathed out the words all at once.

"I think that's pretty obvious, Maryanne," Harlen said. "We need to get word out good and fast. Send out a rider to the new fort near Cripps Brook."

"That's still a goodly ride, Harlen," she said, sitting back down at the well-polished table. "Even if you took two horses and changed every hour or so, it'd take a day or so to get there. From what these poor people have said, these Bjornmen could be here at any moment."

"I don't know any faster way, Maryanne. We're just going to have to do the best we can alone for a time."

"What about the beacon?" Kainen spoke up, his voice sounding too high for his liking.

"Beacon's gone, boy," Harlen said, confused. "You told us that yourself."

"The beacon is but the hill's still there." Kainen explained. "It won't be as good, but surely all we need is a big fire. The cottage and the wood from the tower would do for that, wouldn't it?"

"I imagine it probably would, at that," the smith said, as a broad smile grew on his bearded face. "That's a rare one you've got there, Maryanne."

"I'll go." Cedril spoke up, from the bar. "I want to see him anyway and a flame burns brighter at night."

"You can't think to go now?" Maryanne said. "You'll blunder right past the trail in this dark. Leave it to the morning!"

Erinn extricated herself from Harlen's arms and made her way to the door. She suddenly needed air. The place was stifling, filled with too many opinions, and it was too loud for her to cope with right now. She stood on the front step, watching more carts arriving through the gates. The steady stream of them had slowed slightly, and they were only arriving in groups of ten or twelve now, but they were still coming in. She wondered idly where they were going to put them all, as she stepped down to the edge of the road and walked slowly towards the church hall. The night was cloudy, the faintest hint of the tiny crescent moon peeking through the clouds as they drove across the sky. Torches were burning outside almost every home and lanterns shone bright in windows. There would be little or no sleep in Widdengate tonight.

The hall was bustling. Lanterns were hanging on hooks by the double doors, the light a welcoming sight. Those lucky enough to have found chairs sat in them, but most were on the floor, wrapped in blankets. They huddled in small groups, sipping from steaming cups of tea and bowls of soup. Children, ever resilient, ran here and there, laughing as their parents enjoyed their first hot meal in days.

Hannah worked her way through the crowd, handing out blankets. She spotted Erinn in the doorway and made her way over to her.

"Come to lend a hand, dear?" she said, in the mildly condescending voice that parents always seem to use with children they haven't yet realised are grown.

"I came to look," Erinn said, her mouth forming the words without the assistance of her brain. Hannah gave her a strange look.

"I mean, I came to look in on the old man we found at the hill," she went on.

"He's in one of the other rooms with some of the worst wounded," Hannah said, after a moment. "I don't think he's come round yet. Could you help me here for a while first, then we'll go and see?"

Erinn nodded dutifully and Hannah smiled in approval. "Right then, there's lots to do and none of it hard." She stopped. "I tell you what. Why don't you run and fetch Kainen and Devin, and anyone else who's not busy, and bring them all here. It's time we pulled together on this, and there's plenty of those who haven't pulled their weight yet."

Erinn ran to fetch them and, before long, she was handing out blankets, as Devin and others boiled up soup and made tea. It was a pleasant kind of busy, just enough to keep her too busy to think, but not so much that she was run into the ground.

Some time later, she found herself leaning against the doorway leading into one of the back rooms, which had been turned into a makeshift infirmary. The room was full of men and women lying on piles of blankets that served as makeshift cots. Trallen moved slowly through the people, most of whom were asleep or unconscious, checking to see if there was anything they needed or that he could do.

Erinn's eyes roamed through the room and fell on the old man from the hilltop. He looked older and more frail somehow, now that he was cleaned up and in a bed.

"I wonder who he is." Devin said over her shoulder.

She turned to look at him. "We'll have to wait and see when he wakes up, I suppose. He certainly holds the answers to an awful lot of questions."

"If he wakes up." Devin said. "Hannah told me that's a nasty wound he has. The blade might have cut into some of his vitals."

"All we can do is wait, I suppose. I'm going to go home Devin, will you walk me? I'm suddenly all done in."

Devin looked her at with surprise. "If you want me to. Of course."

"I know it's silly. I just don't want to be alone right now."

"Of course," Devin repeated, for want of something else to say. He took her arm and led her gently out into the darkness.

* * *

They worked deep into the night, farmers, hired hands, and villagers. They cut the wreckage of the beacon tower away, stacking it inside the cottage until it almost reached the roof. The larger timbers were lifted and leant against the side of the building until the final structure was almost as high as the tower had been.

Cedril stood near the doorway of the cottage with a flaming torch in his hand. His face was wet with tears, but he was unconcerned by the small crowd of people watching him. "One thing I always said, son," he said, into the doorway. "Don't start the job unless you mean to finish it." He paused, then tossed the torch inside. "I know you'd want to finish it."

The stacked wood had been surrounded by thatch, which had been torn down from the roof, and it caught quickly. Flames licked away at the thick timbers, growing stronger and rising towards the remnants of the roof. Within a few short minutes, the whole cottage was ablaze and the fire soared high into the dark skies, as the villagers drew back from the heat.

Cedril watched the western skies, waiting. The flames were slow to come, but orders are seldom flexible, and eventually the distant beacon flared, followed by another and another, carrying the delayed signal onwards, westwards. The fat miller cried then, silently with his face turned to the darkness as the flames devoured the remains of the tower, the ruined cottage, and the body of his only son.

Chapter Thirteen

She walked into the kitchen to the rich scent of musk. The man himself was unclear, more the suggestion of a man than anything she could have described to anyone else. At the same time, he was so much more male than anything she'd ever known. He smiled at her as she walked in, a hint of dazzling blue eyes and perfect teeth.

"You're not supposed to be in here," she said weakly, knowing it was a ridiculous thing to say.

"I was waiting for you, Hannah," the man said, again with that smile. It wasn't arrogant or rakish. It just screamed confidence and self-assurance. The type of smile that made her go weak at the knees.

"F..for me?" she stammered, hating the way she sounded. Like a young girl who blushed at the sight of a man, not a woman past her thirties. He moved closer and every step was like a strut. Then, she was in his arms, his strong muscles bunching under his loose shirt as he held her tight. His mouth seemed to be everywhere at once, kissing her lips, the line of her jaw, her throat.

She threw her head back and let him do as he would, lost in sensation and the smell of him. He devoured her neck, moving lower to kiss the swell of her breasts, before coming up to kiss her lips again. Her eyes opened for a moment and the man was gone.

Instead a horned creature held her close. Its eyes glowed the colour of a summer sunset, and it grinned as it moved in to kiss her again. She screamed and lurched back, staring at it in horror. Naked and more than ready for her, it had the torso of a man and the lower body of a goat.

It reached for her again, grabbing her arm and pulling her to the floor. It slid a hairy hand up her thigh and under her skirts, tearing at her underclothes. It didn't seem to matter how much she struggled, he was able to hold her down with ease. Then he was between her legs and she felt him against her, his muscles bunched and…

Hannah screamed and sat bolt upright in the bed. Her hair stuck to her face with sweat and her heart pounded like the hooves of a galloping horse. She looked around the dark room in confusion, but saw nothing. The only sounds were the wind against the side of the house and Khorin's soft snoring in the bed next to her. A dream. Another dream.

She shook herself against a sudden chill and climbed out of the bed, padding across to the window. The night was dark and clouded, probably still some hours before dawn, though it was hard to tell. Throwing on a thick robe she made her way down the stairs, taking care not to disturb anyone. Another time, she might have laughed at the thought. It was almost impossible to wake Khorin. The shreds of the dream still clung to her, however, and she could not smile.

The kitchen was dark and cold, but the coals in the woodstove still produced a dull red glow when she blew into them, enough to light a taper so she could light the lamps. She busied herself with clearing the worst of the ash from the stove and lay thin strips of kindling on the coals, before putting a couple of larger pieces of wood on top and closing the door. The kindling flared after a moment as the air was sucked in through the narrow vents, and she moved to the pump to clean out the kettle while the larger pieces caught.

You're losing your mind, she thought, as she placed the kettle on the stove and opened the metal door again. The larger pieces of kindling had caught well and she added two thick logs on the top before closing the door again. Making tea in the middle of the night was a foolish enterprise. It simply took too long for the stove to heat up. She knew though, from the past few weeks, that there was little chance of her getting more sleep.

The thought of going across to the hospital crossed her mind briefly, but she quickly dismissed that idea. If she was needed she'd have been called, and she'd only wake those that needed the sleep if she went in there now.

She replayed the dream in her head and shuddered. She'd had the dreams almost every night for the past two weeks. They hadn't been this bad since right after it happened, before Midwinter. She'd thought she might have been coming through the worst of it, but then this.

The kettle was steaming and she busied herself with the mechanics of making tea. Cup and leaves and strainer. She toyed with the idea of adding a good slug of brandy to it, but settled for a generous dollop of honey.

"You've got to talk to someone," she advised her reflection in the dark windows. The truth was she couldn't talk to anyone though, could she? Not without being thought a complete loon. The disastrous attempts to talk about it with Khorin had shown her that. Besides, reality was bad enough at the moment, what with refugees pouring in through the gates every five minutes. What were a few bad dreams in the face of that?

She blew on her tea and wrapped her hands tight around the cup, seeking comfort from the heat that was just this side of being hot enough to burn her, and waited for daylight.

Dawn came slowly, the sun burning its way through the clouds and shining down on the village. The once sleepy place had roused itself during the last few weeks. The residents had set up a camp outside of the walls to house the endless influx of people, and tents dotted the grass while workmen hurried to finish the larger wooden buildings that had been fashioned to house three or four families.

Hannah stepped out of the little cottage and headed towards Widdengate. The walls looked imposing, even from here, but the influx of the refugees made a mockery of them. There were more people living outside of them than could be protected by them. She doubted that the village could actually hold all of these people now, should it ever be necessary.

The village was already coming alive as the sun crept over the trees and the noises of village life began to fill the air. Smoke was rising from a half a hundred fires as people struggled to heat water. Chickens clucked and crowed amid the sounds of early morning, the low murmur of conversation, and clack of pots.

"They always manage to grab a chicken," she said to herself as she made her way through the already open gates, past the young guards scratching at their new uniforms, and on towards the church. She glanced over at the hospital as she climbed the stone steps. *How quickly it has become the hospital, instead of the hall and school*, she thought.

She felt a sense of peace wash over her as she stepped into the church. Perhaps it was just that it was a few degrees cooler and so much quieter than the outside, but it never failed to give her a sense of calm. It was an impressive structure, even more impressive when she thought about how quickly it had been built. High stone walls with expensive, leaded glass windows gave way to a vaulted ceiling. Rows of silent pews led towards the altar, with its beautifully engraved lectern, behind which stood a statue of a hooded figure depicting the Lord of New Days. The figure held one hand out in welcome, as if asking the viewer to take it.

Hannah walked softly between the rows of pews, heading for the altar. Even at this early hour, all of the tall thick candles were lit. A woman stepped out from behind the deep red curtain that concealed a doorway leading to the back. It took a moment or two for Hannah to recognize her as Sarah, the miller's wife. She stopped as she saw Hannah, and rested the broom on the floor. "Can I help you?" she asked, in a proprietorial manner.

Hannah cleared her throat, unsure of her own voice. "I…I was looking for Father Trallen, if he has a few moments?" she asked.

"I'll go and see," Sarah said, looking her up and down with disapproval, though at what Hannah could only guess.

The church suddenly felt cold and Hannah hugged herself, rubbing her arms, as she examined the statue again. Despite the fact it was carved from white stone, it seemed sinister and a chill coursed through her. The figure was supposed to be asking to hold hands, to show you the way. To Hannah, however, it seemed that the figure sought to lead you astray, to lead you onto darker paths. She chided herself for being ridiculous, and then turned as the door behind the curtain creaked lightly.

"Hannah," Trallen said with a warm smile as he stepped out to take her hands. "I didn't expect to see you until later on this afternoon. You were up so late in the hall."

"I know, Father," she replied, a slight quiver in her voice. "I wondered if maybe you might have time to talk for a few minutes?" Her voice was hushed and hesitant, and had none of its usual calm assurance.

His expression changed to one of concern. "Of course, my dear. Why don't we go into my office?" He opened the door and ushered her through. The back of the church was simple, a small kitchen and living quarters and a cosy study. She followed him silently through the narrow hall, ignoring the almost possessive look she received from Sarah as she passed.

Trallen went into the study and settled into a comfortable looking chair behind a large desk. He waved her into a chair and folded his hands on the desk. "Now, how can I help you, Hannah?" he asked, gently.

"I don't know where to start." she laughed, suddenly nervous.

"Is something bothering you? I must say, you don't look yourself." Trallen said, his voice full of paternal concern.

She looked around. The room was lined with bookshelves housing more books than she had ever seen in one place. Deep red curtains hung at the window and a large fireplace filled another wall. She wondered for a moment just how much wealth this church had. Trallen had certainly spared no expense since the day he arrived. She forced herself to meet his gaze and swallowed.

"Do you ever dream, Father?" she asked in a voice she hardly recognized as her own. It was small and broken. Desperate.

"Dream?" He looked confused for a moment. "Well, yes, I suppose I do. Don't we all?"

"This *is* just between us, isn't it?" she asked, as the thought occurred to her.

"Of course, Hannah. You needn't worry about anything like that. Now please, tell me what troubles you."

It was hard to get the words out to start with and then, like a dam had failed, they flew from her mouth in a torrent. The strange figure in the kitchen, how he'd changed into that monster, and then the flash of blue sparks as she defended herself with the poker. The distance that had grown between her and Khorin, and finally the dreams that she couldn't seem to shake off. Trallen's face was impassive throughout.

"And so, when Khorin and Devin came in and found you," Trallen prompted, "what did you tell them?"

"Khorin sent Devin upstairs." Hannah pressed her palms together between her knees as her eyes pricked and she bit the inside of her cheek. "We talked and I told him that something had attacked me."

"And what did he say?"

"He didn't believe me. He thought I'd had a walking dream." She sniffed and rummaged in her skirts for a handkerchief.

"What do you think?" the man smiled. "Do you think it was a dream?"

"I don't know, Father. I mean, it was just so real. I had bruises on my hips from where I hit the floor, but I suppose if it had been a walking dream..."

She shook her head suddenly and spoke with conviction. "No. No, it wasn't a dream, I'm sure of it."

"Sometimes, Hannah, dreams are sent to tell us something." Trallen leaned back in his chair and looked up at the small window.

"Like what?" Hannah replied.

"I'm not sure, but the fact you keep having the same dream would seem to support this idea." He stood. "Would you like some tea?"

He didn't believe her. He was being nice about it, but clearly he thought it was all a dream too. It was all too much and she stood in a sharp motion, clutching her handkerchief in a fist. "No. Thank you, Father, but no. I've wasted too much of your time already."

"Now, Hannah," he said, reaching out for her hands. "Don't take it like that. You've not wasted anybody's time."

"Except perhaps my own," she said, with some heat. "It's clear you don't believe me."

"My dear, we all have dreams that confuse and even scare us sometimes..."

She cut him off, raising her index finger in front of him. "It was not a dream!" she said, biting off each word. She threw the door open and nearly barged into the mousy woman in the hallway, who tumbled away from where she'd clearly had her ear pressed to the door.

"As for you," Hannah said, rounding on the woman, "you ought to be home with your husband instead of eavesdropping in here. He's just lost his only child, for pity's sake. It's disgusting the way you're carrying on. The whole village is talking about it!" With that, she swept down the narrow hallway, leaving Sarah with her hand pressed to her mouth and her cheeks flushed, as she exchanged guilty looks with Trallen.

* * *

He awoke, in some confusion, in a makeshift bed. It was little more than a pile of straw, well-covered with thick blankets and sheets, but straw nonetheless. Still, it was warm and the thick blankets under the sheets kept the straw from poking through and scratching too much. He rubbed his eyes and ran a dry tongue around the inside of his mouth, trying to clear the stale taste as he looked around the room. It was well lit, with two large windows and a lantern burning in the corner. A large slate stood on a stand in one corner of the room, stained a paler colour with chalk dust. Tables and benches had been stacked in another, presumably moved to make room for the four beds. He tried to haul himself to a sitting position, gasping in pain as the movement pulled at the wound in his side.

"Oh good. You're awake," a voice said, as he lowered himself back down into the bed with a grimace.

"I suppose I am," he managed, in a weak voice.

"How do you feel?" The voice belonged to a red-haired girl of perhaps fifteen summers. She crouched next to his pallet, her plain grey dress pooling about her feet.

"Tired," he managed. "Thirsty."

"I suppose that's to be expected," she replied. "Do you think you're up to trying to drink some water?" He nodded. She moved to a table in the corner and splashed some water from a jug into a small bowl. Kneeling down beside him, she set the bowl on the floor. "Do you want me to help you sit up a little?"

"Please," he said. His voice was a dry croak.

She pulled gently at his shoulders, forcing him upright, as she wedged folded blankets down behind him. He coughed most of the water out as she supported his head and held the bowl to his lips, but he managed a few sips.

"Is that any better?" she asked.

He cleared his throat and managed a weak smile. "Much," he said. "What's your name?"

She laughed. "That was going to be my next question." Her hand went to her long hair, which was tied back in a plait. "Erinn," she said. "What can I call you?"

He frowned slightly at the strange way she'd phrased it, almost as if she were inviting him to choose one. "My name," he laughed. "It's been so long since I've used it, I've almost forgotten." She looked at him expectantly. "Obair," he said. "My name is Obair."

"That's a nice name," she said, standing and crossing the room to check on the occupant of another bed, an older woman with dark hair. She seemed to still be asleep or unconscious. Erinn glanced back at him. "Are you having any pain?" she asked.

"Some." He twisted in the bed, trying to find a position where the wound didn't pull.

"I can get you something for it, if it's bad. We have a tea."

"Willow bark and birch?" he guessed.

She nodded and he pulled a face. "I think I'd rather be in pain."

"It's not *that* bad," she said, with an amused look.

He looked around, noting the sun streaming through the windows. "What day is it? Where am I?"

"It's Dawnings," she replied. "The twenty-third. We found you five days ago and brought you back here. How much do you remember of what happened?"

"Is it full moon yet?" he asked, ignoring her question. She gave him an odd look. "Not yet, no. Not for three or four days, I think. Why?"

"That's something at least," he said, softly to himself. He looked up at her. "Where is *here*, exactly?"

She flushed. "Sorry, I didn't think. You're in Widdengate, on the edge of The Wash."

He nodded slowly. "What do I remember? I remember a strange man on the road." His gaze slipped from her eyes and drifted around the room as if lost and seeking a place to settle. His forehead creased in thought. "He spoke a language I didn't recognize, which is a bit odd in itself really. He seemed upset about something, but we couldn't understand each other. I gave up in the end but when I tried to move past him, he attacked me."

"What about the tower?" she said, with a catch in her voice.

"Tower? I'm sorry, Erinn, I don't remember anything about a tower."

"That's where we found you. What were you doing there, anyway?" Her demeanour had changed. Her eyes were intent, but her lips were pinched. She was holding something back.

"Am I a captive here, then?"

"What?" She looked shocked and stepped back from him. "No! Of course not!"

"It's just your questions seemed...well...you know..."

"Oh, Obair, I'm sorry." Her face crumbled, and her poise and assurance dropped away from her. For the first time, she sounded like a fifteen-year-old girl. "It's just that when we found you...when I found you...you were with someone who was... close to me."

"Is he here?" Obair looked around at the other beds, but only one was occupied.

"No, he...he was dead when we found you. He'd been attacked." She sniffed, rubbing at her eyes with the back of her hand. "I'd hoped you'd be able to explain things and answer some questions."

He lay back into the blankets and sighed. "No, Erinn, I'm sorry I have no answers for you. Only more questions, I imagine."

"I've tired you," she said, leaning in to look at his eyes. "I'm sorry. I'll leave you to rest."

"No, please." He reached out and caught her arm, but let go quickly as she looked down at his hand. "It's just that it's been a very long time since I've been able to talk to anyone."

"Alright, but only for a little while, or Father Trallen will have my hide. If Hannah doesn't have it first, that is!" She fetched a chair, scraping it along the floor to his bedside. "What would you like to talk about? Where are you from, anyway?"

"A question first, if I may?" He waited for her nod. "What do you know about faerie stories?"

* * *

Hannah was still fuming as she walked into the hospital, but the sounds and smells of the place soon drove the thoughts of Trallen from her mind. The ever-present sound of crying, combined with the low hum of conversation, and the constant smell of boiling water and willow-bark tended to put things into perspective. There were people here who had far bigger problems than dreams.

A blonde woman, in her middle years, looked up from where she crouched next to one of the beds closest to the doorway. A young girl with a nasty cut on her leg, which had turned sour, lay in the bed crying as the woman applied a new poultice. She stood as Hannah approached, brushing her hair from her face with the back of her hand as she turned to face her.

"How are we doing this morning, Lyra?" Hannah asked. The woman had been a godsend really. She'd arrived with one of the first group of refugees, and presented herself as soon as they'd begun turning the school into an infirmary. Though not fully trained, she was a good stretch closer to being a hedge doctor than Hannah would ever be, and Hannah deferred to the woman's judgement as a matter of course.

"We're getting there, I think," Lyra replied, as she stood. "Three more gone since yesterday."

"Gone? I thought we hadn't lost anyone since the first day?"

"No!" the blonde woman laughed. "Gone as in able to leave. Not the other gone."

She laughed again as Hannah breathed a visible sigh of relief.

"Are you about ready to hand over, then?" Hannah asked.

"I think so. There's not much to report, really. Most are on the mend now. Oh, and the old man Erinn found at the tower is awake. She's in there with him now."

Hannah raised her eyebrows at that. They hadn't expected him to live, which was one of the reasons Lyra had insisted on putting him in the back room. "People who are sick don't need to be watching others dying," she'd said. "Getting well is as much in your head as it is in your body, and if you watch others falling by the wayside, it makes you lose hope." It had made an odd kind of sense to Hannah, so she'd gone along with it. Besides, they'd been running low on space anyway.

"Right, well, get you gone then, girl," she said. "You look all done in." She didn't actually. She was one of those annoying people who always looked fresh regardless.

The woman gave her a penetrating look. "I'm fine, Hannah. Actually if anything, you look more tired than I feel. Is everything alright?"

"Yes, fine," Hannah said, with a lightness of spirit that she didn't feel. "Just not sleeping much at the moment."

"Well, don't let this place drive you too hard, okay? You're no good to anyone if you're falling down in the middle of the day."

"Yes, Mother," Hannah said and stuck out her tongue.

"I'm serious, Hannah." she said without cracking a smile.

"I know. I'll look after myself, I promise." Hannah replied. "Now go on with you."

"Now who's mothering?" Lyra teased, as she left.

Hannah stood for a moment as she took in the room. The majority of the beds were filled with people who probably shouldn't be in them any longer, but there was no other place in the village to put them. The camp outside of the walls was barely fit for a dog, and she had problems sending anyone to it. She walked through to the back, returning waves from various patients and visitors on the way.

Hannah stopped in the narrow corridor as her fingertips touched the door of the back room, listening to the voices coming from inside.

"...just stories for children, aren't they?" Erinn was saying.

"Are they, though?" asked the old man.

"Well of course they are, Obair," Erinn laughed. "What else would they be?"

"I'll come to that," Obair said. "Let me ask you this first. What do the fae do in these stories?"

"The fairies, you mean? Well, lots of things, really. They come in the night, and steal cakes and food. They pester farmers, and bother sheep and pigs. Oh, and sometimes they steal babies and replace them with a fairy child."

"Hardly topics for a child's story, wouldn't you say?" Obair said. "Can you think of a single story where the fae are nice? Or friendly?"

There was a long pause before Erinn finally replied. "You know, I don't think I can. Isn't that odd? I never thought of that before."

"So then these tales are not so much stories, as they are warnings, then." Obair said.

"I suppose you could look at it like that." Erinn giggled suddenly. "Are you saying that the fairies are going to come out from under their toadstools and get us all, Obair?"

"Did you ever play chase as a child and hold up your crossed fingers to stop someone from catching you?" the man asked.

"I suppose." Erinn's confusion at the change of topic was clear in her voice. "We'd all shout 'fainites' and that would make you safe for a minute or two."

"It's not 'fainites', Erinn," Obair said softly. "It's 'fae nights'. It means that everything stops on the nights of the fae. All games and all foolishness cease because, on those nights, mankind must do everything it can to stay safe."

Erinn laughed uncomfortably as he carried on. "What about the old skipping rhyme, 'Iron to Keep the Fae Away'?" He hummed a few bars.

"'I'm to Keep a Fairer Way'? I know that one," Erinn said.

"Sing it for me?"

"I suppose," she said, and sang in a clear, high voice:

"I'm to keep a fairer way,

With horses' shoes and miller's weigh,

From wax to waning moon, we pray

Keep us warm 'til light of day."

He applauded with a weak clap. "How old would you say that song is, Erinn?"

"Oh, it's ages old. My grandmother taught it to me and she said her Nana taught it to her."

"What if I told you there were older words to it? That your words have just replaced the original ones over the years?"

"Really?" She sounded intrigued.

"The version I was taught by my master went like this." He sang in a quavering voice that lurched unsteadily from one note to the next:

"Iron to keep the fae away,
Horse's shoe or music play,
From wax to waning moon, they prey
Scarce safer in the light of day."

"That's interesting, Obair, but I think I'm a little old to be scared of things that go bump in the night," Erinn said.

"Of course you are. But are you old enough to wonder what is actually causing the bump?"

"You're confusing me," Erinn replied.

"I don't think so," Obair said. "I think you were already confused. Perhaps you're just starting to see the truth."

"What truth?"

"That there is a meaning behind the stories, songs and games. Something that the druids have kept us all safe from for hundreds of years."

"The droos ? What have droos got to do with anything?"

"Druids, Erinn. Not droos." he corrected her with a sigh.

Hannah jumped as a door crashed open inside the room and she jerked away from the door for a second.

"I think we have heard quite enough of *that,* thank you," Father Trallen said, in an outraged tone, as he stormed into the room. "Erinn, thank you for your efforts. You may leave."

Hannah stepped back from the doorway before it opened. Erinn rushed out and disappeared down the hallway. Hannah looked over her shoulder to be sure the girl had gone before moving closer to the door again. A hope was kindling inside of her. A sad, quiet hope, but a hope all the same, and she held it tight, nurturing it, like a candle in the night.

"I appreciate you are still unwell, sir, but I for one will not tolerate that sort of talk in here." Trallen's voice carried easily through the door Erinn had left ajar.

"What sort of talk?" Obair asked.

"Nonsense about fairies and droos. Superstitious bunk,"Trallen said. "These are good people here. God-fearing folk who have embraced the word of the Lord of New Days, and I won't have this foolishness."

"Lord of New Days?" Obair asked.

"Yes, the Lord of New Days. The Saviour of the Righteous, leading us from the superstitions of the past to the glory of His future."

"I can't say I've ever heard of him," Obair said.

"That doesn't excuse your behaviour, and I won't have you corrupting these people."

"Corrupting them?" the old man asked, a hint of amusement in his voice.

"Yes, corrupting, with that sort of heathen nonsense,"Trallen snapped. "I will have someone look at you and determine if you are well enough to leave. I think it may well be best if you were on your way, before you do any more damage."

"I'm sorry, Father...?"

"Trallen," the priest supplied.

"Father Trallen. I don't mean to offend you or anyone else here. I was simply asking the girl some questions."

"Well, I will not tolerate that sort of foolishness sir. Not in my church hall. The holy text is quite clear that our task is to move beyond the superstitions of the past," Trallen explained, his pompous voice irritating Hannah.

"I wonder how it is that I've never heard of your faith before, Father?" Obair asked.

"We are a fairly new church,"Trallen explained. "The First had the truth revealed to him only six years ago. The faith has been spreading ever since."

"Interesting," Obair said.

"I'm sorry, I can't stop to talk about this right now."Trallen said. "I really must get on. I'll send someone to check on your recovery, and we'll get you up and about as soon as we can." His tone seemed somewhat mollified as it carried towards the door.

Hannah realised, almost too late, that the priest was approaching the door. She dashed down the hallway and ducked into a small cupboard as she heard the footsteps approach. Holding her breath in the dark, she bit her lip to keep from laughing as the priest passed. "Hiding in cupboards now, like a naughty child," she muttered, as she clambered out, and brushed the dust and cobwebs from her skirts. She glanced once down the corridor to ensure she hadn't been seen and then hurried into the back room.

He lay back on the pillows, with his eyes closed. His face was old, the kind of age that comes from a lifetime of hard and relentless work, rather than just the passage of years. She stepped to his side, her soft shoes making little noise on the plain wooden floor. Despite this, he opened his eyes and looked up at her curiously.

"Hello," he said. "I seem to be very popular this morning."

"You have had a few visitors," Hannah admitted. "I'm sorry about Father Trallen. He has some odd ideas sometimes."

"You heard then?" Obair cocked a bushy, grey-white eyebrow at her.

"It was hard to miss." She fought down a flush and coughed into her hand.

"Has he been here long?" He tried to pull himself back up into a seated position and she placed her hand on the thin nightshirt to support his back whilst she pushed the pillow and folded blankets in behind him.

"Almost a year, I suppose. He arrived last spring, out of the blue." She checked on the sleeping patient in the other bed, before pulling over a chair.

"I have a confession to make," she said.

"Oh?"

"I heard a little more than just Trallen ranting at you." She laughed an embarrassed little laugh. "I'm afraid I may have eavesdropped a little bit."

"Did you now?" His voice was flat, emotionless.

"You were talking to Erinn about fairy tales." She ignored his accusing eyes and forced herself onwards. The question was burning inside of her.

"Was I?" He gave her an appraising look. "Just indulging a child's curiosity, Miss." He chuckled softly. "Sorry, that just sounds wrong on a grown woman. Do you think I might ask your name?"

She laughed along with him. "Sorry, Obair, my name is Hannah."

"So you heard that too, then?" He raised both eyebrows this time and gave her a pointed look.

She gave in to the flush and her cheeks reddened as she nodded.

"So, have you come to scold me for corrupting the young, Hannah?" He laughed, but the sound died on his lips and he peered closely at her. "No, you haven't, have you? You've come to me with a question. I can see it on your face. You've seen something, haven't you?"

She nodded and glanced over her shoulder to the door. "Not here. I can't talk here," she said quickly. "Let me have a look at your dressings. Trallen has made it clear he wants you gone. If you're well enough, you can stay with my family."

"I don't want to cause you any trouble, Hannah." His face was serious.

"Obair, something happened to me some months back. Something that has nearly ended my marriage and that I still can't explain." She rubbed her upper arms as if feeling a sudden chill. "For a time, I thought I might even be going mad. If you can take this from me, as I hope you can, then you'd be welcome to stay for the rest of your life, let alone a few weeks."

She stood, businesslike as she brushed down her skirts. "Now," she said, as she took hold of the blankets, "let's take a look at that wound of yours, shall we?"

* * *

Rhenkin sat back in his chair and glared at the pile of papers before him on the desk. The room was bright and airy, twice the size of any office he'd ever worked from before, and handsomely furnished. The desk alone would probably pay any honest soldier's wage for a year. He went to the window, looking out at the courtyard below and watched his men drill at the pell post. Hacking and slashing first one way then the other. Darting in with low thrusts and pulling out quickly, before the return blow could land. "Lords and Ladies, I miss it," he said, his breath fogging the glass.

He turned back to the desk, glancing with hate-filled eyes at the pile of paperwork. "To the frosts with it," he swore, and made his way to the door. A man wasn't built to stifle indoors, drowning under papers, while children played at being soldier out in the good, honest air. Working up a sweat would help him, anyway. He laid a hand on the door handle just as the knock came at head height. He jumped and swore at himself, glancing around the room to make sure no one had seen, despite the fact that it was empty. He stepped back behind the desk and picked up a random sheet of paper before calling out. "Come!"

"Sorry to disturb sir," the sergeant said, as he entered the room. "Only he insisted it was urgent." He jerked his head at a man in the hallway. Rhenkin recognized the scout immediately and nodded. "That's fine, Sergeant, send him in."

The man was stubbled and travel-stained but he stepped in and moved smartly to attention. Rhenkin looked him up and down. Usually impeccably turned out, he was a mess. His uniform was torn and stained with grass and dirt, and a dirty bandage covered the back of one hand.

"Roberts," Rhenkin said, with a nod. "Report. Where is Stibbons?"

"He's dead, sir. Well, presumed dead," Roberts said. His blue eyes met Rhenkin's and his gaze did not waver as he spoke.

Rhenkin moved back around his desk and sat, waving a hand at one of the two chairs facing him. He leaned forward and planted his elbows on the desk, steepling his fingers.

Roberts sank into the chair and collected himself for a moment before he spoke.

"We proceeded, as planned, through the Wash and into the Reaches," he began, breaking eye contact and staring at a fixed point in space as he remembered. "We made good time, but left the horses at the last garrison. From there, we left the roads and cut across country."

"Get to the point, Roberts," Rhenkin said.

"Yes, sir," Roberts replied, his face colouring slightly. "So far as we were able to tell, the Bjornmen have moved inland and taken all the territory within forty miles of the coast. We saw villagers fleeing inland with whatever they could salvage, but the villages themselves have been burnt to the ground."

"All of them?" Rhenkin was aghast. "There must be ten or twelve villages in that stretch of land!"

"We didn't have a chance to check every one, sir, but we did see four that have been razed. They seem to have fired the barns, storehouses and crops as well, in those places where it was dry enough."

"Nothing to come back to," Rhenkin grunted.

"Sir?"

"The Bjornmen. They burn the villages and then the crops. They leave the peasants nothing to return to, just the scorched earth," Rhenkin said. He closed his eyes, leaned back in the chair and ran both hands back through his dark brown hair.

"What about the peasants themselves? Are they slaughtering them or just driving them off?" he asked.

"They appear to be just driving them off, sir, for the most part."

Rhenkin studied the man. There was more to this, something he wasn't saying. "Continue," he said.

"They seem to have established a patrol cordon beyond which it's extremely hard to move about easily," Roberts said. "They've established at least three villages that we could see. They're heavily defended, with high palisades, ditches and stakes for two or three hundred yards from the walls, and then farmlands out from there. The patrols are frequent but all on foot. We saw no sign of cavalry, or any manner of mounted troops."

"What about their numbers? Could you make an estimate of their troop strengths?"

Roberts shook his head and looked down at the floor. "Impossible to say with any certainty, sir, but more than sufficient to keep us from getting close. They don't have troop encampments that we could see, but they have thrown up the villages in a remarkably short space of time. If I had to base it on the patrol strength alone, I'd say at least twenty thousand, but I think it could be far more than that."

"Thank you, Roberts. We'd better relay this to the duke." Even as he said it, Rhenkin realised how ridiculous it sounded. The entire staff knew Freyton was all but incapacitated by noon each day.

Roberts cleared his throat. "There is one other thing, sir."

Rhenkin paused, half out of the chair, and looked up. "Oh?"

"Yes, sir. The Bjornmen. They've brought some kind of beasts with them," Roberts said in a low voice, as if embarrassed.

"Beasts?" Rhenkin fixed the man with a stern look. "Explain."

"I can't say that we ever saw them clearly, sir. It was when we were on the way back. We'd taken to travelling in the dark, as it was just past the full moon and, most nights, it was easy enough to see."

Rhenkin nodded and motioned the man to continue.

"Well, the first we knew, there was some kind of flute or music playing, and then this high-pitched laughter from whoever was leading them. Then they loosed them on us through the trees. Three of the bastards, that I saw. Dark and horned, with claws like knives. We fought them off as best we could in the dark. But the way they fought, sir...I've never seen anything move that fast." He clenched his fists and leaned against the desk, shaking his head as he drew in a shuddering breath.

"I'm not one for tall tales, sir, and I hesitate to tell you this, even now. I fear you'll think me mad, but they came at me and I slipped down onto the ground. One leapt right atop me and the moon caught its face. It had a man's face, sir. Eyes, nose, even a beard. But the moonlight was shining off the horns on its head. It'd have had me then, sir, if it weren't for Stibbons. He kicked it off me and led them off into the trees. I tried to follow, sir, but he was already screaming by the time I'd stood up and I had to get the report in." He looked down at his shaking hands before meeting Rhenkin's eyes. "I ran, sir. I ran like a scared child and that probably killed him."

Rhenkin stood and walked back to the window. He clasped his hands behind his back as he looked out at the grey skies. "I don't think you failed anyone, son," he said without turning. "Your first duty was to get back here and report. Stibbons knew that and I don't think he'd blame you. A word of advice though, keep this to yourself. Men don't need to be worrying about things like this, not with what's already coming."

"It's okay, sir." Roberts said, in a quiet voice. "I wouldn't believe it, either."

Rhenkin turned and moved to stand beside the scout. "I didn't say I don't believe you. You've no cause to lie to me and I've been living this life long enough to recognise real fear when I see it, Roberts. You've done your job well and you've a bright future ahead of you. Don't ruin it by telling others things they can't accept, no matter how much you know them to be true." He held out a hand and hauled the scout to his feet. "Now, we're going to go and see the duchess, and you can give her your report."

* * *

"I'm sorry, your grace, I didn't know what else to do," the maid repeated, as she led Selena to the polished mahogany doors. "I knocked and I knocked, just as you said, but he made no sound."

"It's alright, Claire, you did the right thing," Selena said, as she took hold of the doorhandles. "I'll deal with this. You may go."

"Yes, my lady." The diminutive maid bobbed a curtsey and left, her walk just a shade away from being an outright run.

Selena watched her pass along the hallway before going into the sitting room and through to the bedchamber. She opened the door, grimacing at the smell that wafted out. It was the stench of dried sweat, coupled with the sickening smell of vomit and sour wine. She gasped and scrambled in her sleeve for a lace handkerchief to press to her nose, before stepping into the gloom.

The curtains were drawn across the tall windows with just the barest crack allowing a slit of sunlight to cut across the room, illuminating the dust that hung in the air. She marched across to the one window and pulled them apart and then forced open the stiff window frame. The spring air caught the curtains, and they billowed out like scarlet sails, as she moved to the other window to do the same.

"Freyton!" She tried to shout, but the stench had robbed her voice of its strength, and it came out as little more than a croak. She tried again. "Freyton, wake up!" She grabbed hold of the heavy drapes surrounding the grand, four-poster bed and ripped them open wide.

The foul stink filled the chamber again as she took in the scene. Freyton lay fully dressed on his back. His face was pale and his eyes were vacant, as he stared lifelessly at the canopy of the bed, one hand still cradling the bottle of brandy to his chest. Vomit trailed from his mouth, running along the line of his jaw to where it had pooled beside his head.

"Oh, Freyton," Selena said as she looked at the man who had been her husband for little more than half a decade. "You poor, stupid, little man." She reached out and removed the bottle from his hand, ignoring the cold touch of his fingers, and gently brushed her hand over his eyes to close them. She took one last look and backed away calmly, stepping out into the sitting room and closing the doors firmly behind her. She tugged on the bell-pull and perched on one of Freyton's frightful scarlet divans while she waited.

"Claire," she said, smiling a greeting as the little maid appeared around the door. "Could you please make sure that His Grace remains undisturbed for the rest of the day? He's feeling rather unwell."

"Yes, my lady." She curtseyed. "Should I send for a healer?"

"No, I don't think that would be much help to him," Selena said, quickly. "Just leave him to rest. He'll call if he wants something. Let him sleep. Is that understood?" She fixed the brown-haired maid with a firm stare until she nodded. "Good, and send Hanris to my rooms please."

"Very good, my lady." She nodded. "Should I direct Captain Rhenkin to you, as well? He's been asking after you with some urgency."

"You know, Claire, that might be just the thing." She ushered the maid into the corridor.

Rhenkin was waiting for her as she came into the parlour. He snapped to attention as she made her way to her usual chair by the window with its little side table.

"Rhenkin," she said. "I understand you've been scampering all over the grounds looking for me."

"Indeed, your grace," he replied. "I have a scouting report from the Eastern Reaches."

She stood at that, all thoughts of Freyton forgotten. "And?"

"It's not good, my lady." He cleared his throat. "The Bjornmen have pushed some forty miles inland and driven off all of the peasants they came across. They have razed at least four villages to the ground, and we suspect many more."

"To what purpose?" Selena said. She was seething. Years of work developing these lands was going to waste at the hands of that barbarian rabble.

"It appears they are building their own villages, heavily fortified, and also beginning their own farming efforts.

"On my lands?" she cried. "Damn them! Damn them all!" Selena cried, clenching her hands into fists and digging her nails into her palms. "What are their numbers? Can we push them out?"

"We were unable to obtain a clear picture of their numbers, my lady, but it would be perhaps, unwise."

"Don't dance around it, Rhenkin," she growled. "Can we force them out or not?"

"I don't think so my lady, no," he admitted. "Without the King's forces to support us, I believe any campaign would be doomed to failure."

"Yes, well, King Pieter would appear to be a bit less than concerned about our situation." She strode to the map filling the rear wall of the chamber. "Which ones?"

"my lady?"

"Which villages, Rhenkin?" she grated.

"Frenton's Cross, Selene, Harton's Fields and Sonlan have been burnt to the ground. I don't have information on any others as of yet." He paused as she fumed to herself under her breath. "They...um...also appear to have torched the fields in a number of locations."

"I won't have this, Rhenkin," she said, in a low voice as she glared at him. "I have dragged this duchy back from the edge of the abyss with these villages and this expansion. I won't have it turned to ash by some hairy idiots from across the seas who want to play farmer!"

"The refugees have largely settled at the edge of The Wash." He gestured to the map.

"Where?"

"Widdengate, mostly, your grace."

"*Where?*"

"Widdengate," he repeated as he searched over the map. "It's a small village near to one of the beacon towers we had built. I believe it's in this area, but I don't think it's marked on this map."

She frowned at the spot he was pointing to. "That's it, then. I refuse to lose any more lands." She turned to him. "Where did you have the garrisons muster?"

"Carik's Fort," he said, pointing again.

"Fine. Move them all to Widdengate and fortify it. We will *not* lose another village."

"I'll see to it, my lady."

"One more thing, Rhenkin," she said as the thought occurred to her. "This delay in communication is crippling us. I want you to go there and personally take charge."

"Me, your grace?"

"Oh, don't bother to hide your joy, Rhenkin. Your hatred of paperwork is legendary." She allowed a wry smile to flicker across the edges of her lips. "Who is your second?"

"Coulson, my lady," he said. "He's a good man."

"Sort out an introduction before you go." She ran her hand lightly down his arm. "Protect my lands, Rhenkin, but come back safe to me. I'd miss having you around the place."

"I would miss being around the place," he said with a tight smile.

"See if you can have someone find Hanris, would you? I can't think what's keeping him."

She did not have to wait for long once Rhenkin had left until Hanris arrived. Hanris was dressed in his elegant black coat and white shirt, as usual, and his spectacles perched on the end of his nose. He entered the room and bowed.

"Hanris, I'm afraid we have a problem," she said, dispensing with the pleasantries.

"Your grace?"

"Shut the door, Hanris." She chewed on the inside of her lower lip, as she considered how to begin. He closed the door and turned to her, cocking his eyebrow.

"Freyton's dead," she said, simply. "I think he choked during the night. It looks like he was drinking again."

He didn't bother with condolences, to do so would have been hypocritical. "I will send messages at once to inform the family," he said simply.

"You will do no such thing!" Selena snapped in a shocked gasp.

"Your grace?" Hanris said in confusion.

"Think, Hanris. What happens if Freyton dies?"

"Well, of course you will be provided for, my lady, but the duchy would pass on to the next male in the line of inheritance. A cousin, I believe, since there is no direct heir."

"We are at war, Hanris!" She bit off the words as she glared at him "Do you really think we can afford for another bumbling idiot to take control now? Now, of all times?"

"I really don't see that there is any other choice, my lady," the stuffy little man persisted.

"There is always a choice, Hanris, even when it isn't immediately apparent." She walked over to the sideboard and filled a goblet with a pale, white wine. She was normally not much of a drinker but today, Lords and Ladies, today she needed it. She took a deep drink and turned back to the chamberlain.

"Where is the will, Hanris?"

"With the palace records, my lady. With the deeds and suchlike."

"And has anyone inspected it in recent years?"

"No, your grace, why would they?"

"So no one would know whether it had been updated or not, then?" She watched his face, as understanding finally dawned on him.

"No, my lady, they would not," he replied, picking nervously at some unseen piece of lint on one arm of his jacket. "Of course, any alterations would require your husband's signature."

"Oh, come now, Hanris, you do Freyton's signature better than he ever did himself," she chided.

Hanris flushed and coughed into his cupped palm. "Even if that were true, my lady, it would be highly irregular for the duchy to pass to yourself. It flies in the face of tradition recognised for scores of generations."

"I am quite aware of that. It would never pass to a mere woman," she said, with a twist to her lips. "What if I were pregnant however?" she asked, her eyes flicking towards the barracks and Rhenkin's office, before darting back to Hanris's face.

"A regency, you mean?" Hanris mused. "Yes, that might work. Of course, when the baby failed to appear..." He trailed off.

"Women lose babies all the time, Hanris," she said, gently. "For that matter, it wouldn't be that difficult for me to get pregnant, you know?" He looked genuinely shocked at that.

"What you're suggesting, my lady, would be nothing short of the grossest form of fraudulence."

"Needs must, Hanris. Needs must," she said. "The Bjornmen have moved forty miles inland. They are burning villages to the ground, and driving the peasants before them. Do you want to wait until they are ready to torch the palace itself? Or do you want to work with me to save the work we have put all our time and effort into for the past few years?"

He stared at her in horror for a long moment, before shaking his head slowly.

"Just do it, Hanris," she grated. "I don't have time for moral objections right now. Do what needs to be done and then bring it to me once it is ready for signatures."

"I...my lady...I..."

"Now, Hanris!"

He gave her a hurt, worried look and then fled.

She sat for a time, staring into space, and didn't really even notice she'd moved until her hand was pressed against the wall. She stared at the map grimly. "No more," she whispered.

Chapter Fourteen

Hannah held the mug tightly between her hands and looked down at the table. It was sturdy and well made, polished by a thousand hours of having flour and pastry scrubbed off its plain surface. It showed scorch marks in more than one place where she'd had to put a pot down quickly and had nowhere else within reach.

"I don't know where to start." she confessed as she glanced up at Obair.

He sipped his own tea and nodded. "Was it night-time?"

"Late evening," she replied, looking down again. "Maybe ten of the clock?"

"Go on..."

"Devin and Khorin had gone to the inn. It's something they do once every few weeks. I think they need the time to just be men without me tutting at them." She smiled at the thought.

"Anyway, the animals were making a fuss, so I went out to check on them. When I got back, there was a stranger in the kitchen, here." She gestured across the room to the counter near the woodstove.

"So much of this was like a dream, you understand? I couldn't really even tell you what he looked like, but I knew he wasn't Khorin. He walked over to me, pulled me close and kissed me, and I wanted him to..." She looked at the old man and blinked away the brimming tears. "Do you understand what that feels like?" Her voice was fierce as she forced the words out. "I wanted him to. I wanted it all. And in that moment, I didn't give a damn about Khorin or Devin, my family… any of it."

"What happened then?" Obair prompted, watching her intently.

"Then, something happened. I remember him jerking back away from me, almost like he'd been burnt, and he wasn't a man anymore. He was some kind of beast." She laughed a bitter little laugh and shook her head as she looked away from him. "Listen to me. This sounds crazy, even to me."

"Can you describe it?"

She looked at him curiously for a moment before she spoke. His eyes were eager and he was leaning towards her, across the table.

"It was short, not much taller than Devin," she began. "I remember it had the face of a man, except for the horns. And its eyes. It was the eyes I remember most. They were the colour of sunset and solid, no whites at all." She shook her head and her eyes followed the steam curling from her cup as she stared unseeing at the shapes it made. There was a long silence before she spoke again. "This is hard to say. I can't help but think that it all sounds like some nonsense from a child's tale. It's no wonder Khorin wouldn't believe me. You won't either." She stood and moved to the window, it was too dark to see out. It didn't matter, she wasn't really looking. It was just a means not to see the scorn she knew was coming

"The creature you saw," Obair said, in a quiet voice. "It had the legs of a goat, as well as the body and face of a man." He carried on as she spun to face him. "It was probably mostly naked, perhaps with a belt, and it almost certainly had a knife made of horn or bone." She nodded in silence, as her mouth hung open in disbelief.

"You've seen this thing?"

"Thing? It's called a satyr. There are many more of them too, Hannah, and they're coming," he replied.

"Who *are* you?" she said.

"Me?" His laugh was every bit as bitter as her own had been. "I'm a man with a terrible secret. A truth about an enemy that would make the Bjornmen look like children. And now that it's finally come time to tell it, I doubt there is anyone outside this room who would believe it, or not laugh in my face."

She sat back in her chair. "But who are you, though? What were you even doing near that tower?"

"I'm sure you've heard of the druids, Hannah," he said, meeting her eyes with his own. "What was it Erinn called them? droos ?"

She was across the kitchen before she realised she'd left the chair, hands scrabbling for a knife from the rack. "You just stay back. Stay away from me!" she cried, pressing her back against the counter.

"Hannah," he said, with a tired smile. "Look at me. Even if I wanted to do anything to harm you, I couldn't."

She looked at him then, really looked at him. A tired looking old man hunched over the table in clothing cobbled together from what the village could spare. His eyes were sunken under his shaggy grey eyebrows and he was thin, painfully thin. He was no threat to her, or to anyone.

"Most of what you will have heard about the druids are tales they created themselves, anyway," he explained as he watched her slowly uncoil.

"Why would anyone do that?" she asked, easing away from where she'd pressed herself into the corner, but the knife was still held firmly in one hand.

"To ensure they were left alone, Hannah. The druids had just barely survived the purges and so it was decided then to spread the stories you've heard."

"So, it's all nonsense then?"

"I expect that most of what you will have heard of them is, yes. The tall tales of druids sacrificing virgins on stone altars and wielding terrible magics are tales they created themselves. Mostly they were simple men and women devoted to an impossible task. One they couldn't trust to anyone else."

"So, the stories about the droos are all false?"

"Honestly, Hannah? I have no idea," he admitted. "I haven't heard them all, or even half of them, I expect. I began my task as a young child. All I know is what my master told me and, in truth, that wasn't much."

"But you are one of these, druids?" She tested the word, rolling it around with her tongue. Her eyes were still a little wide but beyond the shock was a curiosity.

"That's broadly true, I suppose, but I'm more of a caretaker than anything else." She gave him a puzzled look and he returned a sad smile. "You need to understand, Hannah, that there is no secret store of knowledge. I'm not some all powerful wizard from a children's tale. My earliest memories are of working with my master…" He glanced at the doorway, as heavy footsteps crunched down the steps to the kitchen.

Khorin stepped in quickly, closing the door fast against the draft behind him, then looked at Obair with surprise.

"So you're up and about, then?" he said.

"Yes," the old man replied. "I seem to be on the mend."

"Just be careful of your ears, then," Khorin said, with a perfectly straight face. "You'd not be the first to fall victim to her."

"Stop it, you!" Hannah swatted at him but he danced out of her reach, laughing.

"And what are you two talking about, then? Look at the pair of you, thick as thieves." Khorin chuckled as he walked to the stove.

"Nothing much," Hannah said, in a panic, as she shot pleading looks at Obair.

"I was asking about your lad, Devin," Obair said, not missing a beat.

"He's a good lad," Khorin said, as he filled the kettle from the pump. "We couldn't love him more if he was our own."

"He's not yours, then?"

Khorin turned at that and shot Hannah a puzzled look. "He's a foundling. I found him in the woods. Must be almost seven years ago now."

"There's a tale worth telling in that," Obair smiled.

"You don't know the half of it," Khorin said. He waved a cup at the two of them and cocked an eyebrow.

"Please," Obair said, as Hannah nodded.

"Found him all wrapped up in ivy at the base of a tree. It was like something out of a fairy tale." Khorin poured hot water through the strainer and then added honey to all three cups.

"He was freezing to the touch too. I thought he was dead when I first saw him. Even when I got him back here, he took three days or so to wake up, didn't he?" he said, looking over at Hannah, as he carried the cups over.

"How did he wind up there all alone?" Obair asked, genuinely curious.

"That's the thing, I've no idea really. He had some tale about his mother getting sick and some fanciful stuff about a creature in the woods helping them for a time, but it sounded like a fever dream to me."

"That's not all of what he said, Khorin," Hannah said, sitting up straight. "Not even close. You've missed more than half of it."

"You tell it then. You've always told a better tale, anyway."

Obair turned in his seat and watched in silence, as she blew gently on her tea for a moment and collected her thoughts.

"What he said was that his mother was sick. They were lost in the woods and had been wandering for days with little food or water. His mother had been hurt and she was becoming feverish. He said she was hot, so I think that's what he meant." She looked at Khorin for confirmation and he nodded.

"It's all so long ago, it's hard to remember, but I do remember this part clearly. He met a woman in the woods, someone strange who helped them both. There was some mention of a ring of stones in the woods, of finding his mother dancing around it in the night, caught in a fever dream or something. Then later the woman and his mother vanished into the stones. That's the last he remembered before Khorin found him." She looked up from her tea and faltered as she saw Obair's ashen face.

"What's the matter?" she asked in concern, reaching out to touch his forehead. "Are you feeling ill again?"

"Did he mention the eyes?" Obair managed, in a strained voice.

The blood drained from Hannah's face as she made the connection. "He did. They were the colour of sunsets. The same as…"

"…as the satyr you had in here." Obair finished for her.

"Hold on. What's this?" Khorin said, as he looked from one to the other. "You told him about all that?" He stood, his face like thunder as she nodded, and he leaned over the table, stabbing one thick finger down towards Obair as he spoke. "Listen, old man. I'm not one to throw someone who's sick out of my home, but I'll not have you upsetting my wife or filling her head with nonsense."

"I understand, sir," Obair said, flinching back from the finger. "You need to know, though, that what happened to Hannah was not a dream. There are things you need to hear. This woman that took Devin's mother was no fevered imagining, just as the creature that attacked your wife was no dream. They were both quite real and if the fae have a woman that danced around the stones...stars above, this explains everything!"

"What do you mean?" Hannah asked.

"Devin's mother would be a tool, Hannah. The fae who held her could use her as a gateway to this world. The Wyrde would be no more effective a barrier than a wet sheet of paper!"

Khorin's face creased in disgust and he stepped back from the table. "I'll not stay here and listen to another word of this." He turned towards the door.

"Khorin, you've not even had any lunch!" Hannah called, but he waved her protest away and stamped out of the cottage.

"Give him time, Hannah," Obair said, softly. "It's a lot to accept."

"If he ever does," she said, hearing the break in her own voice. She looked down at her hands and her hair fell forward over her face, veiling her misery.

"He won't have a choice, Hannah. The fae are coming. Pretending it isn't so won't help."

"What do you mean?" She tucked her hair back behind her ear as she looked up.

He sighed. "I'm doing this all wrong," he muttered to himself. He sipped at his tea and pulled a face. "Have you got anything stronger?" He tipped the mug meaningfully.

"That's a good idea." She gave him a wan smile. "I think I could use one too." She retrieved a dark brown bottle from the pantry and poured them both a generous measure of brandy in fresh mugs. He took a large mouthful at once and then coughed and sputtered as the fiery liquid burned his throat.

"Let me start at the beginning," he said, twisting the mug on the table as he thought. "My earliest memories are of working in the glade with my master, as he taught me the ritual that kept the fae away from us. I don't even remember my family and I remember little of how I came to be with him."

"There was a power that kept the fairies away?"

"Not fairies, Hannah, that's a word that leads to silly tales. They are the fae." His voice was low and serious.

"Fae then." She cleared her throat. "If you and these druids were keeping the fae away somehow, then what happened?"

"I don't know," he admitted. "The Wyrde was always a strange thing to me. Maintaining it was a bit like holding your breath, but with your mind. I had to keep a grip on it at all times, even whilst sleeping."

"This Wyrde? This was the ritual you mentioned?"

"No. The Wyrde was a force, a barrier that served to keep the fae from entering our world. The ritual helped to maintain it, but it wasn't the whole of it. Think of the Wyrde as being a bit like a dam. The ritual was a few sections of wood bracing the dam but it wasn't the whole of it."

"Then what's happened?"

"It's been slipping slowly out of my grasp for years." He breathed in deeply and sighed. "It's never been perfect anyway. Things like the satyr that attacked you have been slipping through in ones and twos for centuries. It just needs to be the right phase of the moon and the right place." He looked up at her, checking her expression. "The only things that could never pass through were the fae themselves. The Wyrde never let them through."

"There should have been hundreds of people across the world performing the ritual, but in the end I think there was only me left. I could feel it slipping more and more. I felt, a pressure, something pushing at the fabric of it, tearing at it. It's gotten a lot worse over these past five years or so, though I have no idea why. Then, finally, they found me."

"Who?"

"Satyrs, though now you've told me about Devin's mother, I wonder if there weren't fae as well, at times." He drank again and swallowed without a blink. "The satyrs hounded me at night, killed my livestock and made it clear that the Wyrde was weaker than I'd ever imagined. I'd gone to look for help, to warn people, when that man attacked me. That's when I lost it."

"Lost what?"

"When I lost my hold on the Wyrde. I felt it finally fail."

"Can't you just begin it again?" she asked.

He laughed a sad little laugh. "I wouldn't know where to begin. I was like a boy trusted to put twigs on a campfire to keep it going. I have no idea what formed the sparks and I don't know how to fan the coals." He sighed and looked her square in the eyes. "The Wyrde is gone, Hannah, and as soon as the fae realise this, they will come."

"More of those fae things that attacked me?"

"Well, satyrs are more like foot soldiers than anything else. Fast and strong, but not terribly bright. The fae themselves are something quite different. They're supposed to look a lot like us. We'll find out soon enough, I suppose."

"There you go again with that. You said they were coming. When?" she demanded. "How many? Isn't there anything we can do?"

"As to the first, that I can answer. The fae do not live in this realm. Their own home is another place, far removed from here. Even with the Wyrde gone, they can only cross over when our worlds touch, between the full moon and new moon. Even the fae using Devin's mother as a gate would have been bound by that."

"But it should be full moon tomorrow!" Hannah said in alarm, as she stood. Obair nodded sadly as he looked up at her. "We've got to warn people! How many will there be? What do they want with us?"

"Hannah, nobody would believe us. Think! If we go darting around the village warning of an invasion of fairies, how are people going to react?"

"They'll either laugh, or think I've cracked," she said quietly, sinking back into the chair.

"Exactly. As to your second question, I have no idea, that knowledge is lost. There could be a score, a thousand or an army. They may not even come here. They have the whole world to visit. The worst will not come on the first night, anyway."

She noted the catch in his voice. "What do you mean by that?"

"On the first night, if anything, it will only be a scattering of curious satyrs or something similar. The worst will come on the third night. That's when the hunt will come."

"The hunt?"

"The Wild Hunt." He spoke in little more than a whisper. "This place, this village, it takes its name from something much older. The stones that I was tasked to watch, where I worked the Wyrde, were once known as the Withen Gate. My master told me it was there that the fae begin their Wild Hunt."

"What do they hunt?" Hannah said, in a sick voice, her eyes already screaming the answer to her question.

"What do you think, Hannah?" he said, softly. "They hunt us."

"Lords and Ladies," she swore. "Is there nothing we can do? Surely the soldiers…" She left the rest unsaid.

"Steel will not harm them. It would be like fighting a raging bear with a twig."

"What then? There has to be something. Damn it all, Obair, you must know something!" She slammed her hand onto the table hard enough to make the mugs clatter.

"It's all lost, Hannah, all the knowledge we had about them was destroyed centuries ago." His face reddened behind his grey whiskers as his temper rose. "Damn it all to hell, don't you understand? They're coming and we know almost nothing about them. I told you, there is no secret store of knowledge. We'll be like children to them. Iron will hurt the satyrs, but for all I know, it has no effect on the fae at all!"

Both Hannah and Obair jumped as the door flew open and Devin all but fell down the steps. "Soldiers!" he gasped, between ragged breaths.

Hannah rose to her feet. "The Bjornmen?" she asked.

"No, not Bjornmen. They wear Duke Freyton's colours. I think it's an army!" Devin replied looking curiously at Obair and his reddened face. He shrugged and hurried them outside. The flood of troops marching along the road towards Widdengate dwarfed those who had worked to fortify the village and build the signal tower on its distant hill. The land immediately outside the walls was covered in men working to erect tents. More men moved amongst the refugees' tents, taking them down to make way for a more organised pitch. Still they came, hundreds of men followed by cavalry and endless wagons.

"Surely this must make a difference?" Hannah asked the old man in a soft voice.

"It might at that, Hannah, but not in the way you think." He began to walk towards the village.

"Where are you going?" she asked, as she realised he wasn't simply trying to get a closer look.

"To try and talk to the man in command." He stopped and turned. "If you are going to try and talk to people, then I would suggest you do it today."

* * *

Rhenkin sat astride his horse and surveyed the village sourly, as he reached forward absently to pat the big animal's neck. The northern side of Widdengate nestled close to the woods, while its fields stretched off to the distant forest to the south. A small river cut its way out of the woods and through the long grasses, before passing close to the village and snaking off to the south.

He took in the village with its palisade in one long look, before glancing at the unprotected mill and scattered farms that lay outside the walls. He heard his second pull in slightly behind him and clear his throat.

"What is it, Larson?" He didn't take his eyes from the village.

"I've given the order to strike the refugee camp, sir, and informed the village council that you will be speaking to them shortly. They'll be sending a man to meet you," the Lieutenant said.

"Very good. What do you make of it all?" Rhenkin waved an arm vaguely at the village and surrounds.

"It's certainly not ideal, sir." Larson ventured.

"No, it's certainly not that. Don't walk on eggshells, Larson, I'm not going to send you off digging latrines if you miss something," Rhenkin said. "I need a second pair of eyes. Tell me what you see."

"Yes, sir," Larson replied, sitting up higher in the saddle. He assessed the area for a moment before he spoke again. "The existing defences are inadequate. That palisade wouldn't hold for long. Any force that issued from it would be ground to pieces against their own wall. That's assuming the refugees weren't out there and in the way. I would suggest leaving it in place and then erecting a larger defensive perimeter farther out. We also need some proper watchtowers. This land is depressingly flat and the ones they have there are nowhere near tall enough."

"I'd say you're right about the palisade. It looks like it was thrown up by children, anyway." Rhenkin snorted. "Build me something larger. I want three rows of ditches leading up to it. Something for their cavalry too, assuming they have any." He looked sourly at the woods and scowled. "I hate building defences out of wood. What I wouldn't give for six months and a good supply of stone. Still, we work with what we're given and at least we have the wood right here. Talk to the section commanders and get the men to work. I want to see something big enough to give any invaders pause for thought by tomorrow morning.

"Find a scout and send him to me as well, would you? The Bjornmen's last known location was only about three days away if they travel in any kind of force. I don't want them catching us with our britches down."

"Yes, sir." Larson saluted in his saddle and set off towards the village.

Rhenkin nudged his horse into a slow walk, letting it more or less pick its own path, as he continued to scan the area.

The Bjornmen would have cut through here like a hot knife through butter. The wall wasn't worth a damn and he doubted he'd find anyone within the village that he could consider even half-trained. His mood grew blacker the closer he got to the walls.

The transformation was dramatic. The refugee camp was cleared away and incorporated into the growing military one. Within a few short hours, a large ditch had been dug, encircling the village and outlying farms and men were hard at work creating two more. The sounds of logging carried from the woods and the beginnings of the larger palisade were already visible.

Rhenkin had put off his meeting with the council longer than he really ought to have and it was beginning to get dark by the time he strode into the inn, but still he chafed at the necessity and lost time.

It was very clearly a family place. Well lit from both lamps on the walls and candles at the tables, it was clean and smelled more of freshly baked bread and roasting lamb than ale and wine. It made a welcome change from some of the low dives he'd been forced to pass through on the journey here. A stout man he assumed must be the innkeeper looked up and met his eye as he walked in, and nodded politely as he finished filling a tankard for an old farmer leaning against the bar.

"Reckon you'd be the one in charge of this lot, then," the farmer said, as he looked Rhenkin up and down. Some men were impressed with authority and impressive uniforms. Farmers, Rhenkin had noticed, tended to take the world as they found it. Overall, he found it refreshing.

"I am," he replied, shortly. "I was told I could meet the village council here."

"Council!" snorted the farmer as he took the tankard from the innkeeper. "Bunch of self-important fools, is all they are."

"Samen, you don't want to be talking like that if you're going to keep drinking in my inn," Owen muttered from behind the bar, just loud enough for the farmer to hear. He looked past the cantankerous old man at Rhenkin. "If you'll follow me, sir? We've a room in the back we use, so we can have some privacy." He shot Samen a look as he said the last, which prompted another snort, and the old farmer raised his tankard in a mock salute.

The back room was filled with villagers, all looking at Rhenkin with nervous and expectant expressions. The innkeeper took a seat at the end of the long table that dominated the room and motioned for him to sit. Rhenkin ignored the offer. Sitting too often led to drinks and long discussions, and he hadn't the time for either.

"I'll keep this brief," he began, before they could start with the introductions. "I have much left to do and am short on time. Duke Freyton has ordered that this village be properly fortified against the Bjornmen threat."

"Are we in danger from them, then?" an older woman with fading blonde curls asked, in a tremulous voice.

"Of course we're in danger, Maryanne," a fat man with sad eyes snapped. "Any fool can see that. My son's death should have taught you that!"

"Shall we let the man speak?" rumbled a man Rhenkin marked as the blacksmith. The size of him alone would have indicated it, even without the burn-scarred hands.

"I don't want to cause a panic," he continued, "but I do want to be honest with you. I expect this village to be their next target if they continue to push as they have been doing. My men and I will be building a larger wall around it and other defences, as required, but anyone who wishes to leave needs to do so soon and understand that I cannot guarantee their safety."

The meeting collapsed into a series of protests and repeated questions after that, as he'd known it would. Villagers were the same the world over. He finally extricated himself from it and fought his way out of the inn. He walked quickly to the corner of the building and ducked into the darker shadows, breathing in the cool night air.

"Captain?"

He whirled in place, his hands darting for both sword and dagger, until he picked out the old man in the darkness. "What do you want, old man?" he said, straightening from his fighting crouch and pulling his hands away from his weapons.

"You are Captain Rhenkin, then?"

"I am. I'm also in a hurry, so make it quick."

"I understand you're to take charge of the defence of the village," the old man went on, holding up a hand as Rhenkin made to interrupt. "There are some things you cannot defend against. Things you would scoff at, were I to go into detail, but which you cannot ignore."

"Look, I really don't have time for this." Rhenkin made to push past the old man, but stopped as he raised a finger.

"I ask nothing of you, Rhenkin. Just that you use your eyes and ears tomorrow night. I expect we will be speaking the following morning." The old man stepped back into the shadows as he fell silent.

"What do you mean by that? Do you know something?" he demanded. The man simply shook his head and carried on walking into the night.

"Crazy old fool," Rhenkin muttered. "As if I don't have enough to worry about." He drew his cloak tighter about himself and headed back to the camp.

* * *

"Devin!" Erinn's voice cut through the noise of the village and he turned with a smile, as she weaved easily through the press of villagers, labourers and soldiers towards him. Overnight Widdengate had gone from a hamlet struggling to cope with an influx of refugees, to a military camp. The village itself was dwarfed by the camp and where once Devin had walk for ten to fifteen minutes to get into the village itself, now the ditch and beginnings of the wall were a mere five minutes away.

He moved to meet her, smiling. "Erinn," he said. "It feels like ages since I've seen you."

"It's only been a couple of days, you know," she smiled back. "Besides, I've been busy in the hospital and you've been… What have you been doing?"

"Khorin has me nailed to a plough," he said, with a grimace. "Well, he did have before Freyton's men arrived. There doesn't seem much point now."

"Don't be so dramatic," she laughed. "I doubt you were pulling it yourself. I seem to remember seeing two rather large horses in your barn. As for the other, you mustn't give up hope, you know. The Bjornmen might not even come here."

"I didn't mean it like that," he said, stepping aside as a labourer struggled past carrying a long length of wood. "It's just that with them digging ditches and building these spiked logs that they are dropping all over the place, there isn't much point in ploughing a field."

Her face fell. "Oh! You're right, I suppose. Is the farm going to be alright? I hadn't thought about things like that what with..." She waved vaguely around. Then it dawned on him. With the influx of troops her father and his apprentices must have more work than they could handle at the moment.

"I expect we'll make it through. If the worst come to worst, I'll come and ask your father for work." He laughed at the thought. Whilst Harlen was a nice enough man, he was known to be a harsh taskmaster and Devin could think of nothing worse than being cooped up in a hot forge all day long. It was bad enough that Hannah had made him promise not to hunt anymore for the time being.

"Listen, Devin, I need to talk to you about something," she said. The serious expression seemed out of place on her sunny face, and he looked at her in concern.

"Um, okay."

"Not here." She grabbed his hand, leading him between two of the new cabins the soldiers had built that morning. "It's about your mother. She's been all over town talking to people."

"She does do that on occasion, you know?" Devin said, with a crooked smile.

"I'm serious, Devin," she scowled. "She told my father to make sure I was kept in tonight. That something was coming. She's scaring people and, to be honest, she's not sounding like herself."

"What did she say was coming?" he asked. She'd seemed fine that morning, although a bit quiet. "I'm sure it's nothing," he added, with a confidence he didn't feel.

"You'd better find her, Devin," Erinn said, with a frown. "Some of the things she's saying...well, they aren't good."

"Like what?"

"There's no time, Devin. Just find her." She darted past him into the street, pausing long enough to give him a serious look and was swallowed up by the crowd.

He wandered out of the alleyway. Despite the addition of the extra cabins, Widdengate still wasn't large and there were only so many places Hannah could be. The mid-afternoon sun was slanting down, slicing through the haze of sawdust that seemed to have been floating over the village all day. For want of a better idea, he headed for the church.

His short trip took him past the smithy and he paused for a moment to enjoy the sight of the sparks flying. He might not want to work in there, but ever since he could remember he'd loved watching them.

"Devin!" a voice called from inside. "Hey Devin! Get in here!"

He took a hesitant step forwards into the shade of the building and saw Harlen staring out at him. "What are you up to, lad?"

"I was looking for Hannah," he replied, feeling a bit foolish.

"I expect she'll turn up. Come and give me a hand here for a bit."

There was no polite way to refuse, and Devin found himself being put to work on a bellows as Harlen pounded away at the forge. By the time he managed to extricate himself, the sun was close to setting. His ears were still ringing from Harlen's hammer strokes as he made his way to the inn.

* * *

The setting sun was warm on Trallen's shoulders as he walked along the well-trod path to the woods, fuming to himself. It was simply unacceptable. First Erinn and then Hannah. Running around filling people's heads full of stuff and nonsense. "Damned old fool." he burst out. "He's got the whole town jumping at shadows." He spat and kicked at a pebble on the track, sending it skittering across the packed dirt and into the grass.

They'd all been so helpful when he first arrived, Sarah and Hannah especially, settling him in and helping him to get to know the villagers. Sarah had even helped him to organise the choir, though she claimed she hadn't the voice for it herself. And now, since the old man had arrived, all his hard work was beginning to fall apart.

"Honestly, it's no wonder I need a break," he muttered.

He passed into the woods, following the clear path made by woodcutters over the years, and hurried along to the little clearing where he knew Sarah would be waiting. As usual, he felt the combined twinge of guilt and excitement as he walked. He resisted the urge to glance back over his shoulder to check he wasn't being followed.

It was darker under the trees and cooler without the sun on his black robes. He found the birch easily, and turned to part the bushes and step into the clearing. The expectant smile fell from his face. It was empty. She must be delayed. He knew she'd come, though. She'd not been able to deny him once since that first forbidden encounter in his study. He shuddered slightly, with remembered passion, as he settled down against a broad horse chestnut tree.

Still, she was married. It was probably part of the attraction, the forbidden nature of it all. It definitely wasn't her mind that drew him to her. He laughed softly to himself at the thought. She was definitely not the sharpest woman in the village. Conniving, certainly, and with an eye to a man with some money, if her miller husband was anything to go by, but no, she didn't have a quick wit. That said, he wasn't meeting her for conversation. They talked, of course, but that was usually afterwards.

Unbidden, the memory of Hannah came back to him, and he stood without thinking and began to pace back and forth. "It simply makes no sense!" he told the uncaring trees. "Why suddenly become this superstitious fool? She's like a peasant farmer, all of a sudden." He laughed at himself as he realised what he'd said and turned back towards the tree.

He stopped dead in his tracks as something fluttered down in front of him. It had the wings of a dragonfly and they shone brightly as they reflected the light of setting sun. He watched, his mouth agape. It was a tiny woman, flying slowly through the clearing, her black hair trailing out behind her.

She was barely bigger than his hand, but perfectly formed. She wore only the briefest of tunics, which exposed her long smooth legs and bare feet.

"Beautiful," he breathed, without realising it was he who spoke.

Movement caught his eye and he spotted a second figure and then a third. Before he had time to draw three breaths, the clearing was filled with them, the sunlight making their pale purple skin glow as they darted here and there in an aerial dance.

He became aware of the sounds of their speech and laughter as they dashed past him, and he spun in place, arms outstretched, as they flitted past his fingertips, their gossamer thin wings brushing his skin. He laughed in delight but the sound died on his lips as a hundred tiny heads snapped round to face him, as if only just noticing his presence. They flocked to him, circling him slowly to form a wall of winged bodies.

He gasped again at the beauty of them, the simple existence of them, despite everything he had learned and preached from the Book of New Days. Then he jerked in pain. He looked down at his hand, wondering at the small trickle of blood oozing from the barely visible slash.

They circled faster, as he sucked the blood from the cut, and a rasping sound accompanied the glint of a hundred tiny knives. The whirring of their wings became a roar, as they whirled past him in a torrent of purple and flashing teeth.

The cut on his hand was forgotten as he felt tugs on his robes, first on one shoulder and then on the other. The creatures buffeted him, their bodies striking him with glancing blows that were not enough to make him fall but enough to knock him slightly off balance.

A long slash across his cheek made him cry out in pain and he blundered forward into the swarm seeking a way out as he held a hand to his cheek. Then the pain was everywhere, as the torrent became a hurricane. He twisted and jerked, as lines of fire appeared all over his body at once, and his robes were shredded to tatters in moments, the pieces falling from him like autumn leaves. He screamed then, high and terrible, as the cuts criss-crossed his body. He heard the winged women laughing and mocking him, as the blood coursed down.

"Help me, Lord!" he cried out, and then finally, he could take no more and sank to his knees.

The onslaught stopped. The last thing he saw, as his face met the soft earth, was a purple figure, licking the blood from her pale white knife, no larger than a thorn, and smiling at him coquettishly.

* * *

Devin pushed his way through the crowd. It seemed every refugee with money, or soldier who had managed to get away from the camp, had made their way to the inn, and it took him a good few minutes to make it to the bar. He had just waved an arm to try and attract Owen's attention, when the church bells began to ring.

The taproom fell silent in moments and people looked nervously at the windows. Someone in the corner hushed a couple of people still speaking loudly. "What's the matter," one slurred. "Can't you hear the bells properly?"

"Bjornmen," a voice carried from the crowd, and then Devin was moving with the press of the crowd as the inn emptied. Devin ran. Later he would not be able to explain it, but he ran towards the church as if his life depended upon it. The bells ceased before he was halfway there, but that just spurred him on.

As he drew close to the dark stone building, he heard raised voices.

"…had no right, Hannah. The agreement was only for signs of attack. Not for some feeling you have because of that old fool you have staying with you! I don't know what's come over you. Father Trallen will be furious. Honestly, how are you going to explain this to those that fled into the village? Don't you walk away from me! Hannah!"

Devin drew to a halt as he watched Hannah stride away from the irate miller's wife. Her head was bowed but, even at this distance, he could see the satisfied smirk on her face. She looked up, noticing him for the first time.

"Devin?" The single word was filled with concern. "Where's Khorin, I thought he was with you?"

"I haven't seen him since mid-afternoon."

She looked up at the darkening sky and then at the first hints of the full moon rising over the trees. "Oh no!" she whispered. "That stupid, stupid man. I told him to leave them!"

"What?" He was at her side in two steps. "What is it?"

"Your fool father. I told him he needed to be inside the walls before sunset."

"You know how he is, Hannah," Devin smiled. "He'll not settle down until the animals are sorted."

"You don't understand, Devin. He has to be inside. Something is coming. Something terrible." She rounded on him and grasped his upper arms firmly. "You have to get him. Run. Steal a horse if need be, but get him!" Her eyes were wild and her hands gripped him hard enough to hurt as she shook him slightly. He felt a sense of dread wash over him and, without another word, he turned and sprinted for the inn.

The stables were untended at this time of night and Devin slowed his pace, so as not to spook the horses. He didn't bother with saddle or tack, but brought out Bessie, Kainen's serviceable mare that they'd both ridden for years. She wasn't the fastest horse, by any means, but she knew his scent and wouldn't object to carrying him bareback.

He grabbed a handful of her mane and threw himself upwards, trying not to pull too hard and pressing down on her neck for leverage. Scrambling onto her back, he urged her onwards and set off for the gates at a dead run.

The gates of the palisade had yet to swing closed, despite the rapid approach of nightfall, and troops and villagers were still passing between them. Devin pressed himself low over Bessie's back and urged her on, ignoring the indignant cries of those who threw themselves out of his way. Something in Hannah's voice had sparked a fear in him. It was a nameless, shapeless fear, but it burned hungrily within him as he charged out through the gates and into the darkness.

* * *

Khorin darted out of the cottage as he heard the goats cry out, and stopped as he turned the corner of the cottage and saw the figure near the barn.

"You there!" he shouted. "Hey! What are you doing?" The man was short, probably a boy from the village up to no good. He strode forward and then stumbled to a halt as the clouds parted, and the moonlight spilled across the barn and played over the thing's horns and goat-like hooves. Its eyes shone a deep orange in the reflected light and a grin split its face. "A manling, a manling!" it cried, and ran at him.

Khorin turned and fled. Like a young child running from a noise in the woods, he ran with no thought of falling, just with all the speed he could muster. And then there were three of them. Peeling out of the darkness, they ran in from both sides. He turned desperately but the closest crashed into him, and they tumbled to the ground in a tangle of arms, legs and hooves.

It was faster to rise than he was and, as he pulled himself up to his knees, they crowded around him, laughing and mocking. One pulled a set of pipes from its belt and played a tune, as it began to dance.

"A manling, we have found tonight, as our Lady spills her light!" they sang, as they skipped around him.

Khorin made to stand, but a hoof caught him in the back, knocking him to his hands and knees, as the breath crashed out of him.

"A steed! A steed!" one of the things cried. "Shall we see if it's for riding?" Khorin felt a weight strike his back as the creature leapt astride him. It grasped his hair in one rough hand as it gripped him tight with its furred legs.

He bucked, desperately trying to force the thing from his back, but it just held on tighter.

"It needs to be broken!" cried one.

"You have a wild steed." The other laughed, and ripped a stretch of bramble from the ground at its feet. It passed it up to the creature on his back and laughed again. "Ride him. Ride him. Break him for the hunt." it urged.

"Bear me steed. Onwards to the hunt!" the creature sitting on him cried, as it whipped the brambles down at his rump and legs. The thorns tore at his trousers and ripped the skin from his bare back. He shot his hand forward to balance, lurching from the pain.

"That's it, little donkey," it shouted, in glee. "On. Onwards!"

Khorin collapsed onto the grass and rolled to one side, throwing the hateful thing from his back. He scrambled to his feet and lurched towards the village, "Help me!" he yelled.

"Your steed has fled," said one.

"Poorly trained," noted another.

"Bad donkey, you come back here!"

They ran after him, catching up with him easily, but making no effort to stop him. Instead, they cavorted around him, shrieking "Run manling, run and hide!" and screeching with laughter. As he passed the cottage, they were on him again. He flew sprawling to the dirt as the hoof caught him high on the shoulder, driving his face into the ground and jarring his head so badly, he thought his teeth must break. Another kick followed, hard to the ribs, and he curled up reflexively, only to have another find the small of his back. A moan of agony broke from him that took the rest of his breath and he squeezed his eyes tight against the pain.

He forced them open again when he heard the thudding of hooves and, through his tears, saw a horse approaching. The creatures turned to watch it and he took his chance, forcing himself to his knees.

He was about to run, when he recognised the rider. "Devin!" he shouted, weakly. "Devin, run! Don't stop, just run!" He gasped out the last word, as a hand caught his hair and jerked his head back, the claw-like nails scraping at his scalp.

"This steed is no good. Too old to train." Laughter rang out and then he felt the knife at his throat. "Run!" he roared, but his shout was cut off as the blade hissed through his skin. He fell to the ground, gurgling, his hands clutching at his throat as he fought to keep in the jet of blood that arced through his fingers. A distant, small part of him took comfort from the thud of the hoof beats growing distant, and then all was pain and darkness, and the wild laughter.

Devin wheeled the horse as fast as he dared in the dark, and pushed it into a gallop towards the village. His body shook and his mind reeled as he made it through the gates. He let the horse slow and then stop, sliding numb from her back. He could hear shouts and screams in the distance, but he stumbled, as if half-asleep or drunk, towards the inn. He blundered into the stable, vaguely aware that Bessie had followed him, and then it was all too much. He fell to his knees and then lay on the straw-covered ground, as shock and grief took him with huge wracking sobs. He stayed there, wrapped in shock and grief, as long-buried memories climbed to the surface and images of creatures with burning amber eyes filled his mind.

* * *

Rhenkin walked the walls, his eyes drifting back over the village and the camp the new wall had enclosed. The torches had been lit and the evening air was heavy with the smell of burning pitch. The palisade had been erected at a blistering rate, but even so, the defences looked a lot more robust from the outside than they did from within the village. Work on the walkway had only just started, and Rhenkin had only a few hundred feet of wall on which to pace. It was enough to be seen though, and that was what mattered. One of the first things he'd learned about being in command was that you needed to be visible.

He passed the sentry, who was leaning against the freshly cut wood with an air of utter boredom, as he stared into the darkness beyond the wall.

"Keep those eyes open, Son," he said softly, fighting a smile as the young man pulled himself upright.

The night was still and everything was quiet, despite the earlier business with the church bells. For all the chaos it had caused, Rhenkin had been glad of it. It had proven to be a good practice run and everyone from the outlying farms seemed to have made it into the village.

He was five feet past the guardsman, when the figure threw itself out of the darkness and bounded up the vertical palisade. It traversed the wall in two easy bounds. He barely had time to catch a glimpse of golden eyes before it was gone, down into the camp and headed for the village. The sentry fell at his feet, blood gushing from his neck, his sword still sheathed.

Rhenkin threw himself at the ladder. The ground was clear between this stretch of the new wall and the village, and the figure was covering the distance in a shockingly fast time. He sprinted after it and charged into the streets themselves. They were largely deserted, so he had no problems picking his enemy out in the shadows. He ripped his weapons from their sheaths as he ran and screamed out, "Intruder in the camp!"

He barrelled around a corner and saw the man had crashed into a group of three soldiers. One lay on the ground already, with blood staining his chest black in the dim light. The others circled the man warily, their swords held low as they looked for an opening. As Rhenkin closed the gap, he saw the man dart between the soldiers, with a speed that defied belief. His eyes widened in shock as he drew closer and got his first real look at the attacker as it slashed once, twice, with its knives and was gone. The guardsmen grabbed at the vicious gashes as the blood ran. Giving them no more than a cursory glance, Rhenkin ran onwards after the nightmarish creature.

Troops began to form up into small squads on the streets, with sergeants and corporals yelling orders in the confusion. Curtains twitched and villagers poked their heads around their doors to see what was going on. Rhenkin charged past them all, the creature's laugh carrying back to him as he ran, his heart pounding. The figure was managing to stay ahead of him, seemingly without effort, spinning, and almost seemed to caper along with a mad, wild laughter, as if this were all a child's game.

A door opened ahead of them and a girl in her late teens leaned out, the lamplight catching her red hair. With a gleeful cry, the creature ran to her and grabbed her arm, dragging her into the street. It pulled her around in a spinning dance, whooping as she whimpered in terror and fought to get away. Rhenkin closed the distance and crashed into its back, knocking all three of them to the ground.

It was up as quickly as it fell, rolling with a smooth, easy motion as it turned to face him with its curious knives held ready as he found his own feet. It darted in, with slashes to his face and thigh almost before he was upright and Rhenkin was forced to stagger back awkwardly to avoid having his thigh laid open, as he parried the attack at his face with his knife. The thing, whatever it was, turned to grab at the girl, who was still pulling herself upright. Seizing the moment, Rhenkin swept his knife across its back, but the blade did not penetrate the skin. Instead, it bounced off, as if he'd hacked at a pell-post leaving a dark black line but causing no real damage. The thing hissed in pain and spun to face him, whipping the girl round in front of it as it brought its knife around in front of her. It fixed him with a grin, the human expression looking odd on its bearded face and those amber coloured eyes shining in the lamplight.

Rhenkin raised his sword to thrust as he realised the monster's intention. Even as he began the move, he knew there was no way to save the girl. He caught a flicker of movement behind the creature and then the night exploded in blue fire. Rhenkin threw his arm up across his face as the brilliant light threatened to sear his eyes, his sword flying from his grip, as he dropped to one knee. As the light died down, he pulled himself warily to his feet, holding his dagger loosely. He blinked, trying to clear away the blue-green after-images, and approached the charred wreckage of the creature. The big man Rhenkin remembered from the town council had pulled himself up from where he'd fallen back against the doorway, and was staring at the hammer in his hands in amazement.

"What did you do?" Rhenkin asked, in an awed voice.

The man met his eyes and shook his head dumbly. "I...I just struck it in the head. I..." He trailed off and stared at the large black hammer again, turning it in his hands as if looking for something.

"What is that thing?"

"This?" Harlen said, raising the weapon. "It's just a forge hammer." He looked as though he was about to say more, but the girl at his feet moaned and tried to pull herself up. "Erinn!" Harlen dropped the hammer and knelt beside her. Rhenkin stepped towards them to help, but then whipped his head around as the sound of distant screaming carried through the village.

The satyr cut through the village like a scythe through a wheat-field, crashing into homes and dragging villagers from their beds even as others tore through the massed camp of troops and refugees. Chaos reigned, and the fact there were only a small number of the creatures worked in their favour as the village twisted and coiled like a confused serpent, trying to respond to the attack.

Finally, the creatures seemed to tire of the game themselves and fled into the night, their bodies covered in thick, black lines where sword blades had struck them.

* * *

Devin stormed through the village in a rage, his hands clenched into tight fists at his sides and his cheeks streaked with tears. His hair and clothes were covered in straw, but he was oblivious to how he looked as he walked into the hospital. The main room was packed with wounded, spread out over the floor on blankets and sheets. He looked around blankly, as snippets of conversation carried to his ears.

"Apparently, she's in a right state. She found Trallen in the woods, all tore up to pieces!"

"Sarah? What was she doing in the middle of the woods at that time of night?"

"What do you think?"

He picked his way through the wounded on the floor, struggling to find places to put his feet in the press of people. They looked up at him as he passed, but their faces might as well have been the faces of strangers to him.

"...nearly had Erinn. Dragged her out of the door when she stuck her head out to see what all the noise was about. If Harlen hadn't been there, anything might've happened."

"She's luckier than our Karren then. They found her half-naked and sobbing, her dress all torn to shreds. She's not spoken since."

Finally, Devin spotted Hannah and Obair. They were crouched down by a wounded soldier in a far corner. Hannah's face was haggard and tear-streaked, but she gave him a feeble smile as she looked up and rushed over to him, her arms outstretched. He clung to her like a lost child, for a moment, before pushing her back. "You knew." It was not a question.

"I knew there was a chance of them coming," she said in a low voice so as not to be overheard. "I didn't know what would happen to all these people or how bad it would be."

"How could you know those things were coming? They were like something from a nightmare. How could you possibly know?"

"Obair knew. He told me nobody would believe us and it's true, Devin, nobody did."

Devin turned and glared at the old man. Pushing his way past Hannah he grabbed the old man, pulling him up by his robe. He was still not a large man but work in the fields had given him strength in his arms, and the old man felt as light as straw as he swept him up and slammed him against the wall.

"You knew!" he shouted into the man's shocked face.

"Devin, please!" Hannah pulled gently at his arm and he slowly let the man slide down the wall to the floor.

"He couldn't have done any more. It's not his fault," she said, a plea in her tired eyes.

"I can't believe you're taking this so calmly," Devin said, accusingly.

"I had a couple of days to get used to the idea." She smiled.

And then it all made sense to him. "You don't know, do you?"

Her face fell as he spoke. "Know what?"

"Khorin's dead, Hannah. Those things killed him."

And then she crumbled. He sank to the ground beside her and wrapped his arms around her as they cried. Her in shock, him for the loss he'd known about already.

Chapter Fifteen

Obair stepped back from the boy and his mother. Their display of grief had turned heads, and now they held each other in a widening circle amid the bustle of the hospital, as refugees and patients looked on awkwardly. He turned away to find cold blue eyes appraising him from across the room. Rhenkin cocked his head towards the door and left.

The sun was warm on the steps and the sky clear as Obair stepped out through the double doors. It appeared to have all the makings of a beautiful day, almost making a mockery of the events of the night before. He caught the sweet smell of burning stourweed and turned to see Rhenkin sat to one side on the steps as he sucked his pipe into life.

"A young scout came to me a few weeks ago," the soldier began as he held a glowing taper and puffed on the pipe until it was burning to his satisfaction. "Told me that the Bjornmen had brought some kind of beasts with them." He met Obair's eyes, "He was terrified. You could see it on his face. It's funny really, if he hadn't been so scared, I don't think I'd have believed him."

Obair nodded and waited for the man to go on.

Rhenkin drew deeply on the pipe and stared across the village in silence for a moment, watching the flow of the crowd. "For all that, I would never have believed what happened last night if I hadn't seen it with my own eyes. I've been a soldier my whole life, old man. I've fought in border skirmishes that we all pretend didn't happen, and I've seen men piss themselves as the enemy charged. I've never, in my life, seen or heard of anything like those things last night." He stood and turned to Obair. "Which raises the question of how you knew they were coming, and just what they were."

Obair met the younger man's eyes. "What exactly did you see?"

"I chased one of those damned things across half the village and watched it cut through my men like they weren't there. I've never seen anything move that fast.

And then, when we fought…" He looked down at his feet, shaking his head.

"When you fought?"

"When we fought, my blade just bounced off it. It barely left a mark." His composure cracked for a moment, showing the briefest glimpse of the turmoil he was feeling, and then the mask was back in place, cold and immovable. "How did you know they were going to attack?"

"Let me ask just one more question first, if I may?"

Rhenkin grunted.

"Do you believe your scout? That the Bjornmen brought these things with them?"

Rhenkin pulled the pipe from his mouth and scratched at a day's growth of stubble before answering. "No, I don't. That thing I fought last night had weapons. It had intelligence. Whatever it was, it was too strong to be controlled by any man. It was no beast set loose by a handler."

"You're right, of course, they are nothing to do with the Bjornmen at all." Obair said. He glanced down at the wooden steps leading up into the hospital. "Do you mind if we sit? It's been a long night for me too." He eased himself down onto a step and gave a contented sigh. "No, they are not the Bjornmen's pets. They are part of the fae."

Rhenkin coughed, stifling a laugh and fixed his face into a glower. "The fae? I came looking for answers from you, not children's tales."

"Perhaps you should look to the children's tales for the answers?" Obair said, with a humourless smile.

"What?"

"Think on it, Rhenkin. What have you witnessed? Creatures no man can say they have ever seen, that move through your troops like wind in the long grass. Eyes that glow in the dark and skin that your blades will not cut." He glanced at the soldier's face and noted his troubled expression. "Did you happen to see the one that was killed?"

"See it? I watched it happen!"

"What did you see, then?"

"The smith. Harlen, I think his name is. He stove its skull in with a forge hammer."

"And what do you suppose the hammer is made of?"

"I see where you're going with this, but I don't think I'm quite ready to accept the idea of faeries coming to get us in our beds."

"Isn't that exactly what happened, Rhenkin?" The captain opened his mouth to protest, then closed it again slowly.

"There are more coming, Captain. These few were simply playing, toying with us because they could, like a cat with a mouse. Tomorrow night, the real force will come and we must be ready."

"Who are you?" the captain breathed.

"That's one place to start," Obair said with a small smile, ignoring the sound of the doors closing behind them. "My name is Obair, but there are far more important questions to ask right now, and we are short on time. Do you think you can just accept that I am someone who knows more of these creatures than you, for now?"

Rhenkin nodded. "For now, at least."

"Good," Obair replied. "Now, how many of them do you think there were?"

"If I were to base it on the number of wounded and the damage caused, I would have said upwards of fifty, maybe even a hundred," Rhenkin said, as he stared into the distance and puffed on his pipe.

"But you know that isn't the case."

Rhenkin grunted his agreement.

"Would you believe it was only five?" Obair pressed.

"Five? That few?" Rhenkin pulled his pipe from between his teeth.

"Just five," Obair nodded. "Five satyrs alone did this much damage. Tomorrow night, we face the full host, a force that will hunt us down like a rabbit before a pack of dogs."

"And just what would you have me do, old man?"

"We have one chance, Rhenkin. This is the first time in probably a hundred generations that we will face the Wild Hunt. We must meet them as they arrive and strike at them before they form up into any real force."

Rhenkin snorted. "Even if I did as you ask Obair, we don't know where they will muster, and how do you propose to attack creatures who can face good steel without a scratch?"

"With iron, Rhenkin. You saw yourself what Harlen's hammer did to the satyr. As for the other, I know precisely where they will muster."

Rhenkin sighed. “I can’t do it, old man. The Bjornmen are on our doorstep. I have reports that their main strength is pulling back, consolidating, but they have a force moving on a village less than ten miles distant. Even if I could spare the men, which I can’t, what would we use for weapons? My sword didn’t even scratch that thing.”

“Have your field smiths make iron weapons,” Obair said softly.

“I told you, I don’t have the men to spare.” Rhenkin said flatly. “Besides, iron is too brittle to make a good sword.”

“So make spears and arrowheads.” Devin interrupted from behind

Rhenkin turned in surprise. “You’ve quiet feet for a farm boy,” he said with raised eyebrows.

“I’m no farmer, I’m a hunter,” Devin said shortly. “Those things killed my father last night. I know I wouldn’t be the only one willing to lend their arm.”

Obair looked at Rhenkin, one eyebrow raised.

“I’ll not strip the walls for you, but I’ll give you what I can,” the captain said, with a sigh.

* * *

Klöss stood on the hilltop overlooking the village, watching the line of carts and people as they fled from the rear gates.

“You should not be here, you know?” Tristan rumbled from beside him.

“So you’ve said,” Klöss replied without taking his eyes from the village.

“If something happens…”

“I know,” sighed Klöss, glancing at the big man. “If something happens then the plan is affected.” He grimaced. “I’m sick of hearing this Tristan, I’m no more important than anyone else at this point. The plan is finished, all we have to do now is hold what we’ve taken.”

“I was going to say if something happens, your uncle will have me flayed,” Tristan said, without expression.

Klöss laughed and punched him in the shoulder. “You’d better stick close to me then, hadn’t you? I imagine a man as big as you looks a little odd without his skin.”

He waved vaguely at the village. “They’ve thrown these walls up quickly, haven’t they? This place was only scouted three weeks ago.”

The village was surrounded by a wooden palisade, twenty feet high, with a deep ditch immediately before it. Armoured men could be seen standing on a walkway inside it, above the thick double gates.

"They work fast," Tristan agreed. "They don't seem to learn, though," he said, pointing to the two lines of catapults behind them, in front of their own massed troops.

"No," Klöss said, with a grim smile. "Wooden walls are never a good idea." He turned to an older man, who stood beside the rows of catapults. "Are your preparations complete, Weaponsmaster?"

"Just awaiting the permission for a ranging, Shipmaster," the grey-haired man replied. "It's an easy shot with no boat shifting."

Klöss grinned and drew his sword, pointing it towards the walls. "Then loose!"

At the Weaponmaster's echoing shout, a single catapult lurched forward as it lofted a barrage of rocks towards the walls. Klöss watched carefully as the stones fell and noted they fell short by just fifty feet. A jeering cry rose from the defenders as they watched the barrage miss but silence fell swiftly as older, more experienced men explained what was really going on. The gates closed at the far side of the village. Even from this distance, Klöss could make out the small crowd of villagers trapped inside, being forced back by armed men.

A small flight of arrows flew futilely from the walls towards the Islanders, but it was a vain hope. Klöss was well aware they were far out of range of anything that wasn't a siege engine.

He watched as the old weaponsmaster supervised the adjustments to the catapults, and turned to Tristan. "There is something that feels wrong here, though."

"How so?"

"These people are not idiots. They must know the fate of the other villages."

"You expected something more from them?"

"I don't know, Tristan. I expected something." He turned and waved at the village vaguely. "They're doing the same as all the others. Trying to defend the village, trying to stop us from taking it. They ought to know by now, that's not what's going on."

"Stupidity is not that uncommon, Klöss," Tristan offered.

Klöss glanced at the preparations again and watched as the old man signalled to him from one of the farthest machines, holding a white baton aloft. Klöss gave an exaggerated nod and the baton cut down through the air. Half a hundred catapults lurched forwards, straining against the ropes staking them firmly to the ground, and rocks and stones rained down on the walls.

The barrage cracked timbers and smashed through sections of the palisade in some places. Men screamed as parts of the wooden walkway collapsed and others were flung off it like wet rags, as the fist-sized stones fell like rain. At the catapults, men rushed forward and emptied huge, smoking pails into the cradles. The weaponsmaster held a red baton aloft and looked at Klöss again for the nod, before giving the order to loose.

The lighter missiles flew farther than the rocks and soared over the walls into the village itself. From the hilltop, there seemed to be little effect other than the occasional scream when a glowing ember worked its way through armour and clothing to skin.

Klöss watched intently, whilst behind him he could hear the clatter of stones as the catapults were reloaded. As the weaponsmaster gave the order to fire again, Klöss heard the distant cries of dismay as tendrils of smoke rose from the village. The tiny glowing coals had lodged themselves in the thatch of half a dozen homes and, as the steady breeze fanned them, the fire kindled and began to feast eagerly on the tightly packed straw and wooden beams. In a matter of minutes, flames were soaring high and neighbouring roofs were beginning to smoke, as sparks and embers flew into the air.

A rumble of hooves heralded the attack before it began. From around the edges of the woods to the north, a company of mounted men approached at full gallop with weapons drawn.

"Well, bugger me, they *can* think!" Klöss muttered. "Weaponsmaster, maintain your barrage. Section leaders, prepare for horsemen!"

The men moved easily into their positions. Shifting in a manoeuvre which had been practised so many times as to be second nature, the spearmen formed a long line and knelt low, with their weapons braced against the earth. Two other men knelt on either side of each spearman, bearing bulky and awkward arbelests loaded with heavy, iron bolts.

The horsemen crested the last rise and charged, bending low over their horses as they swept down towards the waiting Islanders. As they got within fifty feet, their lances lowered like a breaking wave, and then the arbelests fired.

The bolts they were using were not the standard quarrels. There was no wood in the shaft and the fletching was more for the sake of convention than anything else, as the effective range of the weapon was little more than fifty feet. The arbelests had been brought along with only one purpose in mind, and it was for this reason that the bolts slammed, not into the riders, but into the horses.

The air was split with whinnying screams as the heavy bolts smashed legs and tore into the unprotected chests of the horses. Mounted men fell en masse and the charge dissolved into chaos, as the horses behind smashed into those falling or already rolling on the ground. The few that made it to the Islander's lines were met by the waiting spearmen, who stabbed savagely into the animals' necks and skipped aside as they crashed to the dirt. The stricken cavalry were ill-prepared as the Islanders charged and, within a few short minutes, they were slaughtered to a man.

Another barrage of rocks smashed into the walls and the hastily-built defences began to sag as the wooden posts that formed the palisade split under the onslaught. Finally, as a great section of the wall crashed down to the ground, the gate swung open and the defenders poured from the village.

The Islanders quickly reset their lines as the section leaders screamed orders, shifting to meet the defending force.

"Spare none?" Tristan asked, quickly.

"It's the standard order, Tristan," Klöss replied, as he checked the straps on his shield and settled his helmet.

"Weaponsmaster! Cease the barrage," Klöss shouted. "Arbelests, reload and prepare for horsemen!" He watched as the defenders formed ranks and began the march towards them. He'd chosen their position carefully. What began as a gentle slope became a serious incline after a few feet, and the villagers would be feeling the weight of their armour before they made it halfway to the top.

There were fewer than two hundred of them, but Klöss had learned never to underestimate people defending their own homes. Finally, as he decided that there would be no more of the horsemen he'd come to dread facing, he turned to Tristan with a tight grin. "Think you can still keep up?"

"You still need me to play nursemaid and keep close to you?" Tristan grinned back.

Klöss lifted his sword high and screamed "Charge!" and the massed Islanders sprinted down the hill.

He ran with the others, sword in hand and a grin plastered to his face, as they barrelled into the enemy ranks. A sword crashed off his shield and he turned to its owner, a boy of no more than twelve summers. The boy's expression was one of terror, as Klöss rammed his blade into his chest. He slipped off the end of Klöss's sword with a hurt and confused expression, and sank to the earth.

The fight was short and ugly. The Islanders swarmed over the enemy, overwhelming them in what felt like moments. Then it became a wanton slaughter, as they chased down those who sought to flee, cutting them down one by one. Sickened by it all, Klöss made his way up the hill and sat on an old stump as he watched the wreckage of the village burn. His men were moving through the remains, touching torches to any buildings left intact. The storehouses had long since been emptied.

He looked up as Tristan flopped down beside him. "Not a good fight," the big man said. "These men in the village. They were not warriors. More like farmers taught how to hold a sword for a day or two."

Klöss grunted in agreement and watched idly as his troops began work on constructing an encampment for the night. The sun was already close to setting and the smoke from the village painted a dark stain across the sky.

"This is the last one we have to do for a time, though," Klöss said. "They've nothing left standing in the lands we've taken. No reason to return, other than revenge. We've done all we can."

"You think it will work?" Tristan asked.

"Would it work on you?" Klöss said with a tired smile. "No, I doubt it will stop them trying to return. They'll send troops soon enough and probably more than just the handful of horsemen we saw here, but it might stop some of the peasants coming back. We didn't come to conquer the people, after all. We just want the land." He rose slowly to his feet. "Let's go and see if this lot have remembered how to make a camp, shall we?"

* * *

The moonlight reflected from the stones, painting the trees in shades of grey and making the leaves dull and lifeless. The glade was silent. The stones clustered around the monolith like children begging for a story. Delighted laughter suddenly echoed off the trees and silence fled as bare feet stepped out of nothing and onto the grass.

Three sets of eyes that glowed faintly amber in the moonlight were filled with amazement and then delight, as the fae moved slowly around the clearing, reaching out with long, elegant fingers to touch the grass and the stones. Other figures passed through into the glade and the fae stepped aside as the satyrs passed through, first in twos and threes, and then by the score. Before long, the glade was filled with the sounds of music and wild laughter. A single harsh clap called for silence and the hush fell almost instantly.

She stood at the monolith, leaning against it in a graceful pose of idle relaxation. Her skin shone white in the moonlight but if a man were to look closer, he would have noticed the pale green swirls and sparks coming from her bare skin where the light touched her. She looked down at her simple clothing and a shimmer passed over her form, as if her image were a reflection in a pool of water disturbed by a fallen leaf. Her form twisted in the half-light and then she was clad in a gleaming breastplate, greaves, vambraces and a shining winged helm.

The assembled fae and satyrs laughed and hooted at the glamour and then stood and listened attentively as she spoke to them in a lyrical tongue. She spoke quickly, explaining her wishes in simple terms they could understand and then she fell silent and pointed into the trees with the unmistakable air of command. Moving fluidly, the host coursed out of the glade without a sound, moving with a grace that belied their blistering speed. The three fae followed close behind with long easy strides that matched pace with the charging satyrs.

In a few hours, they emerged from the woods and drew to a halt, gazing down upon the field of campfires that lay before them. Hundreds of tents stood pitched near the still smouldering village, and the light of the campfires cast a ruddy glow as smoke curled up into the moonlit sky.

Teeth bared in feral grins, the fae called out soft commands in their musical tongue and a hundred bone knives tasted the cool, night air for the first time in a hundred generations. The armour-clad fae, now shining in the moonlight, cried out a single word and the satyrs flowed out from the forest and fell upon the Islander's camp like a black wave crashing upon the shore.

The first who fell died silent, startled deaths as they stood on watch with bored eyes looking into the darkness. Then a terrible scream cut through the quiet and the camp came alive, as men scrambled from their blankets to grab weapons and roll to their feet. By the time the first horn sounded, the satyrs were well into the camp.

The fae stood at the edge of the forest, cruel smiles on their lips as they watched and waited.

* * *

Verig kicked savagely at the sleeping men through the sides of the tent. "Get up, you motherless dogs! Enemy in the camp!" He put the horn to his lips again and sounded it high and clear. A dark figure hurtled towards him and he dropped the horn as he ripped his sword from its scabbard and sank into a low stance. The figure flew at him, wielding two long horn knives as it thrust in high at his throat. Rather than risk the second blade slashing downwards, Verig twisted away, allowing the knife to scrape along the face of his shield, as he stepped back and to the side of the line of attack.

He held his blade low and ready, the weapon steady in his palm, although his heart began to race as the firelight revealed the attacker for what it was. The satyr grinned as it moved towards him, its hooves moving on the grass lightly. The knives twisted and spun in their own dance as it approached, and the creature let out a small laugh as it neatly sidestepped the blade Verig flicked out.

The attack came with no warning. Verig had a lifetime of experience in the arts of war and had spent years training others to watch for the signs of attack. A slight crouching to brace for a lunge, a tightening of the grip, a dropping of one shoulder. This time however, there was no warning and his experience failed him utterly. The satyr was upon him before he could react. He staggered backwards in a desperate move to distance himself from the blades. The air hissed as the horn knife passed within a hair's breadth of his throat and then he fell, as his boot hit the tent's guy rope.

The breath blasted from his lungs as he landed heavily, and he twisted and rolled to the side as the knives followed his fall. His sword had fallen from his grasp as he hit the ground, and he lashed out savagely with his shield, feeling it slam into the creature's face with a satisfying crunch. Verig felt, more than saw, the thing stagger backwards and he flailed about desperately for his sword. His hand closed on a wooden handle and he hurled the object hard as he rose to his feet.

The heavy wooden mallet smashed into the satyr's forehead with a deep thunk and the creature dropped to the ground like a poleaxed cow. As he searched about for his sword and pulled it from the tangle of the collapsed tent, he saw dark forms moving through the camp like a deathly wind. Blades bounced off creatures' skin and although they screamed in pain, they barely slowed as they reached out with their bone knives, slashing at the Islanders' eyes and thrusting their blades into their throats.

Shining armour caught his eye even as he heard the calls from behind him, ordering men to form ranks. The woman was tall and beautiful, although her amber eyes were cold. She regarded him evenly from beneath her winged helm as she crouched to retrieve a sword from a fallen man. She lifted the weapon and turned it curiously so it caught the moonlight.

Though she never took her eyes from him, she seemed intrigued by the weapon, testing its balance and even sniffing the blade with a delicate motion. A slow smile spread across her face, revealing brilliant white teeth. She leapt towards him, covering ten feet in a single bound and landing lightly just beyond his weapon's reach. She waited calmly, as he sank into a fighting stance and then she struck.

He moved easily away from the line of the attack and thrust hard as she overextended beside him. The grin that had been forming on his lips faltered as he encountered only empty air and the fae moved lightly around the thrust with a speed no man could hope to match. He shifted backwards and moved smoothly to meet her next attack, steel striking steel and singing the song he'd loved his entire adult life.

She was fast, there was no denying that. She seemed unused to the weight of the weapon though and lacked any apparent training with a blade. Despite this, her natural grace and inhuman speed made her a deadly opponent, and he let all other thoughts fall away from him. Flowing easily from form to form, he matched her attacks with blocks or slid away from them on light feet.

Her armour seemed impossibly light as she moved, and it was only when he scored a light touch that he realised the truth. It wasn't steel at all, or any form of metal despite the way it shone. Instead, it was something soft and yielding. If it wasn't for the evidence of his own eyes, he would have said she was wearing nothing at all, save the thinnest cloth.

She sprung back from him easily escaping his reach, before speaking in perfect, though oddly-accented Islik. "It has been a long time, manling. I thank you for the bout."

"Bout?" he roared back at her. "This is no game, you damned hell-witch!"

"What else is there?" She laughed then, a cold laugh filled with mocking as she eyed him with her contempt obvious in her amber eyes.

He moved forward on swift feet and thrust hard, his body uncoiling like a snake and his knee sinking low as his other leg extended out behind him for balance. His blade stretched out and caught her hard on her thigh, an inch above the knee. Again the armour seemed to afford no protection but the blade did not penetrate. He rolled to the side, rather than attempt to pull back from the thrust, and then rose smoothly to his feet as the smile slipped off her face like water from a leaf. "You dare?" she hissed and hurled herself back into the fight.

Verig danced through the forms with a speed he'd never matched before, shifting from stance to stance smoothly as he moved through strike, block, side-step and riposte. He blocked the fae's clumsy strikes with ease. Her rage was making her intentions as transparent to him as a student who'd never held a blade. Her speed was astonishing, however, and it took all of his concentration to keep her thrusts and slashes from him.

She grew more and more irate as they moved back and forth, crying out what were clearly curses, but in a language he did not recognise, but which were clear from the tone of her voice. Finally she cast the sword aside in disgust and pulled two long, oddly shaped knives, from her back before sinking into an alien stance and weaving them in an intricate pattern. She moved in, like silk over glass, thrusting at his face with one blade even as she other slashed down at his thigh with the other. He raised his shield to block the one blow and slashed his sword down to counter the other. Too late, he realised the move had been a feint and she spun to the left, her body arching around his sword and arms twisting high over her head with the knives in a graceful sweep, only to plunge down and bury them both in his side behind his sword arm.

Verig gasped as they tore through his boiled leather armour as if it were no more than sackcloth. He staggered and fell to one knee as she ripped the blades free and stepped back to watch him, a broad smile on her alien features under the helm as he sucked in a ragged breath. He fell into a fit of coughing as a bloody froth erupted from his lips. Gasping, he fell to the moonlit grass and, as the darkness grew at the edges of his vision, he saw her lean in close to watch the life leaving his eyes.

The fae tore through the Islanders like a bloody wind and men fell in droves before the satyrs as they spun and danced their deadly dance. Some of the creatures fell too, their bones broken by the efforts of a score of men, but it was clear the night would belong to the attacking force. The battle raged for hours, slowing as the Islanders formed ranks and began to respond in a coordinated fashion.

As the moon began to sink towards the horizon the fae turned, as if responding to some inaudible signal, and fled into the night. The Islanders reeled in their wake, as units staggered to a halt and confusion reigned in the darkness, until the cry to stand down was repeated through the force.

As dawn broke, Klöss picked his way through the carnage, his shield slung on his back and his face drawn as he stepped through the field of bodies. Entire units lay dead at his feet, still in formation. He shook his head at the slaughter, only half-hearing his name being called from behind him.

"Klöss, you are needed." Tristan said, as he caught up with him. "The men need direction."

"They all know what needs doing," Klöss replied, as he scanned the field of corpses surrounding them both.

"This is not like you, Klöss, to leave the men like this." The question was unspoken but clear enough and Klöss could see the worry in the oarsman's face as he glanced at him. He had just opened his mouth to reply, when he caught sight of the person he had been searching for. "Verig!" he shouted, as he darted past Tristan.

The man lay on his side, curled against the pain that still showed on his cold face. Klöss slowed as he approached and walked slowly towards his old teacher. The grass around him was soaked with his blood. He sensed Tristan moving up beside him.

"Should we take him back with us? Frostbeard would want to see him," the man said, in a low voice.

"What?" Klöss frowned. "No. No, we'll build a pyre here. I'll not take him from his battle."

Tristan waved a man over and gave the order to begin cutting wood. "What were those things, do you think?"

"Some form of elite unit, I imagine," Klöss replied. "Though they were like nothing I've ever seen."

"Why send them now? It makes no sense that they were not there to defend the village," Tristan objected.

"Perhaps they arrived late, I don't know." Klöss shook his head. "I'll tell you one thing, though. Uncle Aiden will be furious about our losses and even more livid about Verig. These people will pay a tithe in blood."

* * *

Devin stood at the edge of the clearing looking at the remnants of Obair's life and tried to imagine what it must have been like to live here. The cottage was a tangled ruin and the barn and outbuildings were little better. He glanced over at Obair, who was watching the setting sun, and shook his head as he considered a life spent so utterly alone.

The clearing was filled with as many men as could be crammed into it. Iron spikes extended from the ground around the circle itself, angled towards whatever might charge out of it into them. The ground was liberally strewn with tiny chunks of iron, whatever scraps that Harlen had managed to throw together in the end.

Devin pulled an arrow from his quiver and fingered the rough iron arrowhead. "You're sure about these?" he called across to Obair. The old man was dressed in another set of rust-stained robes, which he had retrieved from the cottage, and held a new black iron staff, given to him by Harlen.

"I'm sure of nothing, Devin," the old druid said with a small smile. "Except that the fae will arrive here this night and that they see us all as their prey under the Wild Hunt."

Devin thought about all the times he'd been in the woods. The countless hours he'd spent stalking prey with bow in hand. The thought of suddenly being that deer, that prey was not an appealing one.

Obair nodded at him once, as if he knew what he was thinking, and then walked through the press of men towards Rhenkin.

"This is one hell of a gamble, old man," the captain said, as he drew close. "If the Bjornmen attack while I'm here…"

"I imagine the Bjornmen have their own problems right now," Obair replied. "The fae are everyone's problem and the sooner humanity realises that, the better."

"So you don't think we'll stop them here?"

"No. This is merely to buy us time, although it may just teach the fae that we're not the frightened rabbits they think we are." He leaned the staff in the crook of his arm and scratched his scraggly beard.

The village men and Rhenkin's small contingent moved uneasily around them, stretching their legs and fingering the unfamiliar weapons. Rhenkin had sent his field smiths to work with Harlen's forge and they'd worked the day through. Each man was armed with an iron-tipped spear and a short iron dagger. The weapons were crude and unwieldy, but at least they would be more effective than steel.

The conversations started to drop off as the sun sank behind the trees. The men huddled closer together and large fires were lit for both light and warmth. The light from the fires extended no further than the men, and the stones remained dark as the first glimpse of the moon peeked through the trees. Rhenkin glanced at Obair and called out to make ready, but nothing came of it.

A low mist began to form in the middle of the circle, lending an eldritch feel to an already otherworldly scene. The men began to mutter and look about nervously, as the moon crested the treetops and its pale light shone down onto the stones. Devin found himself holding his breath as the light moved slowly across the circle towards the monolith at its centre. He nocked an arrow but held the string loose, aware of others following his lead, despite the fact that they were soldiers and grown men, and he a boy not yet sixteen.

As the moonlight struck the monolith an audible hiss sounded throughout the circle and men shifted and swore. A burning smell filled the clearing and the moss on the outer stones began to curl and blacken, before falling away to the ground.

"Listen!" someone cried, and silence fell as everyone strained to hear.

"I don't..." someone began, but he was quickly hushed by those around him.

Devin strained to hear something, anything, but there was nothing more than the shifting of men, the crackle of the fire and the distant sound of birds. Then slowly he became aware of the music, a faint sound of flutes and bells coupled with a laughter that put him in mind of the Midwinter's dance. He stroked the fletching on his arrow, and watched the circle.

It was like watching something step out of a pond, if the pond were somehow on its side. The air seemed to ripple slightly and then a leg extended, followed by another. The creature was man-sized, and dressed in a simple tunic and leggings. Around the circle, men moaned as they caught sight of its amber eyes. Then more passed through, fae and satyrs arriving, two or three at a time to start with, and then in groups of ten or more. They were laughing and chattering in an unknown tongue that somehow spoke of music and dark red wine.

Devin drew back on his bowstring, sighting on a satyr dancing near the centre of the circle. He glanced at Rhenkin, wondering at the delay. The reason was clear on the captain's face. He stood entranced, his mouth agape and his eyes filled with wonder. Men around the circle were dropping their bows and smiling, as more and more of the fae stepped through.

Devin looked around in dismay at the enraptured men and gritted his teeth. He took aim and drew back on the bowstring, sighting a fae close to the monolith who stood with his eyes closed, drinking in the light. He drew in a breath and held it, and then a female fae stepped through the portal, dragging a black-shrouded figure behind it on a length of silvery chain.

His mind reeled as he took in the figure in black. Something about the way it moved called to him. The fae smiled a slow smile as she looked around at the men surrounding the circle and then her eyes met his. She hissed and a broad grin filled her face as she reached out to the hooded figure beside her. "Fie, fly, flee, little manling," she whispered, yet the sound carried easily to his ears as she ripped away the shroud.

Age had ravaged her. Her eyes had sunk into her wizened face beneath a mass of wrinkles and her cheeks were hollow, but he could not fail to recognise her. Their eyes locked and she reached towards him with one hand. Hundreds of tattered memories coalesced in one blinding moment. "Mother," he whispered with lips that barely moved, "Mother."

A low moan swept through the men as a long, hoofed, foreleg stepped through into the clearing, but Devin barely heard it. His mind was on fire with pain and loss, and his eyes were filled with tears. He drew back on the bowstring. She would pay, this creature who had shaped his life in this most cruel of ways. He wiped his eyes on his bicep and took careful aim even as the massive creature stepped fully into the world.

The arrow flew straight and true. He didn't even realise he was screaming until it veered from its path and spun harmlessly into the ground. He stared, stunned, at the buds and leaves sprouting from the shaft of the arrow and then looked to the centre of the stones.

The creature had the body of a stag and the torso of a man. He stood in a stance of undeniable authority, holding one hand up as if he had halted the arrow by force of will alone. Moonlight washed across his bare shoulders and tiny sparks danced over his pale green skin, as he turned his antlered head to survey the crowd.

"It seems we have guests, my children." His voice was low, melodic, and utterly, utterly alien.

As if his speaking had somehow lifted all restraint, Rhenkin screamed "Fire!" and arrows flew across the clearing into the centre of the circle and the massed fae. The antlered creature made a fist and his skin grew visibly darker as, with a splintering crack, every arrow shaft twisted, warped, and then snapped.

"Spears!" cried Rhenkin and hurled his iron-tipped weapon into the crowd of fae. Four score more followed in its wake. The weapons were hurriedly made and poorly balanced, but some flew true. Blue fire flared as fae and satyrs fell screaming to the dirt, but more were already passing through into the circle in a steady stream that was still increasing.

"Do you think to stop us with your toys of iron and wood?" the creature spat, his voice heavy with disdain. "To keep us from what is rightfully ours, with your little iron needles?" His eyes found Rhenkin's. "Watch closely, foolish manling."

He threw his shoulders back and closed his eyes as he lifted his face to the skies. The light twisted in the air and the clearing grew dark as shafts of moonlight formed and flocked to him. His body glittered with dancing sparks and when he opened his eyes, they glowed bright with amber fire. He raised one hand, palm upwards, and a shimmering mist appeared at his feet. "Follow, my children! Follow to the hunt!" he cried in a mighty voice, and he stepped up into the insubstantial air, the mist dancing at his feet.

The creature cantered upwards in a spiral and the growing horde of satyrs followed, rising up above the crowd of awe-struck men on a path of shimmering mist. The fae sounded horns and waited. With a clatter of hoofs, pale white steeds charged into the circle to be held and swiftly mounted. Yet more fae, clad in silvery armour, rode into the circle, their white horses ascending, sparks flying from their hooves. Devin watched, helpless, as Miriam was dragged onto a horse and carried up into the night. He stood still, as silent tears ran down his face. Arrows shot into the sky but they had little effect. As the host rose into the skies, the horns began to sound anew, high and clear, calling the fae to hunt.

About the Author

Graham began writing with children's books for his own kids. Fantasy is the genre he has always read himself though, and this is why he started The Riven Wyrde Saga, a fantasy series beginning with *Fae - The Wild Hunt*.

Visit his blog at grahamak.blogspot.co.uk where you can sign up for e-mail updates and be the first to hear about new releases.

Find Graham on Facebook at on.fb.me/1pMyWmK.
He loves to chat with readers.

Follow him on Twitter at www.Twitter.com/Grayaustin

Graham can be contacted at
GrahamAustin-King@Hotmail.co.uk or through his website:
www.GrahamAustin-King.com.

Acknowledgements

Thank you for taking the time to read *Fae – The Wild Hunt*. If you enjoyed it, please consider telling your friends or posting a short review. Word of mouth is an author's best friend and much appreciated. —GRAHAM AUSTIN-KING

CPSIA information can be obtained
at www.ICGtesting.com
Printed in the USA
LVHW102021130223
739353LV00003B/406